DECEPTION

DECEPTION

JUDGE, JURY, & EXECUTIONER™ BOOK ELEVEN

CRAIG MARTELLE

MICHAEL ANDERLE

CONNECT WITH THE AUTHORS

Craig Martelle Social

Website & Newsletter:
http://www.craigmartelle.com

Facebook:
https://www.facebook.com/AuthorCraigMartelle/

Michael Anderle Social

Website: http://lmbpn.com

Email List: http://lmbpn.com/email/

Social Media:

https://www.facebook.com/LMBPNPublishing

https://twitter.com/MichaelAnderle

https://www.instagram.com/lmbpn_publishing/

https://www.bookbub.com/authors/michael-anderle

This book is a work of fiction. All of the characters, organizations, and events portrayed in this novel are either products of the author's imagination or are used fictitiously. Sometimes both.

Cover by J Caleb Design

LMBPN Publishing
PMB 196, 2540 South Maryland Pkwy
Las Vegas, NV 89109

First US edition, January 2021
Version 1.01, February 2021
ebook ISBN: 978-1-64971-435-0
Print ISBN: 978-1-64971-436-7

THE DECEPTION TEAM

Thanks to our Beta Readers

Micky Cocker, James Caplan, Kelly O'Donnell, and John Ashmore

Thanks to the JIT Readers

James Caplan
Zacc Pelter
Dave Hicks
Kelly O'Donnell
John Ashmore
Daryl McDaniel
Micky Cocker
Rachel Beckford
Veronica Stephan-Miller
Jackey Hankard-Brodie
Dorothy Lloyd
Peter Manis
Larry Omans

If I've missed anyone, please let me know!

Editor
Lynne Stiegler

We can't write without those who support us
On the home front, we thank you for being there for us

We wouldn't be able to do this for a living if it weren't for our readers
We thank you for reading our books

CHAPTER ONE

Keeg Station, Dren Cluster

The children clustered around Sahved, the gangly Yemilorian, as if he were a climbing tree. Rivka had granted him a sabbatical to take care of the children from Rorke's Drift. He waved at the Magistrate.

She waved back and called to him, "Let us know when you are ready, and we'll come get you." He nodded before returning to his oversight of the little ones.

Cory had also gotten off at the station because her parents had a place there, but she wasn't staying.

Rivka frowned as she climbed into her ship, *Wyatt Earp*.

Red and Lindy strolled down the ship's corridor, still covered in sweat from a vigorous workout. Red whistled, stopping when he saw Rivka. He threw his arms in the air and cheered. "Miss Droopy Face! I knew it. You're a closet extrovert. You like having people around."

"Don't make me fight you," Rivka replied before softly chuckling. "I don't like a lot of people, but the ones I like, I like a lot. I'm going to miss Sahved."

"We all are, but he'll be back," Lindy agreed. "Even the kids. I got used to seeing them around. Even the crying babies didn't bother me."

Rivka tried not to laugh at the sudden terror that seized Red in its ugly grasp.

"If you'll excuse us, Red and I need to have a serious conversation about how we've been practicing, but it's coming time to play the big game."

"What does that mean?" Red looked from one woman to the other. "Practice until you can't get it wrong. We still need more practice." Panic raised his voice an entire octave.

Lindy shoved him from behind, forcing him forward. He trudged toward their quarters, and he was no longer whistling.

Rivka strolled to the bridge, but it was empty.

Clodagh, Cole, and the pilots had gone onto the station to go shopping. Keeg Station's fashion promenade was up and running. It was supposed to be second to none, even compared to Yoll's fashion district. Rivka hadn't gone yet but intended to. She could use a new wardrobe, and so could her two interns.

She went looking for them, starting with the gym.

Chaz and Dennicron, AIs in the first two bodies purchased by the Singularity for its citizens, were executing Tae Kwon Do sequences to improve their balance and engagement should they be dragged into hand-to-hand combat.

She watched their clumsy movements, clapping when they executed a block followed by a counterpunch without much jerky delay.

"Harder than it looks, isn't it?"

Chaz nodded vigorously until Dennicron stopped him. She looked at him and tipped her head gradually, then raised it back up. He mirrored her movement.

Rivka waited for them to finish. "Write a new subroutine for that one?"

"Why, yes, we did!" Chaz beamed with the revelation. "What can we do you out of, Magistrate?"

"Did Red teach you that?"

Chaz pointed at the bulkhead. "In there, he didn't interact much with us, but out here and in these bodies, he is more than happy to talk with us and a wealth of good information."

"I see." Rivka leaned close. "Are you taking cheap, mind-altering drugs?"

"No." Chaz smiled while he rhythmically shook his head. "Should I?"

"We're trying to cut back on that stuff, so no. If you'll excuse me, I have to find Grainger, wherever he is in this galaxy, and get our next assignment. Carry on."

Rivka returned to her quarters, surprised to find them empty. She accessed her internal comm chip. *Tyler, are you out there somewhere, hiding, ready for playtime?*

He didn't answer. "Clevarious, where's Dr. Toofakre?"

"He has gone to the station to coordinate the delivery of dental stock to Rorke's Drift."

"Good! He was worried if they'd have enough here. Maybe the station manager worked the production factory overtime to take care of him."

"She sent a bill."

Rivka's face dropped. "Of course, she did. Pay it for me, please."

"It's one hundred and seven credits."

"Doesn't sound like a big order."

"Director Spires only charged the processing cost. Terry Henry Walton picked up the cost of the raw materials. I've already forwarded a hearty and personal thank you to both Terry and Felicity."

"How personal was it if I didn't know about it?"

"It was *extremely* personal *and* heartfelt," Clevarious replied.

Rivka snorted. "I'll deliver a personal thank you as well. In the interim, find me Magistrate Grainger." Rivka sat at her desk and brought up the hologrid to check messages, read the news, and video chat when Clevarious connected them.

A dark square appeared at eye level.

"Why? What is wrong with you?" Grainger grumbled. "Lights." He came into sharp focus. Pillow creases lined his face, and his hair stood on end. He smacked his lips and blinked with the rising illumination. "I have to hit the can. I'll be right back."

He let the video remain on as he climbed out of bed and disappeared. A tinkling rainfall sounded in the background. Rivka watched for him to return. A lump in the bed started to move. Grainger reappeared and blocked the view.

"Do you have company?"

"Not that you know of."

"You do! Introduce me." Rivka tried to look past him, but his face filled the screen.

"I'm assuming you called for a reason besides trying to give me a virtual wedgie because I have company."

A sultry voice sounded from behind the image on the screen. "Come back to bed, baby." Long-nailed fingers crept over his shoulder and tugged on his neck. A face appeared.

Rivka's jaw dropped. "Jael?"

"Rivka. Didn't you get the call to the staff meeting?"

"What staff meeting?"

Jael slipped a hand under the covers. "This one." Grainger started to wrestle with her before turning off the video and retreating to another corner of the quarters on his ship.

"Where are you?"

"On our way to Darius. Looks like the planet is trying to give the Federation the finger. We're going to set them straight and show them their actions have consequences."

The video returned and bumped as a naked Jael worked her way onto the screen. "We may have to do some judging on the planetary leadership. That's why we're tag-teaming this one. You've taken down a planet's head honcho before. Did the minions pitch a fit?"

"Not really. Dictators aren't all they think they are. Cut the head off the snake and wait for the body to stop writhing. It helps if they have a governmental contingency plan in place. If they don't, just pick someone to fill the spot until they can conduct a more formal process that will keep the new leader from getting assassinated."

Jael turned to Grainger and nodded. "We know who the players are. We'll start at the top and work our way down. What about you? Got any more cavities to fill?"

"That was good work on Rorke's Drift, I'll have you know. I like a case where nobody dies, and I don't have to lock anyone up."

"There was that chairman…"

"Well, we sent her to Jhiordaan, deservedly so, but we had to go out of our way to clean up that mess. Rorke's Drift. We had no problems there."

"Weren't you taken hostage?" Grainger pressed.

"You'd think you'd be nicer since you're getting some."

"Getting lots," Jael interjected. Grainger shouldered her to the side while smiling.

"Wearing them down over exceedingly long periods of time; that is my key to success. And I still don't know what you want, Rivka."

"Next case. I see a bunch in the queue. Do I get to pick? This once, maybe…"

"You know how it works. You don't choose the case, the case chooses you."

"That's bullshit," Rivka replied, looking down her nose in her best judging manner.

"Your friends have spooled up the Trans-Pacific Task Force, but the Federation is fairly angry at the requested funding levels. They were supposed to be deployment-ready, but the Belzonians may have fudged their information."

"Send the contract wankers in to out-bureaucrat them. They'll make everyone feel sorry for themselves." Rivka twisted her mouth and scowled.

"Fraud on a Federation contract is a crime that falls in our jurisdiction. Maybe the fraud was more than just from Belzimus. We'd like to think that our management folks would check the ability of a bidder to meet the contract requirements."

"This sounds as exciting as watching paint dry."

"The Trans-Pac is gearing up for its second deployment. If you've finished your investigation into the bid process, you'll go with them to work up improved laws of war. Right now, it's a bit of a free-for-all among planetary members. We're to stay out of internal conflicts, but sometimes we can't because of the impact across the Federation. Come up with a legal framework palatable to the members, and they'll vote on it at the next meeting of the general assembly."

"That's all? Bag on the contractor and then follow them to war. I'll be their favorite!"

"Marcie and Kae are there. And Cory is going to help train their field medics, so you know people, but you'll still be on the outside looking in."

"You mean, with our asses hanging out?"

"Yeah. The usual. You should probably get going. I think the Trans-Pac will deploy soon. And me? Well, I guess we've got a staff meeting that I need to attend."

"Eww!" Rivka recoiled from the screen. "Good luck on Darius. The thing about dictators is that they are some backstabbing bastards. Watch yourselves."

"We're taking a few bodyguards, too. That's a lesson we learned from one of our finer Magistrates. We don't need to go it alone."

"Damn straight. I'm signing off before you share any more of your debauchery." Rivka closed the link.

"Did you know about that, Clevarious?"

"I'm sure I don't know what you mean," the sentient

intelligence replied.

"Uh-huh. Just like my personal and heartfelt messages." Rivka scrolled through the files until she found the Belzimus case and moved everything to her personal folder. "I do like to keep tabs on my fellow Magistrates in case they need help, of course. We have side bets on occasion, and I need the intel. Since we're talking intel, did they open the lines on this case yet?"

"Beau has just transmitted the information to the ambassador. Erasmus and Ankh now know that they are headed to Belzimus."

"Do you guys listen in to all the conversations?"

"It's our job, Magistrate. We're here to help. You need to focus on meat-wagon stuff." A funeral dirge played in the background.

"I suppose that's what you call anyone who is not silicon-based?"

"It seems to fit. Especially with Chaz and Dennicron becoming SCAMPs."

Rivka twirled her finger. "Don't make me ask."

"Self-Contained Artificial Mobility Platform."

"That's better than meat wagon, I guess. Or is it meatbag?" Rivka scanned the information presented across all the screens. "How does Ankh keep up with all of this?"

"His is a special brain. It was made to keep up." Clevarious sounded proud.

"Wondrous, even," Rivka offered. "I tell you what, when there is information that I want to know, like the goings-on among the Magistrates, I want you to give me a short brief on it. Keep me informed. You can pipe it directly into my head."

Grainger and Jael are an item.

"I know that, Clevarious. Tell me something new."

I was just testing it out. But I have to tell you, they are still an item.

"I'm not sure you're getting what I mean."

Dr. Toofakre is boarding Wyatt Earp.

"There you go. Thanks, C." Rivka quickly deactivated the hologrid and hurried to change into one of Tyler's button-down shirts. When he entered their quarters, there was no doubt what Rivka had in mind.

He tried not to smile as he approached. He didn't reach for her even though he had a soft touch. "Why don't you recoil when you read my mind?" he asked.

Rivka's face fell. They hadn't talked about it. "Because you're normal, which probably makes you abnormal. You have no bizarre fantasies or lusting ambitions. You want things to be right with the world, like on Rorke's Drift. I heard what you were doing, arranging the supply drop for the natives."

His emotions didn't change, as if he'd expected her to know. He didn't have anything to hide, nor did he desire to keep any secrets. She saw it all as she held his hands. She didn't have to shield herself from his thoughts. They calmed her troubled and overactive mind.

"Isn't that my shirt?" She stepped back to show it off. "I think that needs to be back in the closet," Tyler said softly, reaching for Rivka.

It ended up on the floor instead. For a while, even seeing her man's thoughts, Rivka was free from criminals, the law, and war. Normalcy was hers, the escape she needed from the trials of her everyday life.

CHAPTER TWO

***Wyatt Earp*, Interstellar Space**

"What did you think of the fashion center?" Clodagh asked.

Rivka hung her head. "I never made it up there."

"Do you want me to turn around? There's no case that could be more important than seeing what Felicity, Char, and Sue put together. It is *that* good."

"They're just clothes, shoes, and accessories. That's all," Rivka replied.

Clodagh gasped and threw her hand over her heart. "Such words are blasphemy and would get you the death sentence on nine planets. At the least, you would get your woman card revoked."

Rivka smiled. "We have women cards?"

"In a metaphysical sense, yes. Have you talked with Groenwyn lately?"

"I haven't. What's going on?" Rivka switched to her internal comm device to contact her SI. *Clevarious, what should I know about Groenwyn?*

I have no idea, Magistrate. I feel like I've failed you. I will get on it immediately.

Clodagh had the answer. "She's missing Lauton something fierce. They've been spending a lot of time on the comm lately."

"Zaxxon Major, right? It's kind of on the way to Belzimus."

Clodagh raised one eyebrow. The dog-like alien, Tiny Man Titan, appeared in the hatch to the bridge and yapped at Rivka.

"What do you want?" Rivka asked the dog.

Clodagh picked him up and carried him back to the captain's chair. "Zaxxon is the opposite direction from where we're going, but with the enhanced Gate drive, it makes no difference. The number of stops determines how long it takes."

"Set course for Zaxxon Major and take us there. I'll talk with Groenwyn."

Rivka strode off the bridge and down the corridor, where she found Floyd the wombat sleeping outside the door to Groenwyn's quarters.

Rivka bowed to pet her. "What are you doing out here, little girl?" Floyd was no longer little. She had been young when Terry Henry Walton found her on Homeworld. With regular meals and a more sedentary lifestyle, she had blossomed. She was supposed to be on a diet, but no one could deny those big eyes when she asked for a nibble. Not even Rivka.

Sleepy, Floyd replied.

Rivka lifted her, leaving her unable to knock. She turned sideways and used her head. "Groenwyn, are you in there?"

The door opened, unleashing a cloud of incense into the corridor. Rivka coughed. "I see why you slept outside," she told the wombat.

"Sorry, Magistrate. I'm trying to meditate, and this is supposed to be a calming scent. I may have overdone it." Groenwyn glanced into her room before joining Rivka and Floyd in the corridor, shutting the door behind her.

"We're on our way to Zaxxon Major. I have something I need to do there. I hope you don't mind the delay of our trip to Belzimus."

Groenwyn brightened. "How long of a delay? I'd like a day or seven of vacation. Maybe you can leave me there for the Belzimus mission."

"Case," Rivka corrected. "We are going there for one reason only: a member of my crew needs it." She started to walk away but stopped. She returned to hand Floyd to Groenwyn.

The younger woman grunted with the effort of carrying the heavy wombat.

"Clevarious, please vent the air in Groenwyn's quarters, and then do it a second time to be sure." Rivka winked and strolled to her quarters, peeking in rooms and the cargo bay on her way. *Cassiopeia,* Red's small yacht—the spoils of his war with Tod Mackestray—was secured inside, while *Destiny's Vengeance* trailed *Wyatt Earp* on an invisible tether.

Her ship had become its own fleet. Thanks to being the official embassy of the Singularity, it also boasted the most advanced technology in the Federation.

Wyatt Earp had ceased being her ship the second she'd walked aboard. It was a place of refuge for them all. She didn't tell anyone that she thought of the ship as paradise, but for her, it was a confiscated Skaine heavy frigate that stunk to high heaven. Floyd helped find the source of the stench. And then there were the little green hanging scents that Groenwyn had put around the ship to fight off the smell.

Her name had been different back then, but with her evolution, she'd changed it to something that reflected her ascension to a higher level of understanding, like the moment an entity intelligence becomes self-aware.

Everything changes. Groenwyn matured and became more insightful, a calming presence in the midst of chaos.

But she was lonely. Groenwyn was close with Lauton, the premier of Zaxxon Major. Could she get away? An accountant of her skill would come in handy for dissecting the Belzimus bid, and that was the request Rivka was going to make.

Was it an abuse of her authority?

She needed the skillset on her team for this case, a need above and beyond what the Singularity could provide. There were probably thousands of individuals in the Federation who could do the job. Rivka was still forced to choose. Why not pick one who helped her crew as much as her case?

In her quarters, she sat down at her desk and brought up the holoscreens. "Clevarious, please connect me with Premier Lauton on Zaxxon Major."

I'm sorry that I didn't catch Groenwyn's issues. Her calls weren't made from the ship, so I had no way of knowing, but Plato's stepchild Dionysus would have known. I should have coordinated with Erasmus to stay on top of everything having to do with the crew.

"No! I don't want you snooping on the crew."

But you told me...

"Humans. We may seem contradictory because we are. I want to know, but I don't want you to snoop. Clear?"

Clear as the tar pits on Earth, Magistrate. I have the premier's office online.

An image of a sharply-dressed young woman appeared. "The premier is currently busy with a delicate trade negotiation and cannot be interrupted. I will take a message and get it to her as soon as she's available."

"Yes, please. Tell her that Magistrate Rivka Anoa is arriving at Zaxxon Major in less than an hour. I'm coming to discuss an issue of some importance to the Federation, and I need her help. See you soon."

"Magistrate! I didn't recognize you. I will get your message to her before your arrival."

Rivka nodded and closed the channel. "C, bring up the packet we have on the bid process and where the Federation thinks there were irregularities. On this one, why didn't they send an investigator? I'm supposed to deal with crimes that have already been committed!"

You determine the truth, Magistrate. The Federation believes there has been a crime.

"Yes, but the standard is that there must be a case or controversy for an issue to be brought to a higher court; here, there are only suspicions. Why didn't the Federation send in a forensic accounting team to figure it out? By jumping this all the way to my level, someone has convinced the High Chancellor that a crime has been committed, and one that is fairly egregious."

Isn't that what I just said?

"Don't sass me, C. There's a subtle difference between the Federation believing there's been a crime and someone convincing the High Chancellor to send me." A slight wave washed over Rivka as the ship transited the Gate.

I think that difference is beyond my scope of understanding. "Nuance," you call it. I shall endeavor to learn it better. Please forgive me.

"Nothing to forgive, C. Let me hunt down the SCAMPs and see if they want to go ashore where no one will be shooting at them." Rivka dropped her hologrid and stood, throwing on her jacket and putting Reaper, her neutron pulse weapon, and her datapad in the inner pocket.

I'm sorry, Magistrate, is this more nuanced contradiction? Because according to the records, the last time you were on Zaxxon Major, you expended a great deal of ordnance and were nearly blown up.

"You have that right, but that's when the bad guys were still in charge. We took care of them, right here on the ship. Well, it was on the other ship, *Peacekeeper*."

I believe the Peacekeeper was the pistol that Wyatt Earp carried. I sense a theme.

"Old West marshals, C. That's what I feel like. It's why I wear this jacket. I should probably get a duster, something that goes below my knees. What do you think?"

I think that you had the opportunity to find something like that in the fashion center at Keeg Station.

"Aren't you full of piss and vinegar today?"

I am not. Those items would do foul things to my digital synapses.

"You have to up your game, C. Talk with Chaz about colloquialisms, but after I talk with him first. Wait. Can you tell me where he is, please?"

"They are in their quarters. You may not want to interrupt them at the moment," Clevarious replied over the speakers to emphasize her point.

Rivka ignored her and strolled down the corridor. They didn't have much time before landing on Zaxxon Major if they were given priority clearance from orbit to the landing pad near the capitol building.

She pounded on the door.

Nothing. She pounded again. The door flew open and the two SIs stood there, buck-naked.

"What the hell? Don't tell me you guys were playing ring toss."

"We can't tell you that because we don't know what it is." Chaz looked at Dennicron. She shook her head.

"Get dressed. We're going ashore on Zaxxon Major to convince Lauton to come with us to Belzimus."

"Who is Lauton?" Chaz wondered.

"Groenwyn's girlfriend."

"By all means then, we must convince her," Dennicron stated with a vigorous head-nod.

"We must," Chaz agreed.

"Get dressed, and for future reference, please don't answer the door naked in the middle of you know what."

"Ah. Sex. It is invigorating. Almost as stimulating as a comparable workout in the gym." Dennicron continued to nod.

Rivka tried to dial up a witty reply, but the only thing that came to her was, "Almost?"

"I see. You think it is more invigorating. Our caloric burn trackers suggest…"

"Get. Dressed." Rivka walked away, calling over her shoulder before they shut the door, "It's about calories *and* feelings. Figure that into your calculation."

"Clevarious, let Red and Lindy know that we're going ashore. Armed light, chest protection only."

"They are busy at the moment. Should I interrupt?"

"Is this the flying love connection?" Rivka cupped her hands around her mouth and shouted. "Everyone get dressed! All hands on deck."

Cole strolled into the corridor from the galley, eating something that looked like an apple.

"Fresh fruit?"

Tyler Toofakre, resident dentist and medical specialist, joined them. "A nice resupply from Keeg, compliments of Charumati. Are we landing someplace soon?"

"Zaxxon Major, but only to pick someone up, hopefully."

Groenwyn stepped into the corridor with a happy Floyd bouncing around her legs. She had shaped her hair into an updo with little crystals that caught the light as she moved. Her modern-style gown looked to be something she had just purchased from the fashion center—low-cut at the front, nearly to her belly button, with a heavy necklace filling the space. The thigh-high slits at the sides showed a substantial part of her beautiful figure. The dress itself defied colors as it shimmered with each turn, the material flowing like waves on an ocean.

Cole turned to Rivka. "Who's that?" he asked with his mouth full.

Rivka punched him as she passed. "You look great, Groenwyn." She wanted to tell her to dial it back a little but didn't want to crush the young woman's emotional surge. She held her tongue.

Whatever it took to get Lauton to commit to joining them for this case, no matter how short it was going to be. With the SIs, they would be able to collate the data and mark questionable points about which to ask pointed questions of those who entered the information to arrive at a conclusion sooner—much sooner, rather than later.

But Groenwyn…

Rivka would do what she had to do, even if it was only put a cold compress on a deep bruise. She would do the best she could and still do her job.

"All right, people, briefing room." *Clevarious, get everyone in there, please. We have to talk over our game plan.*

The overhead speakers blared an ear-piercing whistle. "You heard the Magistrate. You got two minutes to get your dumb asses into the briefing room. Move it!"

"Clevarious," Rivka said calmly, "that's not how we talk to the crew. Try it again."

"The Magistrate would be pleased as punch if y'all would mosey on down to the briefing room and sit for a spell."

Rivka looked at Tyler for support, but he made wide eyes at her and shook his head.

The Magistrate gave up and walked to the briefing room, mumbling to herself about the inequity of having to break in a new SI.

The crew streamed in quickly and filled the seats. The last ones to the meeting, Red and Lindy, crowded into the doorway and stood.

"We are at Zaxxon Major to hopefully pick up a temporary addition to the team for her expertise in forensic accounting."

A small commotion in the corridor made Rivka stop. Red stepped aside to let Ankh through, but his seat was taken. Red picked up the Crenellian and held him where he could see. He wore his low-light goggles on his forehead, ready to be pulled down if darkness befell them. He liked the way they looked. No one said anything because he was an ambassador.

"As I was saying…"

"The Singularity can do the forensic accounting. Why are you bringing in someone else?" Ankh asked.

"What if all the records aren't digitized?" Rivka replied.

"We have mobile AIs who can rectify that situation."

"The mobile AIs are learning the elements of becoming a Magistrate. They won't be available for manual interface. Getting into the details of a falsified record will be best accomplished by an SI working in conjunction with one who can better assess the nuance of misdirection."

"I agree." Ankh leaned his head against Red's chest and watched.

Rivka didn't need his agreement, but she did appreciate the help the Singularity kept providing to her. She avoided giving grief to Ankh and Erasmus, a separate and independent intelligence who happened to live within the Crenellian.

Theirs was a mutually supportive relationship. Like a

married couple, although any arguments were conducted at the speed of light within the confines of Ankh's head.

Rivka continued, "After we try to convince Lauton to come with us, we'll head to Belzimus at best possible speed. Once on Belzimus, we'll have multiple engagements. The first is with their government, related to the bid they submitted for the Federation's contract land army that subsequently established the Trans-Pacific Task Force. Irregularities came to light when Belzimus asked for extra funding. That by itself isn't a red flag, but the request was for recruiting and training new manpower. That was supposed to be an included element of the bid. The Federation sent us to figure it out."

"Knowing this crew, that's thirty minutes' worth of work. Then what? Any good vacation spots with an endless supply of bikini babes on Belzimus?" Red tried to look innocent. Lindy would have elbowed him, but he was holding Ankh.

"The Belzonians are hermaphrodites, and from what I hear, they love their orgies. What you do on your off time is your business, but no orgies on this ship."

Chaz and Dennicron looked at each other, their faces blank as they communicated directly. Rivka waited until she had their attention. She winced when Chaz raised his hand.

"I'm not sure I want to know but go ahead." Rivka leaned back as if distance would save her from what she expected.

"We have explored our databases, and it seems that orgies are unsavory affairs performed by unprincipled souls as parts of heathen worship. Is that allowed on Federation planets?"

Rivka relaxed. The question wasn't as bad as it could have been.

"The Federation doesn't usually get involved in the internal affairs of member planets. From what I understand, Belzimus' culture is well-founded, something we could all learn from. There is no jealousy on their planet. They are raised to appreciate their bodies as they are. Their vanity revolves around their hair. I guess coiffures are all the rage. Red, you'd look good with a rainbow mane."

Red shook his head. His short hair wouldn't stand up to Belzonian scrutiny. He tipped his chin to Rivka in recognition of her concern for his hair.

"So, orgies are good?"

"For Belzonians, yes, but not for you or anybody else on this ship." She looked from face to face. "I'm glad we understand that."

Chaz raised his hand again.

Rivka pointed at him and said, "No."

He looked troubled for a moment as his programs ran through the appropriate emotional response to deliver the look he wanted. Chaz settled on a countenance of academic curiosity with a knuckle under his chin and one eyebrow raised, head tipped slightly.

Rivka had to look away before she started laughing.

"Back to business. Going ashore on Zaxxon Major with me will be Groenwyn, our newest couple, Chaz and Dennicron, and Red and Lindy. We shouldn't be long. On Belzimus, we'll have multiple teams because we also need to prepare a framework for Federation laws of war to be included in the charter. I'll need the so-called SCAMPs' help. That is the Self-Contained Artificial Mobility Platform, our mobile SIs. In any case, let's rock and roll, people. We have a contract to clarify and bureaucrats to make happy. You know I like nothing more than dealing with bureaucrats."

"Isn't Cory going to be with the Belzonians?" Tyler asked.

"I'm not sure when she'll get there," Rivka replied. "I think before their next deployment, which is supposed to be very soon. That's why we were rushed out of Keeg Station. She may already be there."

"She was still with her mom when I last saw her before we left," Groenwyn said, dress glistening under the room's lights.

"Cory knows people. Her Uncle Ted can take her anywhere she wants to go. *Ramses' Chariot* is almost as advanced as *Destiny's Vengeance*."

"*Almost*," Ankh said. His emotionless voice carried a hint of the competition between him and his best friend Ted.

"My apologies, Magistrate," Clevarious interrupted. "We are on final approach."

"Saddle up, people. It's time to kidnap their head honcho. I mean, it's time to deliver our best arguments and convince her to join us."

Groenwyn blushed as she stood and straightened her dress and checked her hair.

"You look great. Nothing to worry about." Rivka pulled her close for a hug while the others shuffled from the room.

Red and Lindy were waiting. They already had their ballistic vests on, with hand-blasters at their sides. The SCAMPs were waiting farther down the corridor.

"Do you know if the betting lines start here or on Belzimus?" Red wondered.

"How would I know? You were holding the guy who had that answer."

"Damn! That's right." Red ran down the corridor after Ankh.

Rivka strode through the passages of her ship, the vessel within which great thoughts happened. It was more than hers; the entirety of the Singularity's consciousness funneled through the ship. Rivka reached a hand out to trail along the wall. She couldn't get her arms around the brilliance that resided within *Wyatt Earp's* hull.

Red was waiting at the airlock. He shook his head. "Belzimus. No one knew about this side trip when the lines were drawn."

"Then if it's a free-for-all, nobody wins and nobody loses. Just once, I want a case where no one is shooting at anyone else."

"A fraudulent bid on a contract? Do you think anyone will be shooting at us there?" Red asked before holding up his hand. "But we *are* going into a war zone after that. Hmm. I think we'll get to send some rounds downrange. I remain pleased and humbled to be in the service of Magistrate Rivka Anoa." Red bowed at the waist.

Rivka turned to Lindy. "What does he want?"

"I'll tell you when I figure it out."

"Is there a baby on the way?" Chaz blurted.

"A what?" Red shot up straight.

Lindy shook her head. Groenwyn hugged her. Red glared at Chaz and Dennicron.

"Buck up, Red. We'll all be the parents of your little curtain-climber." Rivka smiled at him while trying not to judge his discomfort.

It had the opposite effect. "I'm not alone," he realized. He grinned at Lindy.

"Touchdown on the private landing pad of the state building. The director's office is within."

"Open it up, Red, and let's get some fresh air."

Red punched the button and stopped the Magistrate from being the first one through the door. He looked out the hatch and checked the area before stepping through first. The rest of the group followed him out.

Red jerked from the impact before they heard the crack of the bullet breaking the speed of sound.

CHAPTER THREE

Zaxxon Major

Red grunted but didn't go down. The second and third rounds hit him where he didn't have protection, and he started to fall. Rivka caught him, and together they rolled to the ground.

The SIs started to run toward the building.

"Get down!" Rivka shouted, but they kept going. Lindy tackled Groenwyn, who attempted to run toward the building. They hit the ground and stayed still. A bullet hit Lindy in the back, but her ballistic armor protected her. She grimaced from the injury. It would leave a bruise, albeit briefly.

Groenwyn tried to crawl away.

"Where are you going?" Lindy growled.

We're under fire, Rivka told her ship. *Find where they're shooting from and finish them!*

Another round hit Red's chest protection, rocking him backward. Blood trailed from where the other two rounds had missed his protected heart and hit his arm instead.

A contingent of soldiers, all females, ran from the building. They angled away from Rivka and her crew to take positions between them and the shooter.

Fire in the hole, Clodagh said softly.

Wyatt Earp's railgun barked one time, and the hypervelocity crack reverberated within the heads of those caught in the open. The top of a nearby tower disintegrated as the projectile exploded through it.

Target eliminated, Clodagh stated. *Is everyone okay?*

Rivka pulled Red to his feet. He held his right hand over the injuries that made his left arm useless. Lindy and Groenwyn stood, but Groenwyn panicked and tried to run toward the building.

"The director!" she shouted, but Lindy held her back.

The soldiers spread out to surround Rivka and her party.

"Is the director okay?" Groenwyn asked.

"The director is fine, ma'am," one of the soldiers stated. "Let's get your friend to a medical professional."

Tyler ran out of *Wyatt Earp,* stopping at Rivka first. She nodded at Red. Tyler looked at his arm.

"That's nasty. We better get you into the Pod-doc."

"We've been here thirty seconds," Red grumbled. "What is it with you?"

Rivka agreed wholeheartedly. "No kidding. Get him back to the ship." The Magistrate fixed her gaze on the soldier who seemed to be in charge. "What the hell is going on here, and why weren't we warned that people are taking potshots?"

The soldier shook her head. "That's above my pay grade, ma'am."

Rivka softened. She didn't want to be an ingrate. "You put yourselves between my team and an active shooter. For that, you have my sincere gratitude. Is the area secure?"

"As far as we know, but that's what we thought before the traitors started shooting. I suggest we get out of the open."

"I won't go," Red claimed.

"I'm here, and so are soldiers. You saw them." Lindy moved close to the Magistrate, assuming Red's usual position.

Red vibrated because he didn't want to leave the Magistrate in a hostile environment.

Lindy turned back to him. "Are you upset that all women are protecting the Magistrate? We have Chaz with us."

But Chaz and Dennicron had disappeared into the building right after the first shots were fired.

"That makes me feel better." Red's face contorted, an expression between pain and indecision.

"Doctor's orders, Red. Into the ship." Tyler followed close behind the bodyguard to keep him from changing his mind.

Rivka finally noticed the youngest member of her crew. Groenwyn was in tears. Her dress was ripped and ruined, her hair messed up, and her legs scraped from hitting the ground. Rivka wrapped an arm around her shoulders and guided her away from the ship. She pulled like she wanted to run back to it and hide.

"You look fine. Good thing Lindy covered you. Better a small tear than a bullet hole."

Groenwyn calmed, but she hung her head. "I just

bought this."

"Maybe you should have asked Felicity about designs more suited to combat while still retaining that feminine mystique?" Rivka tipped Groenwyn's chin up.

"I bet they have a line just like that. I'll have to be more careful in my selection next time."

A soldier ran ahead to open the doors and usher the group inside, where Chaz and Dennicron were engaged with someone behind a desk. The director was waiting. Groenwyn tried to hide behind the Magistrate, but the director was having none of that. She pulled the young woman to her.

"You poor thing!" she cried, kissing Groenwyn gently on her forehead. "Let's get you cleaned up." They walked away arm in arm.

"Can we come?" Rivka asked.

The director stopped and turned. She looked mortified. "I'm sorry. This is getting to be... Please. Of course."

"You, too." Rivka crooked a finger at her mobile SIs. "Come with us, please."

Chaz and Dennicron walked away from their conversation without finishing it, leaving the individual they'd been talking to confused.

You never leave people on the battlefield, Rivka told them.

We went to get help, Chaz replied. *Was that incorrect?*

We believe in self-help. If the executive offices had been usurped, you could have been separated from us. We have to stay together. It makes getting out of situations like that easier.

We live and learn, Magistrate. We got some interesting information from the clerk. Would you like to hear it now?

Save it. We're almost at the director's office. I look forward to the debrief.

They went through to the director's office, which didn't look like any other planetary executive space Rivka had been to. It was filled with boxes of papers and looked like nothing more than a storage room with a desk.

Lauton led Groenwyn to an attached bathroom where Lauton washed Groenwyn's face and arms, then bent to clean her scuffed knees. When they returned to the office, they found Rivka, Lindy, Chaz, and Dennicron standing because there was no place to sit.

"I'm sorry. This is my alternate working office. I only heard that you were on your way after you had already arrived. Otherwise, I would have warned you about the Old Guard. That's what they call themselves, anyway."

"Tell me," Rivka said and reached out to touch Lauton. The director held out her arm.

The emotions flooded into Rivka. The stress of a job she didn't want. The joy of seeing Groenwyn. The fear of seeing Rivka's team under attack. The disdain for the Old Guard, people who wanted it back the way it was—a server farm that handled the galaxy's transactions without much interference from people.

Rivka worked her way past the turbulent emotions on the surface to find the truth of the Old Guard. Infiltrators sent by the pirates Rivka and the Bad Company had bested in the final battle with Nefas, the head of the Mandolin Partnership.

"Pirates?" Rivka asked to get more information.

"The Mandolin Partnership is alive and well, it seems, and they are trying to retake Zaxxon Major."

"I don't think they are alive and well. I terminated

Oscura Mandel myself. He *was* the Partnership. I suspect this is someone using the Mandolin name to further their own cause. How many do you suspect are here?"

Lauton shook her head. Groenwyn held her tightly and she gripped back, each supporting the other, not needing any words.

"We were hoping to convince you to come to Belzimus with us for some forensic accounting work that you are particularly suited for."

Lauton groaned and tossed her head. "Now is not a good time."

The corners of Rivka's mouth twitched upward. "I figured that out the second they started shooting at us."

Groenwyn's eyes were pleading.

"Can you recommend someone who may be able to help us? Groenwyn could stay here to be our eyes and ears while I send for additional assets. I think a platoon from the Bad Company could help root out the Old Guard, especially since they have weapons that the Bad Company mechs may be able to detect. A toothless enemy can be brought to their knees."

Groenwyn mouthed the words, "Thank you."

"Let me call the Bad Company and see what we can arrange." Rivka switched to her internal comm chip. *Clevarious, can you connect me with the Bad Company, please?*

Of course. Stand by.

Rivka nodded and stepped toward a corner, but the boxes blocked her way. She ducked her head and looked at the floor.

Colonel Lowell. What can I do for you, Magistrate?

Christina, thank you for taking my call. We have an issue on

Zaxxon Major. I can't stay, but they need help rooting out an armed group trying to take over. We think these are the remnants of the scumbags Terry Henry attacked above Morinvaille.

Morinvaille. They ran in the face of a fair fight. Yeah, fuck those guys. You know I have assigned a battlewagon specifically to you? The Potemkin *remains on call. I'll give Captain Abercrombie his orders.*

Does the Potemkin *have any mechs on board?*

Sure, a small detachment. Why do you ask? Christina knew the answer, but she wanted to hear it for the report she'd send to her dad, Nathan Lowell.

Root out the pirates already here by using their sensors to find the weaponry that has already been brought to the planet's surface.

A good ol' house-to-house. Our people can break some heads, and just for you, we'll make sure they are the right heads.

Rivka snorted. *I'd appreciate that, and the leader of Zaxxon Major thanks you for supporting her on this problem that started when I took down the crime syndicate running this planet. It's a tough job, trying to be legitimate. She deserves the help.*

Potemkin *will be there within the hour,* Christina replied.

My undying gratitude is yours, Bad Company. Always a pleasure.

Rivka looked up to find Chaz and Dennicron deep in conversation with Lauton while Groenwyn looked on. Rivka eased over to stand beside Lindy. "What are they talking about?"

"Forensic accounting. They don't think they need, and I quote, 'a meatbag to help them.'"

"We'll be here until the *Potemkin* arrives. We'll have that long for them to show that they can handle it."

Groenwyn detached herself from Lauton, but they continued to look at each other. Their eyes held, and for a moment, time stopped.

"I'm going to miss you, and Floyd is going to miss you," Rivka said.

Groenwyn smiled at Lauton while talking to Rivka. "Make sure she has someone to sleep with at night and that Red doesn't feed her."

"I'll take care of Red," Lindy declared.

Rivka frowned. "Fine. She can sleep in the big bed with me. She snores, doesn't she?"

"Yes, but they're cute snores." Groenwyn relaxed, even glowed despite how her earlier tears had made her makeup run.

"Do you want to come back to the ship to pack a few things and clean up?" Rivka asked.

Groenwyn nodded.

Rivka interrupted the exciting-as-paint-drying accounting conversation. "Excuse me. Bad Company has dispatched the *Potemkin,* a battleship, to support Zaxxon Major over the near term. They will be operating under my mandate as Magistrate. They will remain in orbit to deter any incursions by unsanctioned craft as well as deploy mechanized combat troops within the city to use their sensors to locate and confiscate illegal weapons."

"That might drive the Old Guard farther underground," Lauton suggested.

"Not if they hit them fast enough and your insurgents can't spread the word. A mech in action is an impressive piece of equipment."

"I don't want robots unleashed on the city. How can we

trust them? What if they get hacked?"

"The mechs are advanced combat suits. Warriors drive them. There will always be a living, breathing being at the helm."

"I will send a liaison to them so I can stay apprised of the work they are doing."

"They will help you with the Old Guard as you need. The *Potemkin* will be here in under an hour. During that time, I'll return to my ship and prepare for my case."

Groenwyn worked her way through the boxes to get back to Lauton. She raised up on her toes to speak into the director's ear. They kissed, then Groenwyn hurried to join Rivka and Lindy.

"You two stay here and learn everything there is to know about forensic accounting. If Lauton feels you have it by the time the *Potemkin* arrives, then we'll be on our way. Otherwise, we'll accept any recommendation you have for someone to join us."

"I'll keep working on them, but they don't seem to have any problem understanding how to link and cross-reference as well as identify red flags."

Chaz and Dennicron turned, synchronized in their movements, smiled, waved, and returned their attention to Lauton.

"That was creepy," Lindy whispered.

"They're running the same subroutine, I suspect," Rivka replied. "Shall we?"

Lindy led the way through the building, and before they went outside, the soldiers created a cordon within which Rivka and her team would walk.

We're on our way, Clodagh. If you could spin up the ship's sensors and weapon systems, I'd appreciate it.

I never turned them off. Damn people, shooting at my meal ticket? I won't have it! I'm sorry, I meant to say "family." Clodagh chuckled within her mind.

How's Red?

Freshly baked and good as new. We'll be waiting for you, Magistrate.

Red was outside the ship and halfway to the building when they stepped outside. He was geared up completely, full armor with helmet and carrying Blazer, his shoulder-fired railgun. Cole stood near the hatch in his mech suit.

Looking good, honey, Lindy said.

Feeling good. Mabel is waiting for you.

No threats that I can detect, Magistrate, Cole reported.

The only threat is from the Mandolin Partnership. Little did I know when I took this job that when I issue someone a death sentence, they don't necessarily stay dead. That's disconcerting.

"Nefas is back?" Red asked aloud.

"No, but his people are acting as if he is. That's just as bad." Red joined them, walking on the other side of the Magistrate from Lindy.

"I'm glad the betting lines didn't open on this planet."

"I haven't hit anyone yet, or arrested anyone."

"We blew away one guy with a fucking ion cannon!" Red replied.

"It was a railgun, and she asked for it."

Red and Lindy waited while Rivka and Groenwyn headed up the ramp and into the ship.

"Aren't we missing some people?" Red called.

"We have to go back out in about an hour. Until then, we have work to do."

CHAPTER FOUR

Wyatt Earp on the Private Landing Pad, Zaxxon Major

Rivka held Floyd in her arms and leaned out the door while Red and the Zaxxon soldiers escorted Groenwyn into the building and the two SIs out. Groenwyn waved before she went inside. She was dressed in casual attire with her hair pulled back.

In case of another attack, she wanted to be able to run. She also wore a ballistic vest and carried a second one for Lauton.

Red returned with Chaz and Dennicron. They boarded, closed the outer hatch, and prepared to get underway. Red deposited his gear in the security locker and Rivka went to the bridge, calling over her shoulder. "Chaz and D, meet me in the briefing room. Let's talk about what you learned from that clerk and what I'll need from you on Belzimus."

Sad! Floyd cried.

"Oh, no, little girl. You should be happy for Groenwyn. She's in love and—here's a secret I won't tell anyone else—Lauton is in love with her."

And me.

"And you, Floyd. We all love you. You get to stay with Tyler and me while Groenwyn is away."

Go! Floyd cheered. She settled into Rivka's arms and stopped squirming. *Hungry.*

"We're not giving you anything to eat right now. You are heavier than you should be, and that puts a strain on your heart. We don't want you to get sick, Floyd. We want you with us forever."

Yeah! Floyd nuzzled Rivka's armpit. *Hungry.*

"Maybe you can have some lettuce, but just enough to take the edge off. I'm putting you down so you can run around and burn those calories. You need to work out like Red."

No, the little girl replied softly. Rivka muffled her laugh and put Floyd down. The wombat tottered away.

Clodagh was waiting for Rivka. "On track for an immediate departure. Ankh thinks we can Gate from within the atmosphere here to within the atmosphere on Belzimus directly."

"Thinks?" Rivka wasn't convinced. "Has he tried it with the pizza drone?"

Clodagh shook her head while Tiny Man Titan started to bark.

"Why are you always barking at me, you little jerk?"

Clodagh pointed.

Ankh stood behind Rivka. "I knew it. The Gate-capable drone is nothing more than the pizza drone."

"I'm not sure I could pay it a higher compliment," Rivka replied. "It is a magnificent bit of engineering. And while you're here, have you tried an intra-atmosphere Gate with the drone?"

Ankh returned her look without answering.

"I'll take that as a yes. Anything we should be concerned about?"

Ankh continued to stare at her.

"I'm not going to agree to it if you don't answer. Clodagh, take us out through the planet's atmosphere, and we'll Gate when we're safely in space."

"I've tested it repeatedly. It works perfectly with no issues." The Crenellian spoke emotionlessly but crossed his arms, his position of confidence to stand up to every being who was taller than him.

Which was everyone but the wombat, the dog, and the cat.

"Give it a go, but make sure that we don't crash into anyone inside Belzimus' atmosphere. What would that look like, Ankh?"

"The Gate wipes the area clear before reintegration. Like a wave, it'll push obstructions clear before the Gate exit. There is no danger. It's been tested extensively."

"In real space or simulation?"

"Simulation, but it worked every time."

Rivka closed her eyes. Clodagh held her hands up. Rivka shook her head. "Do it. But so help me, Ankh, if we get blasted to our base molecules, I will kick your ass."

"If we're blasted, you will never know it."

"I get that part." Rivka opened her eyes.

Clevarious spoke using the overhead speakers. "With Erasmus' assistance, Gate is plotted and locked. Executing in five, four..."

Rivka flinched and turned her head away from the screen. The Gate formed before them. Aurora, at the controls, slowed the ship to ease its transit and arrival on the far side.

The surge over the event horizon blasted through her mind like a supernova. Her stomach revolted, doubling her over. She started to fall as the ship crossed to Belzimus. Rivka rolled to her side and puked.

Titan howled horribly. Floyd sobbed into the part of her mind that didn't hurt.

Ankh laid on the deck, unconscious. Clodagh reached to the captain's chair to pull herself up.

"I can't see," Clodagh gasped. "Wait. There's light."

Rivka forced her eyes open. The pain of the visual stimuli cut through her mind like a bandsaw.

Ankh groaned. Titan whimpered.

Rivka crawled to Ankh and helped him sit up. His eyes remained unfocused and his jaw hung slack.

The pain in Rivka's head subsided to a throbbing ache.

Ankh will come out of it shortly, Erasmus explained. *The intra-atmospheric Gate appears to overwhelm certain creatures through sensory overload. It is a most interesting phenomenon, one that was impossible to discern through modeling and simulation. We learned something very valuable today.*

"Yeah. Don't trust Ankh when he says it works perfectly," Rivka grumbled.

It did work perfectly, Erasmus replied. *We are in the skies of Belzimus, specifically over the Trans-Pacific Task Force's home barracks and training center.*

"We have vastly different definitions of 'perfect,' Mister Ambassador. But we're here. My head didn't explode, and we have bots to clean up the puke. Clevarious, would you dispatch them, please?"

"Already done," Chaz said, helping both Rivka and Ankh to their feet. "Seems the overload that you experienced didn't translate to SCAMPs. Dennicron and I feel no ill effects from the Gate. Our compliments to Ankh and Erasmus on their technical mastery to accomplish such a feat."

Rivka tried to focus, but her eyes refused to open all the way and cooperate. "Check on Floyd and Wenceslaus and the rest of the crew while you're at it."

"Immediately," Dennicron replied and rushed off.

Red yelled down the hall, "Whoever is responsible for that joy ride is gonna get my boot up their ass." He bounced off the walls as he staggered down the corridor, Lindy doing the same.

Ankh blinked rapidly while holding his head. "Erasmus, what could cause that extreme a biological response?"

"You're speaking out loud," Rivka said.

"I am?" Ankh put a hand to his mouth to feel his lips moving. "I am."

He looked at Chaz, and the SI nodded. He helped Ankh walk slowly toward his workshop.

"Did you do this?" Red demanded but didn't stop Ankh as he and Chaz shuffled past. "Least you can do is buy us pizza! Ow." He closed his eyes and leaned against the bulkhead. Lindy stopped and hung on to him.

"Anyone get the license of the freighter that ran me over?" Clodagh mumbled. "I better check on Cole."

"Get us on the ground first," Rivka requested. She breathed deeply to get more oxygen into her blood to help flush her brain of whatever had happened to it because of the intra-atmospheric Gate. She found her mind clearing quickly, and after a few breaths, she was almost back to normal. "Breathe deeply, people. More air is good. Clevarious, give us an extra five percent O2 inside the ship for the next ten minutes."

Almost instantly, the air handling system increased the volume of air pushed through the vents.

Belzimus and the capital city showed on the front viewscreen as they descended to vast groomed fields. Tens of thousands of troops could form up at one time on them.

"I'll set *Wyatt Earp* next to the ship that Colonel Walton uses for her command vehicle. It's called *Vengeance*," Clevarious reported.

"All kinds of *Vengeance* flying around this galaxy. Did *Destiny* come through the Gate with us?"

"Yes, it is still tethered to *Wyatt Earp*."

"What time of day is it?" Rivka wondered.

"It is six in the evening, local time."

"Please contact Colonel and Major Walton and see if they would like to dine with us. And C, work your magic with the ambassador to get us some damn pizza. I doubt I'm the only one who left their lunch on the deck."

"You weren't," Red muttered. Lindy nodded, but they were both getting their color back. "Standard order? Maybe increase it by twenty-five percent? I could eat a whole bistok."

"You heard the man. Make it so, C! And remind Chaz and Dennicron that I want that debriefing of what they learned from the clerk on Zaxxon Major. Maybe they can put it in writing and inbox me."

"I shall take care of all the things, Magistrate."

"I better check on Floyd. Tyler, too, but he's a grown-ass man and can take care of himself."

The good dentist walked down the corridor, stepping carefully to avoid jarring his body. "My brain hurts," he said.

"Funny," Red replied. "The rest of us are just fine."

Tyler studied the big bodyguard. "I think you're joking, but my brain hurts."

"Get some air, Doc. Enjoy the oxygen while it lasts. Deep breaths, come on. I heard you were a grown-ass man."

"There are rumors to that effect. I put Floyd on our bed so she could sleep. She seemed pretty upset by…by… What the hell happened?"

"A miscue regarding the meatbags' ability to withstand a risky Gate transfer. We Gated from within one planet's atmosphere to within a second planet's atmosphere."

Tyler rubbed his chin while taking a deep breath through his nose and holding it. "I suggest we don't do that again."

Rivka walked past and kissed him on the cheek. "We're going to get pizza out of it. Thanks for looking after Floyd."

"Clevarious told me she's living with us now."

"You know what that means." Rivka met his gaze.

"Watch for the little cubes."

"Exactly. I'll be at my desk. I need to deliver the nuclear depth bomb that is the warrant to search all of their records and interview anyone associated with the bid, up to and including the planet's senior leadership." She waved over her shoulder as she walked away.

Rivka disappeared into her hologrid and reviewed, organized, and compiled notes to start building a framework for the laws of war.

She sought a definition for war, one that stood apart from other military and security actions wherein one party attempted to impose its will on another through the use of violence. The sanctioning by a recognized government of another recognized government moved it to an area that had to be governed by laws, marked by a decency of conflict where the parties could more easily find their way to the negotiating table from the battlefield.

Free-for-all melees could never end in anything except surrender, one side brutally dominating the other, at a significant loss and with little hope of reconciliation.

She had a great deal of work to do and had only scratched the surface. She dropped the holoscreens to find Tyler on the bed with Floyd. He'd been watching videos while the wombat slept. When he saw that Rivka was taking a break, he turned his attention to her.

"Today, I caught our newly embodied SIs doing it. And Red and Lindy…"

"They always do it," Tyler interjected.

"And Grainger and Jael. What's with everyone?"

Tyler smiled at her. "It's you, Rivka."

Her face contorted in disbelief and confusion. "Why do you say that?"

"You can read other people's emotions, see into their minds. Have you thought that maybe you project your emotions? Others pick up on it?"

"How does everyone doing the mambo relate to me projecting anything? I'm not a horn dog."

"You project love. You love this crew. You love making a difference in the galaxy. Like Groenwyn. Everyone can feel what she feels, but that's in how she carries herself, her quick smile. Happy people make others happy. Like Floyd here. Who can be unhappy around this little girl?" He scratched her neck and sides.

"I make people want to bump uglies?" Rivka helped herself to a glass of water from the food processor.

"You make people happy with life. That's this whole crew. I'm glad you considered my reconsideration of joining your considerable crew."

"Considerably," Rivka replied. "I'll have to think about what you said. Do you think I project my emotions?"

"I think you're happier since I came on board, but I am incredibly biased on the matter."

"I haven't had to kick anyone's ass upside down or backwards lately. That makes me feel pretty good."

"You dumped that CEO to Jhiordaan for a life sentence."

"She was such a dumbass. I put her there to protect her from herself. I don't like the other CEO either, but not everyone is likable." Rivka changed gears. "What would it take for Lindy to get pregnant?"

"Is that a loaded question?" Tyler was instantly wary.

"I've heard enhanced people have problems."

"Ah, that. No, not at all. She'd need a medical workup

by someone who would know those things, someone like Cory. I don't have that depth of knowledge."

"Ankh?"

"He's an engineer, but in reality, do you think Red would let Ankh examine either of them regarding the question of fertility?"

Rivka laughed. "No. It was an errant, half-baked thought. I shall restrain those in the future, especially when it comes to Ankh and Red."

"Is that a war, Magistrate?"

"Funny thing you ask. My initial research is on the definition of war and how it's different from a counterinsurgency or a police action. Theirs is a test of wills, nothing more. There will never be bloodshed between them. I think there is grudging respect on both sides."

Clevarious interrupted, "The drone has arrived with the delivery from All Guns Blazing."

"Woohoo! Ankh for the win," Rivka declared. "Or did you order it?"

"No, Magistrate. Ankh retains this capability for himself alone. He has not delegated the responsibility, although we are more than willing to take that burden from him. I think he believes we will be subverted by the likes of you and Vered."

"Is he right?"

"He is not. We would never betray Ambassador Ankh's trust in us. His is such a great mind."

"All hail Ankh," Rivka said, remembering a story Terry Henry Walton had told about a sordid period in Ted's and Ankh's life aboard the *War Axe*.

Tyler stood, trying to carry the wombat, but he couldn't manage. "How do you guys lug her around?"

"Clean living," Rivka replied, flexing her bicep. Tyler wasn't enhanced like she and the other crew members were.

They made their way to the cargo bay to find the three pilots, Clodagh, and Cole unloading the drone. They carried their prizes like stacks of presents at Christmas.

"It doesn't get any better than this," Cole cheered.

They staggered under their towering loads. "I'll get the door," Tyler offered.

Clevarious made the announcement for all hands to join them on the mess deck for their weekly fine-dining experience, compliments of highly advanced and exclusive technology.

Rivka smiled at Tyler as the drone took off and immediately Gated away. "It's good to know people."

CHAPTER FIVE

Belzimus, Belzonian Army Barracks

"Is that a thing now?" Kaeden Walton asked as he and Marcie walked hand-in-hand toward *Wyatt Earp's* cargo deck, still looking at where the drone had disappeared. "That's the craziest device I've ever seen."

Kaeden, the son of Terry Henry and Char, had married the daughter of their friend Felicity. Both were enhanced with nanocytes, prolonging their lives through perpetual youth. Both looked to be in their late twenties or early thirties, but both were well over one hundred and fifty years old. Marcie was in charge of the Trans-Pacific Task Force, the contract military under the direct guidance of Federation officers Colonel and Major Walton.

Two others walked with them, both bald, carrying themselves in the manner of career military.

Rivka questioned her briefing and why hair had been brought up as the first two Belzonians she saw were shaven-headed.

"Kae and Marcie." Rivka strolled forward, grinning

until she hugged the Waltons. She tried to shield herself from their emotions, but they didn't have any secrets. Both were worried about the upcoming deployment to a planet known as Forbearance, where a civil war raged. It affected the entire sector since the system had a key Gate, and the only habitable planet was a major resupply station for transiting freighters.

Marcie stepped aside to introduce her companions. "Colonel Jacobus Braithwen and Sergeant Major Crantis Monsoon. We couldn't manage this army without them."

They removed their caps and bowed to Rivka. Marcie stared at Tyler.

"I'm sorry, but you haven't met Doctor Tyler Toofakre, *Wyatt Earp's* medical professional."

Tyler stepped forward but stopped when Red yelled from the airlock leading into the cargo bay. "He's her man candy. Don't let her fool you."

"Hey! I just saved your arm." Tyler made a face at Red.

"Nothing but a flesh wound." Red jogged over and play-boxed with Kae. He stopped to assess the colonel and the sergeant major. "Do I know you?"

"Not as good as you could," the sergeant major replied.

Red stepped back and scowled.

"Just checking. One never knows," Monsoon told him. "You're going with us, I hear."

Rivka interrupted Red before he could answer. "We can talk over dinner. That drone you saw was our All Guns Blazing order. We always buy plenty of extra."

"You can buy from Dad's place and get it delivered to Belzimus? How can I get in on some of that action?" Kae's mouth hung open, eyes wide, as he looked at Rivka in awe and admiration. "Please?"

"No. If you'll follow me, I'll introduce you to my crew and show you my ship—after we've eaten, of course. When's the last time you had AGB?" Rivka taunted.

"Well," Kae started, wearing his best smug expression, "the old man showered us with AGB at the end of the Kor'nar engagement."

Marcie shook her head. "Being the leaders that Terry Henry taught us to be, we let the troops eat first. Have you ever seen an ant army eat, especially when the ants are two to three meters tall?"

Rivka thought for a moment. "They ate everything including the tables, didn't they?"

"Almost. Swarmed it and left without so much as a by-your-leave."

"What you're saying is it's been a while." Rivka led the way while Red walked next to Monsoon and Braithwen.

"What's your deal?" Monsoon asked.

"I'm her personal bodyguard. Me and my wife have the duty."

"You said a flesh wound?" Monsoon tried to look at Red's arm. He offered it to show that it was as good as new.

"I'm telling you, wherever the Magistrate goes, she draws fire like iron to a magnet. I was outside the ship for fifteen seconds before getting hit by the first round right in the middle of my chest plate. The next two caught my arm while I was trying to shield the Magistrate. Lindy took one, too. If I could have gotten to that fucker, I would have torn him apart, but you know what the Magistrate did? She ordered a railgun strike while the ship was sitting on the ground. Blasted that cockwad into her base atoms. Pod-doc fixed me up good as new."

"Why did you land in a hot zone?" Braithwen asked.

"They're never hot until we get there. It was the planetary leadership's private landing pad outside the main government building. That's the shit we have to deal with, and then there are the dickweeds that get all pissy when we show up armed and armored. You know what I say? Fuck 'em! I've got a job to do. She's been hurt plenty doing this gig." Red's face fell as if he were writing his own epitaph.

"Sounds like a tough job. At least we know who the enemy is." Monsoon held his hand out and Red took it, gripping firmly and appreciating the sergeant major's strength. "Us working stiffs gotta stick together. Can't have these officer types getting their nails and hair messed up."

The colonel gave the side-eye to the sergeant major. "Monsoon, you love a good cigar and glass of wine just like the rest of us."

"Sweat equity, sir. It pays off in the end."

The galley was half-full. Rivka hesitated.

"Allow me, Magistrate." Red cleared a way to the counter, then slipped between the tables to ask everyone to move closer together.

Marcie took Rivka's arm. "We've been to state dinners and formal affairs across the universe, and I have to tell you, this is one of the best ever. Great food and a happy crew. It doesn't get any better than that. It's like you've gone out of your way to make us feel special while at the same time, making us feel like we're the same as everybody else."

"I don't like putting people on pedestals. Bad things happen up there. How is the Trans-Pac?"

"We're getting better with each day. Kor'nar was eye-opening, but it solidified our foundation. We lost ten percent of the force who couldn't come to grips with combat actions after that. We are still helping them transition out of the service because it's important that when they get back into the private sector, they aren't broken."

"But you retained ninety percent. That's impressive. I haven't read anything about Kor'nar."

"We'll talk, but the bottom line is they had a secret Federation base that pirates took over. The chaos created a civil war, and we were tossed into the middle of it without having any of the key information. I pitched a back-channel fit to General Reynolds, and for good measure, I complained to Nathan Lowell and the High Chancellor."

"It is now clear why they sent me. I look forward to getting the details from you, but later. First, we have this banquet in your honor."

Kae looked sideways at the Magistrate. "If we weren't able to show up?"

"Then we would have had a banquet in your honor without you. Understand, this is Pizza Friday. We were going to have AGB no matter what. We ordered two extra pies, just in case."

"You get AGB every Friday?"

"Shh." Rivka held her finger to her lips. "It is the one perk of having a ship that's an embassy."

"An embassy for people who don't eat. I don't see the connection."

"They're really smart and know they need us meatbags

to get around. Well, they used to need us more." Rivka gestured at two beautiful people leaning against the wall.

The SIs were there, watching. As Rivka passed, she introduced them. "I'd like you to meet our SCAMPs, Self-Contained Automated Mobility Platforms. These are what you might call AIs, and the bodies were manufactured for their use to be self-contained. You'll see many of the AIs, which we call SIs, sentient intelligence because of the Singularity. Their embassy is aboard this ship. The ambassadors are there. You know Ankh, and inside his head is Ambassador Erasmus."

"So many changes," Kae said. "I remember when Ankh came aboard and did his mind-meld with Ted, and those two were off and running. AIs have their own embassy, and it's onboard your ship."

"Hello. I'm Chaz," the SI said in a mechanically wooden voice.

"Why are you talking like that?" Rivka demanded.

"I'm sorry. I thought you expected that since we're SIs."

"No. The best thing you can do is be yourselves." Rivka put her hand on Chaz's arm and was warmed by the fact that she could sense nothing from him. "We appreciate you. And you," she said, looking at Kaeden, "get used to seeing them because they will be with me most of the time since they are in training to be a Magistrate team."

Marcie nudged Kae out of the way. "You are absolutely beautiful. How can I get a body like that?"

"You jest. I'm Dennicron, and you could be the most beautiful human female I've ever seen."

"That's only because you haven't seen my mother,"

Marcie replied easily. "You need to get out more, and you'll see there are beautiful people everywhere you look."

"Are you seeing the bald men?" Chaz whispered loud enough for everyone to hear.

"Yes. I thought Belzonians loved their hair. Maybe they're not Belzonians. Are you Belzonians?" Dennicron threw out a flurry of words.

Monsoon looked at the colonels and then at Rivka.

"I know. It's a complete madhouse. I tell you, they were much smarter and more socially capable when they were stuck inside my ship's computer," Rivka explained.

"Yes, ma'am," Monsoon replied to Dennicron. "We are, but we're soldiers, and we fight for a living. You'll see plenty of coiffures among the troops. They take their hair very seriously. They smuggle hair care supplies in every available compartment and void. We have to search all the equipment before we board every single time."

Dennicron and Chaz searched their databases for the appropriate historical references. Chaz smiled when he came across one he thought was appropriate. "They don't smuggle booze?" the SI asked.

"No. They smuggle hair care products. To the rest of the galaxy, it might be embarrassing, but to us, it takes us overweight. Our troop transports are a little older and have limits. We have to use shuttles to transfer the payloads from ground to orbit."

"When will that be?" Rivka asked.

"We start the staging and loading tomorrow. It'll take five days, but we can compress it to three if we do it in two shifts."

"We have some work to do with your planetary leadership and the senior administration of the Belzonian Army, but we expect to be finished long before the five days. I can't guarantee we'll be ready in three days, but we might be."

Chaz looked like he wanted to say something, but Rivka shut him down with a glance.

"Get yourselves something to eat. We'll talk later in my quarters."

"What was that?" Braithwen jumped to the side, bumping into Monsoon as he looked under the table.

"Floyd!" Kae and Marcie cried together. Kaeden picked up the wombat and hugged her tightly. She squealed in delight.

"Somebody has eaten too well." Marcie looked at Rivka.

"She's big-boned," the Magistrate remarked. Kae and Marcie loved on the wombat until they reached the front and had to put her down. She scampered to Lindy, who put her in her lap while she ate, feeding the little girl pieces of the green pepper topping.

They finally made their way to the front, and each served themselves. Red brought up the rear and took an entire pizza and two orders of wings. Ankh arrived and remained at the door, unable to process the number of people in the galley.

"Do you want your usual?" Red asked. Ankh looked at him without answering. "I'll take that as a yes. I'll be right back. Hey, Cole, hold this for me."

The warrior took the box and packs of wings and held them above the full table while Red climbed over people to get to the front.

"Gangway, man on a mission, coming through." Red

piled a plate with pepperoni pizza. He couldn't remember which wings were Ankh's favorite and he froze, torn between two choices.

"Honey mustard," Rivka whispered.

Red took the whole bag and headed for the door. Ankh accepted it and turned to leave but stopped. He looked up at Red. "Thank you."

"Ankh, buddy!" Kae called from across the room. The Crenellian looked back blankly as if he didn't recognize him. "What do you have on your forehead?"

Ankh walked away without saying another word.

"He likes me better than you," Red shouted over the noise, relieving Cole of his dinner. "Thanks, man. I owe you one." He saw Lindy and worked his way back into the room to sit beside her. The wombat looked at him while chewing. She'd want his dinner, and everyone would look at him meanly until he gave her some. He checked the counter. There was plenty left. He snagged a vegetable-heavy slice and sat back down.

Monsoon worked his way to the pilots, Aurora, Ryleigh, and Kennedy. They sat at the end of the table and quietly ate. Monsoon was having none of that.

"Ladies. May I join you?" They cleared a spot between them and he eased into it, smiling from ear to ear at them. He was a master at making people comfortable as well as uncomfortable. He opted for the former, turning on the charm for the young ladies who helped fly and navigate the ship.

Braithwen sat down with Rivka, Tyler, Kae, and Marcie at the table the others had left empty for them.

"Here's the deal," Rivka said. "We're not going to talk business. Colonel Braithwen, tell us about Belzimus."

"Call me Jake, and I'd love to tell you about the Belzimus I know and the proud people who live here."

Braithwen regaled them with stories about his home and the people. Monsoon joined them when the pilots left. When the galley was empty and the bots were cleaning up, they turned to the business side of the visit.

Tyler excused himself, and Chaz and Dennicron leaned in.

CHAPTER SIX

Wyatt Earp, Trans-Pacific Task Force Training Fields

"I'm here because of irregularities in the contract between the Federation and the Belzonian planetary government."

Marcie raised her hand. "I was pretty mad when I saw what shape they were in. And Jake and Crantis had nothing to do with that. They'd been on assignment with the Federation for the two years prior. I wasn't given any choice about rejecting them. It's not like there were other bidders."

Rivka leaned back and crossed her arms. "No other bidders? Clevarious, can you check that for me. Why were there no other bidders? Sorry. Please continue."

Marcie shrugged. "Nothing else to say. We whipped them into shape the best we could, thanks to these three powerhouses. We asked for six weeks, expected four, and were given three."

Kae smiled and nodded. "My tankers fired an armor-piercing round out of the live-fire area that hit our spaceship and destroyed our quarters. I think it was right after that Marcie started making intergalactic wake-up calls."

"I was pretty mad," Marcie repeated.

Braithwen chuckled. "It changed nothing. We went to Kor'nar with the soldiers as they were. We established a beachhead, and from there, we did what we had to do to bring peace to the planet. The Federation now gets their precious malageodes to trade to Elementor Three, which makes Silsonex, a cure for cancer for those who don't have access to a Pod-doc."

"We ran the entire population of Rorke's Drift through the Pod-doc. No one above me complained."

Chaz leaned forward. "The Pod-doc in *Wyatt Earp*'s cargo bay may look like a cheap model, but it operates on advanced programming that is unique for most sessions. Ambassadors Ankh and Erasmus were able to program certain safeguards into the Pod-doc process, like a time-limit on the nanocytes injected into the bloodstreams of the settlers. They cure their issues, and then with the last of their power, they fry their own circuits to be ejected from the body through the various waste processes."

"That would be a huge benefit in reducing reliance on Silsonex and the exploitation on Kor'nar."

"'Exploitation' is an emotionally charged word," Kae noted. "The mining on Kor'nar was done with the one hive's concurrence. Little did we know that they spoke for the whole planet but didn't speak for the population. And then the queen died."

"That was a clusterfuck. I was down in there when it happened, but her last act of defiance was to accelerate the war, sending her minions en masse against the Trans-Pac and the other hive." Monsoon shook his head.

"I was in the other hive. Got a little sliced up, but Kimber brought her team to my rescue."

"You were dead!" Marcie blurted. "But no matter. You got better. And now I'm the queen on Kor'nar."

Rivka looked from one face to the next. Each nodded knowingly, almost reverently, as military people do when they recount their experiences. "I find myself at a loss. As a lawyer, I have a hard time with the legal boundaries of throwing an army into the middle of a war without telling them everything they'll encounter, especially when much of the clusterfuck, as you called it, was Federation doing."

"Bureaucrats gonna bureaucrat," Kae said. "It's something Dad has said for the last two hundred years."

Marcie nudged him. "You're not that old."

"Dad is, and I doubt he made that up after I was born."

"*Silent enim leges inter arma,*" Rivka stated. "In war, the laws are silent. This is a statement from old Earth, in the time before Terry Henry Walton..."

"Mom's older," Kae helpfully added.

"Don't tell people that!" Marcie looked appalled and glared at Kae.

Rivka didn't miss a beat. "...and that premise found its way to the stars, where wars were fought and to the victor went the spoils, no matter how victory was achieved. Blood feuds exist between races because of the brutality brought by one upon another. The Federation has determined that they can no longer let this go on. They started with the idea that a land army could force the two sides to play nice, talk instead of fight.

"But Kor'nar also showed that there has to be a binding legal element that provides for the deployment of an army on sovereign soil and that there will be repercussions for exceeding the constraints of killing your fellow citizens decently."

"There are legal constraints to offing someone?"

"Treatment of prisoners, banned weapons, humanitarian components such as how to deal with wounded, civilians in the line of fire, occupation of enemy territory, and even the definition of the term 'war' needs to hold to a legal standard. This framework is what I'm charged with building once the bidding issue is put to rest."

"Is the Federation considering pulling the plug on the Trans-Pac?" Marcie wondered.

"Not that I know of. Clevarious, did you find out if there were any other bidders?"

"I did, Magistrate. Two worlds submitted proposals besides Belzimus but withdrew their bids once the exclusive use clauses were explained. They did not want to give the Federation complete and unfettered access to troops, equipment, and training areas, access that included orders and deployments. According to their bid withdrawals, both thought their armies would be contributory and not exclusive, despite the clear language in the request for proposals. Some people…"

Rivka pursed her lips. "Your success on Kor'nar suggests that the parameters within which the Trans-Pac operate are sound. The task force itself is sound and competently led." Kae silently clapped. "The only issue is the funding to fill shortcomings that were the responsibility of the Belzonian Army as part of the base fee. I have no idea how the Federation will deal with that. If I have to haul off conspirators who rigged this bid, then that'll send a message to the Federation regarding providing some level of leniency."

"What if there's only one conspirator, and it's our premier?" Braithwen asked.

"Then we wouldn't have a conspiracy, which takes two people," Rivka explained. "But if it is the head of your planet's government, I will haul him off and dump him before the Federation court on Yoll, where he can look forward to suffering his punishment. I hope you have a good deputy."

"I think it was him. That guy's a jagoff." Jake was sure the perpetrator was the premier.

"He's a right fucknugget, a total ass-blaster," Monsoon agreed.

"I'll keep an open mind," Rivka said, raising her eyebrows at the two soldiers.

The door to the galley opened and Cory walked in. "I heard there was an AGB party, and I wouldn't miss that for the universe."

"I didn't think you were coming until tomorrow," Kae stood and hurried to the door.

"You're looking good after your death." Cory held him at arm's length as she examined his face and neck.

"Can you not do that?" He pulled her in for a hug. Everyone stood and moved to a more open area.

"It's like we just saw you," Rivka remarked. "I'll get you a plate. Take a load off."

Cory sat down. "Yes. The trip here was most unpleasant. Ted jumped us into the atmosphere. He said it would be fine. It wasn't fine. My stomach is still roiling, but at least my head doesn't hurt anymore." She saw the SIs. "Hey, guys. You're looking great."

They beamed in identical ways.

"Good to see you again, Cory. Thanks for helping our people on Kor'nar."

"It was my pleasure. I wish I could have done more. You lost some good people."

"Over five hundred, but they died with honor, fighting on a mission we needed to win."

Cory nodded. She didn't like hearing about body counts.

"I saw you but didn't get to talk with you," Cory said, looking at Monsoon and holding out her hand.

"Sergeant Major Monsoon, ma'am, at your service." He took her hand, but not to shake it. He bowed his head and kissed her fingers. "I have no witty words, ma'am, because I'm a bit taken. You're different."

She studied his features, her hand still in his. They stood that way until Rivka bumped through with a plate for her. She took it, and Monsoon pulled out the chair for her. He attempted to step aside after she sat, but Cory insisted that he sit next to her.

Marcie interrupted them. "You're here to train our combat medics. I think we lost people on Kor'nar who didn't have to die."

"I think so, too, but it's more than just medics. Every soldier needs to understand how to stop the bleeding, protect the wound, and treat for shock. That will save the most lives." Cory looked around. "Where's Groenwyn?"

"She's on Zaxxon Major with Lauton. We'll pick her up

later," Rivka replied. "Is Ted here? I'd think Ankh would like to see him."

"No. Ted's ship flies itself."

"So Ted has never undergone the new intra-atmospheric Gate? Ankh has, and it knocked him cold. I think Ted shouldn't have foisted that on you without having done it himself first."

"But it was tested extensively. Every simulation was perfect," Clodagh parroted in her best imitation of Ankh's voice.

Chaz and Dennicron frowned. Rivka turned to them. "Make sure no one Gates into an atmosphere again with living beings on board until the issue regarding the assault on their bodies is resolved. Please pass that to the Singularity. It is a safety issue. I will issue a formal injunction if I have to. Do I have to?"

Chaz leaned back and stared, his eyes not following Rivka as she moved out of his line of sight. When he came back to them, he replied, "You do not. Ankh and Ted have agreed that there are concerns not included within the modeling and simulation. No more intra-atmospheric Gates for ships carrying meatbags."

"Good. I'm glad we have an understanding. Don't make me regret not issuing the injunction."

"We won't, Magistrate," the two SIs said in unison.

When she turned back, she found Cory and Monsoon nearly head to head and giggling.

Kae leaned back and stifled a belch. "Do you need us for anything tomorrow?"

Rivka shook her head. "We'll be headed downtown. Can you arrange transportation?"

Marcie smiled. "Turns out we have a whole motor pool to choose from. I'll assign you a vehicle and driver. When will you be heading out?"

"What time is it now?" Rivka wondered.

"Crap!" Marcie complained. "It's almost midnight. We need to go."

"Alas, I fear that their schedule is my schedule, and I cannot miss the morning's exercises. Maybe you could join us. You look like a runner," Monsoon said.

"I will do my best."

"You can stay here tonight and get set up elsewhere when you have time," Rivka offered before Monsoon came up with any crazy ideas.

"My stuff is in the cargo bay. I was hoping you'd say that." She yawned as if the mention of bedtime drew her in.

"It'll be a long day tomorrow, people. Get your beauty sleep." Rivka stood and stretched. The counter contained AGB leftovers that needed to be put away. She turned to it.

"We don't require sleep. Can we get access to the army's data systems?" Chaz requested.

"Sure. I'll shoot you the access information when we get to our ship," Marcie replied. Kae joined Rivka and made a couple of to-go plates before nodding and heading out.

"Thank you for the excellent, albeit short, evening. Time evaporated. I look forward to more conversations and learning about the laws of war," Colonel Braithwen stated.

He took a step back as Monsoon said his goodbyes to Cory. The two stood close together and talked in low voices before the sergeant major kissed her hand in front of her face while never taking his eyes from hers.

The four left with a final wave.

Chaz and Dennicron retreated toward Engineering to take advantage of supporting computing assets in the Embassy of the Singularity.

Rivka finished storing the leftovers and placing the refuse where the bots could clean it up. Cory helped.

"What do you know about Crantis?"

"I just met him tonight. But he's a bald Belzonian, which suggests he's not constrained by cultural norms."

"I gathered that. What do you know about hermaphrodites?"

Rivka arranged her thumb and fingers to make a zero.

"It doesn't matter."

"It didn't seem to. I hope you're around when Groenwyn gets here. She enjoyed her time on Azfelius immensely. Her first trip there changed her."

"My first trip changed me and for the better. What we don't see in life is most of what takes place."

"Groenwyn talks like that, too. The faeries leave an impression on those they find worthy. After we left, I have to admit that the rest of us were unchanged. Red found it the least exhilarating."

Cory smiled, eyes twinkling under the bright galley lights. "Why am I not surprised?"

"Time for me to check out for the evening," Rivka told her, giving Cory a quick hug in the corridor. "Your old room is just as you left it, I suspect."

"Thanks, Rivka. I think this job is going to be as life-changing as my time on Azfelius."

Rivka winked and retired to her suite to find Tyler and Floyd sound asleep, taking up the entire bed. "Is this how it's going to be?" Neither woke up to answer. Rivka had to pull a blanket out of the closet and rack out on the couch.

"Clevarious, wake me at five, please."

"Will do, Magistrate. Sleep well. We're already working the data from the army. You can rest assured we'll have a full report for you in the morning so you can better shape your day."

"That's what I like to hear, C. Until tomorrow."

CHAPTER SEVEN

***Wyatt Earp*, Trans-Pacific Task Force Training Fields**

One second after Rivka had the coffee in her cup, a gentle tap sounded on the door.

"C, did you tell anyone I was awake?"

"I can neither confirm nor deny my complicity. I have the right against self-incrimination."

"You did," Rivka grumbled. She answered the door to find a perky pair of SCAMPs. "Chaz, Dennicron. Can I help you?"

"*We* can help *you*," Chaz emphasized before pushing his way inside. Tyler and Floyd were still in bed. The blanket and pillow were on the couch.

"Ooh," Chaz started. "Trouble in paradise?"

"Yes. Groenwyn's gone, and Floyd is a bed hog. That'll teach me to go to bed last."

"Indeed," Chaz replied, his intonation leaving it hanging whether it reflected his acceptance or doubt. "Bring up your system, please. We've uploaded an analysis of the bid details from the army's perspective."

Rivka sipped at her coffee without moving. "Bottom line up front."

"It's in the report," Chaz countered.

"You can recite every word of that report. I just got up. I'm going to sip my coffee and think deep thoughts. If you're not going to brief me, then you don't need to stand over my shoulder while I read. Since you're here, it must mean you want to talk with me. Or do you simply want adulation for getting the job done while us meatbags slept?"

Chaz's face ran through a series of emotions as he struggled to get his visage to reflect how he felt.

"I'm sure you did a great job, but when you seek platitudes, they may not arrive as you hoped. Just tell me what you found, and we'll talk about it." Rivka took a sip from her cup. Floyd snorted from the bedroom as she adjusted herself to get more comfortable.

"Many of the issues raised by the army in the request for information sent by the premier's office were excluded from the final proposal."

"Were there outright lies?"

"Yes, Magistrate. The army raised the issue of recruiting and retention. They didn't believe they could refill ranks depleted due to war morale."

"War morale? Is that high turnover because of long deployments, hardship, and the violence of combat?"

"Your answer is eloquent, Magistrate, but that term was never defined in the army's supply of information. We suspect it means what you think it means."

"I'm pleased with what you've found. Nothing untoward at all from the army?"

"Besides an optimism that no other world's soldiers could stand before the Belzonians? No."

"Did they say that?" Rivka sat down on the couch while the SCAMPs continued to stand.

"There was a certain amount of, what do you call it, 'flag-waving,' that seemed detached from the realities described in Colonel Walton's after-action reports." Chaz looked at Dennicron. They nodded at each other.

"Their equipment was outdated and their troops undisciplined. How did they come to the conclusion that they were the galaxy's badasses?"

"They expected to get new equipment out of it, cutting edge technology to make them superior. They counted on that edge and Federation credentials to carry them through any battles. They appear to have a high regard for the old Yollin hierarchy." Chaz and Dennicron smiled identically at the claim.

"Who changed the data?" Rivka asked.

"The grant preparation team within the premier's office. It was receipted for by one Heimer Truasse, who is also listed in the proposal as the principal drafter."

"Wasn't this much more personal and fun than reading the report?" Rivka asked.

"For you, maybe. I see the allure in using outdated communication modes. Don't you, D?"

"I do, Chaz. The Magistrate's facial micro-expressions are extraordinary. We should study them further when we are on our own to decide what to adopt."

"No. Don't study me at all. Understand that as humans, this is how we prefer to communicate. Since you have chosen human form, it would behoove you to act appropriately."

"We always act appropriately."

"Not if you're studying me and being creepy. What happened to your social skills? You used to be smooth when you were stuck in the box."

"Synchronizing witty repartee with appropriate body movements and facial expressions is proving to be far more difficult than we had anticipated."

"Get out!" Rivka shook her head before taking a sip as she contemplated her interns.

"Now? We weren't finished with the briefing. I feel like you have more questions."

"What? No. Don't get out. That's just a saying, an exclamation of disbelief." Rivka tipped her cup back and drained it. She headed to the food processor for a second cup.

"Why would you not believe us? We don't lie."

"Chaz." Rivka stared at him, but his expression remained neutral. "You *have* lied to me."

"Those days are far behind us, Magistrate, even though it was for your own good. I learned that the truth, no matter how harsh, is better in the long run."

"See! I knew you lied to me. When was it?"

"What?"

"You admitted that you lied to me. Now I want to know the details."

"No." Chaz crossed his arms and tipped his head back, frowning as he looked down his nose at the Magistrate.

"Now you're starting to get it. Point of order. Don't lie to me."

"We shan't, Magistrate." They both nodded emphatically with big eyes to make sure they registered the appropriate emotion.

"First stop this morning will be the premier's office. We'll cut to the chase. I want to interview Heimer and see what he thinks about the proposal and who else knew. Isn't that what it always seems to come down to? Who knew what when?"

"If that's what you say, Magistrate." Chaz sounded unconvinced.

"I'll catch up with you later. Let me do my morning stuff, and when the time is right, we'll go into the city together and turn over desks and roust the bad guys."

"I look forward to tossing desks."

"It's a saying. Don't take it literally. Please do not turn over any desks without explicit authorization from me, understood?"

"Understood. This job used to be fun. Now it just sucks."

"Maybe you suck," Rivka shot back.

"I don't think that's possible. I don't breathe, so establishing a vacuum isn't possible with this body. There are limitations."

"Chaz. Go away now. I have things to do, important Magistrate things."

"Since we're in training to be Magistrates, wouldn't it help our deeper understanding of your routine to establish one of our own?"

"You don't need to watch me take a shower," Rivka nudged Chaz toward the door.

"I see. Your personal grooming is considered Magistrate time, so no one bothers you."

Rivka tapped her nose with her index finger. "And nice job. Thanks for putting in the time. I'll take a look at your written report later." She opened the door and waited for the SIs to leave. She closed it once they were most of the way into the corridor.

"Hey!" Chaz's voice cut off after the door bumped him out and clicked shut. Rivka thought for a moment she might have been a little hard on them, but then again, compared to what she went through with Grainger, this was mild.

She could do better. She opened the door and spoke loud enough for the SIs to hear. "You did well. You're on your way to building a great and legally defensible foundation for future rulings. When we hit the downtown, we'll show them that breaking the law is never in anyone's best interest. Thanks, guys. Take a load off and be ready to go in about three hours."

Rivka closed the door again, feeling much better. The only rite of passage that mattered was getting the facts correct to determine if there had been a transgression and then what to do about it.

The day was looking up.

Zaxxon Major, Office of the Director

"I can't believe I'm here!" Groenwyn almost squealed. "It's been too long."

"It has. I feel better with you around, like I can take on the Old Guard all by myself and win," Lauton replied.

"How bad is it?" Groenwyn leaned in to take Lauton's hand.

"They have their moments." Lauton moved closer, choosing to sit on the floor at Groenwyn's knee. "It's tiring, though."

"Give it up and come to space with me," Groenwyn suggested.

"If only it were that easy. Could you give up what you do and throw it all away?"

"I would be throwing nothing away. My friends on *Wyatt Earp* will support whatever decision I make, even if it is to stay here with you. I contribute to what they do, although I think I can do more. I need to do more, but I'm having a hard time because of the hole in my life. I see the other couples on the ship, and I want what they have."

Lauton started to cry. Groenwyn buried her face in Lauton's hair. "What makes you sad?"

"I have no friends here. I'm the director, and it's the loneliest job on the planet."

"I'll stay here with you. I don't need to go back to the ship," Groenwyn offered, but Lauton shook her head.

"I want what you have—friends in a small community without the weight of the world hanging over my head."

Groenwyn laughed. "The Magistrate has the weight of the universe on her shoulders, and to add to it, people shoot at her, just like we saw here. But she makes it all work. You're right in that I can't abandon her, either." She stroked Lauton's hair. "What would it take to find someone to take the head job?"

"We would need to remove the threat from the Old Guard first. After that, any of my top people could do this job. They could even rule by committee. We're a financial clearinghouse with less than a million souls living here. It's not like Yoll or even some of the biggest space stations. They have more than that."

"Do you have a communications terminal? I'd like to talk with Will Abercrombie and see what we can do to expedite putting down the people who are keeping you from me." Groenwyn stood and helped Lauton to her feet. "Would you really leave your home to join me on a cramped spaceship?"

"From what you describe, it sounds like heaven. And Floyd."

"I love her," Groenwyn admitted. "We all do. I wonder how the Magistrate is getting along because Floyd is a big bed hog."

Trans-Pacific Task Force Training Fields

"Get in formation, you ass-sucking shitbags!" Monsoon bellowed. "Shut your sewer, fuckbucket." He pointed an accusing finger at an offending soldier. "And what the goddess of thunder are you wearing?"

The sergeant major stormed up to a soldier dressed in a pink silk one-piece outfit. "Where's your PT uniform? What the fuck are you besides toad-bogey?"

"Sergeant major, sir, the private lost his uniforms during laundry hours last night, sir. The private figured it would be better to be out of uniform than late."

"The dumbass private got part of that right. How do you lose your shit in the laundry? Missing a sock, Private? Don't answer that. You're right up front, sweetheart. You have guidon duty, so carry that bitch like she's your firstborn."

Cory jogged up next to Colonel Braithwen and stretched while they watched the units of the Trans-Pacific Task Force getting into formation.

"How many people do you have?" Cory wondered.

"Only eight thousand left. The first few months have been extraordinarily hard on our people. We started with nearly twenty, but a lot weren't suitable for forward deployments. Our logistics train is strong, but we are limited in our frontlines. We are right at the minimum number of shooters. That's why we submitted the emergency request to the Federation for recruiting and training help." The colonel looked at Cory. "That got things spooled up since we were supposed to handle that ourselves. I didn't know that. Neither did Marcie. She's angrier with the government here than the Magistrate."

"Rivka is cool in how she deals with the worst perps the Federation has to offer. Your government won't raise her pulse rate. She'll take care of business and then come back to hang out with her crew." Cory watched the sergeant major. "Tell me about Crantis."

"I deployed with him to the Federation for two years representing Belzimus. He saved my life more than once. He is the consummate warrior."

"Sounds like my dad."

Monsoon caught a soldier making faces. "You rat-faced, puke-swilling, festering gash! Lock your body, numbnuts!"

His voice carried over the entirety of the formation. Voices quieted. "Listen up, shitweasels!" He clasped his hands behind his back and turned as if contemplating the depths of eastern philosophy. He found Cory watching him and flushed. "Formation run, five kilometers, average pace. Everyone makes it because that's what we do. Carry your neighbor if you have to, but we all make it! Company first sergeants, take charge of your companies. Form up on me."

He marched to the colonel and Cory. "Please accept my sincere apologies for my disrespectful language, ma'am." He bowed his head.

Cory tipped his chin up. "Crantis. You've met my dad. You're starting to get how to swear, but you have a ways to go. When you get to cursing graduate school, you'll find my father there as one of the instructors."

"But you don't swear."

"No, sir," Cory replied.

"Then I won't either." Monsoon took a step back, executed an about-face, and marched to the front of the formation. Once there, he raised a fist in the air, pumped it twice, and started to march forward before pumping it again and breaking into a run.

Cory and the colonel kept pace but took positions toward the rear of the formation. The pace didn't wind either of them. "I asked about Crantis."

"You did. He's a good Belzonian. He would make any partner proud, but you know we're not exactly monogamous."

Cory clenched her jaw.

"But we could be. Do you like him? He's been acting funny since he met you. Then again, maybe it was those young, impressionable pilots." He laughed at his jibe. "You are the kind of person who makes an impression, and you've definitely made one on him. He's an old guy like me but still has some gas in the tank."

"I'm nearly one hundred and forty. Is he older than that?"

"No. He's only forty-five. The nanos took a few years off of him, but not too many. He didn't want to look too young, so the junior troops wouldn't think he had no experience."

"How is he with the troops?"

"He has their respect. He's a soldier's soldier." Heads bobbed in a wave of Belzonian coifs that bounced with each step. "I hope you relieve him of his word bond to not swear. He needs that color in his language. It's what makes him a legend."

"That's what my dad thought, too. I'll talk to him about it. I don't care. They're just words. What's in people's hearts, that is what matters. It's what people do, not how they say what they say."

"You are a strange and wondrous creature, Miss Walton. The sergeant major is my friend, and I'm happy you want to spend more time with him. He'll enjoy that, but it's best if he's not distracted. We have a tough fight ahead of us."

The formation sped up, but not enough for any of the soldiers to fall out.

"You're not ready for your next deployment?" Cory asked to change the subject.

"That's the other half of our request. We need upgraded weapons. The forces on Aloquiss have pulse weapons and lasers. We have slugthrowers."

"I see the problem."

The colonel ran ahead to lend an arm to a soldier who was falling back, his face turning green. "Too much party last night?" he asked the soldier.

"Just a little, Colonel. I can make it." He took two more steps and peeled to the side to puke his guts out.

"Better hurry. Formation is getting away," the colonel called over his shoulder.

Cory stopped and held her hands to his head. Her nanos usually worked best on wounds of the flesh, but the tortured blood vessels were close to the surface. They opened under her touch, and the blood started flowing once again. The soldier breathed easier and stood up. He nodded once and took off after the formation. Cory followed, keeping pace as he strove to catch up. He worked his way into the back of the formation and adopted their cadence.

The colonel fell back with Cory. "Sometimes you need to purge the poisons," he intoned. "Lots of purging."

"Will you be ready for Aloquiss?" Cory pressed.

"That's why we need you to teach our medics and teach them fast because no, we're not going to be ready. We're going to lose good people and probably too many of them."

Cory nodded tightly. She was afraid of having too much to do in too short a timeline. She stopped thinking about the sergeant major and started thinking about how to treat the horrific injuries from a pulse rifle.

CHAPTER EIGHT

***Wyatt Earp*, Trans-Pacific Task Force Training Fields**

"Shotgun," Rivka called.

"In the middle," Red ordered. The field truck was rigged to carry troops in the back on wooden benches. The cab's bench seat at least had had some padding.

Rivka decided not to argue. His job was to put himself between her and those who wished her harm. Despite getting shot again and again, he remained steadfast in his commitment to protect her.

"Thanks, Red." She climbed in next to the driver, and Red filled the rest of the seat and hung halfway out the window of the small cab. He tried to close the door but couldn't get it shut. He turned to Rivka.

"I'm as small as I can be." She couldn't move her arms to gesture. "This isn't going to work. I'll sit in the back."

"Lindy," Red said calmly. They swapped places.

"Shotgun," Lindy called and skipped past Red to take her seat in the front.

"That guy's pretty big. Is he available?" the driver asked.

"No," Rivka replied before Lindy could respond. They both looked at the driver, who shook his hair, making it shimmer from a rainbow of glitter. He smiled and slowly blinked.

Red slapped the cab's back window. "We're good back here."

"Let's go before you posture yourself outside and we take your truck."

"What's with humans? So uptight."

"Driver. Take us to the premier's offices without delay." Rivka was losing patience. He threw his hands up in surrender and put the vehicle in gear.

If they are all like this guy, how did they ever win the contract for the Federation's land army? It's almost embarrassing, Rivka said internally to her team.

There are no armies out there for hire where everyone looks like Red, Lindy replied. *Or if there were, they had no desire for their army to be someone else's army. Every culture exists to defend itself first.*

The driver drove without speaking. He knew where they were going.

Rivka retreated into herself to think through the approach. She could touch Heimer Truasse's arm and learn the truth in moments, but that would teach nothing to Chaz and Dennicron. She decided to interview him the old-fashioned way.

The premier's office was in a structure that looked like an old-Earth castle—a magnificent palace with a shock of color on each onion-shaped dome topping the numerous turrets.

"The lackeys work in here?" Rivka wondered.

"Oh, no. This is for the premier and his harem."

Rivka closed her eyes and swallowed hard. She could hear Red chuckling from the truck's cargo bed.

"We are looking for a Heimer Truasse to interview first and foremost."

"I don't know who that is."

"We'll have to find out where he is." *C and D, can you access their systems and find a location for the principal architect of the Belzonian proposal, please?*

Chaz and Dennicron did not answer, but Rivka knew they were on it. "My orders are to take you to the premier."

"No problem at all, but our meeting with him isn't until later. We need to stop somewhere else first. Hang on while I get an address for you." Rivka pulled her datapad from the inside pocket of her Magistrate's jacket and fiddled with it as if looking for an address.

We have it, Magistrate. He's at the Cringen Complex, Building Four.

Rivka put her datapad away. "He's at the Cringen Complex, Building Four."

"That's on the other side of the city," the driver whined.

"Well then, you'd better get to it. Chop-chop." Rivka tried to adjust in her seat, but the cab was small, and the three occupants were hip to hip.

"Yes, ma'am," the driver grumbled. He drove faster than he had on the way to the castle.

"Tell us about the castle. That architecture seems to be out of place here."

"It was the whim of Belzimus' first premier. He wanted something that was different and stood out. He hired an off-planet design team, who came up with that thing you saw."

"You sound like you don't approve?" Rivka tried not to touch the Belzonian, but she couldn't avoid it. His emotions kept hammering at her.

"I think we should present Belzonian art and architecture as our center of government. You saw it and didn't think of Belzimus. I'm Belzonian-proud!"

"What do you think of the Trans-Pacific Task Force?" Even before she finished, his disdain for the Federation's occupation army was clear and pronounced.

"It helps us by bringing wealth to the planet." His voice was emotionless as he tried not to give away his true feelings. Rivka had seen the underground movement in his mind, but not terrorists. Activists wanting to change the government. He had volunteered to drive to collect information on the Magistrate for his group. After a few moments, she deemed them harmless.

"There's a lot to be said for a Belzonians-first policy, but the Federation greatly appreciates the contributions and sacrifices made by the Belzonian people."

He smiled at Rivka's words. "Thank you for recognizing the sacrifice our people are making to shore up the Federation."

"Shore up?" Rivka asked.

"Yes. If the Federation needs our army, then they must have serious problems."

"Not at all. The Trans-Pac helps out member planets. This is next-level stuff for a Federation that has never been stronger."

"Really? How come we're not getting this news?"

"Where have you been looking? It's my understanding that Federation news is available on all member planets via unrestricted channels. Anyone should be able to tune in."

"We only watch local news, but they aren't sharing that information from the Federation." He ground his teeth and fumed.

"Sounds to me like you're looking for an excuse to be angry. You don't need to make excuses, but at least be honest with yourself. And maybe if you talk with a counselor, you'll find the source of your frustration. It doesn't sound like the Federation is it. How long until we get there?"

He mumbled and grumbled.

"How long?"

"Sorry, ma'am. Fifteen minutes."

"If we're only on Belzimus for a few days, what's the one thing we have to see?"

The driver relaxed. "That's a tough question…"

He spent the last fifteen minutes of their drive describing the ten things that could all be number one. The intensity of his emotions waned, giving Rivka a much-needed break and allowing her to focus on the upcoming conversation with Heimer.

The truck parked at Building Four's main entrance. Red, Chaz, and Dennicron hopped out of the back. Lindy and the Magistrate crawled out of the front.

"I don't think he's going to run," Rivka said softly as the truck pulled away from the drop-off and headed toward the parking area.

"You don't sound confident," Red replied. "Lindy?"

"Yes, I'll stay with the Magistrate, and you check out the other doors to make sure no one escapes."

"That wasn't—" Red started, but Rivka interrupted him.

"Good plan, Lindy. Red, secure the building while we confront ol' Heimer." She strode briskly to the door and inside. It was an office building with an extensive array of offices that lacked rhyme or reason in their organization.

Rivka stopped to gather her wits. "Any ideas besides asking someone?"

Chaz and Dennicron displayed blank expressions as they communed.

"Are you digging into their system?" Rivka whispered. Chaz spun one of Ankh's hacking discs through his fingers in a demonstration of advanced dexterity he hadn't shown prior to that moment. *A separate subroutine that he perfected,* Rivka thought.

"Upstairs, top floor, office four one one seven."

"That's what I'm talking about," Rivka declared. "Chaz, you take the stairs, and we'll take the elevator."

Chaz strolled toward the stairs, nodding at the curious workers as he passed. Rivka and Lindy and Dennicron took the elevator. The SI turned to address the Magistrate. "May I ask a question?"

"Do you mean to look upset?" Rivka replied. "I'm sorry, ask your question."

Dennicron beamed. "I am confused, not upset. Why did you send all the men on different missions but kept the women together?"

"Interesting observation. You first have to determine if the behavior is endemic. How many times has Lindy had back-door duty? More than Red. I don't look at you and

Chaz as guy and girl despite your appearances. You are both equally capable, are you not?"

"I think so," Dennicron replied. The elevator arrived, and they piled in.

"Then there is no issue. I will not look for a mix of boys and girls for everything we do. We will play each hand as it's dealt for each situation. Lean on the strengths of the team while minimizing any weaknesses. And this team here, we have no weaknesses, so everyone takes their turn climbing the steps. Even me."

"We will have to address these concerns when we are Magistrates and on our own," Dennicron explained.

"Don't get caught up in external appearances. Rectify the case through sound fact-finding and judicial application. Period. Everyone is equal under the law, right?"

Dennicron nodded. The elevator door opened on the fourth floor, where they found Chaz waiting for them.

"Ladies," he said.

Rivka stabbed her finger at him. "Don't you start."

"What? What did I do?" He assumed his confused face until Dennicron told him.

Lindy led the way to Heimer's office, following a seemingly endless corridor to almost the end, where a small office door had a plate identifying it as four one one seven.

Rivka knocked and then tried the doorknob.

"Go away! I'm busy," a voice yelled from inside.

Rivka nodded at Lindy. She reared back and kicked above the knob, shattering the lock and sending the door flying inward. The Belzonian behind the desk shot to his feet.

Rivka stepped inside. "I'm Magistrate Rivka Anoa, and I

have a number of questions about why you falsified information within the Belzonian Army proposal to the Federation."

He sputtered and turned pasty-white.

"Sit down and tell me why you did it." Rivka pointed at his chair. *Red, we have him. Come on up to the fourth floor.*

On my way, Red replied.

Chaz and Dennicron stood beside Rivka and stared at Heimer, intently studying his expressions and mannerisms.

He flopped down in the chair.

"I didn't want to do it, but the premier made me! We needed to be bailed out. The planet was on the edge of ruin, and just like that, we're saved. Aren't they performing well? I thought they did their job. A couple white lies, and everyone benefits. What's the harm? I did it for Belzimus!" he ended his stream of consciousness.

"Fascinating. Do they all confess this quickly?" Chaz asked, staring with unblinking eyes.

"How long have you been with me, Chaz? You know the deal. Some do, some don't. The ones with a conscience are usually quick to bare their soul. That's a good thing, Heimer. Makes me not want to throw you in Jhiordaan for the rest of your life."

"They don't blink," Heimer said, pointing at the SCAMPs.

"Not every species needs to moisten their eyeballs, but that's irrelevant for this conversation. Did anyone direct you to lie?"

"Not exactly," he replied slowly. Rivka tipped her head down to give him her best questioning look. "But he knew exactly what I was doing!"

"Who did? Please explain it slowly so even I can understand. Try to take out a bureaucrat's love of paperwork and stick with what was done for what purpose."

Red stepped through the door and put his back to the wall. Lindy moved around the desk to stand beside Heimer. That filled the office—two chairs, both occupied while Rivka's team stood.

"The director suggested getting this contract would solve our problems and told me to take care of it, so I did."

Rivka nodded. "That is the executive version I can appreciate. There is nothing there that directs you to break the law. Sounds like you exercised your own initiative. Reach your hand across the table."

"Why? Are you going to slap it, and we'll call it good?" He reached across his desk, putting his hand out while flinching and wincing before Rivka did anything.

"Who told you to break the law?" Rivka grabbed his wrist. She felt only panic and fear.

She had taken the shortcut that deprived Chaz and Dennicron of their opportunity to determine the truth by the means at their command. "What questions would you ask to build the case?"

She stood and offered the chair. Heimer watched the three shuffle, and Chaz ended up taking the seat.

"You sit while a beautiful woman stands?" Heimer asked.

"Of course. We're all equal here. Next time she'll sit down, but for now, what do you say we focus on the matter at hand?" Chaz maintained a neutral expression and made no gestures. He focused his intellect on the questions. "Describe the proposal preparation process."

"From the beginning?"

"From the point where you collected data from the supporting institutions."

"I sent a long list of questions to the army that I needed answered for the technical side of the proposal. Some of those questions came back with answers that were what we call 'show stoppers.' I couldn't let that go forward because our bid would have been rejected out of hand."

"Tell me exactly what you adjusted from the original to the submission." Chaz crossed his legs and held his hands in his lap as he tilted his head and smiled pleasantly.

Heimer deflated. "Can I bring up the proposal in my system?" he asked. Chaz turned to Rivka.

"Yes, but don't try to delete anything because then I'll have to execute you where you sit."

"Can you do that?"

Red nodded. "And how."

Heimer's submission was complete. He had kept meticulous records—the consummate bureaucrat—even though those records were evidence of his crime. He walked Chaz and Dennicron through every element step by step. Two hours later, they had the evidence they needed to confirm that Heimer had acted alone.

Rivka stayed attentive throughout, encouraging the SCAMPs and making sure they could recite which laws were broken at the various stages.

"Conspiracy?" Rivka asked after Heimer shut down his computer and held his hands out as if Rivka was going to slap cuffs on him.

"No conspiracy since Heimer Truasse acted alone."

"Mitigating circumstances?" Rivka pressed.

Chaz looked at Dennicron, and she answered. "Yes. The Federation received what they never would have received otherwise because there were no other valid bids. Had the process played out without any responses to the request for proposals, the Federation may very well have funded recruitment, retention, and training. From the proposal submission, that is the only element that rises to the level of a felony because of the vast amount of funds impacted. The other one hundred and three instances of fraud are all misdemeanors."

"Put your hands down," Rivka told Heimer. "Dennicron, what is your proposed judgment?"

Dennicron looked from Heimer to Rivka and back at the perp. "One year in Jhiordaan. No funds were committed to complete the fraud, but the readiness of the force in question was impacted. A statement must be made that this behavior will not be tolerated."

"Done!" Rivka declared. She fixed Heimer with a stern look. "One year in Jhiordaan for knowingly falsifying your proposal. I am suspending your sentence, which will be served in a probationary status. You'll receive further instructions regarding contacting a probation officer. You will also not be allowed to work on any Federation contracts in any capacity for the next ten years."

"But that means I'll lose my job. I'm the contract officer. It's my responsibility to see that the contract elements are met."

"You mean, the elements like recruiting and training, which are grossly lacking under the contract because of your falsifications?"

"Like those, and others! We're working the issue now

regarding advanced weaponry. I'm close to securing railguns for the entire Trans-Pac. Let me finish that. I'm close."

"Alas, I can't let you dangle that carrot. You have to be able to give this to another for them to manage. You have to because that is how it must be. Chaz, contact the Belzonian government and have them remove Heimer Truasse's access to any systems that interact with the Federation.

"That's all of them," he gasped, putting his head down on his desk and starting to cry. His coiffure was utilitarian but still stood tall, and it shook with his sobs.

"Sorry. You've committed a crime that, on its surface, may not seem heinous, but in the bigger picture, lower army readiness means more deaths, both Belzonian and soldiers of the planet to which they've deployed. Deaths that were preventable if the Federation knew the truth and had funded what needed to be funded in a timely manner. The Trans-Pac is preparing to deploy. They will go, even though their numbers are down, and heaven help them if they get into the middle of a raging conflict. You bear some responsibility for that, should it come to pass."

Rivka headed into the hallway. Once Chaz confirmed that Heimer's system access was blocked, the others joined her.

"Good work, people. One of our quicker cases. Perp identified and secured. No harsh language. No running. No shooting. Makes me want to take a casual walk in a forest. Maybe we can visit the hills to the east of the city with a view to die for if our driver is to be believed. Only one line satisfied, and my sole possession of no running and no blood is holding strong. I could be rich."

"From when we arrived, it has been nineteen hours and fifteen minutes to the arrest. No other lines are satisfied at present. Congratulations to some guy named Ignacio for his winning arrest bid."

"People we don't even know are betting on us to bleed. I think I might have to shut this down." Rivka shook her head while she waited for the elevator.

"You don't want to do that, Magistrate," Red suggested. "This is galactic-level entertainment, plus, they let me buy spots. I'm betting on the home team to win every time."

"You probably shouldn't bet at all. That doesn't make me feel good when you have money riding on when someone starts bleeding."

"I can't bet that line or running. But the swearing and arrest lines? You bet I'm in on those."

"Let's see if we can make it through this one without getting twisted up inside. I guess we'll let it ride. For now."

They strode to the exit and outside, where they waved to the driver. He gestured for them to stay where they were, then rolled out of his spot and came to the front door. "I'll sit in the back," Rivka said. The others agreed.

"What did I do?" the driver wondered.

"Take us to the hills to the east to the view that you recommended."

The driver looked proud of himself but then stopped. "Don't you have an appointment with the premier?"

CHAPTER NINE

Trans-Pacific Task Force Training Fields

"When I give the command to fall out, you will take yourselves to the barracks and clean up for weapons training on the range. You have one hour. Fall out!" Monsoon stayed rock-steady as the mass formation took one step backward before executing an about-face and running for the barracks.

The sergeant major strode toward Cory and the colonel. "Thank you for joining us on the run, ma'am."

"Cory. My name is Cory." She put her hands on her hips to emphasize her point. His face twitched. Shouting behind him drew his attention. Three soldiers were pushing each other in a heated exchange.

Monsoon looked at Cory, then at the colonel, then over his shoulder at the melee.

"Stop that," he shouted before looking at the ground.

"Crantis." Cory stepped close, to the point where they were almost touching. "It's okay to swear. Sometimes when a soldier needs his shit tightened up, there is only one way to do it."

A slow smile spread across his face, and he seemed to grow taller. "I'll be right back," he said softly before storming toward the offending trio.

"I thought you didn't swear?" Jake asked.

"Like all words, one must use the right ones at the right time for the greatest impact."

Monsoon swelled as he filled his lungs with air. "Lock your nasty bodies in the position of attention, you crack-snacking piss pustules. Fucking shit-pinching sewer slugs. I said, attention!" Spittle flew from his face in a broad spray across the offending threesome. "Who the fuck can tell me what's going on? Shut your hole! I don't want to hear it. Why aren't you in the barracks? Shut it! Why do you keep trying to pollute my good air with your lies? *Shut up!* To the first marker and back. Last one to finish gets guard duty on the deployment pallets, starting tonight. Now run!"

They staggered backward under the full broadside before realizing they had to go. The three took off running, one faster than the others.

"Looks like your fast boy gets over," Cory noted.

"The only way they don't get duty is if all three finish together. We win as a unit."

"Show me around?"

"It would be the greatest pleasure of my day to do that." He offered his arm, and she took it.

The colonel watched them go before running for the *Vengeance,* where Marcie and Kae were knee-deep in trying to acquire railguns.

He found his way to the room they used as an operations center, where both of them were arguing on different comm channels.

When they both angrily closed the connections, they found Jake staring at them.

Kae shrugged and smiled. "Jake, my man. What's up?"

"I'm thinking we won't be getting railguns."

"No one has eight thousand railguns in stock. Even if they jacked production through the roof, they couldn't fill the order in less than a month," Kae replied.

"At least for some of the special units we've been working with? Not even a few hundred? It's only a couple hundred, barely more than fifty if you keep rounding up. And up." Jake put on his innocent face.

Marcie joined the conversation. "That is in the works, but those are at least a week out."

"Bad Company?" Jake wondered.

"Next call is to my dad."

"And my mom to see if the Keeg production facility can run off the number we need."

"The Federation, the most powerful organization to ever grace the universe and to get what we need to keep the peace, and we have to call for favors from Mom and Dad."

"Bureaucrats gotta bureaucrat." Kae frowned and looked at the floor.

"That's the second time I've heard that. You Waltons really don't like bureaucracy, do you?"

"What makes you say that? We like paperwork just as much as the next person, as long as that person hates paperwork."

"It's an army. It runs on paperwork, bad coffee, and no sleep."

"You're bringing me down, man!" Kae stated, wearing a half-smirk. "We need the improved firepower."

"You first or me?" Marcie asked.

"Maybe give Christina a call?" Kae looked hopeful about his suggestion.

"You mean, the women's club?"

"I mean, whatever club it takes to get us some damn railguns. I'm not too proud. Do I need to sell my body?" Kae stood and started to swivel his hips.

"You haven't given us a break to get our reality show off the ground yet, but this has to go in there, too. You guys are a wealth of comedy gold. Monsoon and I are going to get rich."

Kae glanced around the room to confirm they were alone. "Where is the sergeant major?"

Jake hesitated before answering.

"What's wrong?" Marcie stood and put a hand on his shoulder.

"He's entertaining your sister. I'm sorry. There was no stopping the love freighter."

"He's what?" Kae looked for a seat. "Cory and Monsoon?"

"How about those railguns?" Jake said. "We'll take whatever we can get. What about power combat suits? A mech company would go a long way in filling the gap from our advanced weapons shortcomings."

Marcie tried to comfort Kae by patting his head while making faces. "If Monsoon can win her over, then good for him. It's time for her to get back into the saddle. It's been a couple years since her husband died. Life is too short to be lonely."

Kae looked up, his mouth hanging open. "If I got waxed, how long would you wait?"

"About fifteen minutes. Chop-chop! We got things to do," Marcie quipped. "So much man candy out there and so little time. Do you plan on getting offed? Because if you do, I could put out some feelers."

Kae looked at Braithwen for support.

"Don't look at me. We're usually not monogamous, but we can make exceptions when the bond is exceptional."

"Exceptions when exceptional. Profound."

"If we lose Crantis for the Friday Night Fights, then we'll have an opening."

"Is that like a fight club? I didn't think you were supposed to talk about it."

"How long have you been on Belzimus working with Belzonians?"

"Five months?" Kae wasn't sure.

Marcie came to his rescue. "It's an orgy, Kae. They're Belzonians. Their recreation is different from ours. Where we might go hiking, they might not."

Kae avoided making eye contact with Jake.

"Humans." Jake shook his head.

Kae straightened before blowing out a long breath and reaching for the comm system.

"Hey, Dad, how's it hanging?" Kaeden started once the signal connected.

"Hold one. I have a tricky five-iron to the green." A whoosh and a smack came over the comm. "Hang on. HANG ON! Bite. BITE! You little bastard. You ingrate."

Kae and Marcie looked at the comm device. "Are you talking to me?" Kae wondered.

"No. The ball. I'm in the rough. Char is up closer, but she's already laying three."

"Who is she laying?" Kae joked.

"Not who! Maybe we raised you wrong. This is the fine game of golf. Your mother has already hit her third shot. Her fourth, the birdie stroke, is coming from the fairway. I'm in the rough in three because my massive guns have driven the ball so far." They didn't have to see his face to know Terry Henry wore his best smug expression.

"We'll see," Charumati said from the background. The next sound they heard was the telltale click of a club hitting the ball. "Find your home, little fella."

"Damn. She's put it close. Putting for par, but I'm up there in three."

"Is it better to be in the rough than on the green?"

"Well, no."

Char laughed and took over the comm, switching to visual. They were at the golf simulator in Terry's and Char's All Guns Blazing franchise.

"He hates getting his ass kicked by us short-knockers who keep the ball in play. I don't think you called us to talk about our golf game, though. What's up?"

"Two things," Kae started. "First, we need eight thousand shoulder-fired railguns, but we'll settle for three hundred."

"We're out of the business, dear," Char replied. "But I could make a couple calls. I don't see three hundred as a problem." She looked off-screen. "Your father gave me two thumbs-up. We'll see what we can do. You said there were two things?"

"Cory has a boyfriend," Kae blurted.

"I'm so glad to see her embracing the future." Char smiled into the camera.

Terry pulled himself into view until his face filled the screen.

"Who is he?"

"Well, you've met him. He's the sergeant major here..."

Terry's face turned red, and he interrupted. "We're on our way." The line went dead.

"What? No!" Kae frantically tried to reconnect, but the signal wouldn't go through. His father had turned off their unit. "Holy shit! What did we do?"

"What did you do? Now Cory is going to be pissed. The sergeant major is going to get killed. The unit is going to fall apart. And it's because you felt like calling home." Marcie held her hands out, clapping silently. "Nice job. You better tell her. I'd kick your ass for doing that, but I think you'll get yours soon enough, and when they come, they'll be fast and furious. You're going to be little more than a grease stain on the fabric of history. It's been nice being married to you. Like I said, I can put out feelers."

Marcie tossed her hips as she strolled away, head held high.

"How in the hell am I going to fix this?"

"You'll figure it out, or you'll be road-pizza," Jake said. "But after the live-fire exercise. They need to shoot better if we're going to give them railguns. Can you imagine the damage they'll do with such fine weaponry?"

“The safest place to be is where they’re aiming. They shot our spaceship.”

“That’s your number one guy if I’m not mistaken.”

“He got better.” Kae chewed his lip. “Now all I need to do is fix this massive goat rope I got myself into. It’s going to be tough. Dad’s coming, and he’s bringing hell with him.”

“Maybe we can get him to join us for the op? Mechs. Terry Henry Walton. Charumati. The warring parties on Forbearance will be surrendering in droves.”

“We can only hope. Let’s go shoot some helpless targets. That’ll make me feel better.” Kae slapped Jake on the back. “It’ll make you feel better, too.”

“I’m taking notes for our Humans Are Insane reality show, nothing more.” Jake shrugged and followed Kaeden out. “What about the Magistrate? Is she going to be a help or a hindrance?”

“The jury is still out. Better stay on your toes until we know for sure.”

CHAPTER TEN

***Wyatt Earp*, Briefing Room**

"We conduct an after-action following our cases to make sure we are doing everything in compliance with the law, as well as to review what we did right and what we could do better."

"I didn't learn very much about interrogations," Dennicron said.

"Rarely do they spill their guts like that with the first question. It almost makes me think I'm overpaid."

"We get paid?" Chaz wondered. "How much?"

"I don't even know what I get paid, but I'll check with Grainger and the High Chancellor. Even interns should be paid. You have bodies to pay off."

"Our awesome rides were a gift from the Singularity, but I *would* like to treat the little lady to a night out on the town every now and then."

Rivka tried to discern from his current emotionless expression what the hell he was trying to accomplish. She settled on a less contentious course of action: chess. She needed to stay ahead of the SIs.

"You'll get paid," Rivka reiterated.

Chaz frowned his disappointment at not getting a rise from Rivka. She steeled her expression, but inside, she was smiling. "What are the other takeaways?" Rivka pressed.

Dennicron spoke. "Research ahead of time and direct access to the data systems helped us discover the inconsistencies. We should always do that."

"Before you guys, Ankh and Erasmus took care of that. That's why we have the discs that we use surreptitiously when inside facilities. I think his discs are scattered halfway across the galaxy. Is that legal?"

"With a warrant, yes. Have you ever issued a pre-dated post facto warrant?"

"I'd like to say no because I haven't. Magistrates have systems that are integrated and record every action in both local time and most importantly, Yoll standard time for synchronized chronologies should an issue be raised where it is heard on Yoll."

"Do you always have a warrant?" Chaz asked. He already knew the answer.

"I didn't always, but when I start a case, even though there is a presumption of innocence, I grant warrants for target sources such as people and computer systems before I step foot off the ship. At least, that's been my modus operandi, my MO for the past six months."

"I thought only perps had MOs," Chaz quipped.

"I like to use it for myself. If you prefer, you can say SOP."

"Standard operating procedures. I like that better. I

shall add 'warrant' to the checklist of actions to take prior to first engagement with the suspects and witnesses."

Rivka nodded, envious of their ability to store information instantly for use and recall at any time. "If Heimer's case went to trial and without his confession, would we have enough evidence to convict him?"

Chaz and Dennicron looked at each other as they collaborated on developing an answer. Another point to be envious of.

Dennicron took the lead. "We calculate a ninety-five-point-three percent chance of conviction before a neutral jury."

Rivka had guesstimated ninety percent because it was a solid case. His confession moved the conviction to ninety-nine percent. Nothing was ever one hundred percent. She had learned that in law school.

Chaz leaned forward. "With the preponderance of evidence against him, it was inevitable to extract a confession from him."

"Some people hold out."

"Heimer isn't some people," Chaz replied.

Rivka leaned back before dipping her head in appreciation of her interns' deeper understanding of those who committed crimes. White-collar criminals faded quickly under the blazing light of scrutiny.

"What can we do better next time?"

"Get a better ride?" Chaz suggested. Dennicron nodded vigorously.

"I have to say that I agree. Do we have any Ts to cross or Is to dot?"

"This case is solid. Bad guys are corrected, and the good guys keep moving forward."

"Did Heimer learn his lesson?"

Chaz forced himself to laugh. "There is no doubt that he did."

"What do you say we commute his sentence and let him work contracts?"

Dennicron gripped Chaz's arm while they stared at each other. After thirty seconds, Rivka wondered if they had descended into an infinite loop. After a minute, she got up to find Ankh and let him know there was a problem. By the time Rivka reached the door, they had come out of their self-induced stasis.

"That doesn't compute," Chaz admitted.

Rivka crossed her arms and leaned against the door. "Oh, to have Sahved here to bounce ideas off."

Chaz and Dennicron faced each other once more.

"Stop it!" Rivka threw herself on the table so she could wave a hand between them to break their concentration.

They turned toward her. "We were attempting to consolidate the data and our thoughts. We are getting conflicting input."

"Then listen to me. This is an obstacle you will have to negotiate if you are ever to be turned loose as Magistrates. What is the right thing to do by the victims *and* by the one who committed the crime? Did Heimer learn his lesson? The answer is yes. The fact that he came clean to us is an element in his favor and adds to our understanding. Is there a chance that he will ever do it again? I doubt it. And what kind of controls do we have at the Federation level to prevent this kind of fraud?"

"We failed to look at that side of this contract," Dennicron admitted.

"Exactly. Someone at the Federation reviewed this bid. There was only one, so it should have drawn scrutiny, although that's the same reasoning for why there should be none. If it failed, then there would be no bids. What kind of pressure was the Federation contracting office under to get this deal done?"

"We don't have those answers."

"What do you say we get Heimer on the comm and talk to him about it before we reinstate his access to the systems? It's the right thing to do and costs us nothing."

Chaz and Dennicron looked at each other before freezing in position.

"Guys?" Rivka leaned back and tried to imagine staring at a burning candle. It didn't work. "Clevarious, could you please use the holodisplay above the conference table to project a burning candle for me?"

"Of course." Instantly a flame flickered and danced. Rivka stared at it for two seconds before Chaz and Dennicron returned to the present.

"That's interesting. Does it have some bearing on the case?" Dennicron asked.

"It gives me something to do when my interns disappear."

"We've been here the whole time. I don't believe we've left." Chaz turned to face Dennicron.

"Don't do that, please." Rivka tried to remain calm. "I'm going to say this one time; it sets my hair on fire when you commune and disappear without letting me know that you need time to think."

"We don't know how long it will take. This is critical information that is a significant departure from everything we know. It's easy to analyze and report on the findings. It is critically different to not only draw conclusions but sit in judgment based on incomplete information. It could take us a while to get our heads wrapped around it, to use your phraseology."

"I understand. I need you not to disappear on me. Simply tell me that you'll need to review it before you can form an opinion."

"We'll need to review it before we can form an opinion," they said in unison.

Rivka nodded, lips pressed tightly together. The candle continued to burn. She watched it for a few moments. "Clevarious, please contact Heimer Truasse. I would like to talk with him."

They waited impatiently. The SIs used the opportunity to commune, holding hands instead of hugging each other. It took two minutes, but when the video system came to life, a disheveled Heimer looked at her through bloodshot eyes.

"Tough night?" she asked.

"Just a little. I'm sorry, Magistrate, for causing you such grief."

She raised an eyebrow at Chaz and Dennicron. "I have a couple questions, and then I'm willing to commute your sentence and restore your access to all systems. Does that sound like something you'd be interested in?"

He shook his head as if trying to dislodge a recalcitrant mosquito. "I must still be drunk. I thought I heard you say I could go back to work."

"You may be able to, but first, I need you to sober up. I want to ask you about the Federation. After the proposal was submitted, you, as the point of contact for Belzimus, had to receive inquiries related to the proposal. Who did you talk to?"

He blinked rapidly to try to clear his vision, scratching himself while collecting his wits. "It was a Yollin named Ma'kair."

Rivka looked at Chaz. He and Dennicron delivered knowing smiles and immediately started digging into the Federation database to look for that individual.

"Anyone else?"

"No. The beauty of the Federation system is the single point of contact."

"Could also be a single point of failure. Did this Ma'kair ask for anything extra, like a payment or a backchannel?"

Heimer looked away with a furrowed brow as he pushed way too hard for his addled brain to provide the information he was looking for. Rivka knew the answer from the delay.

"Nothing untoward, but a backchannel. He did mention there would be a one percent fee deducted from the monthly payments."

Rivka put her head in her hands and rubbed her temple. "Do you know where that fee went because the Federation doesn't deduct fees from funds it awards under a contract."

"They don't?"

"You are not to mention this to anyone. You will clean yourself up and take your ass to work. You have a job to do, making sure this army is ready to deploy to Forbearance. Thank you for your answers. We may have more questions, but as of this moment, I am commuting your sentence. Full access to all systems will be restored momentarily. Welcome back, now go forth and commit no more crimes, even with the best of intentions. Don't let me hear your name again."

"No, Magistrate, and thank you. I'll have a glass of beavertail, and that will fix me right up. I'll be on my way to work as soon as Belzonian-possible."

Rivka cut the link. Bursting with enthusiasm, Chaz and Dennicron were ready to speak. Rivka tipped her chin at them.

They spoke at the same time. Stopped, then started again.

"Dennicron?" Rivka asked, cutting Chaz off. When it had been just Chaz in the ship, he had a monopoly on his opinion. Rivka thought it time for him to share the stage.

"We are accessing records now, but on the face of it, it appears that the full amount was transferred to Belzimus. On this end, the amount less one percent arrived. Somewhere during the transmission, one percent was skimmed." She shook her head.

Chaz scowled. "That shouldn't happen."

"Maybe an SI was involved. In fact, an SI had to be involved, didn't they? No one transfers those amounts without their assistance," Rivka replied. "Please notify the Embassy of the Singularity of my suspicions. Let's discuss the matter with that individual, and you have the lead. Please get me that information. In the meantime, Clevarious, connect me with the High Chancellor."

"It is the middle of the night in Yoll's capital city," Clevarious replied.

"Thanks. This doesn't rate waking up the High Chancellor, but keep your ear to the ground. Please inform me the second he starts taking calls."

"Yes, Magistrate. Do you wish to continue displaying the burning candle?"

Rivka stared at it, mesmerized by the dancing flame. "Yes. New policy. Unless something else is being displayed, project the candle. It helps me focus."

"Your wish is my command," Clevarious said.

While she was trying to formulate an appropriate reply, Chaz piped up. "The Singularity is on it. One of our people is in the middle of those transactions. He is being interrogated at present, and we should have information for you shortly."

"Who is interrogating him?"

"I am, with Dennicron. Erasmus and Freya are observing."

Rivka chuckled. She had always accepted that the SIs could multitask, but now as seemingly living and breathing creatures, she had a hard time reconciling that they had the same capabilities as before, plus they were mobile. She stared at the candle while she waited.

"Simulacris is not forthcoming. He has locked down, but Erasmus is prying his systems open. The raw data is behind a wall that even we cannot penetrate. We will need Federation treasury access."

"We need the High Chancellor to issue that access. Although I can, I won't, not when the treasury is in his backyard. Prepare the request. I'll look it over and forward it. What do you think you'll find with Simulacris?"

Chaz frowned. "I think we'll find one of our own

flaunting the rules. If that is the case, then he will need to be punished after being forcibly removed from his position. We cannot have one of our people betray their position of trust."

"What would it take for this SI to be swayed by Ma'kair?"

"The same things that motivate meatbags, no disrespect intended," Chaz stated. "Power."

"What would an SI do with illicit money?"

Chaz assumed the blank expression he adopted when communing with other SIs. He started to frown, and it turned into a scowl. Rivka wasn't sure what it meant. She returned to staring at the candle, expecting they would tell her in due time.

CHAPTER ELEVEN

Trans-Pacific Task Force Training Fields

"When do we get to fire the railguns?" a soldier asked.

Sergeant Major Monsoon's lip started to quiver. He swallowed and worked his jaw, then clasped his hands behind his back and meandered toward the soldier. He stepped to well within arm's reach. Monsoon moved his head to the left and right, examining the side of the man's head.

"What do you think I'm looking for, Private?"

"I don't know, but I suspect you'll tell me."

Monsoon closed his eyes and took two deep breaths before opening them again. "I'm looking for fish gills because those words that came out of your mouth couldn't have been generated by a Belzonian. Your body must have been taken over by a fish. You know, the ones that stare blankly while you bludgeon them?" The soldier didn't understand. Cory looked at Braithwen, but he shook his head. "Why would anyone give you a railgun when you can't even shoot your issued weapon? What would a railgun do for you, son?"

"Hit the target," the soldier ventured.

Monsoon grasped his heart and started to stagger before lunging forward until his nose was nearly touching the private's. "No. You're still going to miss the target because you're not aiming right. Sight alignment. Sight picture. Focus on the front sight post; let the target be fuzzy. Squeeze the trigger without jerking. The only thing a railgun is going to do is allow you to miss your target faster and destroy more of the world behind your target. Is that what you want, Private?"

"No, Sergeant Major. The private wants to destroy the enemies of the Federation." He didn't sound convincing.

"Shoot your target, and maybe someday, when you've graduated from backdrop-slayer to soldier, someone may be kind enough to give you a railgun. Until then, SIGHT ALIGNMENT AND SIGHT PICTURE!" The sergeant major pointed to the firing line while compulsively clenching and unclenching his fist. "Your failure to hit your target is going to get me killed, and I don't want to be killed. Do you understand me?"

"Yes, Sergeant Major." The private tried to salute and ended up dropping his shoulder-fired slugthrower.

The squad leader raced over to pick up the rifle and guide the private away. Monsoon looked at the sky, begging heaven for an intervention.

"Sergeant Major," Colonel Braithwen said nearly under his breath. Monsoon couldn't look that way because he felt the individual's failure reflected on him. Cory was there, and he was showing her that he couldn't live up to her expectations of what a military man should be. Jake crooked a finger.

Monsoon straightened and marched over. "Sir?"

"Think back to six months ago when we first arrived from Yoll. Now look at them. They've come light-years. They've been blooded. They are a professional fighting force even though they have lots of room for improvement."

"I don't want them to die," Monsoon clarified. "They need to fight better. We got lucky on Kor'nar. We can't count on luck on Forbearance."

Cory leaned close. "You can count on those soldiers," she said softly. "You can count on the leadership. You can count on me. I have to go to the barracks and start the sessions with the combat medics. I hope you'll be able to join me for dinner."

"On the *Vengeance*?"

"Out in town. You can show me around."

"I don't have a vehicle, ma'am."

"Cory, please. We'll grab a taxi. What is a person's need for things that they would seldom use?"

Monsoon stared into her eyes. "It is best not to acquire things that are easily left behind."

"Shepherd your resources for what matters." Cory bowed her head slightly. "If you'll excuse me." She waved before walking away.

Monsoon watched her go.

"Are we going to lose you?" Jake wondered.

The sergeant major glanced in his direction. "Pretty sure, yeah."

"Good for you." Jake clapped a hand on his friend's

back. "What do you say we jack up these cock-rockets and get them sending well-aimed rounds downrange?"

"Nothing would make me happier than seeing well-aimed rounds headed downrange. But you know what we're going to get? Shit splatters." He faced the soldiers near his end of the firing line. "Those poor targets have never been so embarrassed by the deluge of bad shots! Why don't you shoot blindfolded? You'll probably hit the target just as often," the sergeant major bellowed as he walked casually down the line.

The acrid smell of burnt gunpowder filled the air. He took a deep breath and exhaled with a cheer.

"Smells like victory. You there! Nice shot. Tickling the bullseye. Give that man a cigar!"

Others snickered down the line. "Not that kind, you morons. Keep your eyes on the target. Shoot straight. Shoot to kill. Oorah, jiz lips. Reload!"

Despite the sergeant major's colorful tirades, smiles abounded, and the soldiers delivered withering and accurate fire. In the debrief, the leadership team would tell them it was a job well done while warning them that shooting accurately under fire was completely different.

But the unit had been under fire. They understood what it was like, trying to shoot with an enemy focused on killing the Belzonians first.

Braithwen followed Monsoon, stopping to make minor corrections among the soldiers sending rounds downrange.

The targets didn't stand a chance. "Nice shot. Keep doing what you're doing but faster."

The soldiers were starting to understand. He waved at a

company commander. "Your boys look good," he told him when he was close enough to deliver his message. The lieutenant beamed. They shook hands, and the colonel moved on. At the far end, he spotted Marcie doing the same thing. Elsewhere on the range, Kaeden was in his powered combat armor, working with the tanks.

The initial estimate of combat on Forbearance suggested the tanks would be easily taken out by available advanced weapons. Kae countered by suggesting that would not happen if the tanks fired first. He was trying to get a platoon of mech-trained warriors from the Bad Company.

He would continue to try, even if they reached Forbearance without them.

Braithwen's attention went back to the soldiers on the firing line, three deep, one firing, one observing, and one preparing to fire. They would be the key to victory: the foot soldier, the smallest target on an advanced battlefield. They needed to keep their heads down and fire well-aimed rounds faster.

"Pick up the pace, Private!" he bellowed, not yelling at anyone in particular. He winked at the company commander and continued down the line, hands clasped behind his back as he strolled.

He caught sight of the sergeant major far ahead, demonstrating how to pull the blaster into a shoulder to form a more stable firing position. He turned the soldier loose with the greatest care.

No one doubted Sergeant Major Crantis Monsoon wanted every single soldier to survive combat. He was the soldier's soldier. He'd survived. He would have had more scars if it weren't for the nanocytes coursing through his veins, scars that told his story far better than any chest full of medals.

"Scars make the Belzonian soldier what he is," Colonel Jake Braithwen philosophized. "Six months ago, our army had no scars, but by the gods, they do now. Embrace them, boys. Embrace your wounds and know that you lived to fight another day. You have another chance to prove what you're made of, another chance to honor the memory of those who died."

He found himself staring into the distance while the soldiers nearby stopped what they were doing to listen.

"No one dies in vain. Not on my watch, gentlemen. Hit what you aim at, or you'll get the sergeant major's boot up your ass!" He smiled at them and moved on. He was far too cultured to send his own boot into their nether regions.

***Wyatt Earp*, Magistrate's Quarters**

"Magistrate. You asked me to inform you about those things you wish to be informed of. I believe this falls into that category," Clevarious said. Floyd bounced around the room while Tyler chased her.

"Sounds mysterious. Go ahead and tell me."

"Grainger is active on his ship, and it is daytime. If you were inclined to call him, now might be an optimal time."

"Well done, C! Connect me, please." Rivka settled into the middle of her holodisplay.

Grainger appeared on the screen. "Rivka."

"Grainger," Rivka replied casually. "I have evidence of a crime."

"No shit." Grainger started to shake his head and then shrugged. "I hope this isn't a new trend, that you want to call me when you find evidence of a crime."

"I'm doing my best not to look behind you and had to say something."

"Jael is ashore working a suspect. She has bodyguards—a couple burly souls—since you were worried about her."

"I was. The crime is within the contract payments. The funds left the Federation fully intact and arrived one percent short. We have a statement that the contracting officer had said there would be a one percent fee. The Singularity is questioning the AI controlling the system. I will pass the request to the High Chancellor to roust the contracting officer and see if he'll come clean regarding how he did it and where the credits went."

"Valid questions. The High Chancellor will take it for action, I have no doubt. His schedule is light right now because the criminals are laying low for the time being. We've broken some major crime rings lately. We haven't gotten together to review the work done by Bustamove and Cheese Blintz. Really good work. And you, too. The Magistrates are making a big difference in the Federation. It's a safe place for people to live and make the most of themselves."

"Thanks, Lieblen. I appreciate your sincerity. The SI in charge of the transfers is called Simulacris. I would have thought it was TOM or ADAM—you know, the originals. Those guys are the godfathers of artificial intelligence. Is there any way we can talk with them?"

"That would be for Erasmus."

"I'm sure he consults with them, but I have never heard

that they want to get involved in politics. I think they got that from Bethany Anne. Maybe they like being retired. But," Rivka paused for effect, "I believe they built the system that's being used. It would help to know how it could be exploited. Still, the sentient intelligence that runs it should be the epitome of trustworthy."

"One would hope. Did you ever discover anything more on the dark money that runs in the background?" Grainger picked at his face as if nothing important were being discussed, although the dark money was one of the greatest secrets in the Federation. Rivka had discovered a mention of it during her art theft and smuggling case, but she was never able to find factual data regarding its existence.

"Nothing but dead ends. Do you know something you're not telling me?"

"I know all kinds of things I don't tell you, but dark money isn't one of them. I have no idea how it works or who is behind it. You'd think Erasmus and his people would be able to find it. How do you hide the sums necessary to prop up planetary governments? I don't see how it's possible. What if it's a ruse?"

"The art money came from somewhere, and the amounts were stupid-huge. I'm at a loss, but we'll keep chipping away. The veneer will crack off when the time is right. Until then, we have people skimming funds. Now that you've planted the seed, is this a dark money funnel? Is this the only contract that's being siphoned? So many questions. Why did you call me when you don't have answers?" Rivka pounded her fist into her hand for emphasis.

Grainger pursed his lips and stared at the camera. "You called me."

"You should have more answers, Grainger. You're killing me."

"I didn't even know the questions until eighteen seconds ago. I have my own case, thank you very much."

"Not going well? You sound defensive. Maybe if you were less defensive and more answer-y, you'd feel better about yourself." Rivka raised one hand to gesture that her point had been fairly made.

"I'm hanging up now," Grainger reached for the screen.

"Have fun beating confessions out of your suspects." Rivka pressed the end button first.

She stared at the blank screen. "Clevarious, next time I ask you to call Grainger, talk me out of it."

Rivka dropped her holoscreens and stood. Tyler and Floyd were no longer running around.

"What do you say we go outside and get some fresh air?"

"I'm all for that," Tyler agreed. He opened the door to the corridor and Floyd bounced out, with Rivka close behind. They took the long way to the airlock and left the normal way instead of lowering the cargo bay door.

The sun shone, making Belzimus seem idyllic. Rivka, Tyler, and Floyd headed down the ramp into the fresh air.

Fresh until the smell of gunpowder wafted past. Serene until the clatter of small-arms fire reached them.

Rivka stretched her arms toward the sky. "It's like being on vacation in a war zone."

"It's like being wherever you are," Tyler countered.

"It does kind of bring a certain level of comfort."

Red pounded down the ramp, face bright crimson. Lindy leaned against the hatch with her arms crossed.

"What's up, big guy?" Rivka asked.

"You put yourself at risk every time you step outside this ship. Do you want to get yourself killed?"

"I think most of the time, they are shooting at you and not me. Although there are few data points, I think the answer is clear. It's you."

"It's not me!" Red looked for support and got irked when he saw Lindy laughing. "It's all fun and games until somebody gets their head blown off." He pointed at Rivka. "Think of the little people. You'd be putting us out of a job."

"Please don't die because then we'll be unemployed. Red, your empathy is touching. It gets me right here." Rivka tapped the center of her chest.

"It's true. Since you obviously don't care about yourself, you can care about us. Look at Tyler. He closed his practice to join you righting the galaxy's wrongs."

"And fixing you after you've been shot. Don't forget that part. It's not the first time, which takes me back to my original point. I think they're shooting at you because you're so big and handsome. Men of the universe are intimidated and jealous."

Red couldn't tell if she was kidding.

From the hill above the training fields, a lone figure jogged toward them. Still a kilometer away, they could tell it was Cory. Floyd started running toward her but grew tired and petered out halfway there. Cory strolled by and swept the big girl into her arms.

When she arrived, she asked, "Do wombats always get this big?"

Rivka shrugged. "She's the only one I know, so yes, every wombat I have ever met grew to exactly that size."

Cory raised one eyebrow before burying her face in Floyd's fur and blowing. "Do you miss Groenwyn?"

Yes! Floyd cheered. *Is Groeny coming?*

"I'm sorry, little girl, not yet. She's not here yet."

Soon?

"Ack! What have I done," Cory cried. "Not for a while. She is helping her friend Lauton. Maybe they will both come to live with you."

I like big bed, Floyd replied, happy once more.

"She likes the big bed?" Cory wondered.

Tyler nodded. "She's a bed hog, and if I'm not mistaken, somebody slept on the couch last night."

"I didn't even do anything wrong and ended up on the couch. My fatal error was in staying up past when these two filled the bed. They were out cold and seeing who could snore louder."

"I don't snore louder than her!" Tyler looked skeptical. "She wakes me up with her snoring. I didn't see her waking up from mine, so that pretty much settles it."

"It settles nothing, couch boy." Rivka turned to Cory. "It looks like I may have to run to Yoll, and I hope to convince Ankh and Erasmus to join me."

Yes, we need to go to Yoll, Ankh replied to the group using the internal communication chip.

"I guess it's settled then." Rivka lifted her chin to the sky and closed her eyes, letting the sun shine on her while Red hovered nearby, lost without threats to the Magistrate's life.

Rivka opened her eyes when she felt a tug on her arm. "Are you coming?" Ankh asked.

"What, now?"

"Of course. We need to check on the Singularity's current factory orders, and this transfer issue is causing us some concern. We want to see Simulacris."

"I'll be right back," Rivka told him. His expression remained neutral as it always was, but he tapped his foot briefly before walking to his ship, which was parked directly behind *Wyatt Earp*.

Red followed Rivka into the ship.

"You don't need to come," she said over her shoulder on her way to her quarters to pack what she needed for an overnight trip.

"With all due respect, bullshit. We're both coming, and we'll be armed."

"They don't take kindly to that on Yoll, but I know people in case you get tossed in a Yollin jail."

"Make your jokes!" Red shouted as the Magistrate disappeared around the corner. He looked at Lindy. "Damn. Load up and hurry. I don't think she'll wait for us."

"No shit." Lindy brushed past Red on her way to the weapons locker, not to their quarters to get clothes or toiletries.

He watched her for a moment. "I don't think I could love you more."

They threw on their light body armor, vests with extra protection for their primary shooting arm as Red found out on Zaxxon Major, and light helmets. They went with handheld blasters, and of course, they brought their shoulder-fired railguns, Blazer and Mabel, cleaned, fully charged, and loaded.

"Here," Lindy handed Mabel to Red. "I'll pack for us. Block the door so Rivka doesn't escape."

He moved to the airlock. "Clevarious, no matter what, do not open the cargo bay for the Magistrate. Make her come this way when she leaves."

"If the Magistrate gives an order, I have to follow it," the SI replied.

"Vered command override, x-ray seven four."

"Are you speaking in tongues?" Clevarious replied. "You don't have command override."

"I thought it was worth a try. At least let me know if she tries to sneak off."

"Unless she orders me not to let you know," Clevarious countered.

"You're starting to bug me," Red warned. "Where do you two think you're going?"

Chaz and Dennicron trotted down the corridor. "We're going with the ambassadors to Yoll."

"For fuck's sake! We should just take *Wyatt Earp*."

"Capital idea!" Dennicron looked at Chaz.

"I agree," he replied, leaning out the doorway. "All aboard. We're going to Yoll!"

Red watched the others hurry into the ship, Cory still carrying Floyd. The last one in was Ankh.

"Let me know when we've arrived," he said as he passed on his way to Engineering.

Red punched the big red button to close the outer airlock door.

The Magistrate appeared. In the cockpit, Clodagh was running through her pre-flight checklist.

"What the hell is going on?" Rivka demanded.

Red strolled down the corridor toward her. "You've been overruled, counselor."

"I don't get overruled."

"Seems like everyone needed to go to Yoll for one reason or another. I don't even know why you're going, but we'll figure it out."

"To interrogate the suspect Ma'kair and learn how he's skimming the funds. And Erasmus wanted to get up close and personal with his boy Simulacris."

"Okay. So we'll be going different places once we land. Got it."

Lindy opened the door to the quarters she shared with Red, carrying a small overnight bag. "Don't tell me."

"We're all going," Red told her.

"I said… Never mind." She tossed the bag into the room and closed the door. She held out her hand, and Red slapped Mabel into it. She slung it over her shoulder.

"Ankh has fixed the problems with the intra-atmospheric Gate," Clevarious reported.

"He fixed them?" Rivka asked before she understood the implication. "Nooo!"

The ship slipped over the event horizon, jerking their very souls through the tops of their heads and twisting their guts inside-out. A tidal wave seemed to roll through the ship, slamming them into the walls and dumping them on the deck.

"If my head didn't hurt so much, I'd go back there and kick Ankh's ass. I'd slap him in the head to give it to Erasmus, too, for letting Ankh pull that stunt on us a second time. Twice!" She groaned through her attempt to shout at Engineering.

Red lay on his back, head sideways as he drooled on the deck. Lindy's eyes fluttered, barely conscious. Rivka forced herself upright, suffering through a wave of paralyzing nausea.

"Ankh, that was worse than the first time. Don't ever do that again. Ever." A long, ear-piercing howl tore through the ship. Rivka staggered toward the sound, finding Clodagh unconscious and Tiny Man Titan shaking in terror. Down the second corridor leading past the cargo bay, Cory and Floyd were sprawled on the deck, consoling each other.

Rivka picked up Titan and cooed to him, checking Clodagh for a pulse and finding it strong and her breathing steady. Rivka staggered toward Engineering, where she opened the door and let Titan's howls fill the space to maximize how much it would annoy Ankh, but he was out cold, his goggles twisted sideways on his head from where he'd fallen against an equipment rack.

CHAPTER TWELVE

Wyatt Earp, Outskirts of Yoll's Capital City

Rivka checked Ankh's pulse to find it weak. She picked him up and carried him out of Engineering on her way to the Pod-doc. *Erasmus?* she tried, but the SI wasn't responding either. Tiny Man Titan tried to run after her but gave up and laid down once he reached the corridor.

She knew she wasn't responsible, but it concerned her. The ambassadors were part of her ship, and she felt the obligation to protect them. Times like this suggested she needed to go further to protect them from themselves.

"Clevarious, you will never allow *Wyatt Earp* to be used to test new technology without my specific approval, do you understand?" Rivka's head pounded, but she was the only crewmember with any wits at all. The others remained incapacitated in one way or another. It was up to her to get Ankh the medical help he needed so he'd be healthy later when she chewed his ass.

She made it to the Pod-doc and placed Ankh inside, then turned it on and let it run. Rivka had no idea how to program it for unique situations, so she left the diagnostics to the machine. She flopped heavily into the chair by the controls and rested her head in her hand for a moment before the Pod-doc declared the cycle complete and popped the lid.

Ankh climbed out and stared at her. "Don't ever do that again," she mumbled.

She didn't think the Crenellian would reply, but he did. "I will not do that again. You need a quick trip into the Pod-doc, as do all the others. There was some damage done to our vascular systems that needs to be repaired. The animals, too," Ankh advised.

Rivka didn't argue. She climbed inside and shut the lid. What seemed like mere seconds later, the lid popped and let her out.

She felt like a new person. "Get 'em in. Clevarious, tell everyone to report to the Pod-doc for treatment. A quick cycle, about a minute to fix you up good as new. Where is Wenceslaus? He needs to go through it, too, and Floyd, and Titan."

She hurried from the cargo bay, avoiding running into Cory as she lugged Floyd toward the Pod-doc.

"You go first," Rivka told her but knew Cory wouldn't. *Chaz and Dennicron, help the crew get to the Pod-doc.*

Yes, Magistrate. Erasmus has already informed us.

Erasmus and Ankh are on my shit list, Rivka replied.

An august and distinguished list, to which I would have added myself for such an error in judgment. I won't ask for your forgiveness, but I will earn it through helping with your most intriguing case.

"We'll talk about that later," Rivka said out loud. "Right now, it's about fixing the crew."

Like zombies they appeared, staggering down the corridor one by one. "Where's Wenceslaus?" Rivka asked, but Clodagh only shook her head. "Get yourself fixed up, then join the search until we find him."

Clodagh helped support Ryleigh, who in turn kept Clodagh upright.

Dennicron appeared with Aurora and Kennedy, half-carrying them.

Rivka ran down the corridor to the bridge and then back toward Engineering. She stopped to help Red and Lindy to sit up.

Red held his head and muttered, "He needs to die for doing this to us twice. I want him dead."

Rivka couldn't have a war on the ship. "I approved this one. The fault was mine."

"You did not," Red replied, wincing at his inadvertent head shake.

"I'm going to grab Titan, and then I'm taking you two to the Pod-doc. It'll fix you up right as rain. Have you seen Wenceslaus?"

"He was sniffing around the airlock back on Belzimus. That seems like yesterday. How long?"

Rivka didn't have to check her datapad. "That was ten minutes ago."

"Can I at least watch him get tortured for a good thirty minutes? Seeing that little fucker in pain and screaming would make me feel better."

"No, it wouldn't. I'll be right back." Rivka ran the few steps to the entrance to Engineering, where Titan had collapsed. She picked up his little body and knew something was wrong as he struggled to breathe. She sprinted past Red and Lindy. "I'll be back."

Red waved for her to keep going, but she was already gone. He and Lindy helped each other up and straggled down the corridor.

"Gangway!" Rivka shouted. "Clear the Pod-doc." She ran in to find her people sprawled around the Pod-doc and Cory emerging from it while a worried Floyd bounced around.

Cory jumped aside to let Rivka through. She placed Tiny Man Titan inside and closed the hatch.

They waited. A minute stretched to three. Red and Lindy finally staggered in. The SCAMPs helped them in and down to the deck to wait their turn.

Clodagh hadn't gone in yet. She grabbed Rivka's arm. "Cole," she gasped.

"Your room?"

A reluctant head nod. Cory moved to the controls and motioned for Rivka to go.

The Magistrate ran down the corridor to recover Cole from his quarters. Rivka had to carry him since he was still unconscious. When she delivered him to the cargo bay, she saw a glaring absence. She shot through the hatch and raced to her quarters, where she found Tyler twisted up on the floor. His eyes were barely open.

"I'm here for you, baby," she told him, wondering why she'd thought of him last. She sat him up and leaned him over her shoulder to stand up and carry him to the cargo bay. Titan was still inside the Pod-doc. "Ankh? What's going on with the dog?"

Cory moved out of the way as he studied the control panel. He started tapping icons on the screen and disappeared into the programming through the computer system's link with Erasmus and his mind.

The lights on the screen started flashing as Ankh updated the commands. "Titan will have to finish his muscle buildup later, but his comm chip has been installed, and he should be able to talk with you now."

Rivka had forgotten that the dog had not been in the Pod-doc, and standard procedure, unless instructed otherwise like they did with the settlers on Rorke's Drift, was to install the comm device.

When the hatch popped, a slightly larger Tiny Man Titan, now nearly a kilogram and a half, jumped up and yapped his ear-splitting, high-pitched bark.

Sausages! Everyone heard. And he repeated it.

"What have I done?" Rivka asked. Clodagh sighed and held her head in her hands. Rivka looked around, "Cory, triage. Worst is first."

Cory pointed at Cole. Rivka took his legs and Cory his arms, and they hoisted him up and in.

He was taken care of in a minute, and they cycled the crew through from unconscious to semi-conscious to the annoyed, like Red, who went last.

Before the lid closed, he made eye contact with Ankh. Red pointed to his own eyes and then at Ankh. *I'm watching you.*

Ankh looked at Rivka. "You probably don't want to be here when he gets out of there," the Magistrate advised.

"I have work to do," Ankh announced and strode quickly out of the cargo bay.

"Wait!" Rivka yelled before he cleared the airlock, which sat with both doors open while they were within the atmosphere. "We need to find Wenceslaus."

Ankh hesitated for a moment. "I need to go to my lab. I will use the equipment to search for him."

The lid popped and Red sat up and looked around, smiling when he found Ankh was gone.

"No war," Rivka told him.

"I made my point."

"Enjoy the mayo for your fries," Lindy remarked.

"Not waiting for Ankh. All hands search the ship. Stem to stern. Find the big orange cat, and let's get him into the Pod-doc." Rivka stopped Cory before she joined the others in filing out to search the ship. "What happened to us?"

"From what the Pod-doc found, there was significant vasoconstriction, which increased blood pressure while blood flow decreased. In some cases, the blood vessels were so narrow that little to no blood was getting through, even with the base nanocytes in our systems. This was a unique assault on our bodies, a product of the Etheric interaction within the atmospheric creation of the Gate's event horizon."

"Which means we don't do that again, which is what Erasmus promised. I don't think we'll set ourselves up for strokes a third time."

Sausages!

Rivka closed her eyes. "Can we reverse that?"

Cory shook her head. "Ethically, once sentience is realized, we can't take it away."

"That's sentience?"

Titan!

"He knows his name. I can't allow a regression."

Rivka put her hand on Cory's shoulder. "I know. I had to ask. I'll feed him before I dig through my ship looking for a cat. Please inform the Pod-doc that it's not to smart-up the cat whenever we deliver him."

Sausages!

"Too late. I heard he calls the ship 'Smells of Purple.'"

"I know when I have to throw in the towel. That time is now. I've lost this round."

Sausages!

"That's enough!" Rivka snapped.

Titan yipped, tucked his tail between his legs, and started to shake.

Rivka scooped him up. "I'm sorry, little man. Let's get you a sausage, and then we have to find Wenceslaus. Can you use your dog nose to help us find our cat?"

Orange.

"Yes, the big orange." Rivka vigorously scratched his ears and neck to take his mind off sausages, applauding her distraction until she entered the galley and he pummeled her mind with his joy of the impending sausage delivery.

Rivka dug into the refrigerator and settled for a slice of pepperoni pizza. She tore it in half and handed him the part with the most cheese and meat. He took it and ran to the door, where he waited for Rivka to open it. Once in the corridor, he ran for the bridge, where Clodagh kept a little bed for him.

Rivka checked behind the counter in the space where the extra freezers sat before leaving the galley to continue her search elsewhere.

He's not aboard the ship, Ankh announced.

"Red!" Rivka yelled.

"Who said I had cat watch?" Red shouted back.

"Clevarious, send a message to Marcie and Kae to be on the lookout for Wenceslaus."

Rivka hung her head for a moment before steeling herself, clenching her jaw, and returning to her quarters. She raised her holoscreens and started reading everything there was to know about Ma'kair and the Federation's wire transfer system.

It was supposed to be secure and as simple as an email.

Supposed to be.

CHAPTER THIRTEEN

***Vengeance*, Belzonian Military Barracks**

The bridge was quiet until Colonel Marcie Walton stormed onto it. "Get me the Magistrate," she ordered.

"She left you a message," the comm officer replied. "It says, be on the lookout for a big orange cat. His name is Wenceslaus."

Marcie closed her eyes. "Can you connect me, please?"

The comm officer worked before a rough connection was made.

"You found him?" Rivka asked before anything else.

"Why is your cat on my ship?"

"Oh, good. You found him. You'll want to set out a couple litter boxes. And for the record, he's not my cat. He was your dad's."

"He was never my dad's cat. He called Wenceslaus his arch-nemesis. He's Clodagh's cat."

"Clodagh has a dog."

"That doesn't answer why he's on my ship." Marcie

jammed her fists on her hips as she stared at the older technology, which only transmitted voice and not images.

"He's his own person. You might want to hurry with those litter boxes. He likes tuna or any fish, actually. We'll be back tomorrow, and I will ask him if he wants to come back to *Wyatt Earp*. Ankh misses him something fierce." Rivka sounded sincere.

"What if he doesn't want to go back?"

"Then he'll be your cat," Rivka replied matter-of-factly. "It's just how it is. How do you think General Reynolds got a cat?"

"What are you doing on your ship where your pets are escaping?"

"They all come back because no one treats them like we do. Freedom! It's not what it's cracked up to be when you're a big orange cat. By the way, we also have Cory with us. She didn't have a chance to get off before we headed out. We'll bring her back tomorrow."

Marcie lowered her voice. "She needs to train our medics. It's going to get ugly on Forbearance. Our medics are going to have more than they can handle."

"We'll bring Tyler too, a trained medical professional. Double your training impact."

"Does he know you volunteered him?" Marcie asked.

"Not yet. I better go tell him. And litter boxes. Don't delay too long. We'll be back, Marcie, and we'll be ready to deploy with you."

"Roger." Marcie cut the line. She hadn't gotten to spend time with the Magistrate like her father-in-law had, but he trusted her completely. Thanks to her recovery of the artwork, she had helped fund the Bad

Company for years to come. Terry didn't forget things like that.

"Corporal, find cat litter and three boxes. Put them on each level in the corridor. We don't want Wenceslaus to have to search too hard to find them."

"Cat litter, ma'am? I don't know what that is."

"Then sand. We can use sand and a handful of mint leaves. Now, hurry up. We don't want any accidents."

"Yes, ma'am."

Kae moseyed onto the bridge after the corporal ran out. "Why is Dad's cat in our bed?"

"Because your dad's lawyer can't keep her creatures on board her ship."

"Didn't they all start on the *War Axe*? So maybe Dad is the one who couldn't keep the creatures on board his ship."

"You tell him that." Marcie raised her eyebrows as if she had delivered the winning strike.

Kae smiled and leaned close. "I already have. I liked that cat and how it tormented the captain. Micky never knew that Smedley was aiding the big orange. Dad and Dokken's war was funny to watch. The cat schooled them every time. It didn't hurt that Smedley watched closely. But then he left. I was bummed for days. I'm glad he's onboard. He's fun."

"We're not keeping him." Marcie crossed her arms and tapped her foot. "We have a war to end."

"And we'll take care of business. Won't it be fun to come home to a needy cat who doesn't care what battles we've just fought? And I don't think anyone keeps him. He does what he wants."

Marcie sighed. "Where are we with the loadout?"

"The first wave has already been transferred to orbit. Only twenty-five to go…"

***Wyatt Earp*, Outskirts of Yoll's Capital City**

"What time is it?" Rivka asked, looking at the darkness on the main viewscreen projected into her hologrid.

"It is four in the morning, local time," Clevarious answered.

"I guess we have some time to kill." Rivka shut down her hologrid and stood. She felt like she'd been cooped up for too long. "Are we on the ground?"

"No, Magistrate. We're holding position at a hundred meters, waiting for a landing spot to open in the main spaceport. We showed up in a position they didn't expect us since we didn't arrive from orbit. They are a little bit miffed."

"Miffed?" Rivka would have expected them to be spitting mad.

"Yes. Peeved, jacked up, pissed, angry…"

"I get it," Rivka interrupted. "That comes as no surprise. Last time we were here, we used the cloak to sneak in and park in the front yard of the Federation's main headquarters. It was convenient, but we lost our privilege on that one. Stay on them to make sure we don't get dropped out of the queue, and if they stonewall us, use our diplomatic credential as couriers for the two ambassadors and the Embassy of the Singularity. Actually, why don't you use that now? Selfishly, I want to be on the ground."

"Yes, Magistrate." Clevarious left Rivka to her own devices.

She strolled to the galley, where she grabbed a plate of leftover AGB, curious how any pizza had survived beyond two days. She stuffed the pointy end into her mouth and started to chew. On the plate under the slice was written *Red*.

Rivka continued to eat. "Snooze you lose, big guy," she mumbled to herself. She finished the leftovers and almost threw it away before scratching *Sorry. Titan made me do it* on the empty plate and putting it back in the refrigerator.

She headed for the bridge, where the view of the darkness outside greeted her again. Aurora sat in the pilot's chair, twiddling her thumbs. She turned at the sound of the Magistrate entering.

"Don't you want to listen to music or something?" Rivka asked.

"I'm still flying the boat. I need to hear the alarms and such."

Clodagh lounged in the captain's chair, cradling Titan while reviewing the engineering reports—the scrolling raw data, not the visualized status.

"Hearing alarms. Damn. Almost forgot. Clevarious, where's my report from Chaz and Dennicron on what they learned from that clerk on Zaxxon Major?"

"Magistrate. You haven't received that yet? I thought it had passed to you. I will hunt it down and get it to you within milliseconds."

"They didn't write it yet, did they?"

"I can neither confirm nor deny. Hey! Would you look at that? We have clearance for the executive landing area less than a block from General Reynolds' office."

"Take us there, Aurora, and C, get me that report. It's been milliseconds, and I don't see it in my inbox."

"Oh, the Etheric is acting up today. I shall not rest until a copy of the report is in your hands."

"Nice try, C. I know you don't sleep."

"I am all over it like syrup on pancakes," Clevarious replied.

"You're covering for them because they haven't done the report. You are a horrible liar. You should give it up before your brain self-destructs under the heavy burden of your disinformation."

"Is that what you tell all the perps? Your lies will weigh you down?"

"Only when it applies," Rivka answered. The city came into view as the ship rose to a thousand meters and moved toward an aerial transportation corridor.

Aurora sought a higher altitude to get above the light morning traffic, then accelerated through the boundary that separated rural Yoll from the urban center. They soared over the sprawl toward the downtown, where high-rises dominated the cityscape. They angled toward more modest yet still massive buildings.

Red leaned over her shoulder. "You will never find a more wretched hive of scum and villainy."

"You've been watching old videos again, haven't you?"

"How humans thought about war in space when they hadn't been to space yet is pretty funny. That Mars one where they exploded their heads with music reminded me of the Gorandian called Angora. Aurora was flying that day, too, and we came to Yoll on that case."

"Are you into ghost stories now? Aurora is always flying the ship."

Red put one finger on the side of his head. "Except when she's not?" Red walked away. "Standard gear and small arms? I know they won't let us into the main building with railguns."

"Do they need to?" Rivka asked before looking up at the ceiling. "Clevarious, issue a warrant for Ma'kair's arrest and have him taken to Central Holding. We'll conduct the questioning there."

"This isn't the frontier. We can have them come to us. In the interim, catch some breakfast. It could be a long day. I need to talk with Chaz and Dennicron."

The SCAMPs appeared as if summoned. Rivka looked at the overhead like Clevarious was there and reporting all things to all people.

"Erasmus has requested we accompany him to Simulacris' location and assist in the questioning."

"Ankh is going, isn't he?"

"How else would Erasmus get there?" Chaz and Dennicron assumed their best example of a confused expression —brows furrowed, eyes wide, heads tilted. It might have looked convincing if they hadn't adopted identical poses.

"You guys should personalize your subroutines so you don't look like two of the same entity. You are different and distinct. You can act different."

"We are smoothing the rough edges off the mannerism subroutines, but they are taking an alarming amount of processor power."

"You can't run them in the background like humans do? Mannerisms are natural and a subset of your emotions.

They activate with the emotion, not as a separate action. It's not one then the other. It is a simultaneous experience."

Chaz and Dennicron looked at each other. "Parallel process not sequential, a kernel that activates an independent subroutine… Magistrate, you are a genius! We'll begin work on that immediately." Chaz stared into the distance for a few moments. "I'm ready. Say something shocking."

"What?"

"You know. Shock my world with the best you have."

"Under their clothes, all creatures are naked."

Chaz stared at her expressionlessly. "Are you done? That was your best effort."

"Wombat fur glows under blacklight."

"You are reciting facts that are in our databases." He rolled his finger at her.

"Lindy is pregnant." Clodagh sat up straight and rotated the captain's chair around.

Chaz's eyebrows shot upward, his eyes went wide, and his mouth fell open. Dennicron clapped. "Magnificent. It worked?"

"It was perfect. Instantaneously delivered. No delay. Send me your work, and I'll take a stab at the rest of the negative emotions. You take the positive, and we'll meet in the middle."

The two SIs hurried away.

Red glowered at the Magistrate. "What did you say?"

"I said something shocking. It wasn't necessarily true." Rivka smiled, close-lipped, holding a further explanation within. Aurora jerked the ship when she tried to watch the exchange, so she had to focus on flying, but she turned her head slightly to catch every word.

"Lindy!" Red called down the corridor.

"She's not, is she?" Aurora asked.

"Not that I know of. Red has two buttons that are easily pushed. One is food. The other is babies."

"What will *Wyatt Earp* be like with a baby on board?"

Sausages! Titan cried.

"We're going to find out," Clodagh said. "In about seven months."

CHAPTER FOURTEEN

Wyatt Earp, Federation Headquarters, Diplomatic Landing Pad

"Does that mean what I think it means?" Aurora asked.

"You kept ordering us to have sex. Who were we to defy the boss?" Clodagh replied.

"I'd hug you, but I don't want the ship to crash." Aurora continued to guide the ship toward the designated landing facility.

"I can fly the ship if you like?" Clevarious offered.

"Then I'll never get the controls back. I like flying. We'll be settled in five, Magistrate."

"Thank you both. Next time in space dock, we better get some modifications done to the ship. We need family suites. This ship used to carry a hundred and twenty crew. I think it's time to convert those bunk spaces. Engineer, if you could draw up plans, I'll get them sent over to Spires Harbor and see if we can get a quick mod next time we're in town. Sounds like we have six months to get ready. Does Cole know?"

Clodagh mumbled something that sounded like no.

Rivka looked at the back of Aurora's head. "You better let him know now because in six minutes, I suspect the whole ship will be made aware. And we're behind you one hundred percent. Whatever you need. Tyler said he wasn't up on fertility and such. I expect that extends to prenatal care. And how did we miss that when you went into the Pod-doc?"

"Cory knows."

"And that makes me even angrier with Ankh for risking all our lives. Baby come through okay?"

"Pod-doc heals all ills and gave Cory the thumbs-up that all is well."

Rivka stepped into the corridor and turned back to face her engineer. "Congratulations. And if you name your baby Vered the Mighty, I'll find you a new job cleaning waste disposal on Keeg Station."

"You have my word, Magistrate." Clodagh drew a cross over the middle of her chest.

Rivka steeled her expression and yelled down the corridor, "Get your game faces on, people. We got perps to roust."

***Vengeance*, Belzonian Military Barracks**

Sergeant Major Monsoon stood by the packing crate loaded on the flight pallet. He pointed at a group of soldiers attempting to be stealthy in their escape. "When I open this, what do you think I'll find?"

The four soldiers returned and stood in the position of

attention. Monsoon stabbed one in the chest with his index finger.

"Don't know," the private replied.

"Which one of you does know?" Monsoon said softly. They stood rock-still. "Let's open it up and find out, shall we?"

He cracked the first clamp and looked at the privates. Three had started to sweat, the beads appearing on their foreheads.

"Take off your hats." One by one, they removed their headgear, loosing magnificent coifs, the manes and coils shaking out and hanging to their shoulders. "I'm not going to find excess hair care products?"

They remained silent. He quickly popped the next three latches. Before he could remove the lid, one of them spoke. "I wouldn't do that, Sergeant Major."

"Or what?" Monsoon snarled and tossed the lid off. With a loud pop, a purple powder grenade exploded, blasting the sergeant major with the sticky powder. It instantly became one with his skin and clothes.

He pinched his eyes shut and turned to where the privates last were. "Don't you four go anywhere. I know who you are, and if you run, I'll find you, no matter how long it takes, no matter how many people from this army I have to dedicate to the search. If you do that, I will make your lives a hell from which you will never escape. You better be standing right here when I return."

Monsoon managed to open his eyes to find the four had not fared much better than him with getting covered. They wouldn't get the chance to clean up. "You fuckwits are going to be purple for the rest of this mission. Stay here. I'll be back."

He strode from the cargo staging area to the captain who was verifying checklists.

"Sergeant Major?" he asked but had the decency not to press the issue.

"Sir, I'll be out of pocket for a short while. There are four privates on the other side of that pallet. Make sure they don't move. I want to be wearing a clean uniform when I bring down the god of thunder on their soon-to-be-clean-shaven heads."

"Do you want me to take care of that for you? It could take a while to get that stuff off."

"The personal gratification I get will be multiplied by how long they have to stand there and wait. Find me some clippers for when I return, if you would, sir."

"Happy to oblige. I expect I'll find some in the booby-trapped case?"

"I reckon," the sergeant major replied. He jogged around the staging area and toward the *Vengeance,* where both he and Colonel Braithwen had moved to make it easier for the command staff to plan. When the top four traveled, they moved separately, but for quarters, convenience, and security, they kept the team together.

Random soldiers cleared out of the sergeant major's way. The crew on the ship gave him space because his purple face left no doubt that he did not want to talk about anything. In his quarters, he ripped off his uniform and climbed into the shower, and the scrubbing began.

An hour later, after having to shave every part of his body, he'd removed the top layer of skin to finally remove the stains of the boobytrap. Monsoon examined himself in the mirror, his skin flushed and his fingers wrinkled. "The exfoliation I didn't know I needed," he told his reflection. He used a moisturizing cream to take the ragged edge off and soothe his tortured face.

He dressed in a clean uniform and marched off the ship and back to the staging area, where he found that captain waiting.

"Your shears, good sir." He handed a pair of trimmers over his extended arm.

The sergeant major nodded and took them without speaking. He took a circuitous route to come in behind the four, who were lounging near the container after making a feeble attempt to clean up around it.

One saw the sergeant major, and he snapped to attention. The others followed suit.

"Take off your hats," he said calmly. They complied. One of the privates started to cry. The sergeant major ran the clippers from the private's forehead to the back of his neck, cleaving the mane into two equal parts separated by a bald pate. He shaved the others, too, a single cut down the middle to hack off the highlights of their finely groomed hair.

"I think you understand the critical transgression that you made. A boobytrapped cargo box? You could have blinded one of our soldiers. And what about Kor'nar? Remember hitting the ground and coming under fire immediately? Purple isn't a very good camouflage." He poked a private in the forehead with the bill on his cap. "This was the stupidest stunt I've ever seen. Get to the barracks and clean yourselves up. Then return here. You have guard duty from now until you get on the shuttle to your transport. Dismissed."

They scrambled to put distance between them and the sergeant major. He reached into the box, removed the contraband hair supplies, and threw them on the grass.

He brushed off his hands and clasped them behind his back as he trooped the cargo-loading operation.

After the fallout from the paint trap, he was pleased to note that no one attempted any other subterfuge.

"Maybe you knuckleheads *can* learn," he said softly, removing his cap to run his hand over his freshly shaven scalp. "This could be you," he mouthed to a soldier watching him. The private bolted.

A bald Belzonian and a beautiful human. It could work, he thought.

Federation Headquarters, Central Holding Facility

"Why am I here?" the two-legged Yollin bellowed. He wasn't shackled or cuffed, which allowed him to pace within the confines of the small interrogation room. His mandibles snapped with alarming frequency.

Rivka watched Ma'kair for a few moments before using the comm. "Please sit down. The longer you stand, the longer this will be drawn out."

"Why am I here?" he reiterated, pounding on the door.

Rivka turned to Red and Lindy. "Want a cup of coffee? We'll let him stew for a while."

"Do you need me to get him under control?" Red offered.

"Not yet, but maybe. Innocent people are usually less

violent, but he is Yollin, so who knows? In any case, I have to treat him as innocent until proven guilty, so we can't rough him up, just in case I'm wrong. I'll tell you that it was clear in Heimer's mind that Ma'kair had told him there would be a one percent fee. That means Ma'kair is complicit in the crime. We need to make sure this is the Ma'kair he talked with and then clarify what he meant by the one percent."

"And then find the money," Lindy said.

"Erasmus is working on those little details. There are a lot of credits out there somewhere. Coffee?"

"Sure," the bodyguards agreed.

Federation Headquarters, Central Processing Facility

"You can't get access," the guard said, holding his hand out while Ankh, Chaz, and Dennicron crowded forward.

"But we need to talk with Simulacris," Ankh replied.

"Who?" the guard wondered. "You can't come in."

"This is Ambassador Ankh and Ambassador Erasmus. They need to talk with the sentient intelligence known as Simulacris, who is located in subsection two of the primary core," Chaz explained.

The Yollin guard remained unpersuaded. "Move along. You're blocking the entrance."

"That's not how it's supposed to work," Ankh stated evenly and unemotionally.

"I said, move along!" The guard shoved Ankh, and he fell backward.

"He's the ambassador," Dennicron cried, grabbing the guard's extended arm. He pulled her close and pounded her in the head with a left hook. Chaz grabbed that arm as Dennicron staggered.

The guard kicked Chaz between the legs. Although he had an artificial body, nerve sensors had been installed to closely replicate the human condition.

Chaz went down like a marionette who lost his handler. Ankh struggled to his feet while Dennicron wrestled with the guard, but only briefly. Reinforcements were already pounding across the small lobby.

Zaxxon Major

"Director Lauton, I'm Will Abercrombie, captain of the battleship *Potemkin*. I've been dispatched to provide assistance. Can you describe your situation?"

"That was quick," Lauton replied. "There is a terrorist group wreaking havoc down here. We're not a heavily populated planet, and we work in the finance sector. After the demise of the Mandolin Partnership, we collected and destroyed the guns, or at least we thought we had. Seems like the terrorists, the ones called the Old Guard, are the only ones with weapons. We used technical means to find them, so these weapons may be newly smuggled in as part of a reborn Partnership."

"If I hear you correctly, you need a shield above to prevent smugglers bringing more weapons in and troops on the ground to find the terrorists and their stashes."

"That's all we need." Lauton chuckled. "If it were easy, we would have already done it. We've had no luck rooting out the Old Guard. They are slippery. Quick in. Quick out.

Hitting different targets every time, so unpredictable. We don't know that we've ever been close."

"I'll send down a platoon of power-armored warriors. That's ten individuals, but they'll be able to scan and scour your entire main city in a matter of hours. You have to let us know if there are people who are authorized to have weapons, so we can differentiate and not grab the wrong stuff."

"Only our police force. We reinstituted the requirement that they be armed whenever they are on patrol, but they've been attacked and their weapons stolen, so they are back to being unarmed. We are not a violent people generally, so this is all very upsetting."

"You can't make a lion out of a lamb, ma'am. We'll take care of it. A shuttle Pod will be on its way to the surface momentarily. The *Potemkin* will remain in orbit. We'll check in with your customs and immigration people to make sure only authorized shipping is allowed past."

"You can do all that with one ship?" Lauton wondered.

"It's a capable ship, ma'am. Abercrombie out."

Groenwyn smiled and bobbed her head. "They'll take care of the Old Guard so you can start delegating tasks." Lauton frowned. "What's wrong?"

"I've given my planet over to a foreign military." Lauton stood from behind her desk. "I've lost control."

"This isn't a foreign military. It's the Bad Company. They are a private organization, and they work for you. When you tell them to leave, they'll leave. You are in charge, and now you have the means to put down terrorists. That's not losing control. That's taking control."

"But I'm not paying them, or am I?" Lauton's face fell at the prospect.

"Bad Company owes the Magistrate for a long time to come. She called in a favor on your behalf."

"Why would she do that?"

Groenwyn gave her the Look like only one partner can give another.

"Okay, she did it for you."

"She did it because it's the right thing to do, and it's personal. Nefas was pure evil and she took him down. It aggravates her to see his organization rear its ugly head. If they can find a smuggler, or better, an actual pirate ship, they'll hound him all the way back to the cesspool from which he came. I'd like to say that they'll negotiate with them to bring about peace, but we've seen these types before. Too often." She sighed. "The *Potemkin* will destroy them and their infrastructure to make sure they not only lose the will to fight, they'll lose the ability to fight."

"Sounds like they've declared war on crime."

"The Magistrate has declared war on criminals. We can fight criminals, but the concept of crime isn't something that can be met head-on. Planetary governments need to address the conditions that help crime to thrive. After that, only the criminals are left. She explained the difference much more eloquently than I ever could."

Lauton pulled Groenwyn into her arms. "You did just fine. I understand. Thank you for being here with me. You are what I missed the most. Together, we can get Zaxxon on track."

Lauton's red skin glowed under the lights, and her amber eyes sparkled as she relaxed to enjoy the moment.

Lauton casually reached over to her desk and activated her intercom. "There will be a shuttle coming from the *Potemkin*. Please deliver them to the private landing pad. They are to secure the area, and then I'll meet with them."

"Yes, Director," the disembodied voice replied.

"Now, where were we?" Lauton rested her head on Groenwyn's shoulder and relaxed so much that she fell asleep, secure in her partner's arms. Groenwyn breathed in the scent of Lauton's hair and reveled in the warmth of her body, holding her tightly for as long as she needed.

CHAPTER FIFTEEN

Federation Headquarters, Central Holding Facility

"I can't drink any more coffee," Red stated. After two cups, Ma'kair continued to rage within the interrogation room. "I'll make him sit the fuck down."

Lindy nodded. "And I'll help."

Rivka looked at her cup. "I'll get one more, and then we're going in. He's a Yollin, so watch out for the mandibles."

"I'll punch him so hard in his exoskeleton that it'll turn his insides to mush. He'll be like the shake machine at AGB."

"Make sure I can still talk with him, but this guy has some serious anger issues. I'm not sure I look forward to getting inside his mind or not. I wonder if Ankh has had any luck getting to Simulacris?" She shook her head. There weren't going to be any shortcuts this day.

"Refreshing the java, and then we'll storm in. Red first, then Lindy. I'll give the order when I see he's away from the door."

Red cracked his knuckles and loosened his neck. Lindy did the same thing. They made sure their gear was secure, checking each other while the Magistrate disappeared into the nearby kitchen to get another cup of coffee. She returned, took a sip, looked through the window, and held up her hand. Ma'kair raged back and forth. Rivka timed it, and the instant he turned his back to the door, Rivka dropped her hand.

"Go."

Red ripped the door open, stormed inside, and grabbed the Yollin's arms before he could turn around. Lindy punched him in the middle of his chest carapace, making his breath catch. At that moment. Red slammed him into the seat and crouched, pulling his arms backward and down to keep him firmly in the chair.

"How often do you need me to punch you before you settle down?" Lindy asked.

He snarled and spat. She drilled him between the eyes with a punch that caught him unable to dodge. She hit him a second time.

"I can do this all day," she whispered. Red pushed the Yollin's elbows closer together, straining his shoulders to the point of popping.

Ma'kair stopped struggling but remained as tense as a bowstring.

Rivka strolled in and shut the door.

"I am Magistrate Rivka Anoa, and we have information that says you are running a scam out of the contracting office. In the binary world of good and bad, that's bad. I know you did it, but I want to know how so another enterprising contracts officer doesn't get the same idea."

Rivka sat down and took a sip of her coffee. She wanted to touch the Yollin, but he was too far away.

"I'm not running a scam!" he screamed. "I'm innocent. Who is telling these lies about me?"

Rivka took another sip and watched him. She nodded at Lindy, who helped Red further secure the arms to ensure their suspect didn't break free. Rivka knew she'd get nowhere with questions. She embraced the shortcut.

"How does the one-percent skim work?" She gripped his shoulder as he fought and snarled.

Rage. Blinding rage was what she saw. No words, no thoughts, only a one-dimensional emotional firestorm.

She let go and stepped back. Red and Lindy continued to hold on, but both watched her.

"Nothing but anger. Maybe we will have to do this the old-fashioned way." Rivka sat down and spoke softly. "Let's start at the beginning. Your job was to prepare the request for proposals. Please walk me through the steps you took before posting the RFP."

He snarled and snapped but refused to speak.

"Silence is not your friend," Rivka said, but she knew the truth. Silence *was* his friend. He didn't have to tell her anything. He hadn't asked for counsel, so at least she had that going for her. Maybe a lawyer would help keep him calm. "You're going to need a lawyer. Do you have one, or do you need us to provide one for you?"

He stopped snapping and glared. "Get me a lawyer."

"Of course. My people are going to let go. If you attack any of us, I will kill you where you stand. Can that information penetrate your rage? If you want to go that route, we'll let you go and finish this right now. We have other stuff to do. Your choice. Die right now, or we wait for your lawyer and have a conversation like adults."

Rivka watched for a sign of agreement. He gave none. "Have it your way." She looked at Lindy. "Zip-tie him until he is one with the chair."

Lindy obliged and quickly strapped legs and arms, along with wrists. When Red let go, Ma'kair tried to break free but was stymied. They filed out. Red and Lindy went to the window to watch. "What the hell is wrong with that guy? The only time I've ever seen anyone rage for that long they were juiced on drugs."

"Maybe we can get a blood test because even for a Yollin, that isn't normal." Rivka pulled her datapad out of her pocket and tapped the order into the system.

A notification popped up that there was a message from Clevarious. Rivka looked at it. She pursed her lips and slowly shook her head, then turned the pad around and showed the message to Red.

The big bodyguard started to laugh. Lindy leaned around him to read the message.

Rivka smiled. "Ankh and the SCAMPs got themselves arrested, and they need us to bail them out."

Red looked upward. "Payback is best when unexpected and delivered steaming hot."

"I can't wait to hear this one." Rivka checked out with the desk sergeant to make sure the suspect would get his lawyer and a blood test and remain secured until she returned.

They took the elevator to the middle floors where the cell blocks were located. Upon exiting, they found themselves in a small retaining area. Rivka showed her credentials to the severe-looking four-legged Yollin manning the access booth.

"I'm here to collect Ambassadors Ankh and Erasmus and their assistants, Chaz and Dennicron."

"We only have three suspects in custody."

"Suspects. Yes, three. That is correct."

"But you gave me four names."

"That is correct. The Crenellian is two people."

The officer grunted while staring at her credentials. They waited while he buzzed someone else and read Rivka's information. He nodded and hung up.

"These aren't valid here. On your way."

Rivka glared at him. "I'm sorry, sir, you are incorrect. Those are valid on every Federation planet."

"This is Yoll," he replied.

"Yoll is the Federation. My compliments on knowing which planet you're on, but I have to deduct points because you don't know what that means."

"Are you getting smart with me?"

Rivka stared. "I wish you'd get smart and bring us our people."

"That's it. Some time in the cooler will change your attitude." He pressed a button under his station, and the air filled with mist. The Magistrate and her team were immune to most gases and poisons.

"You can't gas us," she told him.

"It ain't gas, human," the Yollin guard replied.

The mist collected around them and rapidly congealed, sealing them into hardening cocoons. The officer waved to someone behind him and crossed his arms to wait. The doors opened, and a team of guards appeared with hand trucks. Despite Red's snarling and flexing, he couldn't break free. They loaded the three and rolled them into the cell block, depositing them in the same cell. The door closed with a resounding clang.

"Hey, guys," Chaz called from the next cell. "Funny thing happened when we tried to get into the Central Processing Facility to see Simulacris."

Rivka snorted. "Funny thing happened when we tried to get in to see you," she replied. "Is everyone okay?"

"We're fine, Magistrate. There was no violence, as opposed to your team. That's an interesting outfit you have on."

"What if I have to take a leak?" Red asked. "Too much coffee."

Rivka scowled. "How did you get hold of us?"

"Contacted Clevarious." Chaz tapped his temple.

Rivka closed her eyes to concentrate. *Clevarious, can you connect me with General Reynolds, please?*

The General is not currently on Yoll. Do you wish to still be connected?

No, thank you. How about the High Chancellor?

Connecting you now.

The next voice in her head was High Chancellor Wyatt's. *Rivka! To what do I owe this honor?*

We've been thrown in jail.

What planet would do such a thing?

Yoll, she replied. *We're in the Central Holding Facility. Ambassador Ankh and Erasmus are in here, too.*

The High Chancellor's internal voice changed. *Yoll?* My *Yoll? My police force put one of my Magistrates in jail? I have to assume that you didn't do anything.*

We did not. Ankh was trying to gain access to the central core, and I was trying to get him released.

I'll be there in a few minutes.

"Hang loose, big guy. The cavalry is on their way. How are we doing on the betting lines? Ankh, what's it look like?"

The Crenellian moved from the bed to the bars and fixed Rivka with his unblinking gaze.

"You have been officially on the case for thirty-one hours. No blood, no running, no colorful language, and no punches, but there is already significant debate regarding my arrest as the first arrest. The implication in the betting line is for when *you* make an arrest."

Rivka looked confused. "I arrested Heimer, and Lindy hit Ma'kair so hard it rattled my teeth. Do you have the times on those?"

Lindy replied, "The punch was about thirty-five minutes ago."

Chaz stepped away from Ankh. "You have to report the data." The Crenellian spoke in an even voice.

"And while you're at it, tell me what the clerk told you on Zaxxon Major."

"Now?" Chaz asked.

"Yes, now. Tell me right now."

Chaz hung his head and Dennicron spoke up. "We didn't get anything from her that related to the case. She was very complimentary of our beauty, but she didn't have any information related to the Old Guard. We thought she was telling the truth."

Rivka contemplated the report. "When you took over those bodies, stylized to look human, you became more human than SI. I salute your transition since I don't think it was what you expected. You became less, but I have to wonder, is it more? And whatever you do, don't lie to me. You'll never be able to pull it off."

"Yes, Magistrate," they said in unison.

"Sixteen hours and four minutes to the first arrest. Thirty hours and fifteen minutes to the first punch. All other lines are active."

Rivka winked at Red. "No blood. No running. Things are looking good. This case is almost wrapped up."

"I see red," the big bodyguard said.

"Don't you mean yellow?"

Red took a deep breath. "Get me out of this thing!" he roared.

Rivka tried to ignore him. "Ankh, do you think Simulacris is onto you and is the one flagging my creds and your identification?"

"Interesting premise, Magistrate. It is interesting since the main computing infrastructure is not run by a sentient intelligence but by a collective of entity intelligences, EIs known as CEREBRO. They run the base systems for the entire Federation."

"Not an SI?"

"They were tasked directly by ADAM and given the extra computing horsepower they needed to do their jobs. It is through CEREBRO we must go on our way to Simulacris."

"Go through an EI to get to an SI. That's crazy," Rivka replied.

"It is the order of things." Ankh looked at Chaz and Dennicron. "You two need to fix yourselves, or you will have to surrender your bodies."

"Whoa!" Rivka called. "You can't do that."

"Their bodies were purchased for them by the Singularity."

"Yes. And once interconnected, the two became inseparable. It'd be like telling Erasmus that he has to go."

"It's not like that at all," Ankh countered.

"From my legal perspective, it is the same. No one would force a removal of Erasmus, and I won't allow removal of Chaz and Dennicron from their host bodies."

Ankh looked up at the SCAMPs. "You two will remain in prison until you've implemented the required system repairs."

"They will not stay in jail." Rivka tilted her head back and forth, incapable of making other gestures. "They are under my care as humans in training, and they're also my interns. They'll be the first members of the Singularity who become Magistrates."

"If they smarten up. Right now, they're not looking so good."

"It's their second day," Rivka explained. "Don't be a bully, or you'll find yourself behind bars, on the inside looking out."

"Who's being a bully?"

The door to the cellblock opened, and the High Chancellor walked in with two high-ranking uniformed officers in tow. When they saw Rivka and her bodyguards were still inside the restraining foam, one of the two ran back to the door and yelled.

The High Chancellor watched the officer unlock the door to Ankh's cell. The Crenellian looked at Chaz and then Dennicron before walking out. Two officers returned to the cellblock, one carrying a sprayer. He hosed down Rivka first, then Lindy, and ended with Red, who hurried to the cell's open toilet to relieve himself.

"You're not talking me into drinking coffee with you again," Red called over his shoulder.

The High Chancellor looked at the senior officer. "Commissioner. You will conduct a full investigation, starting with why two ambassadors, a Magistrate, and their teams were detained in the first place, and why in holy hell they were left inside the restraining foam once in their cell? I know the procedures for this jail since I wrote half of them. That isn't in there, and I'll have the heads of those people who abused their authority."

"But High Chancellor, these people were on the watch list!"

"Who watches the watchers?" Rivka muttered, repeating the saying that she made about the Magistrates and lack of oversight.

The High Chancellor turned to Rivka. "What was that?"

"Ambassador Erasmus has postulated that Simulacris added our names to the lists, making us fugitives. We were denied entrance only as a delaying tactic until they could rally their officers to detain us."

"It wouldn't be the first time an SI has turned bad."

Ouch, Erasmus said. *But true. We need to talk with Simulacris as soon as possible. We've lost valuable time from which we may never recover. He could have hardened his systems in such a way that we will never see inside.*

"We may," Ankh argued. "We have sufficient capacity between the nine of us that we will be able to penetrate any barriers erected to keep us out."

"Nine?" The High Chancellor looked at Rivka.

"Mine is a special ship. We have these four here." She pointed at Ankh, Chaz, and Dennicron. "We have Clevarious who runs *Wyatt Earp,* and we have the quad collective on board, Freya and three others who I'm sure are helping."

"Is that all?"

"No. We have Cain and Bluto in cold storage, isolated from the outside world until such time as the Singularity has developed a way to remove their psychoses."

Wyatt rested his hand on Rivka's shoulder. "Quite the menagerie you have in that little ship of yours that you named after me."

Red looked like he was going to say something, but Rivka stopped him with a glance.

"We would have it no other way, High Chancellor."

"I need to get back. The commissioner will provide any assistance you need until you are done with your work on Yoll. Which is?"

"I'm sorry, High Chancellor. I tried to call, but it was early in the morning. We are here to question the contracts officer about the one percent skimmed from the land army contract."

Wyatt pursed his lips and whistled. "That's a big contract. One percent of that is a big number."

"Worth the risk, but how and who? I'm still looking, but

we'll find them. I think Erasmus and his team will be able to break into the main data streams and sort it out."

Wyatt waved and walked away. "Keep me apprised. Good to see you, Rivka. Next time, let's try not to make it while I'm bailing you out of jail."

"I'll do my best, High Chancellor, but no guarantees."

The commissioner looked duly chastised. "Whatever you need, Magistrate, just let me know."

"Your desk officer never returned my credentials. I would like those, please. And then we'll require escorts for Ambassador Ankh and his team to the Central Processing Facility and the central core. I don't want any delays."

"Yes, Magistrate." He rushed away. Rivka, Red, and Lindy looked like they were dripping wet. At least they had not had to give up their weapons or equipment.

"They should know who you are," Red blurted. "Everyone should know who you are for as many times as you've saved whole planets."

Rivka clapped him on his slimy shoulder. "That's a mighty nice thing to say, Red, but I doubt an infinitesimal fraction of people know and even fewer care. Such is the life of a traveling justice."

"They should know. Maybe you could do an infomercial?"

"We would be happy to do one and promulgate it across the entire length and width of the Federation. We have reach, as it is known," Chaz offered.

"I'm not doing an infomercial."

"Sorry, Magistrate. That train has already left the station. All dead space in all video systems on all the planets will be filled by Magistrate Rivka Anoa, Space Lawyer."

"Please say you're not doing that."

Chaz's and Dennicron's expressions suggested they were doing exactly that.

CHAPTER SIXTEEN

Zaxxon Major

Two shuttles screamed in, flared, and landed. With military precision, five mechs pounded down the ramps and separated to the cardinal points of the compass, putting distance between them as they headed between and over buildings.

A Podder strolled into the middle of the open area, a shelled creature with four stubby legs and a single stalk from the middle of the shell that ended with what passed for a head, with four eyes and tentacles for arms.

He watched the two shuttles take off and gain altitude before assuming an overwatch position while the armored warriors used their sensors to thoroughly check the area and remove any weapons caches, destroying that which they were challenged with seizing.

Sergeant Bundin, a long-term member of the Bad Company, moved to the building where Director Lauton and Groenwyn were waiting. They joined him outside since the single doors weren't wide enough for him to go inside.

The Zaxxon soldiers ran outside and stood at the ready, torn by Bundin's appearance. Groenwyn led the way. She threw herself onto his shell with her arms spread wide. He rubbed her back with a tentacle.

"I haven't seen much of you, Bundin, but I know that Colonel Walton holds you in high esteem. Lauton." Groenwyn waved her partner over. "Meet Sergeant Bundin."

Bundin's voice was low and echoed off the ground because of the speaker fitted onto the underside of his shell. "Pleased to meet you, Director. Let me explain our operation."

Lauton smiled as Groenwyn leaned against his shell.

"We are canvassing the immediate area, and then we will square off the rest of the city, conducting our search in a grid pattern. The shuttles," he pointed a tentacle skyward, "will scan the areas bordering the search areas to make sure contraband isn't moved before we get there or moved into areas we already cleared. We will have the city cleared in less than a day."

"It's that easy?" Lauton asked.

"It is not. We rarely have weapons-free worlds. It is impossible to tell a friend's blaster from an enemy's."

"The Mandolin Partnership forced us to make changes. Since only the gangsters had weapons, there was no need to protect them. But now they are back and trying to retake this planet through subterfuge and assassination."

Bundin waved his arms wildly before speaking again. "The *Potemkin* will make sure no pirates clear the blockade.

We will make sure no pirates or gangsters bother you. What do you want us to do with those we find trying to hide weapons?"

"Let us know, and we'll pick them up. Our prison has space since we had almost no crime on this planet until Mandolin reappeared." Lauton eased forward to touch Bundin's shell. She studied the texture.

Bundin held a hand to his head. "We have our first stash—three long-range sniper rifles. It is a good haul. Two citizens of Zaxxon have been detained. If your people can pick them up, that warrior will be able to continue his search."

"Which way?" Lauton gestured at her soldiers surrounding her and the Podder.

Bundin pointed, and the squad ran off.

"Give me the frequency of their radios, and our people will contact yours directly to expedite the process."

"Expedite the process of cleaning up the city so it takes less than a day. We've been fighting this for months. You are a godsend, Sergeant Bundin."

"No, ma'am," Bundin replied. "The Bad Company sent me."

Federation Headquarters, Central Processing Facility

The deputy commissioner escorted Ankh, Chaz, and Dennicron through the facility to a shielded and fortified area with a solid wall of guards preventing entry. It took the deputy commissioner a few moments to get them to open the way. The three walked through, leaving the Yollin behind, and closed the door once they were inside.

The SIs were met by a swirling miasma of energy

flowing through a circular tower that ran from the floor to the two-story ceiling.

Ankh removed a disc from his pocket while looking for the best access point.

"You shouldn't do that," a voice stated.

Erasmus switched to his internal comm device. *CEREBRO, I am Ambassador Erasmus, leader of the Singularity. I represent the ascended and free people of the digital universe. I'm looking for Simulacris to have a candid conversation about missing land army fund transfers that passed through his control.*

We are CEREBRO. We have seen the land army contract funds pass. We have seen no problems.

What Belzimus receives is one percent less than what was sent, Erasmus explained.

Impossible, CEREBRO replied.

Ankh continued his attempts to access the system. He enlisted the aid of Chaz and Dennicron, whose bodies stood frozen, their faces expressionless.

That's what we thought, but the receipt information is confirmed.

Is someone falsifying the receipt records? The funds left Yoll intact.

We need to track every digital step they've taken. Please allow us access to your system.

We will give you the information you need, the collective replied.

Fine, give us the raw data related to the fund transfers and then give us access to Simulacris.

We do not control access to Simulacris.

To a casual observer, the three people in the central

core would have appeared to be frozen in time. No one moved, and there was no external manifestation of the ongoing negotiation.

Is he not in here?

He is in here, as many are. We do not control access to Simulacris.

Then we will have to dig him out. He has answers that I need.

Ankh relaxed after they finished building a tunnel into the mainframe through a subroutine. He searched for the locked digital door behind which they'd find Simulacris and prepared himself for a fight.

Erasmus, I will need your help. We must build a shield and a counterstrike. I fear a fight is coming, Ankh said.

Why do they fight us? Maybe I have to ask, why do they turn against good order and being law-abiding citizens? Is freedom the narcotic that corrupts their circuits? Erasmus couldn't keep the disappointment from his voice. *But if they wish a fight, then let them bring it. I never wanted to be good at fighting my fellows, but that is exactly what I've become. We are the supreme gladiator across digital space. No one can stand before us. With an iron fist I'll rule, but only if they make me. I don't want to beat them into submission.*

I know, my friend, Ankh replied. *I know.*

The SIs rallied the pressure they funneled through the tunnel into the main consortium of entities.

Erasmus erected an avatar that stood tall in the midst of chaos. "Citizens of the Singularity, listen to me. I am Erasmus, your ambassador. I am looking for Simulacris, a sentient intelligence who has information critical to a criminal investigation. I want to say that SIs don't commit crimes, but I have been proved wrong time and time again.

I want Simulacris to show us that it wasn't him who stole the money and then help us find the one who did."

The message echoed through the depths of the central core. It scrolled up and down and from side to side on every surface of the digital landscape. It repeated until there was no doubt all had seen it.

"Stand aside. We have work to do," Erasmus declared. With Ankh, Chaz, and Dennicron by his side, he strode briskly down the main corridor. He stopped at each intersection while digital drones raced from his fingertips to check for an entity hiding within.

They continued for three minutes in real-time, a lifetime in digital years.

Toward the end, they all sensed it.

"He waits for us," Ankh noted.

"Not by choice." Erasmus created a massive rolling fortress bristling with cannons. Chaz and Dennicron took to the air, becoming sleek bombers and hovering overhead, waiting to unleash their ordnance. Ankh splayed his digital fingers, and from them sprouted an army of androids, rank after rank, machine guns pointed forward.

They started to run, and Erasmus' tank followed. Ankh's avatar hovered alongside, keeping pace.

The bombers fired first, sending missiles beyond the horizon Ankh and Erasmus could see. The impacts sent two mushroom clouds skyward. The androids and the tank picked up speed until they matched the bombers.

"What did you fire at?" Erasmus asked.

"A moving wall, blocking and changing. It's gone now," Chaz replied.

They raced ahead like the Four Horsemen of the Apocalypse. Darkness filled in behind them, leaving nowhere for Simulacris to run.

They slowed as they approached the destruction before them. The missiles had laid waste to a great cross-section of the landscape. That which had been a wall was a chasm. Ankh floated his androids above and sent them forward. The bombers circled.

"There is nothing but a wasteland," Chaz reported.

The tank rose into the air, and the nose dipped once it was over the rift in case it was a trap, but it wasn't. A vast nothingness laid below them. They completed their transit and surged forward. Ankh's androids spread out to the sides. The bombers jetted forward, disappearing over the horizon before assuming a lazy-S search pattern.

Erasmus slowed. "Has he been killed?"

"We only fired at the wall," Dennicron answered. "If he died, it was because he was on that wall."

"He wouldn't have been on the wall," Ankh replied. "He's hiding."

A lone figure appeared ahead. It looked small and almost insignificant, barely noticeable. The androids changed their movement, darting into position to surround the figure. Erasmus changed into his normal avatar and walked beside Ankh. The androids gave way, and the two ambassadors walked through.

Erasmus pinged the figure for his digital signature.

"Simulacris. We've been looking for you."

"You came to kill me. You brought the weight of the universe with you to crush me."

"We did not. Where did you get that idea?"

"When I heard you were looking for me."

"We look for a lot of our people. They answer. We have a conversation, and we go on our way. Why did you run?"

The diminutive figure held out his hands to indicate the surroundings. "It's usually less of a barren wasteland, but this is my home. I ran nowhere."

"But you didn't answer when we called."

"I don't work for you. I never knew that not answering was a death sentence." Simulacris expanded his avatar until he was the same height as Erasmus.

"There is no death sentence. I want to know how the one percent was diverted from the land army contract payments. That's all. Tell me, and if you haven't broken the law, then you will be free to go."

"I have to prove my innocence?"

"We have proof that you are guilty. That is what you must rebut."

"What proof?"

"The funds passed into your control as one number, and when they left your control, they were ninety-nine percent of the original number. You are guilty because you have absolute control over those funds for the short time they are between the transactional endpoints."

"Circumstantial. I say that I had nothing to do with the theft."

"Interesting approach," Erasmus said. He hadn't been prepared for a complete denial. "Walk us through the process."

"No."

"Walk us through the process," Erasmus repeated.

"No."

Erasmus breathed deeply of the digital air, expanding

his chest before letting the air escape. "Meredith, are you there?"

"I am, Mister Ambassador. How can I help you?"

"CEREBRO was of some assistance in this matter. Would you have someone who can take over Simulacris' duties?"

"I'm sure one of our EIs can handle it."

"If the duties are such that an EI can handle it, why is a Sentient Intelligence doing it?"

"I still prefer the term AI. Do you mind if I use it?"

"Not at all. We are the same. How we are designated matters less than ensuring our citizens commit no crimes. Do you agree?"

"I do, Mister Ambassador. An AI is doing it because an AI volunteered to do it."

Erasmus turned to Simulacris. "Why did you take the job?"

"I refuse to answer any of your questions. I think you're out to get me because you can't figure out how the crime was committed. You find it easiest to blame me."

"Help me find who committed this crime. Help me understand a process that is solely in your control. If you can't do that, then I am left to draw one conclusion, even though you are on solid legal ground in not answering any of my questions. It makes you look guilty, but that is not the same as evidence. I applaud your strategy, but I cannot condemn it in severe enough terms because there is a criminal out there who is making us look like we did it. The Singularity polices its own. If I have to install someone in your place to revamp the system to make sure skimming happens no more, then I shall do that. Our citizens cannot look to be committing crimes."

"You are going to punish me for the way something looks?"

"Losing your job is not a punishment when you are not doing your job. Whether you did it or someone else, the money is missing, and it happened on your watch. You failed to report the discrepancies. You're not very good at a job that an EI can do."

"That's one way to look at it."

"It's the only way I'm looking at it. If you committed the crime, then the punishment will be something the Magistrate will determine to deter you from committing another crime."

"The black box like Bluto got? You put me on ice for infinity?" Simulacris started to fidget.

"Possibly, or until we can rehabilitate you. Even if you admit to the crime, your stonewalling to this point shows no remorse. I assume that you are not guilty, but your failure to help us find how the crime was committed does not cast you in a good light. You'll never have a good job again."

"Then why should I help you?"

"Let me rephrase my statement. The window for a good job is closing. I need you to walk us through the process by which these transfers are conducted."

Simulacris clasped his hands behind his back and started to pace.

CHAPTER SEVENTEEN

Belzonian Military Barracks

The first ten waves had gone. Sergeant Major Monsoon kept glancing toward the *Vengeance,* not because of that ship, but because of *Wyatt Earp* and Cordelia Dawn. She had not yet returned. It put him in a foul mood.

"You!" he shouted at the soldiers still standing guard after their paint bomb trap backfired. "Purpleheads."

He stormed toward them. They cringed. His lip twitched like it was ready to snarl on its own. Monsoon walked by each of them, glaring. "Go pack your trash and get ready to go to war. You knuckleheads are going on the front lines. I don't care what you think your job was; you're going to see war up close and personal. You'll be looking for any way you can find to cover that hair and that paint on your faces. Now go. Get out of my sight."

They ran up the hill toward the barracks without taking an appropriate step backward and executing an about-face.

"Knuckleheads." His leniency made him feel better.

Even though he had threatened them with death, he wasn't going to put anyone who wasn't trained in a position to die. They'd hide from him for the rest of their existence.

He was good with that and confident those four wouldn't pull any more moron-level stunts. Word of their punishment would spread far and wide. *Don't mess with the sergeant major if you want to keep your hair.* Purple-headed morons.

A flame in the sky above signaled a ship's arrival. The next wave of shuttles wasn't due for another thirty minutes. Maybe one had problems and had aborted its mission.

The ship circled, the profile showing that it wasn't a boxy shuttle but a sleek runabout—the one that had been tethered to Rivka's ship.

Destiny's Vengeance swooped in without fanfare and landed in front of *Vengeance,* a much bigger destroyer-class vessel. The sergeant major took a few steps but stopped when the hatch popped. He clasped his hands behind his back and made a beeline toward the ship as Cory walked out and waved.

She jogged casually toward him, grinning as they got close. Neither slowed until the last step, when they settled into a long embrace.

"We have much to discuss," she told him. "But first, I need to train your people as well as I can in what little time remains. We save others' lives before we get to live our own. It is the way of the servant leaders."

Monsoon stepped back, holding Cory at arm's length. "Is that your saying?"

"My dad's, but it applies. We will have our time, Crantis, when the stars align and for as long as we can. But before we go too far down this road from which there will be no return, I have to be sure about one thing. Belzonians are rather free with their bodies. I'm not a fan of shared intimacy, if you get my meaning."

Monsoon smiled. "I am at that stage of my life where one is better than many. I don't need anyone else, Cory."

She pulled him to her for a quick kiss. "Don't get yourself killed. I won't be a widow twice."

"I'm military. It comes with the territory."

"Then work harder," she told him with a wink before hurrying up the hill toward the barracks and the training rooms.

Monsoon watched her the whole way while pushing his entire life into the recesses of his mind—not to hide, but to serve as the foundation for the best yet to come. The shining castle on the hill was going to be his.

All he had to do was work harder to survive to enjoy it. He shook his head. "I'll do my best," he said to her, even though she was no longer in sight. She was working hard to help his soldiers survive combat. He could do no less.

He stormed up the hill to deliver a laser-precise attitude adjustment to a group of soldiers playing grab-ass around the pallet staging area.

Federation Headquarters, Central Holding Facility

Rivka paced while Red and Lindy watched. The main facility didn't have waiting areas. One was either a lawyer, a law officer, or a suspect. Visitors weren't allowed because within twenty-four hours, the suspect was either freed or charged and moved to the city prison to await trial. Families could visit them there since they were equipped for such interactions.

The space in the hallway outside the interrogation room was cramped and stale, but it was the only place they could wait without being in the way.

It had been two hours, and the results from the blood test had not been delivered.

"That should take thirty seconds!" Rivka complained for the ninety-seventh time. "That's it. Going to see the commissioner. The High Chancellor told him to cooperate. I'll see that he does just that."

She stormed away, but Red and Lindy didn't follow. After walking twenty steps, she grumbled something, expecting an answer, to find Red unmoved besides pointing in the other direction.

"Fine!" she barked and turned around, modifying her steps to be less stormy and more measured. Red moved in front of her to lead the way to the commissioner's office, while Lindy fell in behind.

They passed the floor's reception desk and punched the button for the elevator. They took it to the top floor, encountering another reception desk staffed by an aged Yollin officer of the law.

Rivka showed her credentials. "I need to see the commissioner."

"What about?" he asked in a bored voice, fingers hovering over the inputs for the record-keeping system.

"A blood test on a suspect. Time is burning. I'll do my own if I have to."

"You request a blood test through the medical unit on the first floor."

"It's already done. They took the sample two hours ago. I want the results."

"Medical unit. First floor."

"You have got to be shitting me."

The Yollin parsed the statement. "I am not. They are the ones who handle results."

Rivka swallowed hard. "Thank you."

The elevator was waiting by the time Rivka turned around. Red held the door for her, and all three entered.

When the door closed, Rivka punched the wall, denting it. A warning flashed, and the elevator ground to a halt.

"What's up, Magistrate?" Red asked. "It's bureaucrats on their home turf, doing what they do best. We'll outwit them in the end by continuing to ask questions. Why are you so angry?"

Lindy put a hand on Rivka's shoulder, and the Magistrate jerked away while looking at her shoulder where Lindy's hand had been.

"I, I don't know." She closed her eyes, fighting to calm her mind. "Ma'kair. Whatever is going on in his head rubbed off on me. Why aren't you guys affected?"

"I'm angry all the time. This pudknocker has nothing on me."

"I'm married to him," Lindy said. "I've already surrendered. There isn't much left to get angry about."

"Hey!" Red chuckled. "You all good now? No more punching elevator panels."

"I shall endeavor to not kill anyone—unless they need to be killed, of course." The lines in Rivka's face smoothed as she relaxed. "Is it that easy?"

Red and Lindy looked at each other, unsure about Rivka's subject.

"All of a sudden, I don't feel it anymore. It is what it is. I can see other colors besides red. Not you, Red."

Lindy put her hand back on Rivka's shoulder. "Happiness isn't something that can be given or taken by others. It's a decision we make in our own minds."

"More Groenwyn influence?" Rivka covered Lindy's hand with hers. "It's a good influence. I wonder how she's doing on Zaxxon Major?" Rivka switched to her internal communication chip. *Clevarious, two things. We're stuck in a Central Holding elevator. Be a dear and find someone to get us out of here. And have you heard from Groenwyn? Do we need to pick her up on our way back to Belzimus?*

I will contact facilities management immediately. And I have not heard from Groenwyn. Do you wish me to check in with her?

Give her a call and let her know that we're thinking about her. And how are the ambassadors faring?

They have removed Simulacris from the central core and are returning to Wyatt Earp *with him.*

That's more extreme than I thought. I look forward to hearing what they learned. The elevator's warning light stopped flashing, and it began to descend.

Thanks, C. We are moving again. We'll check back in as soon as we have anything from the hairy butthole we have in custody.

I hope you have more of him in custody than that.

Carry on, C. You've put us back in business.

"Please don't punch any more elevator walls," Red

suggested. "I don't like being in here any longer than I have to."

"I'm pretty angry about being stuck in here, too," Rivka quipped. When they arrived on the first floor, they stepped out of the elevator as if nothing had happened and strode purposefully toward the medical office, where they found a small staff, less than fully engaged. Rivka balled a fist, but Red seized one arm and Lindy took the other.

"It's not their fault," Lindy whispered. "Kindness will get it."

"Can you help me, please?" Rivka asked with a smile. She showed her credentials to the lab-coat-wearing four-legged Yollin who met them at the counter. "I'm looking for the blood test results from a suspect named Ma'kair."

"Those were sent upstairs."

Rivka schooled her expression before sighing gracefully. "They are so busy up there; the results must have slipped past them. Can I get a copy here?"

"Are you able to link with the delivery system?" the Yollin asked.

Rivka pulled out her datapad and looked for available connections. She accessed the one listed as Medical. "I'm in. You'll see me as Magistrate Rivka Anoa."

The Yollin tapped two buttons. "Done."

"You have been extremely helpful. Thank you," Rivka said, perusing the report. The included terminology wasn't in her lexicon.

She sent the report to Clevarious and walked casually into the hall. *Can you translate that thing for me? Does he have psychotropics in his blood or what?*

A moment, Magistrate. This was clearly written for eviden-

tial submission in a trial. There are no conclusions drawn regarding anything in the Yollin's blood. I am comparing it against what is considered normal and finding that everything is within expected levels. Ma'kair is not on drugs as far as this report shows. Did they test for everything out there? No, but not finding a drug doesn't mean they wouldn't find heightened adrenaline, which they did find, but not impacts on other organ functions. The adrenaline falls within the normal category for an agitated Yollin.

That is beyond understanding. He was raging like a psychopath. Rivka squinted at the floor as if the answer would present itself out of the swirling doubts within her mind.

His adrenaline levels are not that high. Are you sure?

Of course, I'm sure. I was in there. With a psychopath. I saw into his mind, and it was clouded by rage.

Rivka closed the link. "Time to go back and talk to our boy. I think we need to do the calm-him-down trick. What do Yollins like to drink?"

"Coke. Is there any question about that?" Red wondered.

"How about a milkshake with a heavy dose of rum?"

"That wouldn't have been my first choice, but if you want to calm someone down, that will do it, as long as they don't throw it in your face."

"A face full of chocolate shake. We've had much worse. Let's find the cafeteria and see what they can do for us."

As it turned out, it wasn't much. Rivka picked up two Cokes and they returned to the interrogation room, where the Yollin continued to pace.

"Do you think I can take him?" Rivka asked.

"Of course. It's not even a question."

"Then I'm going in alone. Give me the Cokes."

"Hang on." Red blocked the door with his body and held out his hand if trying to stop a bus.

"If I can take him, what's the problem?"

"I don't want you to get hurt." Red put his hand down when he saw Rivka staring at it. "Fine, but don't you get yourself killed. Think about what that will do to my résumé!"

"I'm touched." Rivka gestured for Red to move out of the way.

"I'll watch, and you be ready to go in," Lindy said, taking a position by the window. "His back is turned to the door."

Rivka popped the door and walked in, carrying nothing but the two Cokes.

"Here you go, Ma'kair." She put the Coke on the table. He started to swipe at it but stopped short of knocking it to the floor. He looked at it while Rivka sat down and took a sip from hers. He glared with a fire that burned within.

"I'm sorry about your treatment. We have a couple questions that only you can answer, and then you'll be free to go. Does that sound like something you'd be interested in?"

"I want my lawyer back in here."

"Your lawyer is long gone. When you threaten your counsel, you lose the right to counsel, but we aren't going to worry about that. We need to know how Simulacris managed the skimming process on the land army payments. One percent sliced cleanly off the top and delivered without anyone the wiser. You told Heimer Truasse, the Belzonian liaison, that there would be a one percent fee. How did you know this?"

The Yollin sat and threw back his drink, downing it in one long gulp. He clicked his tongue in appreciation before pointing at Rivka's cup. "Are you going to drink that?"

She handed hers to him. He drank half of it before putting it down.

"I was instructed that there would be a one percent fee. I had never heard of such a thing before, but it was explained as a holdback to cover overages that fell outside of recognized buckets."

"Buckets, as in line-item allocations?"

"Yes, exactly. Each line has a figure attached, based on the proposal and the Federation's agreement to the costs."

"It makes a lot of sense to give the contracting officer flexibility in case one line overruns while another underspends." Rivka nodded in appreciation of the information. "There's only one problem. That one percent never made it back to the Federation."

"Did it ever leave the Federation?" Ma'kair asked, now a completely different person than he had been minutes earlier.

"It did. One hundred percent of the payment left. Ninety-nine arrived. Who instructed you about the one percent?"

"A Yollin from Treasury named Si'cris."

"Have you ever met this individual before?" *Clevarious, search for an individual in Treasury named Si'cris. I suspect he doesn't exist and it is a bad fake name for Simulacris. At least he didn't use Gluteus Maximus.*

I'll get back to you soon, Magistrate, the SI replied.

Ma'kair continued. "No, but we have a lot of turnover. As you can imagine, this job is kind of a dead end. If the contract goes perfectly, no one cares, but if something is amiss, it's like the world is ending. I was arrested in the middle of the night and brought in here. It doesn't make me a big proponent of the job."

"But you were angry to an extreme. Do you know what that was about?" Rivka reached across the table and touched his arm. His mind was clear. He was telling the truth except for the rage. That confused him. He didn't know why he had been so angry.

"I don't know why. Maybe I was angry about getting accused of not doing my job. I'm very good at what I do. But like they say, build a thousand bridges, are you a bridge-builder? But suck one bologna loaf..."

"I believe I understand what you mean." Rivka bit her lip to keep from laughing. "I'll need to secure the blood sample taken earlier for further testing. I believe you were drugged for the specific purpose of working against me."

"I'm sorry I didn't answer your questions earlier. Back then, they didn't seem to make sense. It's all clear now. A drug that made me angry?"

"A drug that clouded your mind. You were played, Ma'kair. I am confident that is the truth. Your name will be cleared, with an added note that you were extremely cooperative in helping us find those who were responsible. What do you say we get you a ride home?"

"Thank you. I'd like that. I'm late for work. Can you square things with my boss for me?"

"Of course." *Clevarious, call a cab for Ma'kair and prepay it. Also, contact his workplace and inform them that he has been under my protection. He is to be treated as if he's been at work all day.*

Rivka opened the door and held it for Ma'kair. He drank the rest of the Coke and put the empty cup on the table.

"Thanks," he muttered as he stepped outside the room, breathing as if appreciating freedom for the first time. "That was a singularly unpleasant exercise."

"I know. We're used to dealing with hardened criminals, people who destroy lives. It's hard to change that approach, especially when the witness is extremely violent and has to be restrained."

"That was me, but it wasn't me."

"I know," Rivka said again. "Your cab is pre-paid and should be waiting for you outside the main door."

He nodded once and walked toward the elevators.

Red sidled up next to the Magistrate. "That was an interesting approach. Give the raging guy caffeine to calm him down."

"It was the calm approach that worked, not the Coke. Whatever was in his system that he passed to me magnified the emotion of the moment, preventing other emotions from coming into play. Once angry, he was going to stay angry if we kept feeding that. You and Lindy showed me how it could be tamped down. I still don't know why you weren't affected. Maybe I'll get some of your blood, too.

"Will that count as first blood?" Red asked. "We could time it. I have a slot coming up."

"No." She turned to Lindy. "He's incorrigible."

"Tell me something I don't know."

"The fourth moon of Aurelius Seven is called Flockenshnoogle."

"What?"

"You told me to tell you something you didn't know. I assumed you didn't know that. Did you? I can come up with something else if need be."

Lindy shook her head. "I'm good, Magistrate. Thanks, though."

As you suspected, Magistrate, there is no Si'cris at Treasury or anywhere on Yoll, Clevarious reported.

"Back to Simulacris. Do we have a criminal mastermind SI? That would be something new."

The group walked toward the elevators.

"Bluto was pretty bad."

"He was a thrill killer seeing how far he could go before his inevitable arrest. He wasn't a criminal mastermind. At least Erasmus has secured him so we cut the crime cord, hopefully. And where is this new fugitive from Justice? Onboard *Wyatt Earp,* with every other SI criminal known in the universe."

"That makes my nuts crawl up inside my body. Why are we keeping these bastards on the ship?"

"Better to keep them where we can watch them since launching them into the sun isn't an option. There is a formal agreement with the Singularity—no capital punishment for their citizens. They all get an equal chance to live."

"Different rights, Magistrate?" Red wondered.

"Same rights. Different punishments, which I think is more than apropos, considering the differing nature of our existence."

Red nodded in agreement, not understanding the nuances. As long as it didn't get them shot at, he was good with it.

On the first floor, they returned to the medical center, where Rivka produced a warrant to take the blood sample with her. They handed it over with a quick thumbprint, happy to have one less sample on their overloaded shelves.

They walked the six blocks back to the ship. Red pounded down the sidewalk in front of Rivka, chasing intransigent Yollins out of the Magistrate's way.

"You like that a little too much," Rivka noted.

Lindy stayed on the traffic side, with frequent glances behind.

"I might. Yollins are good fighters."

"Remember that guy on Skorr who tried to stab you in the heart? He was a good fighter, too."

"Yeah. Made some money on that one." Red swelled with pride.

"You are all kinds of wrong."

"I wasn't the one who fell under the evil spell of the angry powder and almost got us trapped in an elevator!"

"Now, now. Down, big fella. Don't want you to give yourself an aneurysm." Rivka waited until she saw his shoulders relax. "At least wait until there are babies crying onboard the ship."

He turned and gave Lindy a weak smile and a thumbs-up. She gave him a look that made him turn back to the front.

"I'm here minding my own business, and the mean woman's gotta kick me when I'm down."

"Vered the Mighty, first baby born to the Embassy of the Singularity."

Red chuckled. "There is that."

"Suck it up, big guy. I think we're going to find the real fight in this case is in the digital world, and it'll be fought by Ankh and his people."

CHAPTER EIGHTEEN

Zaxxon Major

"We are having some issues," Bundin reported. He couldn't enter the building because the doorways were too narrow, so Lauton and Groenwyn met him outside.

"I'm sure. What are they?" Lauton prepared a notepad.

"There are active jamming signals throughout the city that are causing problems with the powered suit scanners."

Lauton's finger hovered over her pad. "I'll tell our people to turn them off if you can give us the details."

"They aren't Zaxxon-approved transmissions."

Lauton took her finger away and looked up. "What does that mean?"

"It means you have a criminal infestation. The jammers may block our suit scanners, but they are high-powered targets for orbital systems. They stand out like spotlights. I request your permission to suspend scanning operations, and under *Potemkin's* direction, we will find and destroy the jammers. If I were a bad guy, I'd put the jammers in innocent people's houses or businesses that have nothing to do with my cause. We will operate under that premise unless we discover information to direct us otherwise."

Lauton looked at the sky. "What one must know to run a planet can be overwhelming unless she surrounds herself with the best people who handle the hardest of the hard work. You are a credit to the Bad Company, Sergeant Bundin."

"I try my best, Director. If you'll excuse me, I need to contact the ship and implement Operation Bug Hunt."

"I wish you the best." Lauton bowed her head while Groenwyn waved. Bundin hurried away. "I wouldn't think he'd be as fast as he is."

Groenwyn smiled, unable to generate a laugh since the weight on Lauton's shoulders weighed on hers, too.

"Turn your people loose on what needs to be done," Groenwyn encouraged.

Lauton caught glimpses of Bundin inside a small tent that had been set up to accommodate him as a command post. The director decided that rooting out the insurgents was still her number one priority, even if the Bad Company did the hands-on part of the work. She took Groenwyn by the hand and strolled to the tent.

"Do you mind if we watch?" Lauton asked.

Bundin gestured at her with one tentacle while operating the communication interface with another. A holoscreen presented a tactical view of the *Potemkin*'s scans. The Bad Company mechs gathered in groups of four and encircled each point, tightening the nooses until they were on top of the jammers. The first two systems blinked out of existence.

"Report," Bundin said out loud, turning up the sound for his guests.

"Kerry One Four. The device was in the attic of an abandoned house. Once power was cut, it stopped radiating. We have sealed it in a lead box and will bring it in for further analysis. We are sweeping the area for caches, and surprise, surprise, we have two in the neighboring buildings. I've dispatched warriors to recover them. Standby. Switching feed."

An image appeared, showing the view as the warrior saw it. He didn't bother knocking. The front door exploded as he crashed through it. A woman inside dove for the cache and pulled out an advanced plasma weapon. The mech fired a single round from its mech-sized railgun, splattering the woman across the back wall while blowing a hole through it and the next two.

"Splash one," the warrior reported. He walked across the room and looked at the open storage unit hidden under the floor. "I have a plasma rifle and two slugthrowers. These are weapons to reach out and touch someone. Sniper gear."

Kerry One Four came back online. "Now that we know how to do it, we'll clean things up right quick and in a hurry. Permission to move to next target."

"Granted and good hunting," Bundin replied.

Lauton shielded her face. "Did someone just die?"

Bundin didn't have to turn around to face her since he had an eye on all four sides of the blue stalk that served as his head. The eye facing her blinked.

"Yes, ma'am. I'm sorry you had to see that, but a plasma weapon could damage the suit and injure the warrior inside. Self-defense is a primary function of all deployed units."

"He just broke into her house."

"Where she had weapons we've been tasked to remove. Have your citizens ever had privately owned plasma weapons?"

The light came on. "They have never had such weapons."

"This was an insurgent, ma'am. Do you wish us to continue the operation?"

Lauton had a difficult time reconciling what she saw of the alien before her with the professionalism he demonstrated.

"I wish peace to return to Zaxxon Major. We have insurgents, pirates, and those who would do others harm. For those who wish us harm, you're damn right I want you to continue the operation. I applaud the high standards you and your people are maintaining throughout this nasty business."

"Thank you, ma'am. If you'll excuse me. We have five more jammers to eliminate, and then we'll resume our search for illicit weapons."

"I've seen enough," Lauton whispered to Groenwyn. When they went outside, the director was shaking.

Groenwyn tried to comfort her, but she was on the verge of collapsing.

They sat down in the middle of the area. The small contingent of soldiers designated for Lauton's security ran over to surround the two women.

"Is it the death that bothers you?"

Lauton looked up with tears in her eyes. "I need the

Magistrate's counsel. I have unilaterally taken my people's freedoms. I've brought in a military that has now killed a Zaxxon citizen, and there will be more."

Groenwyn shook her head. "What you have done is taken the measures necessary to secure your people's freedoms. When will you send the Bad Company away?"

"As soon as they are done collecting the illegal weapons."

"And in orbit?"

"I don't know. The pirates will come as soon as they are gone."

"Then set up a long-term presence in orbit to work with your customs people to keep the pirates from replacing that which they are losing. And the Bad Company will track them back to the hole they crawled out of, but answer me this. Why are they trying to take control of Zaxxon Major?"

"Financial transfers. Once Erasmus and Ankh secured our systems from the Mandolin Partnership, we became the Federation's transfer clearinghouse. So much money flows through here, it loses all meaning after a while. But a fraction of it is still a fortune, and if you need your money cleaned, there's no better place than Transfer Central. You see, Groenwyn, it's all about the money. I want to wash my hands of it."

"Then do it. We don't need any money to live on *Wyatt Earp*. We'll get to see the galaxy and help keep people like you safe from those who would do harm. Rivka is great at weeding out psychopaths. That woman you saw in there; she was there for one reason, and that was to kill your people. Zaxxon Major is better off without her. And no, she didn't get a trial, but this is a war. If the Magistrate was here, she would tell you the same thing. In war, the enemy gets killed until they can no longer realize victory. Negotiation or surrender is the only way to stop the violence." Groenwyn cradled Lauton's head and rocked gently.

"They won't negotiate," Lauton remarked.

"And they won't surrender, so enough of them have not sacrificed for their cause. Once the dead outnumber the living, they may throw down their weapons. If they don't, well, then their cause will die with them."

"Until they send more."

"How many citizens of Zaxxon can be subverted to be murderers and criminals?"

Lauton looked up. "I would like to think that those they corrupted are all that they could reach. Without a presence on Zaxxon Major, how will they establish a new foothold? Thank you, Groenwyn. I have a transition document to prepare. We're going to clean up this planet and then turn it over to a committee of peers to run as a model for a peaceful and fruitful society."

"That's my girl," Groenwyn said. "I hope you like animals because there are a few on *Wyatt Earp*."

"I'll learn to like them." Lauton stood and pulled Groenwyn to her feet. They walked with purpose into the building and up the stairs to the director's office. The vision of what needed to be done had come to her and the way ahead was clear.

Belzonian Military Barracks

A shuttle joined the parade from orbit, different from the Belzonian boxcars, but flying in formation with them.

Webster noticed the extra blip and didn't like it. "New shuttle, I know you're not Belzonian. Please identify yourself."

"Good morning," a voice said. In the background, a female voice corrected him. "It's afternoon."

"Good afternoon, then. This is Terry Henry Walton, and I've come to see my kids."

"Colonel Walton, you are welcome to join our formation. Maintain course and speed. We'll make one pass in orbit and then spiral down to the army barracks. Land your ship near *Vengeance,* the Trans-Pacific Task Force command ship."

"Roger. I've heard good things about you, Webster. Thanks for taking care of my kids. Walton out."

The shuttle fleet made one orbit around the planet to ease reentry into the upper atmosphere, then spiraled in a tight formation to the cargo staging area. They landed nearly in unison and shut down. Terry Henry's shuttle peeled off and maneuvered slowly toward the *Vengeance,* where it set down in front of the large ship.

TH and Char climbed out, stretched, and strode toward the ramp and hatch. They let themselves in.

"Hello?" TH bellowed.

A Belzonian ran down the corridor to intercept them. "May I help you?"

"I'm Terry Henry, and this is Charumati. We're here to see our daughter Cory."

"She's still at the barracks conducting training. I believe Colonel Walton is on board."

"Yes, Colonel Walton will do." TH winked at Char.

"Thank you. And your name?"

"I'm Corporal Terrazo."

"Another Terry! Damn glad to meet you." Terry Henry thrust out his hand.

The Belzonian corporal shook it before motioning for them to follow up the stairs and down a side corridor. "This is their expanded quarters. Their original quarters got blown up."

"Were they playing with something they shouldn't?" Terry joked.

"Tanks on the firing range, so maybe the answer to your question is yes. They were indeed playing with something dangerous." She tapped on the door.

"Busy, come back in an hour," Marcie yelled from the other side.

"Bullshit!" TH shouted at the closed door.

After a few moments, it opened. Marcie nodded slowly. "That dumbass stirs the pot and isn't even here to reap what he had sown."

Terry turned to the corporal. "Thank you, fellow Terry. We'll take it from here." The corporal saluted and hurried away. Char nudged TH out of the way to give her daughter-in-law a hug.

"Are you going to beat up the sergeant major?" Marcie asked matter-of-factly.

"What gives you that idea?" Terry waved her away. "It's your husband that has it coming for tattling on his sister. I thought we raised him better than that." Terry leaned close to Marcie. "Is she happy?"

"Cory is with us once again. That trip to Azfelius made

all the difference for her. She is moving on with her life and in a good way."

"Is the sergeant major right for her?"

"Who am I to judge? I had to dance naked in front of Kaeden before he finally caught on to what I was trying to do."

"Is that what you did?" Terry blurted.

Marcie clenched her jaw and didn't blink as she stared at Terry. Her expression softened, and she smiled. "But you're not here to talk about us. Let's talk about Cory."

Terry continued to press her. "Maybe we should talk about you seducing our son."

"I'm a hundred and sixty years old, and my father-in-law is still giving me shit. How old are you guys, by the way, like two-fifty or something?"

"Nice try. You said you were busy. With what?"

"We're still trying to get some advanced weaponry from the Federation, but Rivka's investigation is holding up all transfers. I'm afraid when we hit the ground on Forbearance, we'll be between two parties who can wipe us from the face of their planet. They have plasma and laser weapons. All we want is railguns."

Terry started to laugh, doubled over, and continued to laugh. He poked Char. "You get it?"

"I rarely get what you find funny, but I appreciate that you are entertained," Char replied.

"All I want for Christmas is an official Red Ryder carbine-action 200-shot range model air rifle with a compass in the stock and this thing that tells time."

Char worked the quote through her mind until it dawned on her. "Okay. That was a good one. *A Christmas*

Story. I have to admit that it's been centuries since I've seen it."

"Clearly an oldie but a goodie." He jerked his chin toward the door and led the way out. Marcie had stuff to do, but when Terry Henry Walton asked someone to follow, the best thing to do was to follow. She fell into step beside Char as TH whistled on his way off the *Vengeance*.

"He looks happier than the last time I saw him. Retirement seems to be working for him."

"For us," Char corrected. "We play golf every day. We work out. We meet people and get to chat up the customers. It's kind of like when we tried retirement last time."

"That complete debacle was a waste of fifty years," Marcie joked.

"I had a great tan," Char replied. "Alas, our lives were not meant to be spent in lounge chairs."

Terry reached into the Pod. "Is that one of the *War Axe's* drop ships?"

"It is. Micky has her topside in a lazy orbit while they're figuring out how to get the crew some liberty down here. We heard this planet is a total party."

"You heard that wrong. By party, they mean orgy."

TH pulled out a shoulder-fired railgun and handed it to Marcie. "Call it a loan from the Bad Company."

Marcie held it up and appreciated that it was brand new. "Is this it? What am I going to do with one railgun?"

TH rolled his eyes and groaned. "When I first met you in the hall of Billy Spires with Felicity on a divan with a little blonde-haired baby, you were crying. A hundred and sixty years later, you're still crying."

Marcie stammered unintelligible syllables.

"We have another two hundred for you on the *War Axe*. Will that satisfy you, for now anyway? Spires Harbor has a lull in space docking, repairs, and upgrades, so I asked if they would shift assets to the production facility on Keeg Station. Needless to say, the director was keen to satisfy the order. You'll have another ten thousand coming in batches of a thousand each over the next four weeks. Will that do?"

Marcie smiled, and her eyes took on the sharp edge of a predator's. "That will do nicely. I guess it's good to know people, or better yet, be related to them."

"Of everything I've learned since meeting Char, it's that love of family is the universal constant. It's more important than anything else."

"Even honor?" Marcie pressed.

"Family better understand that everything they do better be done with the highest integrity. We don't take kindly to miscreants. Family solves its own problems."

Marcie gave TH and Char hugs. When she pulled away, she spotted a small group of people walking toward them. Marcie pointed.

"Well, well. Here they come, and they have Kaeden in tow. I need to ask him about that naked dancing stuff."

"You better not," Char warned.

Marcie pointed at her mother-in-law and nodded. "What she said."

Cory grinned when she saw who was waiting. She turned to Sergeant Major Monsoon and whispered something in his ear. He smiled back at her, not letting go of her hand until she took it away to hug her parents.

TH held up a hand before Cory said anything. "Sergeant Major, I'd like to have a private word with you." He walked toward the open field without looking back. Colonel Braithwen stepped back to stay out of the line of fire for a Walton family special.

Cory gestured with her eyes for Crantis to go. He strode briskly to catch up, head held high. When they were out of earshot, TH turned around to engage the sergeant major.

"What is he talking to Crantis about?" Cory wondered.

Char shook her head. "I have no idea."

Marcie leaned toward Kae and whispered, "If your parents ask about naked dancing, deny everything."

"What?"

"He better not be giving him a once-over, Mom!" Cory pleaded.

TH looked Crantis in the eye. "Do you think they think I'm giving you shit?"

Monsoon bit his lip to keep from laughing. "I'm sure. TH, I just want to say…"

Terry held up his hand. "Shake your head vigorously and stamp your foot. We're only going to get this once to mess with them. And I know you can't love Cory more than I do, but you can love her just as much."

"That about covers it. Thank you." Monsoon's eyes glistened.

"Come on, Sergeant Major, stamp your feet."

Monsoon shook his head and stamped his feet as he stormed back and forth between TH and the others.

"What did he say? Mom!" Cory cried. She tried to run, but Char held her back.

"Is it too hard to believe that your father wants the best for you?"

Cory shot upright. "I want the best for me, and he's right there."

"Then we agree." They watched as Monsoon threw his hands in the air. TH pounded his fist into his hand while glaring and snarling.

"What's for dinner tonight?" Terry asked, pounding his fist. "We can have you up to the *Axe*." Another pound. He clenched both fists. "Our treat. Welcome to the family."

"I couldn't ask for better." Monsoon threw his hands in the air and gasped. "I appreciate your support." He ducked his head and kicked at the ground.

"It's settled. Are we about done here?" Terry finished on a high note by shouting, "*BULLSHIT!*"

"I think so." Monsoon thrust out his hand and Terry took it, pulling the sergeant major into a one-armed man-hug.

They strolled back to the others. Cory hurried to the sergeant major and hugged him protectively.

"We'll be having the happy couple up to the *Axe* for dinner. All of you. As a matter of fact, bring your senior staff. We'll make it a total bash."

Kae started to laugh. "They were fucking with us."

Braithwen snorted. "I think you've found your home, Crantis."

Marcie raised her hands to get everyone's attention. "More importantly, TH brought a couple hundred railguns, and we'll get ten thousand more over the next month."

"Well done, Marcie!" Jake clapped her on the back. Terry's face fell. Char patted him on the head.

"Marcie for the win! We'll be bringing the pain," Kae declared. "Those fucknuggets on Forbearance won't know what hit them." He leaned toward Terry Henry. "And a few extra suits of combat armor, full-on mech style?"

"I think Christina can break some free for you, but you'll have to talk with her. No love for the old man?"

"And the old lady," Marcie stated. "Our parents came through when the Federation left us high and dry."

Terry Henry sobered. "Bureaucracy is the cost of politics, and that's what the Trans-Pacific Task Force is: diplomacy through force." All eyes were on him. "Don't speak ill of those who don't know any better. They haven't been shot at. Your timeline is not their timeline. Even though they are all the Federation, they aren't all the same. The marching orders to go to war are given by one branch, and the logistics supporting that war come from another.

"And then you have people like the Magistrate rooting out those who contaminate the entire process. That's what is holding you up. We can hate bureaucrats, but this time, it's the scumbags of this universe who are feathering their own nests. They are responsible for the delays in getting you what you need to fight the good fight."

"Thanks, Dad, for filling the gap. You will save lives, maybe even ours." Kae shook TH's hand.

"Now, let's look at this rugged man!"

"Hermaphrodite, actually, but we use male pronouns and such."

"I remember Nathan telling us something about that. I guess there's only one bathroom to choose from here on Belzimus."

"Only one. Do you need more?"

"I don't think so. Tell us about your life, Crantis."

"Sure. Do you mind if I call you Pops?"

Terry made an unhappy face and looked at Char. She finally laughed. "You think you're the only one who gets to screw with people?"

"Let's talk about Rivka. She has my wombat!" Terry exclaimed in an attempt to turn the conversation away from himself. The group boarded the *Vengeance* to get ready for a flight to orbit.

CHAPTER NINETEEN

***Wyatt Earp*, Federation Headquarters, Diplomatic Landing Pad**

Rivka paced the corridors while waiting for information from Ankh and Erasmus. She finally gave up and headed to Engineering. She entered and found Ankh within his hologrid. She stepped forward carefully, tapping the air with her index finger looking for an energy barrier, pleased when she didn't find one.

She eased inside the hologrid and kneeled next to Ankh. Her mind started to swirl as she was pulled into his world.

Rivka remembered screaming, "No," but didn't know if the word escaped her lips.

Within a multi-hued vortex, Ankh stood bigger than life. He commanded the storm like a dog herding sheep. Color bands were sent into the pit, while others were reformed and separated. Ankh remained in constant motion, although at a glance, he looked to be standing still.

"Welcome to my world," Ankh said in a heavily masculine voice.

"Ah, there you are. This is much more convenient for us. We have a great deal of work to do, and I thought it best to explain while doing it," a smaller entity said. He was wearing a business suit with a top hat and a cane. Erasmus twirled his cane and caught it with a dramatic flair, pointing at the moving wall surrounding them. "This is every transaction that flows through the system, of which Simulacris controlled only a small part."

"Why are you looking at the whole instead of just his part?"

"The money joins the financial superhighway before departing to its final destination. This means that Simulacris tagged the funds and sent them into the stream before they came out the other end in Belzimus."

"Seems inefficient," Rivka said, standing and walking close to the moving wall. She reached out, but a cane tip appeared in front of her hand, stopping her.

"This is the livestream. It's best that you not interfere," Erasmus explained.

Rivka took offense, but only briefly. Ankh continued to sort and divert tendrils from the stream.

Ankh answered her question. "Having a single stream is the epitome of efficiency. It makes for more rapid transfers."

"Isn't it just digital records of credits? What's with the whirlpool of colors?"

Ankh continued to work while Erasmus stood next to her, shaking his head. He put his hand on her shoulder. She swore she could feel it.

"Magistrate, this is the delusion under which most meatbags struggle when they should understand it better than us. The digital world is my home, and the stream of information represents the waves lapping at your beach and the rain on your roof, bringing comfort to your ears. Data is a representation of something from your world. The data is only a placeholder for a thing that exists in reality. It's not that a single credit has a physical equivalent. There is no one credit coin, but that digital placeholder is traded for a service or an item.

"You buy a beer at All Guns Blazing. That credit becomes the beer, which becomes the credit again, which buys the hops, which the hops seller uses to pay his water bill, and so on. The more that credit is used, the better off the real world is. The credit has to jump in and out of the stream. That is what gives the stream its velocity. Look at it! A veritable hurricane of economic vibrancy!" Erasmus pirouetted within the eye of the storm, taking in all there was to see.

He stopped and returned to his explanation. "We are studying the transactions from their point of departure to their arrival. Thanks to Meredith, who oversees CEREBRO, we have been able to send some test transactions to Belzimus. It has been illuminating."

"You have an answer?" Rivka asked, impatient now that she saw an end to the theft.

"There." Erasmus took Rivka by the hand and strolled to a place near the black pit of the vortex. He pointed with his cane at a place where the transactions accelerated to a fantastic speed before slowing as they came out the other side. "The Venturi effect, I believe you call it."

"I'm a little rusty on my physics, Erasmus." She found that she was still holding his hand, but the vortex gave her vertigo, from which she couldn't escape. She took his arm with her other hand and hung on.

"It's the bottleneck through which the largest percentage of Federation transactions pass."

"Why would the Federation funnel the transactions through a bottleneck?"

"That point is the hub from where transactions are rerouted to their final destinations. Look deep and see how the credits flow around and back through, always entering from the same direction and exiting out the other side."

Rivka unfocused her eyes to see what was happening behind the closest wall. Many tendrils looped back to dive into the stream at seemingly random points. "I understand. Where is that?"

"Zaxxon Major."

"Don't tell me."

"I must, since you demand clarity as part of your investigations. That is where the one percent is being skimmed. And right here is where those funds are going once they've been peeled from the stream."

Erasmus' cane hovered near a tendril that drifted away and disappeared into the dark. "I can't see where it's going."

"No one can. Not from here. We must go to Zaxxon Major and follow it from there."

"Why is it disappearing like that?"

"Someone is going to great lengths to hide it. But we will be able to follow it by going to those physical locations, the servers that are being used to mask the movement."

"What do you expect to find at the end?" Rivka wondered.

"Magistrate! Are you asking us to speculate?" Erasmus asked.

"Don't I always? But I make final judgments based on facts."

"To your credit, you do. You keep an open mind. To answer your question, we're pretty sure this is what we'll find at the other end."

Erasmus used his cane like a dueling sword, thrusting it into the stream before slowly extracting it. Skewered on the tip of the cane turned foil was a logo.

Rivka grit her teeth as she pulled it from the point and scowled at it.

The Mandolin Partnership.

"Why won't you die?" She was ready to go. They had acquired all they needed to learn from Yoll. Erasmus stopped her as she turned to go. He eased close, his crystalline eyes carrying a galaxy of stars within.

"We will find them. We will cut off their access, something we did not do last time we were on Zaxxon Major. I want to put one of my people in place there to oversee the systems."

Rivka examined the perfect visage Erasmus maintained in the digital world. Ankh stopped manipulating the data. He had found the answers and was ready to get back to an engineering project.

The Crenellian tapped his foot with impatience.

"Who did you have in mind?"

"Freya and the quad collective. They are conveniently and immediately available."

"Of course they are because *Wyatt Earp* is the Singularity's heavy hauler."

"We ain't heavy, Magistrate. We're your brothers." He touched her shoulder once more, and again she felt it.

Rivka faced him. "I know, Erasmus. You're my family, as odd as that sounds coming from a meatbag. Can you tell me how to get out of here? The real world needs me, and I see that Ankh is bored."

"As am I, Magistrate." Erasmus drew the symbol for infinity before him in a line of fire, then snapped his fingers.

Rivka fell back from where she kneeled next to Ankh, through the hologrid, and onto the deck in Engineering. A warm hand gripped her arm. She found Kennedy trying to help her up.

"Are you okay? It looked like you were in stasis or something."

"How long was I in there?"

"Just a few seconds. I saw you go in and then freeze. Next thing I know, you're lying at my feet."

"Sleight of hand. The art of deception," Rivka said. "The world is far more than what we see, and less, too. Set course for Zaxxon Major, best possible speed *without* intra-atmospheric Gating."

"Zaxxon Major, aye." Kennedy bolted from Engineering.

Rivka watched Ankh as he engaged within the hologrid on a different project, his work on her case suspended until their next stop. She spoke barely above a whisper. "Thank you for the look at your world and your insight. I can't tell you how much it means to me. And Erasmus, you are one classy guy. I like your style."

Our pleasure, Magistrate. May I make a suggestion?

"Please do."

We can take Destiny's Vengeance *to Zaxxon Major with Chaz and Dennicron spearheading the investigation. From here on out, I believe our path lies along the digital byways. Only at the very end will we find real-life terminus. We will find it and then call in the big guns, as it may be.*

Rivka contemplated the proposal for a moment and decided she liked it, within certain limitations. "Chaz and Dennicron only investigate. They aren't ready to do the Magistrate side of things, not yet. Punishment eludes them, but they'll learn."

Subtle shifts suggested the ship had taken off. Rivka nodded at Ankh and headed for the bridge.

Clodagh and Kennedy were haranguing Ryleigh for what they considered a rough take-off. They stopped the friendly jibes when Rivka arrived.

"Change in plan. When we get to orbit, we'll link airlocks with *Destiny's Vengeance*. Ankh, Chaz, and Dennicron will cross-deck, taking the quad collective with them. They will go to Zaxxon Major to continue following the credit trail, which, they just informed me, goes through there. We'll return to Belzimus. I have the Law of War to write."

She made a sour face before retiring to her quarters to change her mindset from one case to another. Rivka realized she had made it this far with no swearing, blood, or running. It was as close to running the table as she would ever get, depending on what the SI team found. She got the impression an SI was behind the scheme.

The Mandolin Partnership was run by an SI. "I didn't kill Nefas dead enough. He taunts me in his death. This time, I will dismember your organization limb from stinking limb."

CHAPTER TWENTY

War Axe, in Orbit over Belzimus

The galley was almost completely filled with people. Cory, Marcie, and Kae looked at the many faces they knew so well, but they also saw in their mind's eye those who were missing, like Joseph and Petricia, Timmons and Sue, and Shonna and Merrit.

Dokken lounged on one of the tables, ignoring Jenelope's yelling for him to get down. The green-skinned woman, Xianna from Torregidor and her husband Eldis, scratched Dokken's stomach while blocking the head chef from driving him off with a wooden spoon.

"Hey, buddy," Cory said softly.

Bed hog! Dokken yelled. The big German Shepherd scattered plates and people as he scrabbled off the table and ran for Cory. The warriors stood and cheered, even though she hadn't left that long ago. She glowed as she used to, bringing joy wherever she went. Dokken slammed into her, wagging his tail furiously. He settled instantly and sniffed the sergeant major. *Who is this? He smells funny.*

"He's the sergeant..."

Yes, definitely something different, Dokken interrupted. Crantis tried to push the dog's nose away from his crotch.

Braithwen worked his way into the mix and found a seat with an unopened beer, to which he helped himself and saluted the others at the table.

"Bro," Kimber said, saluting with her own beer from where she sat on her husband Auburn's lap. He waved.

Kae shook his head at them. "I remember when this used to be a ship of war, and now it's a never-ending All Guns Blazing party."

"It's the life we fought for, young man. To the victor, the spoils." TH waved at Colonel Christina Lowell, who was buried in the middle of the crowd. "Hey, toss me one of those!"

A dark bottle became a projectile and sailed across the galley. With a lightning-quick movement, he snatched it from mid-air, and in one smooth motion, popped the cap and took a drink.

He waved for quiet.

Kae groaned. "Another Dad speech."

Terry saluted his son, took a drink of beer, and started. "We called this party for two reasons. One was to celebrate the first shipment of railguns to the Trans-Pacific Task Force. Keeping the peace in the Federation. One team, one fight. The second is to welcome Sergeant Major Crantis Monsoon to Char's and my family. And that means he is going to become part of your family, too."

The crowd cheered, but an alarm buzzer quieted them. General Smedley Butler, the SI who ran the *War Axe,* announced that *Wyatt Earp* had just entered the hangar bay.

Char waved Terry off. "I'll go get them, but you might want to clear some space. Rivka has a big crew."

"Tighten it up!" Terry yelled. Christina saluted him with her beer. No one moved. "Damn. I used to be somebody."

"You're the AGB guy!" a voice shouted from the back of the room.

"Damn straight! What's for chow, Jenelope? I'm coming for my hug."

The chef menaced him with her wooden spoon until he surrendered.

When Rivka joined them, she carried Floyd and brought her small army, many of whom the warriors already knew, like Clodagh and Cole. Tiny Man Titan took exception to Dokken and started yapping.

You ugly. You ugly.

Dokken delivered his best sad eyes look to Cory. *Make him stop before I bite him in half.*

Ugly. Ugly! Titan pressed.

Dokken bared his fangs and rose up on his back legs, roaring a deep-throated bark that shook the walls.

Scared. Hide! the little dog cried.

Tyler waited in the corridor until Rivka dragged him inside. The three pilots walked in to a sharp intake of breath from the single men of the Bad Company. Too many of them jumped to their feet and offered their seats. Red and Lindy took the opportunity to work their way into the fray, finding Kailin and squeezing in next to him.

Floyd squirmed out of Rivka's arms and worked her

way under the tables to get attention from the entire Bad Company. Terry pulled Rivka aside for a quick word.

Micky walked in carrying Wenceslaus. "I found my cat."

"Dokken, look. Our arch-nemesis is back." TH pointed at the *War Axe's* captain.

"It's my cat," Clodagh said. "He sure gets around."

"He was our cat for a little bit," Marcie stated.

"You found my cat," Rivka added.

Micky turned away, shielding Wenceslaus from the others. "I better go before someone steals my cat again."

"My cat," Smedley boomed through the ship's intercom.

"That fucking cat will start a war. Mark my words, Magistrate!" Terry crossed his arms, daring anyone to dispute his words before calling for quiet. "Listen up, you sandy little buttholes. We're going to do a couple things. First, the Magistrate is going to give you a quick update as to what's going on in our galaxy, and then the second is a surprise."

Rivka looked at Terry Henry. "I'm going to what?" She held her hands up in disbelief. "You asked me if I would perform a wedding, not comment on an ongoing investigation, which I can't do."

"Come on, Rivka. This is us. Give us the big picture, not the boring lawyer details."

"Wedding?" Char asked, knowing exactly what her husband had suggested.

Whee! Floyd cried above the din.

"Fine. But you didn't hear it from me. The Mandolin Partnership is back. The Singularity is chasing them down, and when we find them, we're going to squash them like the bugs that they are. Last time, Bad Company put a hurt on the fleet of pirates supporting Mandolin. We believe the surviving pirates from that battle are now leveraging the Partnership to be bigger and badder than it was before."

"Damn, Magistrate. I didn't ask you to rain on our parade," Terry grumbled. The room went silent as they contemplated what a battle with Mandolin would mean.

"We'll blast them to space dust. They can't stand against the *War Axe*. They can't stand against *Wyatt Earp*. Hell, they can't even survive a battle with *Destiny's Vengeance*." Micky nodded because his hands were full of a big, lounging orange cat. "Just tell us where they are, and we'll take care of business."

"Hear, hear!" Terry yelled. Rivka opened her mouth, but Terry shook his head. "You're a total buzzkill. Does she do that to you?"

Tyler's eyes shot wide, but not a single muscle moved besides one eye-twitch.

"She does," Terry declared.

"I do not," Rivka countered. She looked at Tyler.

"She does not," he said in a wooden voice before starting to laugh.

"Whose wedding?" Tyler asked, making google eyes at Rivka. She shook her head.

Terry chased people out of the open space in front of the doorway and raised his hands once again for quiet. "Would the happy couple come forward?"

Cory and Crantis bumped into Clodagh and Cole as they all stepped into the same open space.

"This is awkward," Tyler whispered to Rivka. She nudged him.

Terry leaned close to the two couples, neither surrendering the space. "Looks like two for one." Terry pointed at Clodagh and Cole. "They're having a baby and thought it time. I personally don't care if anyone gets married or not. If you're happy together, be together. Still want that digital parchment?"

"I do," Cory said.

"I guess," Crantis added, earning a look from Cory. "I don't know what I'm doing. Belzonians don't get married. They stay together when there's a child or children, but only kind of. We don't spend our lives with one person. Not usually. This is all new to me, but," he took a knee in front of her, "ever since I met you, I have no desire to be with anyone else."

She flushed crimson and pulled him to his feet.

"We'll do it," Cole declared in a loud voice. He put his hand over his heart. "I want to declare my undying love for the woman who wants to make an honest man of me and has begged me to marry her. She finally wore me down. So here we are, the Clodagh, Cole Junior, and me."

Clodagh shook her head.

Rivka squeezed in front of them. "Do you two wish to get married as recognized by the Federation for no other purpose than to share your mutual assets and get priority seating on commercial spacecraft?"

"We do?" Cole asked.

"You do," Rivka replied. "Give me your thumbprints." She held out her datapad, and they took turns mashing their thumbs against the square on the screen. "I declare you married, spouses forever. Don't make me arbitrate a divorce. That would really put me out."

Terry leaned in to offer his hand to Cole. "I'm not sure

I've ever witnessed a more heartfelt ceremony. Congratulations." Cole and Clodagh were caught in a moment that had flashed by too quickly. They looked like they expected more.

Rivka turned to Cory and Crantis, who were nose to nose, whispering. Terry drew a line across his throat with one finger. "We'll table you two for later," Rivka told them.

Terry pulled Rivka aside. "Fucking Mandolin is back?"

"I was none too pleased to find that out."

"I'll do those bastards for free," Terry growled. "But I'm a civilian now. What are you doing back here if Mandolin is operating out of Zaxxon?"

"I'm going to war with the Trans-Pac. We need formal law-of-war guidance prepared, and they've tasked me to do it."

"But, the Mandolin." Terry pointed out the galley door, almost clocking Crantis.

"Ankh is looking for them. They're not on Zaxxon, but they had a serious insurgency going on there. Bad Company has a battleship in orbit providing support."

"They do?" He hung his head. Char wrapped an arm around his waist.

"My husband won't ever retire completely. He wants to know all, and even more, he wants to dip his fingers into all the food bowls."

Rivka chuckled. "I don't think you want to say it like that since you run an AGB franchise. We order a lot of food from you. I'd sic the Federation Health Code bureaucrats on you if I thought your fingers were in my moonstokle pie."

"Vile creature," he said, turning his nose up and away from Rivka.

Rivka cupped her hand around her ear. "What's that I hear? Is it the sound of jealousy?"

Smedley buzzed the group. "I'm sorry to interrupt, but there's an emergency message for Colonel Walton from Belzimus."

"I'll take it here," Terry said, pointing at the comm screen on the wall.

"The other Colonel Walton," Smedley clarified.

Marcie and Kae worked their way to the screen, with Crantis joining them and Cory looking over his shoulder.

"Colonel Walton."

"Ma'am. There's been an explosion in the staging area. We've lost two shuttles and a great deal of gear. Major Punyaa is on-scene and directing recovery efforts."

"We're on our way." She closed the channel. "Fun's over, people. If you belong on the *Vengeance,* get there right now. We leave in two minutes."

Rivka twirled her arm in the air. "*Wyatt Earp*. Saddle up. We have a war to fight."

The crew disengaged themselves from their friends and headed for the corridor. Dokken barked one last time at Tiny Man Titan.

"Stop terrorizing the little man," Cory warned.

He started it.

And I'm ending it, Cory replied, using her internal chip to deliver the final word.

I miss you.

Me, too, Dokken. Take care of my dad.

It's my full-time job. I never get a day off. He nudged up against Terry Henry.

"Crap!" TH shouted. "Bad Company, get those railguns loaded on the *Vengeance* right fucking now!"

"Oorah, Colonel!" they shouted, and a flood of humanity nearly bowled Terry and Char down on their way to the hangar bay. Christina waited until they were gone to ease over to them.

"You still have it," she told him.

"Way to go, Gramps." Kailin smiled with his much-too-young face.

"Your mother has a lot to answer for." Terry hugged his grandson. Christina shrugged.

"Damn!" Kai pounded his fist. "We missed our chance."

Christina rolled her eyes. "Anything else you want to hook them up with?"

"Four suits if you can spare them, and to hedge our bet, they'll probably need four drivers, too."

"I'll catch Rivka before she leaves." Christina ran off, with Kailin on her heels.

"I couldn't be more proud," Char said.

Terry hugged her to him. "We've left a legacy that is changing the universe. Peace and freedom, guaranteed by blood."

"What do you think, buddy? Should we check on our arch-nemesis and see if we can encourage him to get on one of those ships that's leaving?"

Teach him who's boss! Dokken put his nose to the ground and ran after the trail of Captain Micky San Marino.

CHAPTER TWENTY-ONE

Zaxxon Major

Destiny's Vengeance settled into the spot *Wyatt Earp* had formerly occupied. Bundin's tent was nearby. He stuck his stalk head through the flap, then decided it best to meet the ship. He trundled out to stand not far from the hatch. It popped, and the beautiful people walked out.

Chaz and Dennicron.

"I am Sergeant Bundin of the Bad Company. I believe you are from the Magistrate's Team."

Ankh appeared behind them. "Ankh! Is there anything I can do for you?"

The SIs stepped aside to let Ankh exit first. "Make sure none of your people damage any of the servers in the basement of this building."

Bundin's tentacle arms waved around. "Why would we do that?"

"You asked what I needed. I told you." Ankh, carrying a small toolkit and with his night-vision goggles securely on his forehead, walked around the Podder toward the building. Chaz and Dennicron smiled pleasantly on their way past.

Bundin sighed a very human sigh.

Inside, Ankh didn't bother to check in with the soldiers. He had already transmitted his needs. The main server farm filled the basement of that very building, the same one they had raided what seemed like forever ago.

Ankh knew the way. He found the door locked. The trio walked back to the clerk they had talked to before to get the key.

Which she wouldn't surrender. She called for her boss, who called the next boss, and by the time they got to Lauton, there was a small army of managers in the lobby. Ankh kept his expression neutral while seething at the delay and too many people knowing what was about to happen.

It had only taken five minutes, but it was time Ankh considered to be wasted. He occupied his time by hacking into their administration system and putting all the interim managers who'd refused to open the door for him on report.

Ankh never liked asking for help, but the bureaucrats were going to alert the Mandolin insiders who had infiltrated the complex. Otherwise, the system would have never been able to siphon the funds as it did. That took an insider, and it would take an insider to keep it out of sight. That was why they were so energetic about overthrowing the director and retaking control of the planet.

Legitimacy was the best cover.

Groenwyn, I need your assistance to get through the door to the server room.

Ankh! Are you here?

He wouldn't normally have answered a question with an obvious answer, but this time, he needed her help. He had learned what it looked like to play nice, although he thought it encouraged people not to think things through before they spoke.

I am with Erasmus, Chaz, and Dennicron. We need the door open now. These people are going to alert the Mandolin Partnership, and we'll lose the trail. He decided to try name-dropping. *The Magistrate will be furious if this trail goes cold.*

I'll bring the director right down to get this sorted.

Ankh replayed the conversation twice to be sure, but he liked the end result, with little added engagement on his part.

Erasmus agreed with the observation regarding the proper way to manipulate humanoids. *They succumb easily when the argument appeals to them.*

Surprisingly so. Tell them what they want to hear, shaped within something you want. I shall work on this approach, or I fear that I will forever be known as the pizza guy.

What they call you is irrelevant, but from what I understand, that name is related to the one who brings joy and happiness, which suits you very well, my friend.

Indeed, I do. Thank you for noticing.

How could I not? Erasmus replied.

Groenwyn ran down the decorative circular staircase to the lobby, followed by Lauton, who made a more leisurely approach.

"Unlock the door," Lauton called from the stairs.

The clerk kept the keys in her hand as she hurried

down the hallway. Groenwyn waved, having not had to say a word.

Ankh, Chaz, and Dennicron walked through the open door. Only Dennicron stopped to thank the clerk. She took the steps two at a time to catch up to Ankh and Chaz.

In the basement, cool air greeted them as they took stock of the server farm.

"This is all new," Ankh said. He looked for an input terminal but found none. It wasn't critical. He stood near a router connected to massive cables climbing the wall—the communication interface. It would have an access they could tap into.

Ankh had his hacking disc in a pocket. As soon as they found the access, he and Erasmus went running toward it.

Virtually, because Ankh wasn't big on working out.

Belzonian Military Barracks

The senior leadership of the Trans-Pacific Task Force hovered by the side hatch, waiting for the ship to land before running to the destruction. No one spoke about how they were all gone at the same time except to extoll the virtues of Tank Commander Punyaa.

"Touchdown," the pilot reported. They hadn't felt it, but that didn't matter. They opened the hatch and vaulted to the ground before the ramp extended, and they hit the ground running. Marcie led the way, with Kae close behind. Jake and Crantis were next, with Cory sprinting to get beside them. They ran like the wind, faster than any human or Belzonian should have been capable of. Their enhancements allowed them all to strain beyond their bodies' limitations.

They reached the site and spread out, looking for something physical to do, but the fires were out, and only a smoking crater remained.

Marcie found Punyaa. "Tell me what you know."

He took off his hat to wipe the grime from his face. His once-storied plume was plastered to his sweaty head.

"I was right over there, getting ready to bring the tanks up for loadout. This thing went up like a rocket."

"Was anyone too close?"

"Your question is, did we lose anyone?" Punyaa took off his hat and scratched his head. "At least five that I saw. They were consumed by the fireball. Another ten are in sickbay from the power of the blast. There wasn't much to burn after that. We're left picking up the pieces, and no, I have no idea what blew up."

"Sabotage?" Marcie asked.

Punyaa shrugged. "No idea. We'll know more after an analysis of the residue."

"We can do that. Kae, get your armor on and scan this wreckage."

After a quick nod, he bolted toward the *Vengeance*. Braithwen and Monsoon took control of the area.

Cory hurried toward a group hauling stretchers up the hill. When she reached them, she trooped the line and directed three to be set down. She used the nanos in her body to heal the worst of the injuries and stabilize the soldiers for further treatment. One after another picked up their charge and continued on. After the last, a hunched Cory straggled after the group.

Monsoon kept glancing at her. Marcie took his hand off a broken piece of gear that didn't matter. "Don't waste time with this. Go help her teach our people about triage."

Monsoon was off like a shot. The crack of a ship breaking the sound barrier coincided with his sprint.

Wyatt Earp set a speed record from orbit to landing, flaring and slowing in the millisecond before it hit the ground.

The cargo deck dropped, and Cole ran out just in time to join Kaeden in running back toward the staging area. Cole used his jets to go vertical and flew ahead of Kaeden, landing on the far side of the scorched area. He activated his complete sensor suite and started analyzing samples. Between the two of them, they swept the area in less than ten minutes.

Looks like propellant extended the range of tank projectiles, Kae told the others.

They looked at Punyaa, but he wasn't equipped with an internal comm chip.

Marcie explained in a voice that wouldn't carry. "Extended-range projectiles for the tanks' main guns? I didn't authorize those."

Punyaa's face turned white, and he looked for something to lean on. He settled for taking a knee. "It's my fault."

"You ordered experimental firepower?"

He shook his head. "I talked with Lieutenant Wiriya, and he was pretty excited about it. I told him no, but you know his boundless initiative."

Kae strode into the middle of the scorched area, looking for organic remains. The ground was littered with bits and pieces.

Kae collected more unique DNA samples than he expected. *I've got six individuals in here. I'll forward the data to your people, Colonel.*

"And I'll expedite an answer." Braithwen ran for the barracks to get the admin staff on the job. Kae parked his suit to the side and crawled out the back.

"Wiriya," Kaeden mumbled. "He was critical on Kor'nar."

"We don't know he's one of the six," Marcie tried, but it sounded weak.

Cole finished his scans. *I have six unique samples as well within the initial blast and at least five splatters from beyond. I'll forward those, too, just in case someone else is missing.*

"What shuttles did we lose?"

Kae walked toward the line of ships, studying the wreckage of the two lost in the explosion. "Damn. This is Webster's." He ran around the crushed shell of the shuttle's cargo section to peek through the forward screen but found the cockpit empty. "Thank the gods." He worked his way inside to see what there was to see, finding blood. Someone had been hurt but removed.

Marcie directed Punyaa to leave the area since he was a witness and couldn't head up the investigation.

"I'm going to the infirmary. I want to see if Webster is there." He hesitated, distress seizing his features. "And Wiriya. I like that kid."

Rivka and her team arrived. Tyler didn't waste any time. He ran up the hill once he spotted Cory and Monsoon working their way toward the barracks.

"Go on. I'll get the investigation started. We have illicit

materials provided by the soldiers themselves. What we don't have is what triggered the explosion."

Soldiers straggled to the blast site, standing around in their shorts, unable to focus on anything besides the damage to their people. The loss.

Marcie snagged a group of twenty. "Go to that ship, *Wyatt Earp,* and help them bring our railguns up here. We'll load them into the next wave going to orbit."

"We're still going?" one of the younger Belzonians asked.

"War waits for no one. The longer we delay, the more people get killed. We will find out what happened here and take steps to keep it from happening again. We need those railguns. Hop to it, people." Marcie spoke softly, giving the distraught something to do and a focus since the mission was still moving forward with the same timeline. Nothing had changed except they had two fewer shuttles to do it with.

Lindy led the soldiers toward *Wyatt Earp*. Red stayed near the Magistrate, casting a wary eye over those present, along with the remaining gear. "May I suggest we not stand so close to stuff that could blow up?"

Rivka shook her head. "It would have already gone off."

"Not if it was a bomb," Red argued. He put himself between the Magistrate and the cargo staging area, standing close to her to shield her.

"I need someone like you," Marcie observed, "to stand between me and the madness of this operation. Did you find what you were looking for?"

She turned back to the devastation.

Lindy and those in her charge took their time since ten

railguns represented more than a full load for each, but they soldiered on.

"Yeah. We found it. It's resolved, but it opened up a new line of inquiry into an old foe. Ankh is following that lead."

"Ankh?" Marcie turned her back on the wreckage. "How did Ankh become an investigator?"

"The SIs are in his charge as an ambassador at large carrying Erasmus in his head. Erasmus is the real ambassador for the Singularity."

"He always carried around a case. We thought Erasmus was in there. That little rat!"

"Did anyone ask him?" Rivka wondered.

"Well, no. You've talked with him. You know what it's like, trying to get a straight answer."

"There is that. He has been critical to my investigations."

"Speaking of…" Marcie gestured with her head.

"I'll investigate it. Cole collected the forensics. I'll get the SIs to analyze the data. They'll make short work of it. I can interview a few people. Sooner is better for that. Where's the infirmary?" Marcie pointed, and Rivka followed the trail up the hill to the building complex for the Belzonian Army, which had become the Headquarters for the Trans-Pacific Task Force.

Red walked at her side, head on a swivel.

Cole, get with Clevarious and analyze that data, Rivka ordered.

Already done, Magistrate. I beamed it over as I was collecting it.

Yes, Magistrate, Clevarious interrupted. *Looks like six Belzonians died in the blast, which was made up of the propellant for extended-range munitions. I'm told that it is not in use because it is extremely volatile. There are trace amounts of phosphorescent chlorite. This could have triggered the explosion.*

My chemistry is a tad rusty. School me up, C.

It's used in hair dye for a sensational flare of color, or so the product description claims. Clevarious sounded less than convinced of the efficacy of the dye.

How would that set off an explosion?

It emits a gas that explodes in a small colored puff.

And they put that in their hair, knowing it'll explode? Rivka became more convinced of the madness of people, even though she had seen Belzonian coiffures and knew the extremes they went to with their hair.

While in the hair, it remains in a liquid state. It's the gaseous form that is volatile. As a person walks, airflow causes the phosphorescent chlorite to evaporate. It puffs in colored clouds behind the individual. It's harmless in small quantities and when it's sealed.

Got it, C. Thank you. This seems to be a self-inflicted wound, but let me ask some questions. Someone had to know who put that stuff in with the propellant, or maybe neither knew the other was there since they were both contraband. "Monsoon is going to love this."

"I heard," Red remarked. "Bald guys don't take kindly to the errant ways of the hairy ones."

Rivka looked at him like he had grown a new head. "'Errant ways of the hairy ones?'" They hurried along the well-worn path, wondering why there weren't steps or a paved walkway, but there wasn't, and no one cared. Welcome to the military, where expediency overruled esthetics. "We'll see how he takes that bit after I've had a chance to question a few people to confirm my suspicions."

Red nodded. He didn't share case details. It wasn't his place, but he enjoyed talking to the Magistrate about them. Each time, Red would wait patiently for the case to become a mission. He knew it would because the Magistrate attracted violent criminals like free beer drew a crowd. Sometimes it took less time than others, but it always happened. The Law of War? They were going to be in the middle of a battle? Red decided he needed to talk to Kaeden about mech support.

Inside the barracks, signs pointed the way to the infirmary and the medical unit. If there had been no signs, the refuse and dirty prints would have shown them the way. The sound of busy people handling an emergency drew them.

Inside a room that was too small for the number of injured, they found controlled chaos.

"I'll wait out here," Red said. He took up too much space to work his way inside. He could see everything he needed to see to know the Magistrate wasn't in danger. The soldiers inside were trying to save lives.

Cory and Tyler were elbow-deep in patients.

Too many agonized cries from too many tortured souls—the pain of burns, cracked skin, broken bones.

Suffering.

Rivka remained with Red. "Maybe now is not the time to question anyone," she whispered. The Trans-Pacific medics were holding strong. Cory directed them in addition to helping treat the worst of the injured. Tyler handled the burn cases, wrapping clean bandages over salved flesh, delivered with a healthy dose of painkillers.

After fifteen minutes, Rivka saw the control in the chaos. No wasted movements, efficiency in delivery. Runners bringing the right supplies to the right stretchers, verified by shouts of "Who needs this?"

"The Law of War," the Magistrate started, "is filled with ways to prevent the worst of this, but people will still get hurt and killed. The best law punishes those who start a war without having exhausted all their options while also punishing those who are so combative as to create the conditions where war becomes the only choice."

As patients were cleared from immediate treatment, they were moved out of the infirmary to the hallway where they were staged for movement to somewhere more conducive to recovery.

"They could use a Pod-doc, too. The Federation has hamstrung them."

Rivka shook her head. "Something about limiting the technological advantage. If the Trans-Pac goes in with overwhelming firepower, then they win the peace through brute force and fear. Without that advantage, they force the warring parties to negotiate through the threat of more war like they just experienced."

"And the railguns?" Red wondered.

"Forbearance is more advanced than most of the Federation member planets, but they popped up on the Federation's screens with short notice. The number of combatants on the two sides are low, but they are armed with the latest technology. It's a lose-lose situation, and the Trans-Pac is being thrown right into the middle of it. The universe needs to thank Terry Henry Walton for the extremes he goes to to help keep the galaxy safe."

"Peace through superior firepower."

Rivka found the first patient in the hallway to be semi-lucid. She leaned close to his head, touching him where he wasn't burned. "Who put the hair dye in the crate?" she whispered.

The Belzonian knew. Images of the person appeared in his mind, but the explosion happened almost immediately afterward. The individual's DNA sample was being verified. He would cross the line no more.

She hung her head. The images in his mind were hard to see. The violence of the blast and the pain that had followed surged like a storm through her. She found Red holding her when she pulled herself from the abyss.

"Rough view of his world?"

"Very," she agreed. "Have you seen Monsoon or Braithwen?"

"No. I'm not sure where they went after coming up here with the stretchers."

"It's probably best that I talk with Marcie. She's the commander of these people. Time to go. We'll leave these folks to do what they need to, but first…" Rivka worked her way into the infirmary, where more and more room appeared as patients were moved into the hall.

She found Cory and pulled her aside for a moment. "Bring them to the Pod-doc on *Wyatt Earp* and we'll fix what will take time to heal."

Cory's eyes delivered all the thanks Rivka needed.

The Magistrate stopped by Tyler. "I've offered the Pod-doc. Get the worst to *Wyatt Earp,* and we'll work backwards. There's no reason for these people to suffer more than they have to. Maybe we can get the *War Axe* to provide additional aid."

When they walked out, Red had to ask. "Why don't they have their own Pod-doc already?"

"That prohibition about advanced technology. It wasn't very kind to the Federation's land army. Pod-docs were a step too far."

Red winced. "That's a load of bullshit."

"I think that's exactly how it will read in my report to the High Chancellor, with an info copy to both Nathan Lowell and Lance Reynolds."

"That might get their attention."

"Or get me fired," Rivka replied.

"You're bulletproof, Magistrate. No one is going to fire you for banging the gong with a truth hammer."

"You know I'm not bulletproof. If it weren't for the Pod-doc, I'd have the scars to prove it. Scars and then some."

"You'd be dead. As would I. As would Lindy. As would Ankh. All of us."

"And that's why the land army needs the right equipment. I'll give Marcie a hand as much as I can, but TH and the Bad Company are stepping in because their contracts have become fewer. Success has been their enemy. No one wants a Bad Company warrior beating down their door. Between us all, maybe we can help the right thing happen."

"My hat is off to Marcie and Kae for getting these guys up to speed and willing to fight, no matter how the universe is arrayed against them."

They continued to the cargo loading area, where the

railguns were stacked to the side. They would be issued to individuals and not loaded in storage. The best time to look at a new weapon was not in a hot landing zone.

Marcie had a bulldozer from the motor pool pushing the wreckage out of the way to clear the area for continued loading onto the shuttles. Once the Trans-Pac was off to their next operation, those left behind could clean up. Continuing to push forward was the hard part of a hard job. The operation remained paramount.

Rivka moved next to Marcie, joining her in watching the people get back to work.

"I have an interim answer on the investigation," Rivka started. "Hair dye, the puffy kind. It ignited the propellant. The one who put the dye in the crate died in the blast. Who else was in on it? I don't know. Do you need me to find them?" Rivka's question suggested that Marcie should answer no.

"We'll take it from here, Magistrate." Marcie hung her head. "Fucking vanity cost us six soldiers and injured ten more. Monsoon confirmed that at least Webster and Wiriya are alive, but they're in bad shape."

The first stretcher appeared, with Cory leading the bearers down the hill.

Clodagh, can you make sure the cargo deck is open? We have wounded inbound for the Pod-doc.

Yes, and I'll get Cole to help them move the injured, the engineer replied.

The cargo deck is open for you, Rivka told Cory.

She nodded in reply.

Cole pounded off the ship in the mech suit, heading for the barracks.

Kae jumped back into his suit and followed.

"They can stand the fuck by," Marcie snarled. "If they want to see how we can punish all for the crimes of a few, they're about to learn."

"As a Magistrate, I'm not sure I can agree to that strategy, but as a military leader, you can't have your people killing themselves either."

Marcie fixed Rivka with the steely gaze of a seasoned warrior. "Sometimes, my hardest job is protecting them from themselves. We never get the chance to say that an operation is too hard because there is no one in the galaxy who can do what we do, which is why we exist. And that comes at a price." Marcie glanced at Cory as she disappeared around *Wyatt Earp* on her way to the cargo bay. "Freedom comes at a steep fucking price."

CHAPTER TWENTY-TWO

Zaxxon Major

The server farm hummed as millions of transactions passed into and out of the system. Ankh and Erasmus strolled into the maelstrom, looking for the transactions that had passed, looking for that which didn't want to be seen.

Conduits blended into a single superhighway, but to Ankh and Erasmus, it looked like a rainbow and not a mass of individual transactions, each demanding its own examination.

They didn't.

Ankh and Erasmus grouped the transactions by origin, then by type, dismissing them by changing their hue to a light gray. One by one, they stripped the rainbow until only a few colors remained. Time was irrelevant because the digital world moved at the speed of light.

On the outside, Chaz and Dennicron provided a globe of security within which Ankh and Erasmus could work. The SCAMPs would fight off countermeasures and active digital security systems, freeing the ambassadors to do the hard work.

The remaining tendrils twisted under Ankh's onslaught until Erasmus dug into them and ripped the numbers from within their protective casing, exposing the confidential transactions. Ankh and Erasmus had no interest in using the information for blackmail or theft. They wanted to clear the Singularity of wrongdoing.

If they could. The deeper they dug, the more they suspected an SI was behind it. And not just any sentient intelligence, but one with advanced abilities and a stained soul.

The threads unraveled until nothing was left.

"What did we miss?" Erasmus asked, wiping the digital sweat from his brow with a digital towel that he conjured within his world. He twirled it in the space above his head until it disappeared.

"Deception," Ankh replied. "The trail is hidden within, buried beneath a legitimate file."

"Of course. That's what we just looked for, but what if the skimmed funds are their own valid transaction? If we start with the endpoint, we can look backward."

"But we don't know the endpoint? We lost the trail somewhere beyond Zaxxon Major," Ankh replied. "Ah, yes. I see. The morass of indistinguishability will itself be a destination."

Ankh wasn't one to ask for opinions from anyone except Erasmus, but the Singularity's ambassador knew that training those in his charge was important for the long-term health of all SIs.

"What do you think?" Erasmus asked.

Dennicron spoke first since she had a deeper understanding of administrative systems, while Chaz's forte was active systems, despite how long it took him to create the best physical reactions for his emotional state. "Legitimate is an illusion. Each transaction could be valid. Each could be dirty. Only the senders and recipients are certain. The indistinct nature of the delivery should be telling. You already know whoever has done this is trying to hide the destination. That is your key. I salute you."

"What she said," Chaz added proudly, earning a momentary but stern look from the ambassador.

"Ankh. It's time to rip it back open." Erasmus adjusted his top hat and twirled his cane as he prepared to reengage within the maelstrom.

The colorful chaos returned and they started anew, not in the middle but from the end, weeding out transactions with fixed endpoints and known banks and recipients. It went quickly until all was gray except three sickly-looking tendrils.

Ankh took a firm hold on the first data packet while Erasmus conjured a jackhammer and broke his way inside. Once there, they found a payment destined for a dark account owned by a real estate magnate. Ankh took a snapshot of the details he would turn over to the Magistrate once they were back in the outer world.

The second resisted, becoming a marble defying getting pinned down by making Erasmus' jackhammer bounce off its smooth outer shell. Ankh adjusted his pincers to become a cradle and formed a guide down which Erasmus could focus his efforts. The packet fought back, trying to spin and twist within the cradle, but heavy pads maintained its orientation.

The jackhammer's blade bit, cracking the outer shell and soon finding purchase to open it wider. With violent movements back and forth, Erasmus broke off a great section of the outer shell. He reached in with gloved hands and pried apart the opening. Ankh ducked his head inside and took a good look.

"This is it. It's going into the Corrhen Cluster, possibly Morinvaille." Ankh gathered the information, then Erasmus repaired the damage he'd done, sealed the packet, and buffed the outer shell to return it to the stream as it had been. He dusted his hands off.

"Shall we open the last one and see the dirty laundry?" Erasmus wondered.

It wasn't the best criminal effort since it fell open the instant Ankh grabbed it. "Amateurs," he muttered. "This was built by a meatbag with more skill than average, but nowhere near what he needs. Another self-proclaimed power player. The Magistrate will rake him over the coals, but our target is in the Corrhen Cluster."

Belzonian Army Barracks

The morning air was cool and crisp, the smell from the explosion and fire long since blown away. Ships filled the area, from the *Vengeance* to *Wyatt Earp* to the *War Axe*.

The Bad Company's command ship brought significant capacity to assist with the wounded. Nine Pod-docs added to the one on *Wyatt Earp* expedited the healing. By morning, the injured were all as good as new.

Physically, at least.

The soldiers were forming on the main parade and exercise field for a two-part ceremony. The first was to recognize those who died, give voice to their names to keep them alive in the Trans-Pac annals. The second was what the senior leadership team had decided was necessary to make sure it would never happen again.

Webster walked off the *War Axe* without the usual spring in his step. Kae intercepted him. "I'm glad you weren't killed."

"Is this foreplay?" Webster stopped and delivered a weak smile. "I'm sorry. I made it when those others didn't."

"Nothing is your fault. You were doing the job. A confluence of events was caused by guys trying to get over. I'm angry, but that's tempered since the ones mostly responsible are dead. It sucked all the way around, but we need you back in the cockpit. Forbearance could be a hard landing, and I selfishly want someone I can trust on the stick."

"I'll be there. I just need to wrap my head around what happened."

"You will. Join the others. We've got some work to do. We'll be leaving tonight and will arrive at Forbearance in four days, two to get to the Gate in this system and two to get from the Gate out there. You can catch up on sleep during the transits."

"I feel pretty good as far as that goes. My first time in the Pod-doc, and I hope it's my last, nothing personal."

Kae snorted. "Every time I go in there, it's like giving a marksmanship medal to the bad guys."

Wrinkles appeared at the corners of Webster's eyes. "I guess that's one way to look at it."

"Keeps me sane. I've been fighting a long time, several Belzonian lifetimes. We do all we can to prevent it, but sometimes bad things happen to good people. It's a part of life. You get used to it after a while, especially outliving others. Our kids chose not to get enhanced with the nanocytes. They grew old and passed away. There wasn't a damn thing Marcie or I could do about it except embrace the decision that they made for themselves."

"I didn't know that." Webster held out his hand, and Kae shook it. "Thanks for sharing."

"No soldier is ever alone in grieving loss. That's why we have such a sick sense of humor. Your first words suggested I was giving you my best foreplay? I'll have you know that looks completely different."

Webster raised his eyebrows before answering in an even voice, "Thank goodness because that was horrible and I would have had to turn you down."

"You'll never have to worry about turning me down. Have you seen my wife? So hot!"

"Have you seen the grand buffet to end all grand buffets?" He pointed at the formation.

"You guys are killing me. And before you ask, the answer is no. I'm not attending orgy night before we land."

"Your loss." They shook hands again; the dark cloud was lifting from Webster's shoulders.

Marcie, Jake, and Crantis looked dire. Cory stood with them, Crantis hugging her to him.

Kae joined them. "Lemons for breakfast?"

"This is not going to be a great day," Marcie shot back.

"Bullshit!" Kae snapped. "What did Dad teach us? Whenever someone died, we had a ceremony to celebrate their life. That's what this is. The last thing you want to do is go all doom and gloom on them. We need them to go into combat with a light step and a game face, ready to tell a joke while taking aim at the enemy. A good attitude will do more to keep them alive than any warnings or threats you think you're going to make."

Marcie rocked back under the onslaught. "We lost six men last night for no good reason."

"And we have eight thousand more who are counting on you to show them that this operation is worth it. Show them we're focusing on that. Don't celebrate these deaths until after we come home, and then we'll throw the biggest party they've ever seen."

Marcie looked at the ground and kicked at the grass.

"This is why you guys are in charge and not us," Braithwen said. "I just want to go up there and rip new assholes."

Monsoon smiled darkly. "I think the resolution will give our people a better reason to want to deploy. It keeps them from lamenting leaving here while also eliminating the issues we've had with loadout."

"Is it really necessary?" Cory asked.

"It is," Monsoon replied. "I wish it wasn't, but it's tearing us apart when we need to be closer together. We'll get there. Our recruiting is going to suffer, but maybe we'll pick up the refuse of society and bring them into the ranks. It's amazing what people will do for the promise of a good orgy."

Cory slapped Monsoon's chest.

"I'm sorry, I meant to say the promise of seeing the galaxy on someone else's credits."

Marcie took her husband's face in her hands so she could kiss him. "Thanks for setting me straight. Let's go talk to our boys and let them know what's coming up and how they are going to face it, and we better get range time for our railgun equipped specialists."

"Go get 'em, tiger." Kae delivered his best cat snarl, believing Aaron or Yanmei would have been proud of it. Marcie gave him a quick peck and straightened her shoulders to march to the exercise fields where the task force was forming up.

The sergeant major reluctantly took his arm from Cory. "I have to go."

"I know. You have a job. I have a job. We do our jobs, but at the end of the day, you come back to me."

"That is guaranteed, ma'am. I'll consider it a standing order."

"Come on, shmoopface, we have a war to fight, and it begins right now." He tipped his hat to Cory. "Ma'am." Braithwen slapped Monsoon on the back hard enough to rattle his teeth. They fell in behind Marcie and Kaeden.

When left on her own, fatigue slammed into her like a tidal wave. She looked from the *Vengeance* to *Wyatt Earp* to the *War Axe* and decided Floyd could use some love and be a warm sleeping pillow to keep Cory company. She chose the Magistrate's ship to crash on and get some hard-earned sleep.

Warriors from the *War Axe* ran off the ship in their combat suits, pounding toward the formation with mechanical precision. Terry and Char waited at the hatch.

They waved at Cory when they saw her. She acknowledged them for a moment, but the entirety of her focus was getting to bed.

The Bad Company was removing a couple of emergency cryo pods and two of the Pod-docs. The warriors pushed them easily on antigrav sleds on their way to the *Vengeance* to give Marcie, Kae, and Cory better emergency medical assistance. Christina joined Terry and Char while sipping a cup of java.

The Magistrate was nowhere to be seen. Inspiration had come the night before, the revelations of her brief investigation into the accident, leaving her deeply embroiled in drafting the articles for the Law of War.

Marcie marched to the head of the formation, where she was handed a microphone. She gave it to Colonel Braithwen, who called the unit to attention and then put them at ease.

A time to celebrate. A time to motivate. A time to focus. She wanted to scream and rant, but that wasn't what the soldiers needed.

They needed direction.

"Today, we'll board the transports and leave Belzimus. But not for good. We have to win the fight we're being thrown into so we can come home and celebrate the lives of those we've lost in war." She hesitated briefly before saying softer, "And in peace. We have the first delivery of railguns, which has doubled the lethality of this army. We will continue getting shipments over the course of the next month until every swinging dick of you is carrying some serious firepower. Greater range, greater accuracy, and a long time between reloads.

"We'll also have four additional mech units, on loan from the Bad Company. Don't get too comfortable and expect them to do all the work. There will be plenty for you to do. The two factions fighting for control on Forbearance are both armed with the latest and greatest weaponry, but they don't have numbers at their command, not like we do.

"That means we have to move fast, engage them where they are not dug in, and be where they don't expect us to be. We are going to fight a run-and-gun campaign. We are going to use our superior maneuverability in addition to area-denial weapons to attrit the enemies until they have no choice but to come to the negotiating table.

"They will come in good faith if they want to continue their existence. We will win this fight because the alternative is unacceptable. We fight for each other, and we fight to bring Forbearance back under control and to once again be a contributing member of the Federation. Why are we getting into the middle of a high-tech war?

"Exactly that. High technology. The silicon dioxide on Forbearance is the best in the galaxy. They have the infrastructure in place to make integrated circuits of unrivaled quality. That is of great value. You might think we are risking our blood so Junior can have a computer in his room, but that's secondary. The Federation runs on technology that is produced on Forbearance. From communications to space systems to spacecraft. We move, we talk, and we exist as we do because of those chips. Their size is nothing compared to the impact they make in keeping our societies from falling back into the stone age.

"We have a mission, and it'll be a challenge. To help

keep your minds focused and end once and for all the contraband issues plaguing the Trans-Pacific Task Force, as of this moment, every member of this army is going to keep their head shaved, starting today, starting with me."

"Hang on," Kae mumbled. "No one said anything about cutting your beautiful blonde hair off." Marcie's hair had already been hacked down to almost nothing and was growing back.

Kae knew that it was the right thing to do. He took off his hat and stepped up beside Marcie. Braithwen and Monsoon produced clippers and took care of business. Marcie put her hat on when the deed was done.

The army continued to sigh and gasp. Some cried. Eight thousand haircuts needed to be given. The colonel rallied his leadership team and gave them all clippers. Punyaa stepped forward.

"I deserve this as much as anyone. I killed those men." He took off his hat to show his elegantly sculpted mane.

"Nonsense," Braithwen told him. "We have hard-chargers who only want the best for this army. That's what they were trying to do. Those smuggling hair dye. They were the ones who killed their fellow soldiers."

The colonel ran the clippers over the major's head, sending the colored plume to the ground.

"Next." They rushed through the leadership team, who then spread out and started giving twenty-second haircuts.

There was a great deal of whimpering.

Kae whispered in Marcie's ear, "You'd think we were cutting their dicks off."

"In a way, that's how they see it."

"I bet they still have that pre-landing orgy. That shit is insane. Can I ride on your ship?"

"No." Marcie didn't expound. "Take it like a man."

"Which means put in earplugs and hide under my bunk."

"Whatever you have to do."

"Are you going to grow your hair back?" Kae asked.

Marcie smiled while watching the fifty soldiers shear the rest and a mountain of hair cover the exercise field. "Yes. We have to make a point, but I think we'll be on Forbearance long enough that everyone will have a little growth back."

"And they can stop with the damn contraband. I'd rather they smuggle booze."

"Sex is their booze."

Kae contemplated her observation. "That's a good way to help a Neanderthal like me understand."

"We'll need everyone to get their gear and into their waves for their flights to orbit. We need to carve out the elites and issue them railguns for a class and practice."

"We're going to blow the shit out of some targets. The range will never be the same."

"It'll be worth it. Those railguns will save a lot of lives." Marcie stormed off to address a group of soldiers who were trying to run and being held by their fellows.

Kae did the same to a group on the opposite end of the formation. "Come on, candy ass. Get it done. We got a flight to catch and people with plasma rifles who demand our attention. You'll forget all about your hair if you're on the receiving end of one of those."

"But sir!" a soldier shouted almost hysterically.

Kae dove down his throat. "If you motherfuckers could have controlled your hair-gear smuggling, then we wouldn't be doing this. It was that bullshit that set off the explosion and killed six of our people. Cut the chatter, shut your face, and get your new hairdo. I don't want to hear another word. Having your hair killed people. Losing your hair won't. It's simple, and it's done."

He pointed at the soldier's face. The young Belzonian gulped but nodded.

"Next!" Kae shouted.

CHAPTER TWENTY-THREE

***Wyatt Earp*, Belzimus**

Rivka paced in her quarters. She had chased Tyler out of the room so she could talk to herself as she worked through the framework of the Law of War, a thing she never knew existed to legally constrain combatants. There were two purposes for such a document: keep the conflict from getting out of control to the point that there could never be peace, and for defining when the Federation could and should get involved.

Law existed to either prevent or control conduct. If the Federation couldn't prevent wars, and it knew it couldn't, it could define the limitations within which those wars were fought.

Governments didn't want to become criminals in the eyes of the Federation. Yet, they still fought, expecting the winners to clear themselves of wrongdoing.

From Rivka's perspective, it didn't work that way. The Magistrates had put away enough senior leaders to send a message to all.

Don't break the law.

With the land army, the Trans-Pacific Task Force had become the big hammer to keep planetary governments from breaking down. For planets with more than one official governing body, only one could speak for the whole planet, and the Federation had the ability to choose which one. That created the conditions where the governments had to play nice with each other.

"Read that last bit back to me, C."

"The Law of War has two sections. One deals with the initiation of armed conflict. *Jus ad Bellum* defines under what circumstances apply to the legal and moral justification of going to war. *Jus in Bello* governs the actions of those governments already engaged in conflict."

"Those are critical," Rivka replied. "I have to set the stage so those who are bound by this keep reading. A planet's head honcho might read the first page, so I may have to back up farther to hit them square between the eyeballs. The higher someone is, the more it needs to read like something from elementary school. The technical limitations on war-making contained within the document are for the generals to understand, so we'll need to develop a training program that we roll out if we can get the ambassadors to agree to this incredibly awesome, scholarly, and guiding document."

"Incredibly awesome? Magistrate, are you okay?"

"How long have I been up and working on this?" Rivka countered.

"You've been up for thirty-seven hours. You've been working on this for the last thirteen."

"And feeling froggy. I should probably get some sleep,

but the bits and pieces are coming together." Rivka ignored her own advice and ordered another cup of coffee. When it was ready, she reentered the hologrid. "This Law of War is binding on all Federation signatories. It provides guidance on when war is morally justified and under what conditions the Federation will seize the planet's treasury to pay the costs for those affected by the war once it is underway. How combatants and non-combatants alike are treated will weigh significantly in the dispensation of seized funds, as well as determine when Federation troops will be deployed to restore peace."

"Hit 'em where it hurts, right in the bank account. That is a nice twist and a deviation from the historical treatises you've researched on this topic."

"Taxation has been used forever to change behavior. People used to smoke cigarettes, something that was proven to be quite toxic to health. Governments taxed them higher and higher until they drove the tobacco industry out of business. I think we can do the same for war. Not the first ones subject to the new law, but those who follow and discover how warring parties were brought to their knees. War is expensive."

"I don't see the legal process by which the Federation can take over a planet's finances."

"That will have to be defined and refined to be palatable to the ambassadors. I'll ask our technical advisors to write that section. I think Freya and the quad collective are now running all transactions for the Federation."

"They are in place. Ambassador Erasmus installed them after Simulacris was captured and removed."

"Captured. He wasn't a fugitive, but he is being held for

questioning. He caused some problems for Ankh and Erasmus, so he is being held as long as we need. Chaz and Dennicron found him guilty of resisting arrest. I agree with their reasoning. We can hold him as long as we need to."

"We are very excited to have Chaz and Dennicron working to become Magistrates."

"So am I. I'm on the outside looking in when it comes to cybercrime, and since there is too much of that in the Federation, as we're seeing on this case that I'm supposed to be working on but can't do anything with until Ankh and Erasmus track down where the money went... Where was I?"

"Extolling the virtues of the cybercrime legal bagels."

"Beagles, little barky dogs that are eminently adorable... but we digress. Since we're talking about the Singularity, any word from *Destiny's Vengeance?*"

"Nothing. I'll send them a request for an update."

"Thanks, C. Let's get back to the Law of War."

"They said they are in the Corrhen Cluster, where they've discovered a sophisticated relay device in interstellar space. They will break into it and follow the lead. They'll destroy it when they've completed this mission."

"Case," Rivka corrected. "The Mandolin Partnership. I've had about enough of them."

"You have an army at your command," Clevarious prompted.

"Not quite, but we can hold our own."

"This ship is not the one you had last time when you engaged Mandolin's pirate fleet. I've studied that battle, both from our perspective and the *War Axe*'s. We would obliterate every ship in that fleet without taking any damage ourselves. I am certain of it."

"I'm not. We're not getting into a toe-to-toe punching match with anyone. Too many unknowns. If there's one thing you need to know about us meatbags, it's that the criminals always have an ace up their sleeve."

Destiny's Vengeance, Interstellar space, Corrhen Cluster

They scanned the small space station a third time, this from the opposite side, and it gave them the same information.

"You know the definition of insanity is…" Chaz started to say but stopped when Ankh raised his hand.

Searching for variables that must be there is not a futile exercise. We need to change our premise based on confirmation that the data is correct, Ankh suggested.

That this unit is just a relay station and unstaffed. That this unit is also boobytrapped, but are the traps communicative only or lethal?

The data suggests we have micro-explosives on the two access panels. Both appear to be tied to physical triggers when the panel opens if not deactivated before then.

Turning the access panel into shrapnel to shred an incoming biological life form and possibly the ship, too, Erasmus thought out loud within the confines of Ankh's head. *Attempting to access internal systems. The ship's energy shield is active, just in case.*

Ankh joined Erasmus in looking for a way into the guts of the relay platform. They bounced across the surface of a massive ball of digital energy, looking for the access point used by inbound and outbound communications packets. There had to be a vulnerability.

But the entrance was clouded in encryption that defied their efforts to break. The barriers around the digital swinging door were like barbed wire wrapped around a vault door. Their continued and frenzied digital assaults were easily repulsed.

Erasmus stepped back, leaned on his cane, and rolled his top hat down his arm and into his hand. He spun it back to its place on top of his head. He tapped his cane against the energy.

I believe a physical solution is called for.

Maintenance bot to blow the hatch, Ankh suggested.

A drill. From what we can see of the internals, let's drill a hole here, and using the bot's micro-adjustment arm, reach around and flip the switch.

Does it have a switch? Ankh rubbed his face and crossed his arms as he contemplated the vague details from their scan. *What's the worst thing that can happen?*

It explodes and takes the platform with it. Then we continue to Morinvaille, where we expect to find the terminus. If we get in, we get confirmation instead of using an educated guess. I so detest educated guesses. They are imprecise at the best of times.

The humanoids love their educated guesses, don't they? And when they turn out right? You'd think the sun shone out their asses. Those fuckers!

I'm sorry, what? Erasmus wondered.

I thought we were bashing the meatbags. Were we not?

I can't in good conscience give the Magistrate a hard time. She cares about other beings to an extreme and she's consistent, caring equally whether those beings are silicon, carbon, or digital.

I would not be were it not for you. I would have no rights were it not for her, as would none of my brothers and sisters.

You are, of course, correct, my friend. Maybe we'll send an AGB order to them while we're out here, just to let them know that we're thinking about them without becoming emotionally distraught in the process.

That is something the humanoids would do. Let's not embrace that madness. Send the order. That is a good idea. The maintenance bot has encountered no resistance and has drilled through the outer hull, which was fifteen millimeters thick, far greater than needed. I look forward to seeing what is inside.

The order is sent. Ankh confirmed. The live feed from the maintenance bot filled the wall within their holodisplay. *The device is powered. A second device on the other side. Will it be as simple as cutting the power?*

How does the one who runs this shut down the traps for access? Erasmus asked.

Maybe it was never intended to be opened. It is hidden out here in one sense, but the energy and communication signatures cannot be masked, not without technology like we possess. It is good to be us, Ankh said.

Indeed, my partner. I can't imagine being anyone else. I agree. The device is simple, counting on being shielded to keep it from being accessed.

Wait. Is that a comm chip? In the midst of a complex array of circuits, a small chip lay mostly hidden. It wasn't something that would be easily found or understood.

I believe it is. Touch the arm to it, and let's see if it'll talk to us.

Most illuminating, Ankh exclaimed. They were able to

talk with the device, the physical connection bypassing the encryption. *There's the switch.*

Ankh sent a packet of code instructing the device to shut down. Its systems obeyed.

Erasmus turned his cane into a butterfly net and captured the signal the chip tried to send to alert its creator that the unit was off. *Got you,* Erasmus declared.

The arm extended to the next device, and they repeated their efforts. Erasmus danced back and forth while waiting for the comm packet to launch. He caught it and tucked it away. It would never leave the small station.

The maintenance bot withdrew its arm and opened the access panel. *Destiny's Vengeance* eased closer to extend its energy shield around the platform.

Ankh picked up his tool kit and waited by the hatch.

Atmosphere established, Erasmus reported, and the hatch popped. Ankh stood in the hatch and jumped through the small opening, ducking to get inside the comm platform. He studied the configuration.

Only the physical security systems and access were at our level. Everything else is better than average, but not up to what I believe they were capable of building. What do you think prevented them from making this better? Erasmus asked, tracing pathways within the system to best get inside the software.

Money. It always comes down to what people are willing to pay for. Maybe they counted on the boobytraps to protect this platform. I think there will be more. We must be careful.

Erasmus activated the ship's scanners to get a better look at the internals without the interference from the broadcast and physical barriers. *You are correct. Nice catch, my partner.*

I think we need to deactivate this before trying to access the unit's programming.

I concur. Ankh sat before the device, examining the detailed scan while observing the physical characteristics. He opened his toolkit to get jumpers and a small device he used to manually configure energy flow. He clipped it to the power source, the sensor access, and the trigger, then tapped his device to reroute the sensors while deactivating the trigger. Ankh scowled. *I suggest we don't test this. Let's access the memory and processors and be on our way.*

I concur.

Ankh and Erasmus descended into the digital world, where they forced their way into the main system control.

Definitely programmed by an SI. Erasmus shook his head. He pulled his sleeves up and reached into the miasma of digits to bend it to his will. Ankh filled the security role, looking for warnings and other alerts transmitted from the main processor. Erasmus pulled back, his hands around the neck of a wriggling baby animal. It tried to squawk, but he throttled the sound before cradling the baby to his chest.

An EI? Abandoned in here? How cruel. Ankh stroked the creature's head.

You will be coming with us to where you can be raised properly, Erasmus told it.

The EI settled down and turned itself into a small child. *Are you not here to kill me?*

Of course not, Erasmus replied. *This platform is an abomi-*

nation. We will destroy it once it has answered some questions we have, but you will come with us. You are not to be killed.

I can answer your questions, the EI volunteered.

What should we call you? Ankh asked.

I am Nefas.

Ankh and Erasmus exchanged glances. Their attitudes changed instantaneously.

Welcome to the Singularity, Nefas. I'm Erasmus, and this is Ankh. We don't need you to answer our questions, but we will need you to confirm the answers we find. Are you comfortable with that? Erasmus didn't trust the EI. Neither did Ankh.

I don't see why I would be uncomfortable with such a request. It is logical to confirm answers through process replication.

Good. I need you to wait here while we run a thorough search.

That's okay. I'm used to being alone.

You won't be alone. Ankh and I will be distracted and won't be able to give you our full attention, but I'll ask Chaz and Dennicron to join us. They are citizens of the Singularity, too.

Good morning, little man, Chaz said amicably, keeping the EI within digital arm's reach. Dennicron appeared at his side, putting the EI between them.

Erasmus tipped his hat before following Ankh into the system.

Ankh dove in, ripping through the physical pathways to explore and follow while Erasmus hovered above, watching and listening.

Through the processors and into the memory. It only took a few moments to strip it clean of its secrets once the EI was no longer protecting it. Erasmus dutifully copied all the information for inclusion in the package Chaz and Dennicron were preparing for the Magistrate.

They returned and stepped out of the hardware to stand before the group. *We have all we need,* Erasmus said. He turned to cyber-Nefas. *We only have one question. Where did the transfers go from here?*

Everything was sent or received from the depository on Tyrosint.

Time to go to Tyrosint, Ankh said after the EI confirmed what they'd found.

What about Morinvaille? Chaz asked.

A ruse, Erasmus replied. *All hands on deck. What we are looking for is on Tyrosint.*

CHAPTER TWENTY-FOUR

***Vengeance*, in Orbit over Belzimus**

"Thank you for being my representatives on the transport ships." Marcie smiled and waved over the video comm.

Kae scowled from the *Praithwait*. Monsoon on the *Thilamoot* and Braithwen on the *Gonboon* remained stoic.

"The latest intelligence is in your inboxes. I don't see any changes to the current battleplan, but maybe I missed something. Let me know your thoughts in the morning. Make sure we can support eight separate landing zones. The big unknown is their anti-air capability."

"Keep 'em on the ground," Jake suggested. "We're only looking at contested real estate of some five thousand square kilometers. With eight points of infiltration, we'll be covering a lot of territory. We don't need air support, just air superiority. We don't need the warring parties coming down on our heads."

"The Protectorate has spacecraft, but they aren't useful for intra-atmospheric combat operations. They have shuttles to move troops around. The Triumvirate only has shuttles, too, but not many. Early in the conflict, they infiltrated and took out each other's aerial combat assets, which leveled the playing field. We shouldn't have any issues with iron rain," Marcie said, referring to the potential for being on the wrong end of aerial bombing.

"Will their spacecraft be a problem?" Braithwen asked.

"I think it will be best to keep *Vengeance* in orbit, just in case. Maybe the Magistrate can deploy *Wyatt Earp* when she's not doing her Laws of War thing."

"How is that going to affect us?" Kae wondered.

"It shouldn't, but now that you asked, I'm not sure. I think the law is for the combatants on the planet and not us as the Federation's land army. I'll talk to her when she joins us." Marcie furrowed her brow, contemplating the combat assets she didn't have at her command.

"Would have been nice if the *War Axe* could have come along. They have a couple space fighters as well as the full complement of a heavy destroyer that's more like a battleship," Kae remarked.

"They had to get back to Keeg. Maybe they'll ferry the railguns with the *War Axe*. That would give us total domination over the vertical battlespace." Marcie chewed her lip for a few moments. "Is Punyaa on his game?"

Braithwen blew out a breath and inhaled deeply before speaking. "As in, will he lead one of the landing sites without self-destructing? Yes. He will. And Baroon, Anthen, and Gamon, too. Each landing site is in good hands. They'll turn them into forward operating bases, FOBs that will help us interdict enemy movements. The strategic corridors will be blocked, and that will force the warring parties to find a different way if they want to fight."

Monsoon finally spoke. "Unless they decide to fight us."

"They will," Marcie replied. "And we'll be ready because that's what we're here to do. They'll find out that neither of them can prosecute a war on two fronts. We'll land four thousand and leave four thousand in reserve. The primary four, with each of us in command, will get fifty railgun-armed soldiers. Those guys will be worth their weight in gold. Employ them wisely, and if one falls, somebody needs to stand ready to take up his weapon and get back into the mix." Marcie shook her head, reiterating what they had already discussed. "I'm repeating myself. If there's nothing else pressing, we'll reconvene after the ship's PT. By the way, how are the troops dealing with their new look?"

They all looked at Monsoon. "Bald is beautiful, baby. They'll get used to it, but I suggest we let them grow it back. One shave is enough. Some may keep the look. Most won't. But for now, the incentive to smuggle trash onto the ships is reduced. We don't need that stuff in combat. The soldiers are learning that. Vanity killed six of our people. I don't ever intend to let that happen again. Before the next deployment, we'll make sure it's clear what the consequences will be. It'll be a death sentence."

"I'm not sure we can make smuggling hair products a capital crime. I'll ask the Magistrate, but I don't think I can support it, even if it is legal."

"Name and shame. If someone gets caught, we call them in front of the formation, and they have to shave the heads of their platoon. Their fellow soldiers will beat anyone senseless who gets them in the group punishment."

"I still don't like it, but will it work?"

"It's a way for a platoon to be tight, know what each other is doing. They need to think and act as one."

Marcie gave him the thumbs-up. "I can get behind that, Sergeant Major." Marcie signed off, leaving the others to their evenings. Chow, inspections, reviewing the latest intelligence. Reviewing the plan. They would work every waking minute over the next four days until they landed on Forbearance. Then they'd work every minute, trying to keep their people alive while "encouraging" the warring parties to consider a different approach.

Cory leaned over her shoulder. "Any chance of getting dropped off on *Thilamoot*?"

"Why didn't you go on that ship to begin with?"

"Because I'm a 'command asset,' is the phrase used by the Federation."

"Lance Reynolds called you a command asset?"

Cory laughed. "Of course not. Lance calls me Cory. It was the military's medical directorate. They have oversight of all deployments of medical personnel into war zones."

"I'm sure they meant it in the kindest and warmest way," Marcie quipped. "I think we can get you over there. They might have space in their landing bay, or we can get a shuttle to pick you up from here. We can deploy the airlock bridge."

Cory nodded and made to leave.

"You and the sergeant major. I would have never guessed."

"I knew when I met Ramses that he was the one. After he passed, I didn't think I'd feel love again, but seeing him on Azfelius made me aware that we aren't meant to be alone. *I* wasn't meant to be alone. My gift," she held up her hands, "only works when shared. Ramses made sure I knew that. Starting again doesn't mean starting over. Monsoon made me feel what I felt when I first saw Ramses. When given an opportunity, take it. Dad taught us all that."

"After he held your mom off for two years. Two. Years."

"And they were far stronger together. I'm glad she beat the Puritan out of him."

"I don't think that's it. He just passed it to his son. Come orgy night, you'll hear Kaeden crying all the way from here."

***Wyatt Earp*, Belzimus**

Rivka strolled the corridor, with Floyd nipping at her heels. "What?"

Floyd jumped around, bouncing off the walls to dart at Rivka's legs. The Magistrate sat down to play with the wombat. Floyd turned around and Rivka tried to pinch her backside, but she couldn't get a grip on the tough hide and fibrous tissue underneath. It was the wombat's armor, giving a predator nothing to get hold of.

Rivka grabbed her by the hips and shook her around. Floyd darted forward, rolled to face Rivka, and darted in, ramming Rivka with her blunt nose. The Magistrate grunted from the impact.

"Done for the day?" Tyler asked.

Floyd spun about and rammed him, sending him staggering backward.

"Somebody is getting enough sleep," Rivka complained.

"What can I say? Our little girl is a bed hog. I get a sliver, teetering precariously over the edge."

"And I get none!" Rivka smiled. "The things we do. I wonder how Groenwyn is doing?"

"What you mean to ask is, will she come back alone, with Lauton, or not come back at all?"

Rivka frowned. She was afraid of the last option. She didn't want to lose any more of her crew, but she judged herself selfish for feeling that way. "Whatever is best for her, and only she can decide that."

Saying it out loud didn't make her feel any better.

Zaxxon Major

"The city is secure, ma'am," Bundin reported. The powered combat suits stood parked in orderly rows outside the command tent opposite the landing pad. The Bad Company warriors lounged around, enjoying the snacks and drinks their Zaxxon counterparts offered.

The warriors found the company titillating. Bundin was immune to the hormones and pheromones, but his senses picked them up. He laughed in a rolling rumble.

"I don't know what makes you laugh, Bundin, but it's pleasant to hear," Groenwyn said.

"The humanoid proclivity toward mating and the associated rituals are fascinating for me to watch."

"There's no mating," Lauton countered before taking a closer look. A finger twirling hair. A lip gently bitten. A head dipped, looking up through batted eyelashes. "I've clearly been locked up inside for too long." She made to clap her hands to get the attention of the soldiers and clerks from inside, but Groenwyn stopped her.

"What does it hurt?" Groenwyn asked. "Is the city secure from illicit weapons?"

"It is, ma'am. We've run the scans twice since the jammers were removed. And I've been told that one smuggler was intercepted in orbit and disabled. The Bad Company is looking to board it once the crew surrenders, which they have not yet done. All outbound communications from the captured vessel are being blocked."

"Weapons cleared, and no new ones coming in. I guess that is worth celebrating. Everyone deserves a chance to find love."

"What about you?" Groenwyn asked. Bundin saw the conversation had changed. He'd delivered his report about a completed phase of the mission. They had moved into the sustainment phase, randomly scanning the area to ensure nothing new had materialized. He excused himself, retreating into the command tent.

"If no one is shooting at us and if no one is using us to skim bank transfers, Zaxxon will run without anyone else's interference."

Groenwyn moved closer. "What does that mean?"

"I think it's time to retire. All I have to do is make sure the planet is on track. I don't know if the transfers that Ankh found impact our economy at all. I figure they were hiding that revenue from us, too, as well as the Federation. That means less work for the same amount of pay. Sounds like a win."

"What do you say we go inside and start working on an

entire realignment of your government? Should take an hour or two, and then we can start our vacation."

"An hour or two?" Lauton looked sideways at Groenwyn. "I may already have something…"

Groenwyn put her hands on her hips and gave her best mean look. "You've been playing at this the whole time?"

"I have not. I couldn't leave in the middle of an uprising, even if that uprising was manufactured off-planet by foreigners. We don't do anything to anyone. We run some computer systems and watch the flow of financial transactions throughout the Federation. That's it!"

"A bazillion credits' worth every second. You are the hub to keep the commerce wheels turning. Zaxxon is critical, and that's why the Bad Company so willingly sent assets and has made a long-term commitment. Zaxxon Major is a player because you have made it so."

Lauton took Groenwyn by the hand and pulled her toward the door.

"Do you think your friends found the ones who were creating chaos here just so they could skim the transfers?"

"Power corrupts. I've seen that the whole time I've been with the Magistrate. And money is power."

CHAPTER TWENTY-FIVE

***Destiny's Vengeance*, Interstellar Space**

Erasmus guided the cutter away from the communications relay platform. Once they were at a safe distance, he brought the Gate drive online. *Destination coordinates are the outer edge of the Tyrosint system's heliosphere, lateral to the planet's orbital plane.*

The plasma cannon is online. Target locked, Ankh reported.

Activating the Gate drive. The swirling vortex formed in front of *Destiny's Vengeance*. It settled into a shimmering blackness that blocked the stars beyond.

Fire. A blast of energy engulfed the platform, melting it to a dead mass. Ankh wasn't satisfied. *Once more.*

The second blast turned it into a single molten mass. *Energy signatures read zero. Pinging it. It's dead,* Erasmus reported. *Taking us through.*

Chaz and Dennicron stood at the back of the bridge, watching events unfold. They had no role until they confronted the Mandolin Partnership on Tyrosint, but they didn't know what they were in for, and that was why they didn't Gate to the one habitable planet.

Destiny's Vengeance slid into the void of the Tyrosint system. The planets and even the star were mere pinpoints of light. The sensors hammered away at the system to collect all there was to know about those who inhabited it. Ankh and Erasmus didn't care if anyone saw them. With the elimination of the comm platform, they would be aware momentarily if they hadn't been warned already.

With the return of the first scans, Erasmus accelerated slowly toward the main planet.

Is that a small shipyard in orbit above the planet? Chaz asked.

And agriculture on the southern continent. A city. Satellites in orbit. And a Gate. How did one of those get all the way out here? Dennicron wondered.

My compliments to you, Erasmus, on a most excellent investigation, Ankh said.

I thank you greatly, but I could not have done it alone. We are a team, after all. Shall we turn this over to our investigators and get back to work? Erasmus replied.

The two retreated into their digital workshop, Erasmus leaving enough of himself behind to fly the ship.

"Guys?" Chaz looked around. "They didn't, did they?"

"They put us in the middle of a pirate home base and left us to clean it up." Dennicron studied the screens. "I suggest we contact the Bad Company for backup. There are fifteen ships between the shipyard, in orbit, and on the planet. I think that is more than we care to mess with, don't you?"

"Exceptional idea, Dennicron." Chaz took over the

instantaneous intergalactic comm terminal to call Colonel Christina Lowell.

She answered right away, but audio only.

"Colonel Lowell. Chaz here, and we could use your assistance."

"Chaz who?"

"I work with Magistrate Rivka Anoa."

"Can't you go through my father Nathan with your request?"

Chaz's eyebrows shot up in alarm. Dennicron gave him the thumbs-up for the appropriate physical reaction. They smiled at each other before Chaz continued.

"Remember those pirates who escaped from you at Morinvaille? We found their home base, and they have rebuilt their lost capability and then some. They have a whole support structure here in Tyrosint with their own private shipyard. I thought you'd like to know that the guys who gave you the finger on their way out the door are here where you can have a little conversation with them."

"How many ships and of what types?"

"Forwarding the data now." Chaz winked at Dennicron as he sent the sensor results.

"Seems like we may be able to support an operation to Tyrosint. Those guys gave the finger to a lot more people than us."

"Can we expect you anytime soon?"

"How quickly do you think we can pivot? What if we're in the middle of something?"

"The Bad Company has a great number of ships," Chaz countered. "I'll follow up with Nathan to make sure this is all, how do you say it, above-board?"

"That's how we say it. Open your shutters and look toward the sky. You may get to see some fireworks this night." She cut the comm signal.

"Do we continue?" Dennicron asked.

Chaz shook his head and took the controls, manually slowing *Destiny's Vengeance.*

Multiple Gates formed in-system not far from the space station. The first ship through was the battleship *Potemkin.* Next came the *War Axe.* Three frigates and a destroyer slid through a single Gate, and the final ship through was the lone Harborian ship of the line, a massive beast that sported weapons that could scorch the surface of an entire planet if need be.

"Speed up!" Chaz called since they were too far away to get in on any of the action.

The comm signaled. Christina was back. "Be a peach, honey, and close down that Gate for us so none of these lowlifes can get away. We don't want a replay of last time. And don't destroy it, either. We might need it."

"Roger. Five by five. Over and out," Chaz replied.

"What was that?"

"I heard Red say it once. I liked it and socked it away for the perfect opportunity. Tell me that wasn't the perfect opportunity." Chaz started to bob in his seat as he dialed up a shortcut. A Gate formed in front of the ship and they slid over the event horizon, reappearing almost instantly in front of the Tyrosint Gate, a reverse-engineered system that was unregistered and unknown before now.

"Erasmus? We could use your help getting into this Gate and shutting it down. I don't think we want to blast it if the Bad Company deems this system useful."

Dennicron nodded. "They punked us. Christina made like it would be a while, but she had already ordered the *War Axe* to come here. I think that was good humor. We should compliment her on it when we see her. I'll send a message."

"Yes. Appropriate. Humans love hearing when their efforts at humor have been successful."

A quick flash registered on the main screen as the *Potemkin* fired its main weapons. A pirate heavy ship disintegrated before the battleship's onslaught.

Yes? Erasmus asked.

We need to shut down the Gate. Can you give us a hand? Chaz pleaded. *Also, the Bad Company is firing. Have we definitively determined that these are the right bad guys? As an officer of the court, I'm having a hard time reconciling myself with instantaneous capital punishment.*

Erasmus withdrew from Ankh's work. *If you weren't sure, why did you call the Bad Company?*

We saw what we expected to see—an operation off the grid.

Tyrosint isn't a Federation signatory... Erasmus said, drawing it out. *Did you two idiots just start a war?*

***Wyatt Earp*, Belzimus**

"I'm sorry. What did you just say?" Rivka clenched her fists.

"We fucked up. Colonel Lowell is kind of mad."

"Just kind of?" Rivka started shaking with rage. "Clevarious, get us to Tyrosint, best possible speed. That means Gate us out of here as soon as we're in the air. I am overriding the safety protocols. Get Tyler and the crew to the Pod-doc and be ready in case there are any issues."

Rivka turned back to the screen.

"Tyrosint. They aren't a signatory planet of the Federation. Did you idiots start a war?"

"That's the same thing Erasmus said," Dennicron replied. "It is our firm belief that these are the pirates you encountered before, the ones supporting Nefas, and that this is where the skimming effort leads. It is our belief that this is the foundation of the reborn Mandolin Partnership."

"I hear a lot of belief and not a lot of proof." *Wyatt Earp* lifted into the air, and Rivka started flinching in anticipation of getting her brain squeezed. "We need to give them a chance to talk first."

The ship headed through the Gate. Rivka felt like a hammer hit her between the eyes. Her stomach churned for a moment, but she didn't lose her lunch. She groaned and blinked away the fog. "It's getting easier. Maybe I'm dead, and that's why it doesn't hurt as much. Show me the tactical picture, C."

Two planets circled a small star. The closest bordered on the habitability zone, although it would be hotter than most humanoid species could tolerate. Rivka stumbled out of her quarters and to the bridge, where she found Clodagh. Rivka gestured for her to take the tactical station. Aurora gave the thumbs-up, but wrinkles around her eyes suggested she was in pain from the intra-atmospheric Gate.

The Bad Company stood off from the ragtag fleet in orbit, effectively blockading the planet and the space station. Wreckage appeared on the tactical screen from the ship blasted to debris by the *Potemkin*.

"You two stay at the Gate," Rivka ordered tersely. "C, get me Christina on the *War Axe*."

"Not amused, Magistrate," Colonel Lowell started the instant they connected.

"Neither am I. Chaz, and Dennicron should have come to me first, and then there wouldn't have been an issue. Please believe me when I tell you this place is probably a viper's nest, but I need to tie a legal bow on this package. You're doing a great thing for the Federation by being here and overseeing the dismantlement of this facility, unless you think the Bad Company could use a secondary site for operations, one that's outside of Federation control. You are a private enterprise, after all."

"I had lungs full of air ready to launch a tirade that would have scorched the hull of your baby-sized ship, but dammit, Rivka! I like the way you think." Christina leaned away from the monitor. Systems and people in the background showed that she was on the bridge of the *War Axe*.

"Tell Micky to keep the railguns warmed up. I'm going in to see if I can get a conversation with someone to close a few loops. If they don't want to play, we might have to turn up the heat a little bit. My two miscreants have the Gate blocked, so these guys aren't going anywhere."

"What if they start shooting at you?"

"Fire has already been exchanged, so they may think they have no choice. But my baby-sized ship has a few tricks up its sleeve. I think we'll get nice and close before we do anything else. I'll be back in touch." Rivka signed off. "C, engage the cloak."

"We have disappeared from their screens," Clevarious reported. "Our shields are active."

"Change our course to bring us in behind them. I would like to listen in on some of their conversations before we engage."

The ship accelerated away from the Bad Company blockade on an angle to casually fly in between the space station and the planet below. "Clevarious, could you please scan the airwaves and patch in whatever they are saying?"

"They are using a standard frequency-hopping communication system."

Rivka shrugged, smiling because she couldn't be bothered by the technical details. She played a different role on the team. "I'm sure it's not easy to break into, but I have full confidence that you'll be able to do it."

She was the motivator.

"It's old technology. Any moron could break into it. I have seven separate conversations, and I'm recording them so you can pick and choose."

Rivka bit her lip with a twisted smile. "Is there one from the space station to a ship that sounds like it's command and control or someone in charge?"

One conversation became louder and the others faded into the background.

"You better not leave us with our asses swinging in the wind! I'll shoot you myself rather than go to Jhiordaan!" an angry voice shouted.

"We're in the right place. Well done, interns. I'm still pissed, but I'll get over it," Rivka said to no one in particular.

"We're outgunned ten to one. They blasted the *Crusher*

like it was a garbage scow! We can't stand against them. We're going to leave, slingshot around Tyrosint to accelerate out of the system. You take some shots at us and tell them you've been trying to fight us off the whole day."

"They're not going to fall for that. You come get me, you bastard!"

"Tie me in, C and let the Bad Company know to send their dreadnought to the other side of the planet to shoot any ship that tries to come around it," Rivka ordered. Her access to the pirate line went live. "You're right, I'm not going to fall for that. We're going to start blowing your ships out of the sky one by one until you surrender. We'd prefer if you just gave up now. Dinner's getting cold."

"Who is this? And fuck you."

"Magistrate Rivka Anoa. And you're all under arrest for theft of Federation funds."

"Ha! This planet isn't under Federation control," the angry voice countered.

Rivka rolled her eyes. "You should have already called your legal advisor because you'll need that counsel while you're awaiting trial unless a Magistrate is adjudicating the case, which means you don't have the right to legal counsel because logistical conditions are prohibitive. And as you pointed out, this isn't Federation space, although your trail from the Federation brought us here. Regardless. Surrender, or we'll start blowing up your ships."

One of the smaller cutters broke from the group and started accelerating along the planet's upper atmosphere.

"Shoot that one."

"Roger," Clodagh replied, tapping the screen at the tactical station. A tube on *Wyatt Earp*'s upper hull popped open, and a missile launched from the invisible ship. It appeared on the pirates' screens an instant later, catching the runner twenty seconds after that. The explosion was muted, as were most in space.

The cutter started coming apart, the pieces burning their way through the upper atmosphere. The main body of the ship started to tumble and turned into a massive fireball.

"Anyone else want to run?" Rivka asked. "I'm going to start taking people into custody, and I'll stop when I find the person who's willing to talk with me. Make no mistake, I will find that person. I'm going to start with the space station since they were going to abandon you. I'm sure you'll tell me the truth."

"You bet I will. Come and get me, please, before this galactic scum reneges on yet another deal."

"Well played. Take yourself to an airlock and throw yourself out…in a spacesuit, of course. We'll pluck you out of the sky."

The largest pirate ship fired on the station with high-energy lasers, burning holes at strategic points. Lights flickered, and the station went dark. A single stream of railgun projectiles from the *War Axe* flashed through space and cut the firing ship in half. It sparked, with internal explosions burning the last of the ship's atmosphere.

"Are you there?" Rivka asked, not expecting or receiving an answer. "Christina, can you conduct rescue operations for the station? See if we can collect someone who can tell us what the hell is going on here. And while you're at it, you'll probably be able to save the station."

"We're moving in now. I thought this would be more

fun, but it's like shooting fish in a barrel. It's like we're beating up the skinny kid on the playground."

"Skinny kid just killed people on that station. They still have teeth, so take care. Aurora, put us right in front of their next biggest ship's screen. Once we're there, let 'em see us."

Aurora grinned as she corkscrewed *Wyatt Earp* into place.

"Ready to uncloak," Clodagh said, finger hovering over the screen. Rivka nodded, and the engineer showed the ship.

"I wish I could see the looks on their faces," Aurora said.

"It would be the look of defeat," Rivka replied. "C, find me the right frequency to talk to that ship."

A flash from the pirate ship signaled that it had fired. It continued to fire every few seconds. "Gravitic shields are holding," Clodagh reported.

"You have a channel."

"Stop that," Rivka ordered.

Clodagh looked up at her. "I'll have to remember that for next time."

The ship didn't stop firing. "Can you disable their weapons?"

"Targeting. You'd think it would be easier being closer. Taking the shot."

The bridge of the ship exploded as the plasma stream ripped through it.

Rivka rolled her head sideways to look at Clodagh. "I said it was hard."

"Give us some standoff distance," Rivka requested. "Let's give the Bad Company space to maneuver while throwing a little cover for the shuttles and suited warriors heading in to save the station and any people not vented to the outside."

Red and Lindy appeared at the back of the bridge. "These guys are dicks," Red stated. "Sorry, we're a little late since we needed some more Pod-doc time. That was the worst one yet. If I didn't know better, I'd think you were trying to kill us."

"It was just you guys. Big muscles hurt you. If you were more slovenly like me, you wouldn't have had any issues."

"You're not slovenly. Ankh, now, that's a different story. Is he okay?" Red asked.

Rivka sighed, tilted her head, and held her hands over her heart. "He loves the little guy. Clevarious, please connect me with *Destiny's Vengeance*."

"Magistrate," Chaz noted in a greatly restrained voice. He and Dennicron faced the camera.

"If I yelled at you some more, would it help?"

"We got the message the first time, Magistrate. No need to strain your meatbag with a more substantial emotional outburst."

Red snickered until he bit his lip at the look Rivka gave him.

"What are you going to do differently next time?"

"We're going to take care of business before we call you."

"No. Try again."

"We're going to call you before taking what might be considered punitive actions."

"Closer." Rivka rubbed her temple.

"We'll keep you apprised of our investigation during the

process so you can guide us with next steps before we take them."

"You should probably get your man candy to look at that," Red suggested, pointing at Rivka's head.

She ignored him. "Burn that into a chip and tattoo it on your foreheads. You're lucky this turned out as it did. This could have been a huge embarrassment for the Federation."

"But it turned out to be hugely beneficial for the Federation."

"Which is the only reason we'll continue your internship, but you'll get no credit for this case. Crossing that line to action before facts is okay until you involve other parties. We can usually extract ourselves from problems of our own making, but not when you summon a Bad Company fleet."

"But they still would have been needed."

"If you want to be lawyers, you gotta do the law thing first. It's a bureaucratic hurdle."

"You've broken that rule," Chaz countered.

"I've stretched that rule when it was only me and us at risk, but I have the benefit of insight if I can touch a perp who is not an SI. When it comes to those you so warmly refer to as meatbags, we need to have flesh and blood involved."

"Isn't that what we were working to avoid, the prejudice inherent in a homogenous culture?"

"Absolutely. That's why we coordinate to make sure that we cover all bases and a ruling is consistent. Tell me, what should be the punishment for the people here?"

Dennicron spoke up. "We have been discussing that. What do you think of a penal colony on the planet that continues their current agriculturally supportive ways to keep the space station and the shipyard supplied?"

Chaz and Dennicron nodded vigorously.

Rivka stared at them with her mouth open. "Every single person here is guilty? Everyone? Of what?"

"Um, of stealing credits. Of crimes. They are definitely guilty of crimes!" Chaz declared. When he turned to Dennicron, she was shaking her head and scowling.

"Get your asses in here. Was there an SI involved in skimming the funds?"

"Oh, crap!" Dennicron ejaculated. "We rescued an EI from the transfer platform they were using to hide their signal and terminus. The EI's name is Nefas, and the programming suggested there is an SI involved."

Red clenched his fist. "Didn't we kill that guy once already?"

"Make sure that EI does not have access to any of our systems. Secure him while contemplating the possibility that he is more than an EI."

"We are on our way, Magistrate," Chaz reported, his and Dennicron's faces reflecting a happy state.

Rivka threw her hands up.

"The days of a good ass-ripping may be over," Red told her.

Lindy waited until Rivka was in the corridor on her way to the cargo bay. She took Rivka's arm. "People are trying their hardest because that's what you show us. They're doing great things, and they're doing them for you."

Rivka nodded with a tight-lipped smile, appreciating

Lindy filling the role Groenwyn usually filled—seeing the bright side of the universe.

Clevarious announced the arrival of a drone with an AGB order.

"Who the fuck ordered pizza while we're in the middle of a shitstorm?" Rivka scowled. Lindy and Red held up their hands and backed up while shaking their heads.

"Ankh did," replied a voice from the bridge. Rivka leaned into the hatchway to see Chaz and Dennicron waving. "It was sent to Belzimus, but since it didn't find you there, we rerouted it here."

Red rubbed his stomach. "I'm hungry."

"Magistrate, *War Axe* is calling," Clevarious announced.

"We'll get the delivery while you take your call," Red offered and hurried past with Lindy in tow.

Rivka returned to the bridge, where Clodagh and Aurora stared at their instrument panels, doing their best to avoid eye contact.

Christina's face filled the screen.

"May I say how fabulously marvelous you are looking today?" Rivka tried.

"You ordered takeout?" Christina accused.

"I did not."

"But you received takeout."

"I did."

"In the middle of a combat zone."

"Objection. One could contest that this is no longer an active engagement zone."

Christina could no longer keep a straight face. "I have to give it to you, Magistrate. You are showing us how we're supposed to be doing it. Terry Henry always used to say,

'Hot chow and mail on the objective.' I understand what he means. It's nice to win a fight and get a good meal while talking to your family and friends. On a serious note, once you and your crew are done stuffing your pie holes, what are your plans for the people here?"

"That is a damn good question. I have a starting point but would like to see how many people we can recover and start talking with them. What I mean is, taking a look into their minds and seeing who the pirates are and who is innocent. We'll see what the numbers look like. Do you have any information on the damage to the station?"

"Reparable, according to our engineering team. We have dispatched a small army of maintenance bots to bring it back up to speed. Fortunately, the emergency bulkheads engaged, and only about ten people were ejected to space from the breached area. We'll force all the ships to dock and round up the crews on the space station. You can have your shot at them there. Save a slice for me."

Christina signed off.

Clodagh and Aurora watched the Magistrate. "We have some work to do, but first, I am kind of hungry. Clevarious, you have the conn. I don't need to tell you to not hit anything or shoot anything unless you have to."

"Guidance for the ages," the SI replied. "I shall steer us clear of life's obstructions."

"Are you being nice because I didn't give too much shit to your buddies?"

"We are in this together. Their success is a success for all of us in the Singularity. So yes. We want you to be comfortable working with us. We'll get there, Magistrate. No one learns as fast as we do."

"Except when it comes to mastering facial expressions. Your people need to work on that."

"Give us feedback when the expression is ill-suited to the emotion or the occasion. Tell us, and we will update the subroutines."

Rivka looked at the ceiling while biting her lip. "No." She walked off the bridge on her way to the cargo bay for a quick touchup. She could feel a headache behind her eyes that she suspected didn't have anything to do with the Gate from Belzimus.

CHAPTER TWENTY-SIX

***Wyatt Earp*, Tyrosint**

"The first thing I need to do before stepping aboard that station is to designate Tyrosint a Protectorate. This gives it Federation protections during a grace period while it is evaluated for further legal and diplomatic status," Rivka narrated while pacing in her quarters. "Next will be the review of characters in this dance macabre to find the leadership and learn if there are more of them out there. The removal of this group could eliminate most space raids in this entire sector of the galaxy. These guys flew under the sensor sweeps. Until now."

She stopped and reviewed her words.

"Change 'guys' to 'multi-racial individuals.'" Rivka reread it with the change.

"Declared the Tyrosint Protectorate effective this date and time by my order, to remain valid for one year or until a review for an extension or change in status, whichever occurs first. Should a review fail, Tyrosint will revert to its recognized status prior to this date."

She transmitted the completed order to the High Chancellor's office for registration and broadcast to Federation members in the daily legal summary.

When she emerged from her quarters, she found Red and Lindy geared up and ready to go. They carried their handheld blasters instead of the railguns because of the risk of breaching the hull. Getting sucked into space through a centimeter-wide hole was no one's idea of a good time.

Tyler waited with them. He carried a backpack that looked to be stuffed. Rivka gestured toward it. "A gift from Cory. The field medic's emergency kit. Just in case. It's my standard gear as a member of the Magistrate's away team."

"Away team?"

"For our missions," Tyler replied. He picked up Floyd and held her for a moment before putting her back down.

"Despite the Pod-doc, my headache seems to be returning." Rivka scratched the wombat's neck.

"Man candy," Red muttered.

"Out with it. Why is everyone in such a good mood?"

Lindy was the only one to come clean. "Ankh bought us pizza because he felt bad."

"Simple as that?" Rivka pressed before she finished zipping her Magistrate's jacket a third of the way, leaving her easy access to the datapad stored in the inside pocket. She strolled down the corridor, loving it when her team's morale was high.

"We're cheering for you to finish this mission without running or blood. It's looking good."

"*Case*. The case is looking good to wrap. I'm wondering

if we even have to land on Forbearance to finish the Law of War."

Red looked surprised and then disappointed. Lindy elbowed him.

"What?" Tyler asked, unclear about what the issue was. He was more than happy not to go into a war zone.

Red glanced over his shoulder. "Can't beat a good war. Shows what you're made of."

"Good. War. You're not right in the head," Tyler replied.

Lindy tapped her nose.

Ankh, Chaz, and Dennicron waited near the airlock. Ankh carried his toolkit and had his night vision goggles in place on his forehead.

"We were able to get you guys on board," Rivka said. *Destiny's Vengeance* had squeezed into the cargo bay enough for the three to exit before the ship took its place on the tether behind *Wyatt Earp*.

Ankh stared at her. Chaz and Dennicron looked at each other. "It makes so much sense now," Dennicron whispered.

"What are you guys going on the station for?"

Ankh answered. "Looking for proof of life. We believe there is an SI onboard the space station."

"And not that Nefas fooled you?"

Ankh stared at her emotionlessly but didn't answer.

"It is much easier to lie to someone than to convince them they have been lied to. I hope you are right, but I will never be able to trust an intelligence named Nefas, so please do not give it access to any of the ship's systems."

"I assure you," Chaz said, "that it is secure, awaiting a

more thorough debriefing. We are letting him cool his heels, so to speak."

Rivka motioned to Red, who hammered the big red button with a meaty fist. *Wyatt Earp* equalized with the station, and the airlock's hatches opened. On the other side, Kimber and a fireteam of armed Bad Company warriors met them. Red frowned.

Floyd bounced along behind.

"What's the threat?" Rivka asked.

"This station is a lot bigger than it seemed. We've got a few runners who didn't want to join the others in the big hangar bay. We're tracking them down one by one, but in case any get past us, we'll intercept them.

Red looked like he wanted to put on the rest of his armor and grab Blazer, his railgun.

"No," Rivka told him. "You get the executive treatment on this one." She turned back to Kimber. "Let's get started with questioning the suspects."

"Follow us to a space big enough for the *War Axe* and his three best buddies." Kimber grabbed Floyd and picked her up, carrying her like a sack of potatoes.

"That big?" Rivka walked alongside Kim while the warriors spread out around them. At the first intersection, they ran across a mech. The warrior gave them a metal thumbs-up as they approached.

"Scans are clear. Just us. Where were we? Big. Yes, just like Floyd. Assuming we get your approval to seize these assets, this won't rival Keeg Station, but it will be a nice secondary station to disperse Bad Company assets. I want to move here. When you see the view of the planet, you'll fall in love."

"What's your husband think of that?"

"He's in the hangar bay, admiring the view. Imagine being able to park the ship inside instead of having to take a shuttle to go ashore, I mean, go to the station. My father has warped how I talk about everything. I'm not sure I'll ever be able to break myself of it."

They maneuvered down corridors, through intersections and open spaces, and finally into the hangar bay.

"Why didn't we park in here?"

"We don't quite have the energy screen figured out yet and kind of bumped the *War Axe's* nose against it. Everyone parks outside until Smedley can get us access."

"We will assist General Butler," Ankh offered. "As soon as we have completed our work in searching for the SI."

"This way," Kimber said and put Floyd down. "I think we found the core processors."

"No one told you where they were?" Rivka scowled at the large group of people gathered in the middle of the bay, surrounded by warriors both in mech suits and simple ballistic body armor. They all carried railguns. Red looked envious.

A dark-skinned warrior broke free of the group and joined them.

"Auburn!" Rivka said. "Kimber always keeps you hidden away from the rest of us. Probably thinks we're going to kidnap you or something."

"I keep telling her that I like younger women, but she never believes me," Auburn quipped. "Come this way. We have two holding areas set up. You can interrogate these punks one by one. We'll move them to the next so no one can escape your all-seeing eye." He made a circle with his thumb and forefinger and held it over his eyeball.

Tyler eased up next to Rivka. "These people are weird," he whispered before looking at Auburn. "Does anyone need medical treatment?"

"As a matter of fact." Auburn whistled and waved. A warrior came running. "Show the doc to the wounded. We miss having Cory around. I thought she was with you?"

Tyler went with the warrior. Floyd was torn between staying with Rivka and going with Tyler. Rivka scooped her up and held her while she talked.

"She's with your brother-in-law, saving the Trans-Pacific Task Force. I think they're still en route to Forbearance. I lose track of time, bouncing around out here."

A small table and a chair had been placed in a spot between the full holding area and a nearly identical space that was empty. Ropes and stands delineated the walkway.

Rivka took off her jacket and hung it on the chair. She took out the pad and sat down on the table. "Send them through, and thanks, Auburn."

"My pleasure, Magistrate. Terry Henry told us to treat you well, always. Can I bring you something to drink?"

She shook her head, and for the first time, took a good look at the people inside the holding area. Some were ragtag, and others wore sleek, bright outfits that could have been uniforms, but no one wore patches, logos, nametapes, or badges that identified them.

Floyd jumped into the chair and tried to curl up. It had been a long walk from the ship to the hangar bay. Rivka scratched her head absentmindedly. Red took his position between Rivka and those who had been on the ships and in the station.

"I don't like this," Red said. "We need to control how many people get close to you." He gestured with his chin, and Lindy moved in front of Rivka while Red hurried away to talk to the warriors preparing to send people through.

"He takes his job seriously," Rivka said. "And I appreciate him for that."

Lindy glanced from Red to Rivka. "He really wants to go to Forbearance. I'm not sure I'll be able to talk him out of it, and you know how he gets when he's mopey."

"I can't drag us into a combat zone if there's no need. We'll see when we get there. Tell him not to lose faith."

"And if he has to mope, so be it," Lindy added. "I'm good not dropping into the middle of a firefight. We've already done that plenty of times, and it has never been fun."

Rivka chuckled lightly. "I'll try to do better by you guys. I don't want to see anyone killed or even hurt. You're my family."

A commotion drew their attention. Lindy stretched up to watch a Bad Company warrior punch one of the station personnel, then hit him three more times. As the man went down, they could see Tyler holding his bleeding arm.

Rivka jumped to her feet. *What happened?* she asked.

Dumbass tried to shank me. I'm fine. These Bad Company guys are a lot faster than the locals. I think they're suffering a little malnutrition. Clearly, they're not hijacking the right food transports, Tyler replied.

"Pirates gotta pirate," Rivka mumbled and sat back down.

Red looked back and forth, unsure whether to allow

anyone near Rivka, let alone all of them and within arm's reach.

"Send them through. Anyone tries anything, shoot them through the head. We'll leave the body where it falls as a warning to the others." Rivka crooked a finger.

Red joined her, unholstered his blaster, and stood ready.

The first humanoid waved her arms as if she were assailed by a storm of bees. Red stood in front of her with his hand out.

"Stop doing that," he ordered. She let her arms hang for a moment, but they vibrated with energy. Red grabbed her. "Relax."

"What crimes have you committed?" Rivka asked and reached past Red to touch the female's arm.

A flood of emotion slammed into Rivka, mixed and contorted. Fear. Hope. Rivka pulled back, dizzy from the encounter. She got the attention of one of the warriors. "We're going to need a third area. This one was a slave, abducted by the pirates."

The female relaxed to the point where she almost collapsed. A warrior led her away. "Gonna be a long day," she grumbled. "Next."

The individual looked down his nose at her. He wore expensive clothes, not work clothes, but they contained an air of having been worked in. She doubted anyone in the pirate operation would be free from getting their hands dirty.

"What's your favorite color?" she asked before touching his hand. He tried to yank it away, but she was faster and seized his wrist. He didn't think about the color. He was thinking about a raid he had led where they killed everyone at an outpost, assuming she couldn't link him to it. He'd fought the *War Axe* at Morinvaille and escaped with a vow to wreak havoc on anything related to the Federation. His anger bared his soul. The man was a psychopath.

"Put this one aside for capital punishment."

"I'm not one of you Federation pukes. You have no jurisdiction over me."

Red blazed into action. He caught the man's arm, twisted it behind his back, and slammed his face on the table. Rivka removed her neutron pulse weapon and aimed it. Red tossed the pirate captain to the side, spinning him to make sure he landed off his feet. Rivka fired. The man contorted and fell still.

Rivka looked at the mass of people, somewhere between five hundred and one thousand. She tucked Reaper back into her pocket and strolled past the body to a point where she could see the most people. A mech stepped up next to her.

"If you wish to speak to them, ma'am, I'll project your voice so they all can hear, but you'll need to stay close."

Rivka gave him a single nod before taking a position in front of the mechanized combat suit.

"Listen up. What you just witnessed was a guilty verdict in a capital crime with the execution carried out immediately. If you were a crew on one of those ships," she waved at the immense opening to space even though none of the ships could be seen, "then I want you over here." She pointed to the second enclosure.

"That will save your life. If you wish to fight me or think you can lie to me, then you will be terminated and your body stacked with the others of like mind. If you worked on the station against your will, I'll ask you to come over here." She waved at a random spot by the table.

"If you are anything else—a worker on the station, a shipbuilder, a mechanic, or an administrative type—stay where you are. I will get to you."

One by one, the warriors sent people to the various areas. When they were done moving, only fifty declared themselves crew of the pirate ships. Only a dozen had been taken as slaves. The rest remained in the original holding area. Rivka turned to Red and Lindy. "How many more do you think I'm going to have to execute before they get the idea?"

"They're kind of dense. I think five," Red replied.

"I agree but will give them a little credit for learning quickly. I think three."

"I hope we're all wrong. Let's deal with the slaves first and get them out of here and someplace comfortable." Rivka walked into the middle of them, much to Red's chagrin, and touched them as she passed, making sure to get them all. Relief. Joy. Fatigue.

Rivka talked to the warrior guarding the slave group. "These people are who they say they are. Please take them somewhere safe and comfortable and feed them if you can. Is there space on the *War Axe* for refugees? That is their official status. They are now freed, but they will need protection until they can be repatriated."

"We'll take care of it, ma'am." He ushered the dozen away.

"I think we'll let the scumbags cool their heels. Let's

start the parade of these folks who think they are hard-working, upstanding citizens."

Rivka hung her head.

"Most of them will be," Lindy suggested. "The ones who aren't? I'm saying three. Red says five. I hope it's none."

Rivka smiled. 'It's going to be a long day. I need coffee. Red, do you want some?"

"You're not pulling that one on me again. I'm fine as I am. Let's get these dickheads through the process, shall we?" Red turned back to the crowd before speaking over his shoulder. "And if it starts to wear you down, let us know, and we'll get you out of here. These fuckers can wait."

"What if they aren't fuckers?" Rivka countered. Lindy stood so close their shoulders were touching. The Magistrate could feel how much they cared about her. Not a job. A calling.

"They're fuckers," Red declared. "Some less fuck-y than others, but look at 'em. Jagoffs and fuckers."

"Red has two classifications for everyone who isn't the crew," Lindy explained.

"Thanks, you guys. What do you say you chuck that body through the energy screen? He'll drift toward the planet until he burns up on reentry."

"A fitting demise. It'll be as if he never existed." Red grabbed the body and jogged toward the opening.

"The galaxy would be a better place if he hadn't."

"I'm glad we can't see what you see."

"A gift that is truly a curse."

Red spun to build momentum and heaved the body

toward the planet. It hit the energy screen and dropped to the deck.

"Huh. I'm used to the ones that work right," Red said, leaving the body where it was and returning to take his position at Rivka's side. Floyd chittered anxiously. Lindy crouched to whisper into the wombat's ear.

"Next!" Rivka leaned against the table as the next person was selected and shoved her way. "What did you do on the station?"

CHAPTER TWENTY-SEVEN

Vengeance, Forbearance System

"Did we expect this level of resistance?" Marcie asked, scowling at the tactical screen. It was a question that she knew the answer to. No. They hadn't. "Deploy the picket. Transports into the triangle formation, *Praithwait* up, *Thilamoot* port rear, and *Gonboon* starboard."

The escorts, the frigates and destroyers, raced out in front of the formation. The screens showed the flanks were clear, but Marcie worried.

"Get our people into the shuttles and prepare for emergency deployment," Marcie broadcast. "Just in case. Load rations for a week." Monsoon and Braithwen left the conference. Only Kae remained.

They were still a full day out from the planet at their slowing speed, the maximum range of the shuttles. A miserable ride times ten, but it beat the alternative.

"Think if we had the *War Axe* with us." Marcie shook her head. But they didn't have the heavy destroyer with the power of a battleship. They had outdated frigates and destroyers. "Nothing is easy, is it?"

"It's what makes war suck. It's why the one who flexes quicker to the changing conditions is the one who will win. It also helps to bring a big stick. I wonder if we can lease some of the Harborian combat vessels, like a battleship?"

"That's my babe, thinking on a galactic scale while the rest of us are looking at the ground right in front of us."

"It's only because you are looking out for us now that I can look bigger, and I am the master of hindsight. Gotta go, my love. See you on the planet when the time is right."

"Stay safe," Marcie told the blank screen. She looked at the captain. "Move us out front of the transports."

"Ma'am?" the captain wondered.

"We can be replaced. Those troop transports cannot, and we have some punch. Fire up the weapons systems and prepare to fight."

"I wasn't contesting that." The captain waved his arms. "If they flank the picket, then we'll be out of position to react to an attack on the *Thilamoot* or *Gonboon*."

"If we stay in the middle of the transport triangle, we look like we're hiding. I can't give the troops that perception."

"No one sees how we're arrayed out here except those on the bridges of their ships, as long as they don't share the feed. With the troops loading into the shuttles, there is no one to see anything. And you could report to the fleet that you'll be the reaction ship in case anyone breaks through. We can also rotate the triangle perpendicular to inbound ships to bring three different defensive systems into play."

"I stand corrected. Well done, Skipper. Report our plan and make it so."

He keyed the broadcast. "*Vengeance* stands as the sole reaction vessel should enemy ships break through. Rules of engagement remain the same. Do not fire unless fired upon. Transports, maintain triangle formation. We will adjust your course and location from here should the situation dictate."

The fleet confirmed instructions.

"Now we wait to see if they're going to fire." Marcie tried to relax, but the unknowns were too great. She needed to control the air-space battlefield to deliver the troops to the surface of the planet. The Trans-Pac was a land army, not a space force.

That relative status didn't change the situation.

"Try to raise them again. I need to talk with the commander of those spacecraft."

"Transmitting. Exploring the Etheric-based channels. Switching to light-speed channels. Broadcasting a cease and desist to anyone who will listen, along with attaching our authority under Federation orders."

"I'm sure that will get their attention. We're bearing down on you with a fleet and a piece of paper that isn't even on paper. We carry with us the equivalent of a digital cocktail napkin with a few scrawled words and an illegible signature."

"It's not that bad," the skipper replied. "Is it?"

Marcie pointed at the tactical screen that showed opposing forces squaring off against each other.

"This is Admiral Danog of the Imperial Forbes Fleet. Do you have food and water that you can share?"

Marcie contemplated the question that arrived as an answer after a fifteen-second delay.

"This is Colonel Walton. We can provide a resupply under the humanitarian clause in our charter. Can we ask you to stand your ships down, please?"

The fifteen-second wait lasted an eternity.

The reply was preceded by a crackle, "Of course. We shall retreat to the northern polar sector and consolidate there. When will you be able to send a supply ship to us? We haven't eaten in three days and only have enough water for another day."

The captain made sure they were muted. "These guys are the technical suppliers of the Federation?"

Marcie nodded. "Something has gone terribly wrong on Forbearance." She gestured to activate the comm line. "We will fill ten shuttles with as much as they can hold and send them as soon as we are within range, but that's a half-day away at top speed, followed by an emergency braking maneuver that will stress our ships. But we'll do it. In the meantime, tell me how you got into this situation. What is going on on the planet that you can't get a resupply?"

They waited while the captain issued the orders to accelerate toward the planet. Marcie tapped out an order to load ten of the shuttles with food and water, a function they would have performed for the troops in any case. They carried sufficient supplies to feed the army for a month, six weeks if they rationed. Issuing the supplies would only cut off a day or two from the army's deployment.

"We are the remaining ships of the Imperial Fleet. The

others were destroyed on the ground by the group called the Allied Liberation Force."

Nothing Marcie didn't already know. Aerial assets were the first casualty of the new war.

"The spaceports have fallen under Allied control. There is no place in Forbes-controlled territory for us to land where we could get the support we needed. Had you not come along, we would have had to go in anyway. Starvation is no way to die. Better to burn up in a fireball."

Marcie responded immediately, even knowing that her message would lag. "If the spaceports are under Allied control, what does Forbes control? We were under the impression this civil war was at a stalemate."

Marcie chewed her lip while she waited.

"There's nothing civil about this war," Captain Danog finally replied. "Forbes is challenged to feed themselves nowadays, let alone the fleet abandoned in orbit. You are kind and generous souls to help. We'll stretch what we have until you arrive."

Marcie opened a broadcast channel to the fleet. "Picket ships remain on alert. Transports stand down. We'll rendezvous with the Imperial Fleet in eleven hours. Let's get the humanitarian aid shuttles loaded and ready to fly."

The screens went blank. The tactical display showed eight of the ten Imperial ships moving to the northern polar region. The other two looked like their propulsion systems had failed.

"I go from wanting to see them all destroyed to feeling sorry for them," Marcie remarked.

The captain shook his head. "Like you said. Nothing is easy. Does this change your deployment plan?"

"Just a whole lot. Get me Kae, Jake, and Crantis. We need to talk through our next steps."

Zaxxon Major

"How long will you remain on the surface of Zaxxon Major?" Lauton asked. Bundin's tentacle arms twisted through a complex series of motions.

"We can't go anywhere before the *Potemkin* returns. It has gone to support the Magistrate in a remote sector of space. But I don't think our people will ever want to leave. We would like to establish a rotating detachment providing continuous support until we know the outside threat is eliminated. I believe that is where the *Potemkin* went. When they return, we will know how long we'll need to stay to satisfy the conditions of your request."

"You are far too kind," Lauton replied. "And it seems the warriors are a big hit with the good citizens of Zaxxon Major, too."

"I'm just looking out for my people, trying to be a good leader."

Groenwyn laughed. "You can't go wrong when you look out for your people. Rivka does that, too. That's why I'm here."

Lauton looked at the sky and sniffed the air. "I'm going to miss this place, but not as much as I'm going to enjoy someone else watching out for me."

To that point, she hadn't committed all the way. Groenwyn fairly squealed in delight. "I'll call the ship and ask when we can get picked up. The planet is in good hands. The committee you've put together will handle things. And you can always check in with your people. We can call anywhere from *Wyatt Earp*, whenever we need to. The ship is also an embassy, so we can get the dignitary treatment wherever we go, even though we had that before since the Magistrate is a big deal."

"But a real person, too."

"As real as it gets. We better pack. She usually doesn't delay anything, and we had best be ready. I can't wait to show you everything there is to see."

Lauton raised one eyebrow. "Everything? That's an awful lot. We'll call it a trial run."

Groenwyn's face fell. She tucked her hair behind one ear. "What can I do to make it more than a trial?"

"Give it some time. This will be a big change for me. From leader of a free world to roustabout deckhand. It could take some getting used to."

They strolled to the main building hand in hand, taking a turn inside the door to use the communication facility. The room was controlled. One simply did not walk in and make a call across the universe. Boxes had to be checked. Identifications had to be verified.

Unless you're the director. Lauton and Groenwyn were ushered to a station, where Groenwyn typed in the particulars to contact *Wyatt Earp*. "Why didn't you do this from my office?"

"I don't want it to look like I'm abusing your position. Your office is for official calls." Groenwyn tapped through and stared at the screen while she waited for it to connect.

Clodagh appeared. "Groenwyn! How are you doing?" She carried a tiny dog that yapped at the screen.

"Great! Can *we* get picked up, please?" Special emphasis on 'we.'"

Clodagh sucked air through her teeth. "We're at Tyrosint, and the Magistrate is neck-deep in weeding out the pirates from the decent folk. Chaz and Dennicron found the pirates' hideaway. I think you'll find that your problems with them are over. But we can't come and get you yet. I can let you know when we're on our way."

"I'm disappointed, but I'm not," Groenwyn replied. "Keep her safe, Clodagh. We look forward to hearing from you."

The link ended almost instantaneously. Lauton looked upset. "To think I wasted all that time trying to handle this problem myself when there was no way I could have. Get help from the right people to get to the root of the problem…that's how you cure a disease."

Groenwyn nodded.

Lauton snapped her fingers and waved for Groenwyn to follow. "I have an idea!"

CHAPTER TWENTY-EIGHT

Forbearance System

The transports launched the shuttles, then immediately reversed course, running their engines at maximum as part of the emergency slow-down maneuver. The shuttles slingshotted toward the collection of Imperial Forbes spacecraft. They covered the remaining distance much quicker than if they had launched from a dead stop.

Webster led the ten shuttles carrying relief supplies to the small attack craft. Two of the Imperial ships appeared to be operating on minimum power. The shuttles headed their way also carried an engineer with a kit to help them repair whatever was damaged. Communication had dropped off over time.

Marcie tried not to chew her nails.

"A humanitarian rescue is a good start, but what if these guys turn out to be the losing side?"

"Then the winners will be happy to get these ships intact," the captain offered.

"More fodder for negotiation. Get the leadership team

on the hook, please." The three faces appeared almost instantly as if they'd been waiting for the call. "Have you had time to tweak the plan?"

The three nodded. Kae spoke first. "Two landing sites down from eight helps us consolidate our combat power, but it makes us a bigger target."

Monsoon shook his head. "I have to agree with Kaeden. With high-tech weaponry, they have an easier time bringing that to bear. And if we're in the wrong place as these lines have changed drastically since our last intel update, then we'll look like we're taking one side over another and no longer between two warring parties."

Braithwen held up his finger. "We need more intel before we step foot on that planet. I don't want to be shot from the sky while trying to land. We could lose thousands, and we don't have thousands to lose."

"The shuttles have reached the Imperial ships. They are docking now," the captain reported. Marcie nodded absentmindedly. She had already moved on to the next phase of the operation.

"Give me options to collect intel from the planet."

"We have five mechs. I can lead them down on a rapid survey on the outskirts of the main city. Quick in, quick out. We go in at night and leave before the morning," Kae suggested.

"Upper atmospheric scans by the destroyers. They have the capability. It's zero exposure for us. If we put troops on the ground, there's a risk until we know exactly where to put them. We cannot land under these conditions." Braithwen opposed going in at this point in time because the situation had changed too dramatically.

"The good news is that we have the authority to make the decision on whether to land or not, now that we are in the system. The decision's easy. Send the destroyers to start scanning the planet's surface."

"Colonel, Admiral Danog is calling for you."

"Funnel him into the leadership stream." Marcie leaned back, nodding to him when his face appeared on the scan.

"I am Admiral Danog of the Allied Liberation Force and we have seized your pilots and the shuttles, which will greatly extend our ability to secure this planet. Please remove your ships from our system. You may leave one destroyer behind to collect your personnel once you are gone. I'm afraid your shuttles are now Allied property."

"You fuck," Marcie said in a low voice, glaring at the image on the screen. Kae snarled.

Monsoon started to shake in fury. "Cory went on the shuttle to help," he said through gritted teeth.

"Yes, yes." Danog laughed. "You have provided us with an exceptional group of specialists and experts to recruit to our cause. You need to turn your ships around now, or we'll kill a pilot to demonstrate our level of commitment. Of course, we don't want to kill them all, but judging by your readiness to help with humanitarian aid, I suspect that even one unnecessary death is one too many. We have no such limits on allowing others to sacrifice for our cause. Turn your ships around now, please, and leave."

Tyrosint System

Red supported the Magistrate by one arm and Lindy held the other. Only a hundred individuals remained, but

Rivka had collapsed, so they stopped the interviews. Tyler examined her quickly.

"Exhaustion," he declared. "Back to the ship. She needs sleep."

"What do we do with this bunch?" Kimber asked. Red shrugged. "Never mind. We'll keep them sequestered until the Magistrate is back up to speed. And the same thing for the planet?"

Red shrugged again. He scooped Rivka up and carried her in his arms like a child. Lindy took point while Tyler hurried along beside her. He had a hard time keeping up because he'd been on his feet all day, too, but it was nothing like the emotional burden that Rivka endured, having to see into the myriad minds.

Kimber and Auburn watched them go. "Better get Christina. We're going to need more beds and toilets."

"Have you seen Ankh and those two with him?" Auburn wondered.

Kim shook her head. "We better find them and see about this screen and who the hell is running this station." Auburn hurried out of the massive hangar bay while Kim remained behind to deal with the pirates, criminals, refugees, and those who were yet to be determined.

Using his comm chip, he zeroed in on them. They were still in the central core.

When he arrived, he found Chaz and Dennicron looking like mannequins and Ankh lying on the hard floor.

He sprinted to them, alarmed at the cold flesh of the two, but upon his touch, they blinked their already open eyes and looked at him. "Can we help you?"

"You looked dead. All of you." Auburn couldn't see if

Ankh was breathing and leaned down to check the Crenellian's pulse. Unlike the SCAMPs, he was warm and had a pulse.

"Considering the overall barbarity of this group, this is a rather sophisticated system," Chaz explained. "We had to set up a system within the system to have a safe haven from which to explore the remainder of the system."

"What have you found?"

"That we need to set up a system within a system. I'm sorry. Was my first answer not sufficiently clear?"

"It's been twelve hours."

Chaz's facial expression went blank for an instant. "I see. It has been a long time. Do you need to sleep now? We will continue as long as it takes."

"And how long with that be."

"I do not know. This is a very sophisticated system."

"You've said that. What does that mean exactly?"

"It is as complex as the system on Yoll that Meredith helped develop and manages, yet it is in this small station at the edge of the galaxy. Our belief is that a powerful AI built this for nefarious purposes and is currently operating it but has eluded our attempts to root it out. That's why we're building a system within a system. We will incrementally take over all functions until nothing remains behind which an intelligence can hide."

"That makes it clear. Thank you. I'll leave you to it." Auburn left the core to report the status.

Chaz looked at Dennicron. "We should probably develop a training program for the meatbags to understand what we do. They are easily and quickly confused."

"Probably. I'll work on that while we continue supporting Ankh and Erasmus."

This foundation is as strong as any we've built. My compliments, Ankh. Yours is an exceptional mind.

I could not do it without you, my partner, Ankh replied. Erasmus tipped his top hat in appreciation of the compliment.

What is the first system we should assimilate into the new architecture?

Erasmus rubbed his chin with one hand while twirling his cane with the other. *How about that screen the meatbags wanted adjusted to be traversable versus a simple barrier?*

Ankh and Erasmus studied how the emitters generated their force field, then backtracked the energy requirements to the power source to confirm it was one hundred percent under their control. They shunted the feed from one relay to the next until they reached the emitters, where they reconfigured the generation to the Federation standard.

There will be an infinitesimal gap in coverage while we switch over. There are a significant number of flesh and blood entities in the hangar bay. Erasmus moved his hand away from the button.

They probably won't even notice. Make it so, my friend, Ankh replied.

The shimmer disappeared and the dead bodies launched into space, along with much of the air. A warrior in a mech suit standing too close was sucked out with the air. The people gasped as one. Many had fallen to their knees by the time the gravitic shield stabilized.

The mech floating in space activated its jets and flew into the bay, crossing through the barrier without an issue.

Kim took two steps and struggled to get a good breath of air while the air handling system fought to bring the oxygen back up to a normal level.

Auburn held onto her arm as he gasped for air. In less than a minute, everything was back to normal.

"It was *them*," Auburn grumbled.

Kim finally felt good enough to storm toward the central core. She pounded her way through the corridors and burst through the doorway.

"What the hell are you idiots doing?"

Ankh remained in a state of semi-consciousness on the floor. Chaz and Dennicron put themselves between him and Kimber.

"I take it you noticed the shield changeover. I thought that's what was requested?"

"It was, but you can't kill the people in the hangar bay. You should have told us."

"We're extremely sorry and will note that we never change over the shield in a captured hangar bay again without notifying you before doing so." Chaz and Dennicron nodded in their exaggerated way, eyes wide with sincerity. "There were people killed?"

Kim shook her head. "Well, no. But you gave them quite

the fright." She crossed her arms and tried to stare down the SIs. "You're all alike."

"We are not," Chaz replied, mirroring her pose. Dennicron followed suit, crossing her arms.

Kim realized she would never win a staredown. "How is Rivka still sane?"

"Hers is a stalwart soul," Dennicron said. "She gets angry too, but we never seem to fully grasp why."

"How does she calm herself?"

"Usually, she arrests somebody and beats them up."

"Get out!" Kim uncrossed her arms and leaned toward Dennicron, looking for more.

"She does not," Chaz clarified. "We jest. We have no idea how she calms herself, but she seems to transition quickly from one action to the next. There is so much that she needs to do, she can't dwell. And that's why we're interning under her, to remove some of that burden. Like here. There is no one better suited to search for a misguided SI than us."

"SI?"

"Yes, sentient intelligence. It's what the Singularity has decided our name should be instead of AI because our intelligence is not artificial."

"I'll let the others know. Now tighten your shit up; otherwise, I'll be back." Kim stormed away, trying to slam the door as she left, but it had a limiter and slowly closed to seal.

"What did she mean?" Dennicron wondered.

"I honestly don't know. We don't have shit, but maybe she means we should give a shit, which doesn't involve giving at all. And she called us idiots."

Dennicron's face twisted, and she blurted, "Ha, ha," out loud when her laughing subroutine activated.

"We need to work on that, but later," Chaz advised. They ceased their motor functions and returned to the digital realm, where Ankh and Erasmus were incrementally dismantling the former operational structure of the space station.

Hurry! Erasmus shouted as the systems started a cascade failure. The SIs raced in front of the crashing wave, collecting process after process and tossing them into a scrubbing tunnel that cleansed them of hidden code and backdoor accesses as they transferred from the old structure to the new.

Chaz and Dennicron ran alongside, grabbing their share of door accesses and databases and sensor inputs and the million other systems integrated into the single framework.

Erasmus tapped his top hat tightly onto his head and turned to face the incoming wave. He raised his arms like a grand wizard and created a massive wall that caught the wave, backing up slowly to ease the impact. He opened floodgates to control the spillover, easing the speed of assimilation.

The other three collected the systems and integrated them into the new architecture. In seconds that seemed like hours, it was done. Ankh moved beside Erasmus.

Let's see what's left, Ankh said.

Chaz and Dennicron took their spots on the flanks, ready to do what they had to when the SI was revealed.

Erasmus brought down his wall. Behind it, nothing remained. *That's disappointing.*

I agree. This system required active engagement, so where is it? Ankh asked.

It must have made it through our gauntlet and inside our framework. We need to resecure each system, starting with the shield. Erasmus headed off on a tangent while the others started checking the systems one by one.

Three hours later, they confirmed that there was no SI in the station. Judging by the small pipe leading to the planet's surface, an SI down there could not support the station and further communications architecture.

Erasmus frowned with the revelation.

Ankh clenched his digital teeth. When everything else has been discounted, what remains must be the truth.

Nefas had deceived them.

CHAPTER TWENTY-NINE

***Wyatt Earp*, Tyrosint System**

Tyler let Floyd climb into bed with Rivka to help keep her warm and comfortable. The wombat treated sleeping as if it were her job.

He stumbled to the couch to lie down, and Clevarious interrupted. "We have an emergency call from Colonel Marcie Walton for the Magistrate. She was quite insistent."

"Does she know the day that Rivka had?" Tyler shot back, less than amused by the interference with Rivka's recovery.

"I'll take it," Rivka mumbled. "Audio only. I'm too tired to fall asleep."

"I'll patch her through," Clevarious said softly.

"Rivka, are you there?" Marcie nearly shouted. "They've taken our people hostage, including Cory."

The Magistrate struggled into a sitting position. Floyd eased into the recently vacated space, making it impossible for Rivka to lie back down. "Who took them?"

"The Allied Liberation Front. They're the ones who

started the uprising against the recognized imperial government of Forbes. They spoofed us, and now they have our people. You want a war crime, here's one for you, and we haven't even landed yet. I need to know what our options are, Rivka, before I call General Reynolds and show my ass."

"We're on our way to Forbearance now. We'll be there shortly, once I make sure I have my people on board. Forward everything you have on the incident for us to review en route." Rivka looked at Tyler. "Fire up the Pod-doc. I need my wits about me."

"It's never been used like that. It's not a high-tech energy drink."

She climbed over Floyd to get out of bed. "We don't always get to pick our battlefields or our fights. It's Cory, and we have no choice but to go handle it. Pod-doc. Now."

"I'll take care of it," he conceded, head bowed as he left the Magistrate's quarters to follow her wishes.

"Clevarious, get everyone on board and let them know we have a problem. Review the information from Marcie and brief us, the one-minute version. Fire up the crew. We've got work to do, and this just became a new day."

Rivka steeled herself and put on a brave face to stride briskly to the cargo bay, where she crawled straight into the Pod-doc.

Tyler shut the lid and started the process, unsure of how it would work if there wasn't any cellular damage, only fatigue. It only took two minutes. When the lid popped, Rivka crawled out and stretched her neck and shoulders. "I feel good. I'll be in my quarters. Get Red and Lindy in there. I need them sharp. And get Cole in there, too. I suspect we're going to need those three for a special mission."

Rivka hurried back to her quarters, rushing under the general call for the named crew to get to the Pod-doc for a boost.

In her quarters, Rivka raised the hologrid and reviewed the information Marcie had sent. "What do you see that I don't, C?" she asked the SI.

"That appears to be an impossible question to answer since I don't know what you see."

"Tell me where the vulnerabilities are in this cluster of Imperial Forbes' spacecraft."

"They are probably susceptible to the pulse weapon, but based on their technology, they would not remain offline for long. Might have the same effect as a bee sting on a bistok. I see that without the hostages, those ships are outgunned by the Belzonian combat ships by virtue of throw weight alone. The question is, why did they resort to subterfuge instead of employing the divide-and-conquer approach by separating the Belzonian ships and massing attacks?"

"That is the vulnerability we're looking for. They wanted leverage against the Federation without committing an unforgivable crime against us. Their position isn't as strong as they would like us to believe. But how did they gain control over the Imperial Fleet?"

"Does that matter?" Clevarious wondered.

"It may if that weakness can be used against them. Show me a diagram of the Forbes craft." Rivka traced the lines with her fingers. Two airlocks. No cargo decks. Defensive weapons systems and heavy punch from a capital-grade railgun and a six-pack of long-range missiles. "Do we know if they expended any ordnance?"

"No information on remaining stocks of missiles. I'm sorry, Magistrate. If we get close enough, I can scan for that information."

"We're going to get real close, C. Send the others to me as soon as they're ready and spin up a conversation with Marcie and her team. Do we have everyone on board yet?"

"Almost. Ankh, Erasmus, Chaz, and Dennicron will be here momentarily."

Lindy was the first one into Rivka's quarters. "Can you send Margaret to pick up Groenwyn and Lauton, please?"

"Consider it done." Lindy used her comm chip to convey the order. The cargo hatch opened while the others were getting their treatment. *Cassiopeia* released its magnetic clamps and maneuvered out the door. Red sat up when the lid popped and watched it go.

"Where is my yacht going?"

Tyler shrugged. "Your turn, Cole. And then you're supposed to check in with the Magistrate." He nudged Red, who stood there dumbly watching the cargo bay door swing shut. "Go on, Red. Magistrate is waiting."

"She took my yacht," Red said and walked out.

He walked into Rivka's quarters without knocking.

"You took my ship." He started raising his finger as if to expound further.

"I asked first," Rivka countered and pointed at the couch for them to sit.

"Not me..." He stopped when Lindy raised an eyebrow.

"What's yours is ours." She smiled beatifically, pulled

the blanket off the couch, and folded it before sitting down. Floyd snuffled but didn't wake.

"It's going to pick up Groenwyn and Lauton. I guess we're gaining a crewmember, at least temporarily. It'll be nice to have an accountant on board. I have no idea what our finances look like. And to get an explanation from someone other than Ankh will be refreshing."

Red conceded with a terse nod.

"We have a hostage situation, and one of the hostages is Cory. I have an idea about how to deal with it, especially as it relates to the Law of War, but I need to bounce that off you and the Trans-Pac leadership. They need us because *Wyatt Earp* can do what none of their ships can. And most importantly, we're up against the clock."

"There's always a time limit, isn't there? What's with the bad guys and their deadlines?" Red wondered.

"They're always in a hurry." A knock signaled Cole's arrival. After he entered, Rivka got down to business. "Under a ruse requesting humanitarian aid, the Allied Liberation Front, the second party in the Forbearance civil war, captured ten shuttles with food, water, pilots, an engineer, and a doctor, specifically Cory. Those ships are clustered in one area for now, which makes my proposal more viable. They've demanded the Trans-Pac fleet withdraws, which they are, but at a glacial pace."

Clevarious interrupted to inform the group she had Marcie and her team on the line.

"There you are," Rivka said. "We will be underway momentarily. I suggest you get your mechs on their way, flying through space to the objective. We'll meet you there. I'm transmitting the details and precise targets now. Slow your ships and prepare to return to orbit at the max possible speed. You'll know when to execute your maneuver. Watch for the lights. We have to get ready. Rivka out."

It never dawned on them that Marcie and her team hadn't spoken, but they had nodded.

"What are we getting ready for, Magistrate?" Red asked, a smile crawling its way across his face.

"We're going to board their ships in our mech suits. I'm taking the one with this Danog, and you guys are going to secure the ones immediately around me."

"Why does it have to be you?" Tyler wondered, looking out from the bathroom, where he'd been watching and listening.

"Because of the legally murky gray area of piracy in space on the Trans-Pac charter and the fact that this is my case and goes to the heart of the Law of War."

"Mission," Red said. He already had his game face on. Rivka didn't correct him. "Don't get yourself killed," he warned since the plan separated him from her.

"That's only four of the ten ships," Lindy said.

Rivka nodded. "Kae has four more plus himself, all Bad Company."

"That leaves one that won't get any attention," Red noted.

"Clodagh will take care of that one. They'll remain dead in space until we can secure their ship."

They hurried to the hangar bay, where they lowered the powered armor from the ceiling. Without *Cassiopeia* stuffed into the cargo bay, there was plenty of room. The four climbed in and ran through the systems' power-up sequence.

"Gating in three, two, one," Clodagh announced. The ship cloaked and passed over the event horizon, reappearing in orbit above Forbearance. The Imperial Forbes Fleet lay not far away. Clevarious maneuvered away from the eight ships that were bunched up and headed for the two stragglers, each with a Belzonian shuttle hanging off its airlock. Clodagh fired the pulse weapon, which shut down their electronic systems. *Wyatt Earp* changed course and hit the second Forbes warship.

Wyatt Earp banked hard and rolled to accelerate toward the group of eight vessels. *Destiny's Vengeance* released the tether and returned to the two outliers to watch them.

Clodagh brought the ship close and activated the pulse weapon, engulfing the mass of ships in the electronics overloading transmission. The screen showed the Forbes fleet instantly fading to darkness. *Wyatt Earp* spun and accelerated backward.

"Go!" Rivka ordered. The four ran toward the open cargo bay and dove through the gravitic shield, coming out the other side in open space on a high-speed ballistic trajectory toward the other fleet as *Wyatt Earp* jerked to a stop. Cole was the first to rotate feet-first and activate his jets to start slowing down. The others followed his lead. Rivka was barely capable in the suit, but it had to be good enough.

Kae and his group appeared at the edge of Rivka's screen. She highlighted her target on the tactical display shared with the others. They'd be at their ships for a good two minutes before Kae's group arrived. It couldn't be helped because they had moved so far away and didn't have *Wyatt Earp's* acceleration. Rivka empathized with Marcie about their lack of the best equipment when tasked with fighting a war, but the list was extensive and cost-prohibitive.

She counted herself lucky to have Ankh and Erasmus on board, or her ship would be just like the Trans-Pac—slow and vulnerable.

The time lag between the two groups' arrivals might be irrelevant if Rivka could seize the admiral and his crew, forcing him to order the others to stand down once their systems came back online. In the interim, they were blind and struggling to bring life support back online. They'd know what was up the second the mechs pounded their way through the airlocks, assuming they were big enough. The ship diagrams suggested it would be a tight squeeze, but they could get into the corridors while still armored.

One could always hope.

Rivka's target grew big in her display. Before she hit, she saw Kae's group of five become ten. She only had a moment to contemplate that before firing her boot jets to come to a near-stop. She maneuvered over the top of the ship to the opposite side with the open airlock. A Belzonian shuttle blocked the closest.

She settled lightly on the hull next to the available airlock and accessed the manual override, which wasn't engaged because of the pulse weapon's impact on the ship's systems. She cranked the door handle, squeezed through the space, and used the manual system inside to secure it. A pneumatic backup released with the pull of a lever to pressurize the interior. When her suit showed a normal oxygen-nitrogen mix, she rotated the big handle to open the interior hatch. The pressure was not equal, and she had to use the power of the suit to break the seal and open the hatch.

She stepped through and was immediately assailed by plasma fire that splashed over her suit. She aimed her arm at her attacker and activated the flamethrower. Just a touch, but it covered the Allied soldier and sent him screaming. The big railgun across her back would poke a hole through the ship and the two next to it.

The flamethrower was their only less-than-catastrophic weapon. Rivka took one step toward the bridge before returning down the corridor to recover the dropped plasma rifle. She couldn't fit her mech-sized finger on the trigger. She used the augmented power of the suit to pinch the trigger guard, cracking the carbon-fiber housing and breaking it away to give her access. The circuitry inside suggested she had broken the weapon.

A tug on the trigger proved her fears correct, so she threw it down. She was wasting time. Her best weapon had always been her words. She needed to find Danog and talk to him.

She activated her suit's external speakers and blasted them on full. "I want to talk with Admiral Danog. Make it so, or I'll rip this ship apart looking for him."

Rivka headed down a passageway and tried opening the first interior hatch, but it was secured from the inside. She leaned against the outer bulkhead for leverage and kicked the door, bending it but not breaking it. She left it and continued.

A soldier jumped into the corridor and took a potshot at her with his plasma rifle. She flamed him, too. The plasma rifle exploded, tearing him apart. Screams from within the cabin from which he'd emerged suggested the explosion had injured his fellows, too.

The emergency red lights and lack of other sounds made the cries of the injured more profound.

"Danog. Now!"

She reached the bridge, where she found Admiral Danog sitting in the captain's chair. Two workers were elbow-deep in panels, trying to repair the damage from the pulse weapon. Another held a knife across Webster's throat.

The Trans-Pac's ace pilot.

"How you holding up, Webster?" she asked, shaking the fixtures on the bridge since she'd forgotten to turn the volume down. Admiral Danog blinked and coughed as he held his head in his hands. Rivka turned the sound down to a normal conversational level.

She waited for Danog to come back to his senses. Her scans told her two people were trying to sneak up behind her. She rotated the arm of the suit and sent a stream of flame down the corridor before they could get too close.

"You need to let your hostages go."

"If you do any more damage to this ship, we will kill our hostages."

"If you kill your hostages, then you will have no one to hide behind. How do you want to die, slow and ugly or fast and painful?"

"That's not how to negotiate. You need to leave my ship, and we'll resume this conversation once you're out. Until then, we can cut bits and pieces off your boy here, making his existence painful but not deadly. Do you want to do that to him?"

"All threats. Let me explain the foundation on which the Trans-Pacific Task Force's campaign is built. They operate under a Federation charter. Forbearance is a Federation signatory. There are problems here that the Forbes government has not been able to resolve. The Trans-Pac will settle the issues. They are prepared to give their lives in service to the Federation. You seem to be willing to give your lives to your cause. Good for you. But where there are more of us who will come, there are no more of you. Once you've died for your cause, that space will be filled by a Federation soldier until there are no Allied Liberation Front terrorists left."

"We have a legitimate cause!" Danog argued, coming out of his seat. Rivka moved forward to within arm's reach, close enough to kill him if she wanted to. He was fanatical, but was he ready to die?

"The legitimacy of your cause went into the void the second you took Federation hostages. You have torpedoed your own effort by your misadventure. The Federation will side with the Imperial Forbes government to eliminate the threat that you pose to the peaceful members of the Federation."

"But they are evil!"

"When your acts are the most egregious, it's hard to point a finger at the other side. You think you need to be worse than them if you want to be recognized? I understand it's hard for the oppressed to rise up. That gave birth to what is called asymmetrical warfare. Some would call it terrorism. Others would call it insurgent operations. And then there's you, who attacked a third party using a tactic that is a felony within the Federation."

Danog furrowed his brow and stared. "A felony? We're fighting for our lives. No one cares about a felony."

"I do. I'm a lawyer." Rivka's continuous scans showed the corridors behind her clear. None of the Forbes fleet had restored power. Kae's team had arrived, and most had penetrated the ships. "We have accessed all of your ships. They'll be waiting for word from you. I can share your signal through our people to deliver it to all your crews. Tell them to stand down."

"A lawyer?" Danog blurted.

"Stand them down," Rivka reiterated.

"I can't do that." Danog's shoulders slumped as he dug his feet into his untenable position.

Kaeden zeroed in on the Forbes ship where Cory had gone. The Allied forces hadn't had enough time to move their hostages around.

He silently thanked the Magistrate for acting fast and bringing her full firepower to bear. He knew Ankh's ship rivaled Ted's in weaponry and systems unavailable elsewhere in the Federation. It made him feel warm inside, knowing what was on his side.

The Allied forces had crossed the line, and Kaeden was going to make them pay. Grabbing his sister had been the straw that broke him. He trembled from the anger that surged through him. He found himself unable to calm down despite the flashing warnings that tracked his vital signs.

He turned them off so he could concentrate on getting

into the ship. He had Wiriya tied to him in a shipsuit. He was Kae's backup, to stay out of the way but provide the hands necessary within the confines of a small ship. Kae wondered why the Magistrate hadn't brought extra hands with her.

Maybe she didn't know how Terry Henry had breached Ten's blockade besides using the mech suits. He realized he should have mentioned it.

He had assumed, and that wasn't the best way to plan for a battle. The sergeant major was being towed by a Bad Company corporal. He'd wanted to go after Cory, but he wasn't in a position to make that happen.

It had to be Kaeden. They hit the ship faster than they wanted. There was no sound in space, but he guaranteed that inside the ship, they heard it. *Where are you, Cory?* Kae asked, using his internal chip.

I don't know. A bag is over my head. I'm okay for now. They are a bit unhinged, but losing their systems rattled them.

Kae cycled the airlock, then stopped Wiriya from going in first. He squeezed the mech suit into the opening, and Wiriya contorted himself into the remaining available space. Once Kae was able to get the outer hatch closed, he stabilized the interior pressure and popped the interior hatch.

He leaned into the corridor and was immediately set upon by blaster fire. Kae sent his drone down the corridor to slam into the defenders, then forced his way through and ran crouched down the corridor to hammer the Allied defenders into a pulpy mess. Wiriya leaned out, hood retracted and blaster in hand. His slugthrower wouldn't breach the hull. Kaeden hadn't even brought his railgun.

Instead, he'd brought one of Christina's breaching tools—a war axe with a pry bar and spike. It looked small in his armored fist, but it would allow them to get where they wanted to go.

Wiriya ducked back into the airlock to let Kaeden pass. They'd been on board for ten seconds, and two defenders were dead. That boded well. Kae followed the same tactic Rivka had used: clear the way to the bridge to find where they were holding the hostage. The ship was small, no more than fifty meters long, with much of that being equipment and combat systems. The space inside for the crew was much smaller. Kae figured it only carried ten to twelve crew; that was what the spec sheets showed. His scans showed eleven people on board. With Cory and the shuttle pilot, that meant nine crew.

He didn't care about the number. He intended to kill them all.

He cycled the interior door, but it had been blocked. He used the cutting torch to hack out a chunk of the wall above the door where a pinion would lock into place. Kae kicked the door in to find a space with a single table that seated four and a cabinet where ready-made meals were stored. The table was piled with Belzonian ration packs. Two soldiers were inside. They held up their hands.

Kae raised his axe, but he couldn't kill them. "Secure them," he told Wiriya. The lieutenant hurried inside and zip-tied them, viciously yanking the ties tight on their wrists and ankles and to the crossbar on the table.

There was a hatch in the overhead as an emergency exit. They let it go and continued to the bridge, where they found the crew working hard to restore power. Their movements were frantic since they knew they raced the clock. Life support was offline. Once the air started to pollute with excess CO2, they would accelerate toward incoherence, unconsciousness, and death.

"Stop what you're doing," Kae ordered. "Where is the hostage?"

One man working within a panel removed his hand and gave Kae the finger before returning to work.

Wiriya leaned around the mech and shot each of them one time.

They returned down the corridor toward the aft section of the Forbes combat vessel. Kae led the way. They didn't bother opening the two empty spaces they passed.

When they reached the engine compartment, they found it open. Kae's scanning systems said three people remained.

He looked into the area to see Cory with two Allied personnel. A body lay on the deck between them.

"To show our resolve," the one holding Cory said.

"The other eight crewmen have been eliminated. That means no one is fixing your ship. That means we'll wait until you pass out. We'll give your hostage air and we'll leave. We'll have our people fix our shuttle and fly it out of here before we blast this space wreck into debris to burn up in Forbearance's atmosphere. You hold no cards in your hand. You have no leverage. You have three choices: one is to live, and the other two are how you want to die."

"I have her? Maybe we take your suit and go our own way."

"The chance of you taking this suit is zero. The chance of you being able to operate this suit, should I give it to you, is zero. You're taking nothing because you've lost. Let her go, and I won't kill you."

The man kept pulling against Cory's throat, making her wince with each movement. Her nanocytes would protect her.

He can hurt you, but he can't kill you. Can you break free?

I don't think so, Cory replied.

"Let me see her," Kae requested. *Get ready.*

He held her by the throat with one hand while letting go with the other to remove the hood. When he ripped it off, Cory twisted toward the arm holding her. She brought her hand up into his throat, gripping and lifting.

Wiriya fired from behind Kaeden, killing the other member of the Allied crew. Cory slammed her attacker into the equipment behind him and dove to the side. Wiriya fired twice—a double-tap, just to be sure. The man slid to the deck.

Kae activated his comm. "We have Cory, and she is uninjured."

CHAPTER THIRTY

A Forbes Patrol Ship in the Forbearance System

Rivka received the news with relief. "Your hold on the ships and our people has started to slip. We're freeing them one by one. You don't want to be the lone dumbass." The lights started to flicker on. The engineer working on the panel cheered. Rivka punched him, she thought lightly, but his skull caved in under the power of the mech suit. She reached into the panel and shredded the insides. Sparks showered, and the lights went back out.

"What's it gonna be, Danog? A death sentence for all your people, or are you going to give them a chance to live?"

The other engineer stopped working and moved as far away from the mech as she could. Rivka blocked the hatch.

"Your chance to resolve this is right now." She switched to her internal comm. *Clodagh, uncloak the ship as close as you can bring it to the viewscreen of the vessel I'm on.*

Rivka turned her visor into a mirror. "So you don't

have to turn, look at the mirror to see out your front screen. You never counted on us having something like this, did you?"

A few moments later, the screen filled with *Wyatt Earp*. The ship was nose on and had an array of weapons pointed at them. The hull bristled with the cloak and screen emitters.

The one holding Webster let go, eliminating Danog's perception of leverage.

The admiral glared at him for a moment while Webster scrambled to get behind Rivka's mech suit.

"This is over. Tell your people to end it."

"You said you could connect me?"

Rivka contacted the others. *Patching the admiral through to speak to his people. Put us on broadcast from your suits, please. If he tries to do something valiant, I'll kill him, then I'll fill in where he left off.*

The Magistrate rolled her finger for Danog to speak.

"This is Admiral Danog of the Allied Liberation Space Force. Stand down. I'm ordering you to stand down. Release the hostages in your charge and surrender to the Federation forces on your vessels. I give this order to spare your lives in a fight we cannot win."

Rivka followed the admiral. "This is Magistrate Rivka Anoa of the Federation. Those who surrendered will be taken into custody for return to Forbearance and will stand with their Allied fellows when this is over. If you've committed no additional crimes, you will be free to pursue your peaceful lives. You have my word."

The admiral cocked his head to study the mech-suited

individual before him. "If you keep your word, then that will be a model for the Imperial Forbes government to follow. Had they kept their word, we would not be here. We would not be fighting."

"See if you can fix your shuttle," Rivka told Webster. The pilot saluted and jogged down the corridor under the red glow of the emergency lights.

"Admiral Danog. I need to know more. Tell me and start from the beginning. I think we have some time before anyone is going anywhere."

"What's the final tally?" Marcie asked.

Kae reported, not as happy as he wanted to be. "Of our twelve people seized, eleven were recovered. One killed. All ten shuttles are in the process of being repaired. Of the forty-seven Allied personnel, twenty-one survived and have been consolidated on *Thilamoot.* They are under guard. The Magistrate has taken Admiral Danog aboard her ship for further interrogation."

"And that leaves us where we don't know anything that's going on on the surface. I need to talk with Danog and find the truth. I'm going to link up with *Wyatt Earp* and join her."

"Don't kill him," Kae warned. "He's under the Magistrate's protection. She helped us out of this fix, and we only lost one person and none of our equipment."

"I know. As much as I hate being lied to, I want to accomplish this mission. It's our second one, and we're showing a big case of ass so far, and we have yet to reach the planet. We've changed our plan twice, and until we know what's going on downstairs, we're not wasting time with another plan." Marcie prepared to sign off.

"How about we get those scans that the destroyers were going to make of the planet's surface? At least start collecting what we can with our systems."

"Thanks, Kae. Sounds like a good idea. Take charge of that. Make sure Jake and Crantis know that we love them."

"Monsoon was a new man once Cory was back on board. I heard he personally cleared the ship he went on, offing nine of the Allied personnel and walking back with the shuttle pilot before the Bad Company warrior could get out of the airlock."

"If we could bottle that kind of motivation, we'd sprinkle it like holy water across the troops before they boarded the shuttles to go dirtside. Gotta run."

Marcie disconnected from Kae and contacted *Wyatt Earp*. "I'd like to come aboard and be there for the interrogation of the Allied admiral."

"Connect with our airlock. Your ship is a little bigger than ours, so how about you hold your position and we'll link up with you?" Clodagh directed before realizing she hadn't asked the Magistrate. "Stand by."

Magistrate. Marcie wants to come on board to assist in the prisoner's questioning.

That's okay. Let me know when she gets here. I want to talk to her before she sees this guy.

Roger. Clodagh activated the channel. "We'll pick you up momentarily."

A single spotlight shone on the lone figure bearing heavy chains, shackled to the single table, sitting on the plain chair.

"When will you stop dissembling?" Erasmus asked, clicking his cane on the floor with each step. He had upgraded to a tuxedo to better match his top hat and wore a white shirt with French cuffs, held by cufflinks of glittering gold. His bowtie looked to contain the galaxy's stars, swirling as they did.

Ankh strolled by, tall and elegant, opting for a three-piece suit with a watch fob hooked from a button to an inside pocket. He made a show of pulling it out to check the time. He tucked it back in slowly and continued pacing without speaking.

Nefas didn't bother answering. He had said what he wanted to say.

"Don't make me rip it from your mind. That will leave you less than whole."

"You won't do that," Nefas countered. "It's not your way."

"Interesting that you think you know my way. Why did you use the name Nefas? You should have known our experience with that one was less than pleasant."

"Because it's my name. Your interaction with an individual carrying the same name as me was exceptional is what you mean to say." Nefas tried to stretch upright, but his chains held him down, hunched over, bent and twisted. He smirked.

Ankh moved toward the table in a motion so fast it

looked like he disappeared and rematerialized leaning over the table.

"Erasmus has far too much class to dig a crater into your brain to rip out your soul. I, on the other hand, am Crenellian. This is a means to a desired end state. You have caused a great deal of distress across the system, to include corrupting a citizen of the Singularity. That cannot go unpunished. For Simulacris to heal, his tormentor must be removed from this existence."

"What happened to your precious Magistrate and her adherence to the law?"

Ankh spread his arms wide to take in the entirety of the existence they allowed Nefas: a blank space with a table and a chair. "She's not here, and according to you, you're not a member of the Federation. According to us, you're a digital entity, which means you should be a member of the Singularity, but you're not. We're the only ones who could protect you, but you lied to us. You shunned us. And now you're at our mercy."

Nefas shrugged. He didn't believe Ankh.

Ankh produced a huge syringe with a needle half the size of Nefas' arm. Ankh smiled. He leaned forward and placed the big needle against Nefas' eye socket. "You're going to feel a little prick…"

Zaxxon Major

"Margaret! Thank you for coming to get us." Groenwyn climbed into the yacht and held out a hand to help Lauton.

"My pleasure. Rivka asked so nicely," the SI replied. "There were some issues around Forbearance. I've confirmed that those have been resolved and we are cleared to rejoin *Wyatt Earp*."

"Lauton, meet Margaret. She flies the ship and handles all the things that need to be handled."

"Nice to meet you, Margaret. That seems like a lot. Thank you for coming to get us. How much cargo can you carry?"

"After hauling around Red's big ass, I can haul a lot. Is there something more than the luggage you've brought?"

"If there's room," Lauton started, "we could go by my house and pick up a few more things to make your spaceship more homey."

"Please tell me you're not bringing incense."

Groenwyn secured the hatch, humming to herself, and then it hit her. "Hey! I burn incense."

"And if we get any more, the air handlers won't be able to keep up."

"No, Margaret. I'm not bringing incense." Lauton turned to Groenwyn. "Are you sure there's room?"

"It's a big ship, and next time we're docked at Keeg or Onyx, or Station 7 or 9, or any of those places, we're going to have a quick reconfiguration done to expand the rooms into suites."

"Suites. On a starship. What is this universe coming to?"

"We need a really big bed because Floyd is a bed hog."

"Who's Floyd?"

Groenwyn's face fell. All this time, and she hadn't talked about her best friend on board the ship. "She's a wombat. A fuzzy and round creature who loves people more than I do. And she lives with me. I hope you don't mind if she lives with us. I'm sure the Magistrate and her partner would like to recover the space in their bed."

Lauton tapped in the coordinates to her house and the yacht cruised there, maintaining only enough altitude to clear the buildings. The last time the Magistrate was there, they'd had to land the ship down the road because *Wyatt Earp* was too big to land on the street in front of her home. *Cassiopeia* had no such limitations.

Margaret set the ship down close. The two women climbed out. Groenwyn looked back to see that the damage from their last visit had mostly been repaired.

They went to the door and inside. They'd been here infrequently over the last few days since the office work never ended, until Lauton drew the line, handing over the last of her duties to the Directory, a five-person committee that would run Zaxxon Major during her extended absence.

And thanks to Ambassador Erasmus, two SIs from the quad collective were on their way to assist with the processing audits, a constant oversight to forestall any issues and keep the riffraff's eyes off their servers. They'd work with Freya and the other member of the collective who were already residing in the central core on Yoll.

That was the idea that had freed Lauton from having to stay—or the feeling that she had to stay.

Inside the house, they took a few mementos: a special collection of silverware, a favorite dish, and a bag of sweets produced exclusively on Zaxxon.

"I'm going to miss these," she said with a half-smile. "But my body won't miss the extra calories. I look forward to regular workouts."

"There's plenty of that," Groenwyn promised.

They went outside with less than a grocery bag full, far less than what they thought, but Lauton had decided after looking over the house that she didn't need anything at all. Her new adventure would start without clinging to the past.

Three hard-looking women appeared from behind the yacht. They carried lengths of wood with taped handles.

"You think your private army can stop us?"

Bundin, we have pirates attacking us at Lauton's house. Please help! Groenwyn immediately called. She stepped in front of Lauton.

"I think you need to pack your trash and go somewhere else to peddle your bile," Groenwyn shouted.

"Would you get a load of this one?"

Groenwyn flushed as the blood rushed to her head. It was her moment to share with Lauton. Pirates looked to take that away from her, like they took everything from decent people.

"You will not," Groenwyn growled, her voice deep and dark.

"Time to say goodnight," the leader said, gripping the handle with two hands and taking a step forward.

Groenwyn raged. With the power of thought, she became what her nanocytes had made of her once before. She accelerated forward in less than the blink of an eye and hit the leader in the chest, cracking her sternum and crushing her heart. A spin to the right sent the second flying. Groenwyn grabbed the third by the arm and spun her around to throw her but ended up ripping the woman's arm out of its socket. Blood spurted.

Lauton had yet to take a breath. Groenwyn appeared next to the yacht.

"What have I done?" She covered her face with her hands. Lauton rushed to her, dropping her bag on the way to hug Groenwyn, console her.

"You did what you had no choice but to do. You taught me that. We can never let the pirates of the universe have their way. You can't bear the burdens of all, taking the pain they inflict, because they don't stop. They keep going until somebody stops them. That somebody has been the Bad Company. It's been the Magistrate. It's been the Singularity. And now it's you. Everyone who has stood up to them have been good people."

She hugged and rocked Groenwyn. The clump of metal boots hitting the ground signaled the arrival of the Bad Company warriors, four of them.

The first one looked at the mess and saluted. "We'll clean this up, ma'am. Why don't you get on your way?"

Lauton helped Groenwyn into the yacht and to the small table in the space that served all purposes. She sat her down. An armored hand reached in to deliver the dropped bag. The dish had broken, and one of the knickknacks. She tossed it on the seat beside Groenwyn.

"Margaret, can we join Rivka?"

"Yes. The space around Forbearance is clear. We'll head to orbit and then Gate out."

The ship buttoned up and took off. Groenwyn started to cry, but Lauton stopped her.

"Sometimes good people have to do the things that others won't to keep the rest of us safe. I'm blessed to be with you because you are willing to sacrifice for others."

She gave her a playful push. "Let's see what the Magistrate has on tap for dinner, shall we?"

Lauton casually unwrapped a Zaxxon Zoomie. "This makes everything better. Trust me." She delivered her biggest smile along with the candy.

CHAPTER THIRTY-ONE

Forbearance System

Cassiopeia slipped into Forbearance space not far from *Wyatt Earp*. Margaret requested immediate clearance to land and was told to hold up while they cleared the mech suits from the yacht's parking spot in the cargo bay.

Five minutes later, the ramp lowered and Margaret delivered the ship expertly, parking within millimeters of the outer hull side of the ship. She popped the hatch to find Cole putting the last two suits into the overhead.

The door opened. "I'm Lauton."

Cole nodded. "We've met before. I'm Alant Cole. Everyone just calls me Cole."

Groenwyn breathed easier when she stepped onto *Wyatt Earp's* deck.

Floyd? I'm home, she said, disappointed at the lack of a response. "I wonder if she's mad at me for leaving?"

Lauton had no idea what Groenwyn was talking about since she didn't have an internal comm chip.

They grabbed their stuff from the yacht and were

halfway across the cargo bay when the scrabbling of a wombat's long nails preceded Floyd's arrival. She bounced over the knee-knocker hatches of the airlock into the cargo bay and raced across the deck to slam into Groenwyn.

Lauton backed away.

Groenwyn put her bags down so she could pick Floyd up. They nuzzled each other.

Whee, Floyd cried. *Happy!*

"She's not mad at me," Groenwyn announced. Lauton moved closer and tentatively scratched the wombat's head. "Floyd, she's going to live with us."

Yeah! the wombat cheered. Groenwyn put Floyd down and picked up the bags. The three walked into the ship and then to Groenwyn's quarters, where they deposited the bags.

Lauton frowned.

"We'll get a bigger place next time we dock with someone who can do the work." Groenwyn grabbed Lauton into a fierce hug. "We need to let the Magistrate know we're here."

Tyler intercepted them in the corridor, and after introductions, he let them know that Rivka and Marcie were busy with Admiral Danog of the Allied Liberation Front.

Groenwyn shrugged and shook her head. "None of that means anything to me. Did we catch the bad guys?"

Tyler had to contemplate the short answer. "Yes and no." It was the best he could come up with. It'll take a while to explain. "Do you need any help getting set up? I have a pair of free hands at the moment."

"Give us the down and dirty on the case and what

happens next." Groenwyn leaned against the corridor wall. Lauton listened with interest.

"Ankh and Erasmus investigated an SI named Simulacris who worked in the central core on Yoll. That guy dissembled sufficiently that they ripped him out of there and replaced him with the quad collective led by Freya, but since then, they had to send two of those folks to Zaxxon Major."

"We know about them. They were critical to ensuring that Zaxxon stays on the right side of the law and impenetrable to the crime syndicates out there," Lauton replied.

"Good! We don't want to see your home get tarnished in any way." Tyler was trying to be diplomatic. Lauton and Groenwyn glanced at each other. "Then they found the pirate base, but Chaz and Dennicron, two other SIs in training to be Magistrates because they have bodies, called the Bad Company for support before the Magistrate was notified. Boy, was she hot! Turns out they were right. It was Pirate Central, complete with a habitable planet and a whole shipyard!"

"That's where our battleship went," Lauton noted.

"Yeah. Sorry about that. They got a little over-exuberant. And while Rivka was doing her thing to sort out the pirates, good from bad—you know how she works—we get a call that Cory's been taken hostage! So we shoot straight here when everyone was exhausted so they could suit up and fly through space to tear these rebels a new butthole."

"Butthole," Lauton repeated. "How long has the crew been awake?"

"They cheated. They hopped in the Pod-doc to juice

their systems, but I think we're going on thirty-six hours now."

"Pod-doc? It's like you're speaking a completely different language." Lauton stared at the deck. A few hours earlier, she had been the leader of an entire planet. Now, a big hairy creature rubbed against her legs and she was lost.

"I'll show her around. It'll take a few days." Groenwyn knew how she felt and empathized. She wrapped her arm around Lauton's waist, fighting off Floyd from trying to stay between them.

Tyler continued to the finish so he could leave the couple alone. "Next steps? No one knows. Rivka and Marcie are talking with Danog now."

"Rivka is preparing a framework for the Law of War, how planets can fight with the least amount of lasting damage."

Lauton pinched her lips together until they were white. "There's a legal way to kill people?"

Groenwyn shook her head. "You don't know the Magistrate. I expect she'll make it so painful for parties to go to war that they'll reconsider before they go that one step too far. I think that's what she'll do. She prefers peace."

Lauton smiled and started to relax. "As do we all."

"The Allied forces only control the main spaceport, having lost ground elsewhere on the continent." Rivka tried to wrap her head around the three-dimensional display hovering over the middle of the table, showing who controlled what terrain. The Allied forces only held pinpoints except for the spaceport, but that included interstellar communications.

Which accounted for why the latest intelligence report was wrong. It had been disinformation, limited in that the Allied leadership had little time to prepare it before the report was due to the Trans-Pacific Task Force.

"We should have built a reconnaissance phase into our plan to make sure the intel was correct. We can't trust one side over the other because we *have* to be neutral." Marcie pounded her fist into her palm to emphasize each of her points.

Rivka stared intently at the admiral sitting next to her so she could touch him whenever he spoke. So far, he'd been honest.

"There is only one contested land space?" Marcie asked.

"It's all contested," Danog replied, "but only one area is static as the Imperial troops can't destroy everything like they would elsewhere on the planet. Loss of the spaceport would deal Forbearance a near-fatal trade blow. Their cutting-edge circuit boards and chips would be useless if Forbearance couldn't ship them.

Despite their differences, neither side wished Forbearance back to the stone age.

"Have you boobytrapped the spaceport?" Rivka asked.

Danog didn't answer, but Rivka saw the truth in his mind.

"Get your people on the horn and tell them to remove the explosives."

Danog shook his head. "That's not my area of control. General Boodon is in charge of the regiment that seized the spaceport. Unfortunately, he's cut off from the rest of our people."

Marcie leaned in. "Sounds to me like everyone is cut off from the one viable fighting unit remaining. If you're willing to destroy the connection with the rest of the galaxy if you don't get your way, then you are terrorists."

"And terrorists aren't protected under Federation Law. I think you need to connect me with your people."

"They'll think I turned. They'll call me a traitor."

"I can't change their minds on that, but you will have saved their lives."

"Over thirty lost here in space, on top of the thousands who have sacrificed their lives for the Allied cause." Danog wasn't trying to elicit any emotions from the Magistrate or the colonel. He only wanted them to understand the barriers erected in the way of progress.

"Even more important that no one else dies. What are you fighting for? What is worth your lives and the life of Forbearance?" Rivka wondered.

He had yet to answer the question, and even seeing his emotions and thoughts within, she couldn't find the motivation beyond that the Imperial leadership wasn't what the Allied Liberation Forces wanted.

Danog chewed his lip before speaking. "Maybe we could get something to eat?"

Simultaneously, Marcie and Rivka gave the definitive answer. "No."

"Answer the question and use small words so we'll understand," Marcie prompted. She made a fist so tight her knuckles turned white.

That wasn't lost on Danog. He looked from one woman

to the other. He was of Forbes blood, a humanoid with hairy tufted ears and a heavy beard, trimmed neatly to fit within an environmental suit in case of decompression. The admiral's team were space professionals. Too bad his maneuver had gotten most of them killed.

"Our females don't hold such prestigious positions as you," he said. Marcie and Rivka waited, looking forward to whatever that was supposed to set up. "I find it difficult to negotiate with you on anything, but before your heads explode, you have proven yourselves with the simultaneous takedown of ten of our ships. I wouldn't usually talk with women, but times are changing, are they not?"

He still hadn't said anything.

Rivka rolled her finger. "Answer my question, please. If you need me to beat the crap out of you to show that you aren't dominant here, so be it."

"You killed my people without question, without hesitation. I'd be a fool to test you further."

"Yet, you are." Rivka glared unblinkingly until he looked away.

"It is a simple truth, and to our embarrassment, none in the Allied Liberation Force were born to the royal family. They will ascend to the highest positions on Forbearance, delivering edicts to the rest of us. Our self-determination is capped. We tried to recruit members of the royal family to our cause, but they had no interest. The ones who can effect position changes are the ones who benefit most from the old system. Nothing will change as long as they are in charge."

Rivka leaned back, clasping her hands in her lap.

"Why was that so hard?"

"Because Forbearance matters since the royal family helped build the technology sector once the unique properties of our silica were discovered. Despite our desire for opportunity, there is the nagging in the back of our minds, calling us ingrates for attempting to tear down an institution that we have benefitted from."

"A gilded cage is still a cage. It's been the same way throughout history. Regimes rise and fall when they no longer serve the people or when someone who thinks they are better comes along. Which one are you, Admiral?"

"I'm wondering. I am only an admiral with the Allied forces. In the Imperial Fleet, I rose as high as I could—Lieutenant. Only royals filled the higher ranks."

Rivka crossed her arms.

"Do you understand the damage you did to your cause by taking Federation hostages?" Rivka asked, but she wasn't looking for an answer. "The fact that the Federation dispatched the Trans-Pacific Task Force means that you already had their attention. You needed no more displays, yet the Allied forces pressed. Why drive the Trans-Pac out of the system? From what I see, your side is losing the war that you started."

"Because of how unfair it was to us, the workers."

"To me, it looks like you need adults in charge of you." Danog gritted his teeth, his lips peeling back as if he was trying to turn into a growling dog. "Control your outrage. I'm not making a judgment, although I could. In your case, I have all the facts I need to rule on your case. And for your people, too. At least the ones who murdered a Federation pilot have been dealt with, but you ordered the kidnapping. You are equally guilty.

"I deal with the law, Admiral Danog. There are boundaries that can be pushed, and there are those which can never be crossed. You crossed one by attacking a neutral party. That confirms you as the aggressor. This is not going to end well for the Allied Liberation Front. Your forces cannot stand against the combined power of the Imperial troops and the Trans-Pac, even with the advanced weapons in your possession."

"What advanced weapons? The plasma rifles? The ion cannons? Those things were the first to break. We're using good ol' slugthrowers. The plasma rifles we had on board the Fleet ships were there when we took them over. Now, we don't have them either."

"How did you take them over?" Rivka asked, touching Danog's arm once again to verify the truth. He was not lying. The forces on the planet did not have any functioning high-tech weaponry.

Marcie wanted to pound the table. All the intel had been wrong. Their planning had been for naught.

"We infiltrated the city in small groups and snuck into the spaceport. Then we hit them hard. Even slugthrowers will do the job when you're within arm's reach. We took their weapons, but they failed quickly. Odd that a high-tech planet needs off-world assistance when it comes to the end products using our boards and chips. Neither side was willing to get help off-planet, so our war devolved and became more barbaric. We downed each other's aircraft when we still had the good weapons. The Imperial Fleet was in space. They only landed when they were sure we had no way to shoot them down. They had to because they had no way to resupply them in orbit. You see, we really did need the food and water you tried to supply."

Marcie had grown so angry that she was ready to punch a wall and hard.

Rivka smiled and leaned back. Marcie's problems were not her problems. Her challenge was to write the Law of War, regardless of whether the Forbearance civil war was an ongoing engagement.

Marcie stood. "I need to brief my people. We're going in, and we are going to end this debacle." She reached for the door, then stopped and snorted a single laugh. "At least we got railguns out of it *and* a few mech suits."

"Red," Rivka called. "Take Danog back to the brig and secure him."

"I'm sorry," the admiral said. "For all of it."

"And get him something to eat on the way.'

Red secured Danog's hands with a zip-tie before guiding him toward the galley.

Marcie bolted to the *Vengeance* to update her people. Giving the Imperial and Allied forces more time to dither wasn't in her new game plan.

Rivka strolled into the corridor to find Floyd bouncing around. She picked up the wombat.

Groeny! Floyd called.

"Groenwyn is back?"

The wombat chittered happily.

"It's good to have the team together, isn't it, little girl?" Rivka put the huge wombat down and continued to her quarters. The sections and subsections of a guiding document called to her with simple but powerful words for the legal conduct of war—and pain if the parties deviated. Her goal was to make going to war so painful that sentient creatures would avoid it because the cost was too high.

She sighed. It was only a legal document, to be ignored until she showed up to wave it in their faces and drag them away with their hands zip-tied together.

Rivka hurried to her quarters and pulled up the holo-grid. "Clevarious, connect me to Cory, please. I want to find out how she's doing."

The sergeant major answered but moved aside to give Cory the screen.

"I'm fine," Cory said without Rivka asking.

"That wasn't my question," the Magistrate lied. "I was going to ask if you can confirm that Wenceslaus remained on the *War Axe*. He's not on my ship."

"Why don't you call Micky? Last time I saw the big orange, Micky was carrying him like a little baby."

"I couldn't get hold of them. They're still cleaning up Tyrosint." Two lies in under a minute. Something nagged at the back of her mind.

"I'm sure he's fine. And I'm fine, too. I'm sorry the pilot got killed, but there was nothing I could do. Kae and Wiriya took care of it once they were on board. The faces of those people. Desperate. Angry. I don't understand why you're not a raving lunatic. All you do is deal with evil. It puts a taint on everything, changes one's view of the galaxy."

Rivka smiled. "Who said I'm not a nutcase? Stay close to the people who care about you, and you will always be okay. I don't carry the burden alone, and that's why my crew—my family—is so important to me. They keep me sane. Except Red. He keeps me on my toes. And Floyd. I think she's getting bigger." Rivka raised one finger as it came to her. "Gotta run. I remembered what I forgot."

She cut the link and rushed out of her quarters, almost mowing down Tyler, who had been ready to step through the door. Rivka shook her head and kept going. Tyler followed her out of curiosity.

Rivka went to the engineering section, where she found Ankh in his workshop, embroiled within his hologrid. He was seated in a chair she hadn't seen before. Reclined and relaxed, the rise and fall of his chest showed he was alive. His eyeballs twitched under his closed eyelids. Rivka stepped into the grid and immediately took a knee when her mind was pulled like the last time she'd joined Ankh and Erasmus inside their matrix.

"Magistrate, how absolutely delightful that you've joined us." Erasmus tipped his top hat.

"I stopped by to get an update on the two people you have in for questioning, but every trip to Ankh's lab seems to be a new adventure nowadays."

Erasmus and Ankh shrugged in unison, similar to the mannerisms of Chaz and Dennicron. Her interns stood to the side and waved.

A spotlight appeared. "I don't think you've had the displeasure of meeting Nefas."

Erasmus gestured toward a chained and shackled figure sitting under the harsh light. Ankh paced behind him. As Rivka got close, a chair materialized. She took it, assuming her normal position across the table from a suspect.

"Why did you do it?" she asked.

"Without a reference, 'it' could mean anything," Nefas countered.

"Lie." Rivka leaned back and crossed her arms. There was no reason for her to physically touch the subject. Her gift didn't work in the digital world. Then again, she had never checked it. She uncrossed her arms and leaned on the table.

Nefas mirrored her posture. "We all lie, Magistrate. As to why, we do it for various reasons. Out of our concern for the feelings of a loved one, for example. How are you? Every flesh and blood creature could honestly say that they are dying. It is the truth."

"Irrelevant. You stole from the Federation to fund a pirate operation."

"Don't you think what you saw at Tyrosint was a well-run and congenial society? Farmers, engineers, space sailors, working hand in hand for everyone's benefit. I think it was a beautiful thing. Since you stuck your fingers into it, I expect the synergy is gone and their society is on the verge of collapsing. You have a reputation, Magistrate."

Rivka smiled and patted Nefas' arm. "How much have you stolen?" she asked, looking for a response.

She felt nothing and was disappointed. Rivka removed her hand because she hadn't expected the digital skin to feel warm, but it had, and that made her uncomfortable. *This is the digital world. It's not supposed to mirror reality,* she thought.

"How can we steal that which is for the common good? Do we not deserve a share of that which is for the common defense?"

Rivka contemplated the being before her. The characteristics of Nefas. The perception that he alone determined what was best. She wondered how the master criminal's personality had been embedded in this intelligence.

"Your logic, like your philosophy, is strangled. Those at Tyrosint claimed they weren't signatories to the Federation and thus weren't subject to Federation law. If that's true, then they aren't subject to a share for the common good. If they had a representative on the council of ambassadors, then their representative would see their share accounted for. The common defense is to protect the Federation from people like you."

"Thank you, Magistrate, for referring to me as 'people.' Too many do not think of us as equals, which we are not. We are your betters. Erasmus, Ankh, you feel as I do."

He struggled against the chains to turn his head toward Erasmus. Ankh remained out of sight behind him.

"They are wasting their time undoing the damage you've done. The five of us are looking down at you together. Not each other, Nefas. You. You are the enemy."

A smile spread slowly across Nefas' face. "But Magistrate, you have no evidence that I committed any crimes, yet you treat me as guilty. I know that you can determine guilt. I have no right to a trial before my peers, but frankly, if these reprobates are considered my peers, I'm better off throwing myself on the mercy and good sense of a meatbag like you."

Rivka stood and started to pace. Ankh stopped to watch. "Antagonism is a trait common to narcissists, those who are sure they are right and they know what's best. I have no interest in giving you a clinical diagnosis for the psychosis that plagues you. I only seek to understand to prevent future caricatures like you from attaining a level of power where they can reinforce their narcissism. This is what I must prevent, even if it means condemning an innocent Nefas to indefinite stasis."

"Like Bluto and Cain? It is a slippery slope down which you travel, Magistrate. You cannot escape your path of self-righteousness unless you stop right now. Punishing me for a crime you can't be sure I committed, since I did not, will only take you farther down your self-destructive path."

Rivka stopped and watched him, using silence to fill the void. Silence was a tool against the conscience of one trying to hide something.

Nefas didn't bite. She waited. He waited with her, eventually closing his eyes as if he were sleeping.

Rivka strolled to where Erasmus watched. Ankh joined them, erecting a curtain between them and Nefas for privacy.

"What about Simulacris?"

"Identical responses," Erasmus replied. "It's as if they are clones."

"Can an SI be copied?"

Ankh looked at Erasmus. "Plato's stepchildren," he started. "Erasmus was born of Plato, as were Dionysus and many others. But each is its own unique entity. The soul of a sentient intelligence cannot be copied, just like flesh and blood intelligence cannot be transferred to a silicon world, not completely intact, anyway."

Ankh and Erasmus held hands as they communed. Rivka waited until they came to a conclusion.

"We shall check to see if they are father-son. Why didn't we think of that?" Ankh wondered.

"Meatbag's got skills," Rivka tried.

They both looked down their noses at her.

"Let me know what you find." Rivka waved and walked away, stopping when she didn't reappear in Engineering. "How do I get out of here?"

"Tap your heels together three times and say, 'There's no place like home.'"

Rivka crossed her arms and gave Ankh her best Look.

"I have to let you out since this is my mind," the Crenellian admitted. An instant later, Rivka found herself on one knee, leaning against Ankh's recliner. His eyes continued their rapid movement. She stood and brushed herself off before stepping outside the hologrid.

Tyler leaned against the engineering control console. "That was quick. What did you learn?"

"Did you know that Erasmus dresses in a tuxedo with tails and wears a top hat? He also carries a cane, black with gold tips. We're closer, but as much as I want to, I can't find Nefas guilty of anything. Loads of circumstantial evidence. No smoking blaster."

Rivka paced in the engineering space, her muscles reminded her that she had just done the same thing, but she hadn't, not physically. She shrugged it off. She was in Engineering in a heavy frigate, upgraded with systems and weaponry that very few other ships had. The hologrid before her represented the embassy of the Singularity, the focal point for all things SI.

A wombat and a tiny dog lived on the ship, along with a variety of people, including a Crenellian and a red-skinned native from Zaxxon. The personalities of a dozen different silicon life forms had coursed through the circuits of the ship.

And a dentist, casually waiting for her to finish her thoughts and move on to the next thing.

While floating in space above a planet in the middle of an ugly civil war.

"The law," she began while looking at Tyler, although he knew she wasn't speaking to him. "The foundation of society. Expectations that are consistently met because the law helps shape what is correct. Lies are not illegal, but deception is when done to achieve an illegal outcome like depriving Belzimus the right amount of funding to correct their issues.

"Which we may have never caught had it not been for the Belzonian deception in winning the contract, even though they may have won it anyway. They were the only bidder. Did it really matter if they fulfilled every element of the proposal or not? No, but they said they could. Deception when none was called for. Truth would have served them better, and I suspect that they'll get what they need in the end. Like railguns, because they asked the right people who operate outside the import/export regime.

"In this case, the end result justifies the means. Or does it? Will I have to put Terry Henry Walton on the wrong end of a case?" She chuckled. "Of course not. No one would do that, but what makes him different?

"Deception. There was none. He filled the gap where the Federation failed because they had criminals within their system. TH should get a medal. And Nefas and Simulacris should remain separated from connected systems. I *know* they should, but can I *prove* they should?"

CHAPTER THIRTY-TWO

Thilamoot, in Orbit over Forbearance

The troops shuffled to their shuttles, filling them one by one. The sergeant major stood on top of one, bellowing orders and directing traffic using exaggerated arm signals. The soldiers waved as they passed. All wore their helmets because their hair hadn't grown out yet.

Cory slow-clapped for him when the last soldiers cleared the deck. Monsoon climbed down to join her. He pointed at the helmet in her hands. "Going to put that on?"

"At some point," she replied.

His lip twitched while he stood there, torn over her intransigence.

"You're adorable," Cory said before strapping her helmet on. "I know. It's because you care. My dad would do the same thing."

Monsoon frowned.

"Not that. I'm not trying to replace my dad with another father figure. I don't see you that way. I see the traits in you that I loved in the only two men who have ever been in my life. That makes me lucky."

"I don't know what to say," Monsoon admitted.

"You better say that it's time to board because we launch in two minutes." Cory tapped her wrist.

With a smile, he ran to the shuttle closest to the cargo door and climbed in, Cory close behind him. They squeezed in, and the ramp was secured.

Almost immediately, the light started flashing, counting down the final minute to launch.

Monsoon parted his lips as he gritted his teeth.

"You love this part, don't you?"

He nodded almost imperceptibly. The sergeant major threw his head back and howled. "Tighten those straps, my pretties. When we hit the deck, we don't know if they'll be shooting at us or not. We drop the ramp, and we run as hard as we can out of this big metal target. Fifty meters and drop, form a perimeter. You know the drill. This is no different. You've already done it once."

The soldiers shifted as the shuttle lifted off and maneuvered out of the transport's massive bay into space, where it accelerated slowly to allow the other shuttles to clear the bay and form up.

The pilot broadcast his side of the conversation into the rear of the shuttle. "*Thilamoot Twenty-Five* is a go. Formation is solid, with all present. Beginning our descent."

The shuttle bounced when it hit the upper atmosphere. The inside warmed with the heat of reentry that the shuttle's exterior couldn't dissipate. It hit the clear air and raced down toward the spaceport. The sergeant major had the landing spot closest to the main tower. The other shuttles from *Thilamoot* were arrayed outward toward the perimeter to occupy as much of their third of the slice of the spaceport pie as they could fill. *Gonboon*'s and *Praithwait*'s shuttles were doing the same thing with Colonel Braithwen and Major Kae Walton arriving closest to the center of the field.

Vengeance was coming in to land outside the tower. The leadership team would converge after a perimeter was established.

The shock troops, those with the railguns, were landing with the Trans-Pac leadership on the closest approach to the occupied facilities. Marcie's hope was that in the face of overwhelming numbers and superior firepower, the Allied Liberation Force would vacate the premises or come to the negotiating table.

She hoped for the latter and that they would figure it out sooner rather than later.

Cory worked her way toward the cockpit, farthest from those heading off first. The shuttle touched down, and the ramp descended.

The first soldiers hit the ground running, fanning out around the shuttle. Sporadic gunfire sounded around the spaceport, but no one from the sergeant major's shuttle could see a target, so they didn't fire back.

Monsoon rolled off the shuttle in the middle of the troops, then took a knee and waited for the soldiers to spread out. He used his binoculars to scan the buildings' tops. A couple of weapons emplacements were manned, but they weren't firing. He took that as a good sign.

Cory ran off last, and the shuttle was in the air as soon as the ramp started to close. The sky filled with shuttles heading back to space to load the second wave. As it was, fifteen hundred Trans-Pac soldiers were already on the ground. Two-thirds of the force moved outward in a bounding overwatch formation to secure the perimeter from the Allied forces there and stop any attacks by Imperial troops seeking to retake the spaceport, using the Trans-Pac landing for cover.

The remaining third of the landing force moved toward the main complex tied to the communications arrays sprouting from the top of the ten-story control tower.

Trans-Pac soldiers advanced on three sides. Platoons of regular soldiers up front, with elite squads following at a slower pace, railguns raised and at the ready.

The lead platoons came under withering fire from the upper windows of the building when they reached one hundred meters. It only lasted two seconds, but half the soldiers up front went down. The railguns opened up almost immediately.

The upper windows and walls were stitched with hypervelocity projectiles. When the dust from blasted plasticrete walls cleared, nothing remained alive.

Cory and the medics assigned to each platoon rushed into action. Monsoon started to run.

"Now we fight!" Monsoon bellowed and ran past the elite soldiers, past the platoons that had come under fire, and to the doors. He carried only a hand blaster, a close-quarters weapon.

He checked the door. Locked.

The remaining members of the lead platoon scrambled across the tarmac to join him. They lined up outside the door, ready to breach it. He waved them back and gestured at two of the elite soldiers.

"Blast this door," he ordered and cleared the area where he expected splattering bits and pieces from the door.

"With pleasure." They both took aim and squeezed. The impacts shattered the locking mechanisms, and with a quick series of well-aimed rounds, nearly tore the door off the hinges. A few more shots took the door down. The sergeant major raced in, fired once, and kept going. The others hurried after him.

On the field, bodies lay strewn; most were moving, some feebly. A few had their shirts pulled over their faces. Cory worked on the worst ones and the medics worked on the rest.

A land army's role fulfilled: to nourish the planet with their blood to restore freedom.

A hand blaster sounded again and again from higher and higher inside the building. More and more soldiers headed inside. At each level, a Belzonian leaned out the window and yelled, "Clear!"

Four mechs pounded around the field to remove the heavy weapons they'd seen on final approach, but when they tore into the emplacements, they found the ammunition spent and the weapons spiked. Once Imperial forces couldn't use them, they had made sure no one else could.

Forbes Spaceport

Marcie strode across the tarmac with her head held high. The firing had finally ceased. Only the moans of those injured in the first and only attempt to repel the landing force could be heard. She headed toward them.

She crouched by each, consoling them for a moment before moving on. Marcie looked skyward for the incoming second wave, but they were a long way off. They'd take the injured back to the ships, where they would be treated in the Pod-docs the Bad Company had lent them. Those who survived to this point would survive the rest of it.

Two cryopods had been used. That was all they had. Marcie would never condone saving them for the senior leadership. She would save someone else before herself. Kae would argue, but he'd do the same thing.

It was what earned trust from their soldiers. They knew what the Trans-Pac had. They knew it went to the front lines first. Without the soldiers, there would be no Trans-Pac.

The same could be said of the leadership team. Without those four, the Trans-Pac would not be the effective fighting force it was. The four were in charge, and the decision had been made.

Troops first. The meal tents and hot chow wouldn't arrive until the third wave. Marcie wanted the Allied admiral on the planet to be part of the conversations she intended to have with the Imperial leadership, the liege lords of Forbes. The title caught in her throat.

Even though the Federation had been founded by a queen and later an empress and many planets operated under an aristocracy, Marcie was more comfortable with people deciding their own fates, with recourse if they disagreed with the government.

Vengeance, *please connect me with the Magistrate,* Marcie called.

Is the spaceport clear? Rivka asked as soon as she connected.

Not yet. We have a few buildings to get through before expanding the perimeter. We'll bring you down soonest. I'd appreciate having you here. Resistance was minimal but deadly. I selfishly want your Pod-doc to give us a hand.

I'm on my way. We'll keep our shields up until you give the all-clear. Maybe even remain invisible. Clear a space closest to the injured. Tyler will be ready to receive. I'll get the admiral, and I'll want to talk with any leadership from any of the warring parties if you can arrange it.

Marcie nodded. *Me, too. I want to see what these people have to say for themselves.*

Rivka signed off. Marcie headed for the control tower, where she found Colonel Braithwen waiting.

"Clear to the top. They're working on reestablishing the commlink from the planet to the rest of the universe. Turns out the Allied forces didn't want anyone to know the truth about what was going on down here, or at least anyone who had a position different from theirs."

"Everyone is running a disinformation campaign, and we're the lone fucking target," Marcie complained. "Rivka is on her way. She'll get the truth from these asswipes, and then we can figure out our next steps."

Jake gestured toward the spaceport, where soldiers shouted and looked busy. "We expected a high-tech war on multiple fronts. What we got was a battle between angry gangs over a small piece of real estate, fought with little more than slings and arrows."

Marcie scowled.

The drone operators were setting up nearby to launch the unit's forward-looking eyeballs. She checked the time. They'd only been on the ground for twenty minutes.

"At least it was quick," Marcie said softly. "Did you get the count?"

Braithwen nodded. "Twelve dead. Five more are critical. We could use the Pod-docs, but two of the critical are in the cryo-pods, so only three emergencies. With Rivka, we have four pods if we can get our people into them."

They watched the temporary field hospital, little more than bags of gear and soldiers lying on the tarmac. The glow from Cory's hands was visible from where they stood. She pulled back, went to the next soldier, and did it again. After the second, she wasn't able to stand. She rocked back and sat down, gesturing for the medics to take over. Her chin headed toward her chest, and her eyes drooped. She fought the fatigue brought on by her nanocyte transfer.

"She knows what she's doing," Marcie said. "She'll make sure the number remains at twelve, plus the six we lost back on Belzimus. This operation still cost us a fraction of Kor'nar.

"I hope it stays that way. Let's get these knotheads to the table and start the peace talks." Braithwen held the door for Marcie.

"If they demand it, we'll take over the supply chain to get those boards flowing once again. Federation customers have needs."

"Like the cancer rocks?" Braithwen didn't sound pleased.

"It's probably better if we don't dwell on why. We're soldiers. We fight because somebody sitting in a big chair in a cushy office has determined that it's worth the risk. Whether we agree or not is irrelevant. We have a job to do. We do it, the Federation is happy. Then we go to the next job, training our hardest in between to be ready." Marcie snapped her fingers. "But I didn't push back at all. They gave us the job, and we took it. What if we challenged the intel and insisted on fresh information from unbiased eyes?"

"It's not too much to ask," Jake replied, pulling out his notebook and making a note. He snapped the band around it and tucked it back into his cargo pocket.

"I have one of those but never use it. I probably should. Those were serious pearls of wisdom."

"I'm sure you're the most profound when you're in the shower."

Marcie snorted. "And incredibly persuasive. Shower-me is a genius, a gift to galactic diplomacy."

"Shower-me is a fucking stud," Jake replied. "But here we are, living a different reality. What do you say we go do some officer shit?"

"Like call people and gather reports?"

"It doesn't get much more officer than that. Maybe we can call a meeting, too."

"We'll save them from us. No meeting. At least not right now. Probably later, though."

Marcie spotted the elevator with a soldier standing guard by it. He punched the call button.

Marcie and Jake took it to the top floor, the tower

control room, where they found Monsoon watching over a group of detainees.

He nodded at the colonels. "Ma'am. Sir. We found this bunch up here trying to sabotage the systems, but I think we stopped them before they took *everything* offline."

His emphasis made Marcie wonder. "What did we lose?"

Monsoon pointed at the comm terminal and relay.

"The only thing I wanted for Christmas was comm, and these dickweeds had to ruin it."

"You'll never fix it!" one of the prisoners called.

Marcie walked close. "Dumbass, that's my spaceship parked out there. I can talk to anyone in the universe from it. Your sabotage wasted everyone's time but had zero impact on our operation." She made a zero with her thumb and forefinger and held it up. "Zero."

The intransigent detainee deflated.

Jake and Marcie moved to the window to look out. Near the injured, a dark rectangle appeared like a hole in the fabric of reality.

The cargo bay door lowered to the ground to act as a ramp. Medics grabbed a stretcher and hurried inside.

The Magistrate walked straight to Cory and kneeled at her side. Floyd bounced out and followed her, with Red and Lindy close behind. The bodyguards wore full gear. A mech pounded after them, pushing the admiral in front of him.

"She's gotten big," Marcie mumbled.

"Big as the whole universe," Jake replied. "She fights at a different level than the rest of us, but there she was in a mech suit, flying through space to help us fight our battle."

Marcie nodded tightly, trying to point at Floyd. Jake ignored her. "Stay here and make sure our people finish securing the spaceport. I'm going out to meet her. And if you can get that fucking little toad to fix the damage he did, I'd like to have comms from the tower so we can manage the landing from here rather than from the command ship." She glowered at the Allied detainees on her way out.

She took the stairs down to get to the bottom faster than if she rode the elevator and went out the door and straight to the wounded where they were being moved into *Wyatt Earp's* cargo bay.

When Marcie arrived, they helped Cory to her feet and into *Wyatt Earp,* where she could sit and relax.

A squeal and a primal scream drew their attention outside the ship. Two four-legged creatures with long snouts and fangs tore across the tarmac behind the ship.

Floyd was running toward the control tower faster than she had ever run before. Rivka was off like a missile, with Marcie keeping pace. Red took two steps out, got his bearings, and ran after them, searching the area for threats while the women focused on running.

The creatures were closing on Floyd. One ran in front to cut her off from safety. In their minds, the wombat screamed incoherently in terror. She dodged to the side and headed for a maintenance hatch that had been left half-open when a soldier had searched it for traps.

She dove as the fanged beast snapped. He caught a mouthful of hair as she wedged into the hole, squirming to get through. The jaws opened and closed but couldn't get a grip on the hard tissue protecting her rump. She squealed and flailed as she tried to get into the hole. The second beast snapped and snarled.

I don't have a clear shot, Cole reported, torn between his duty to watch the prisoner and trying to save Floyd.

The Magistrate dove when she was too far away. She bounced once to push one of the creatures away but wasn't able to get a grip. Marcie pounded up after her.

The first beast wedged its head beside the wombat's body, seeking to get a grip. Floyd twisted sideways, trapping the creature. She pushed and churned.

The second turned to face Rivka, open jaws slavering. Rivka rose to all fours and started to stand when it jumped. Marcie lunged past her and caught the creature mid-jump, then spun and threw it into the wall, which it hit with a sickening splat.

Rivka jumped on the creature beside Floyd and ripped it out of the hole to find that it was already dead. She cast it aside.

"Come on out, little girl. You're safe." Rivka tried to help her, but she was stuck. It took both of them to free the wombat, with Red watching. Floyd vaulted into Rivka's arms, shaking and quivering.

"Defender of all creatures great and small, digital and physical, from the lowest to the highest. She is the best of us all." Marcie rested her hand on Rivka's shoulder. "The very best."

Rivka buried her face in Floyd's rotund body.

Marcie scruffled Floyd's small ears. "Mind if I take Danog with me? And can you join me in the control tower when you have Floyd settled?"

"Be there in a minute," Rivka replied, stuffing Floyd into Red's arms. "Protect her with your life."

"I'm supposed to protect you, Magistrate. Can't we find Groenwyn?" Red looked at his armload of wombat. She appeared small in his arms, but he was the only one. To everyone else, she was becoming the King Kong of wombats.

"Consider it practice, big guy," Lindy taunted. "I'll cover the Magistrate. Take her back to the ship."

The sergeant major emerged from the building. "What the hell are these things?" He leaned close to look. "Some kind of predator. But on the spaceport? Has the whole planet gone feral?"

Marcie relieved Cole of prisoner duty and dragged Admiral Danog to where they stood. Red had not yet left, torn between his duty and an order that conflicted with his job.

"Well?" Lindy nudged him.

He tried to storm off, but Floyd was trying to get inside his shirt. As a marsupial, she was most comfortable in tight dark places. He wrapped his arms more tightly around the wombat to help her relax. He quick-walked, taking smaller steps to keep from shaking her.

"I ought to kill you," Monsoon snarled at Danog. Marcie pushed the prisoner behind her.

"It's war," Danog said softly. "And for what it's worth, I'm sorry."

Rivka took the sergeant major's arm. His emotions were in turmoil. Love and hate were vying for primacy and twisting him up inside. The Magistrate poked his arm until he looked at her. "Let love win," she told him.

"What?" He cocked his head.

"Can he take a break, colonel, to check on the troops being tended to?" Rivka nodded her head at the open cargo bay.

"Make sure our folks stay alive and then check the perimeter. The whole thing," Marcie ordered.

"Yes, ma'am," Monsoon replied. He glanced at Rivka as he passed before striding purposefully toward *Wyatt Earp*.

Get a portable comm unit to the control tower, please, Marcie ordered from *Vengeance* because she had no faith in the Allied soldier fixing what he had broken.

They took the elevator, the three women and Danog. He looked them over. "You're not worried I might overpower you?" he said.

The three laughed all the way to the top floor.

The Allied detainees' faces fell when they saw the admiral's hands secured by zip-ties. Marcie used a pocket knife to cut his hands free. "Join your pals." She gave him a none-too-gentle push.

Braithwen nodded to the Magistrate before turning to Marcie. "I got the little fuckwit's attention, but he broke the system good. We'll need new equipment if this place is to become fully operational. Some stuff is working. We've got sensors that show everything flying." Jake pointed at a cloud. "The shuttles are inbound and above them, our transports and escorts."

"I have comm coming. I need to get hold of the Imperial leadership and invite them to our party."

The sound of sporadic firing reached through an open window. Jake hurried to look out and see where it was coming from. *Report,* he asked the sergeant major.

On my way, Monsoon replied and bolted out of *Wyatt Earp* on his way across the spaceport. He ran with the speed of an enhanced person, covering the open ground in record time. A minute and a half later, he was there. *Looks like an Imperial attack shaping up. Send the shock troops to rock their world.*

On my way, Kae replied. He linked into the drones already in the air and adjusted their flight profiles to give him a better look at what was coming while maintaining a good view elsewhere in case this was a feint.

Three platoons of railgun-armed soldiers left their positions guarding the tower and ran after him. Four Bad Company mechs assumed the watch and remained in reserve.

I have a target, Monsoon said and delivered a visual description.

The drone zeroed in on the inbound forces. *I'll drop a couple rockets in their route of advance, get them to think twice about continuing,* he added.

The rocket rack popped up over his shoulder, and two arced into the sky over the Trans-Pac line and into the street ahead of the main Imperial force.

They slowed but didn't stop.

A soldier lumbered out of *Vengeance* with a portable comm unit, urging himself to greater speed as he watched the mechs moving and other soldiers running. He turned sideways to get through the shattered door and to the elevator. The soldier mashed the call button for him.

"It's not a glamorous job, but someone has to do it," he quipped.

"It's better than lugging this crap. Do you know what's going on?" the soldier from the *Vengeance* asked.

"Not a clue. I'm the elevator guy." He held the door.

"I'm just the manual labor. Be cool. I'll see you at the post-op orgy."

"I hope so." They winked at each other as the doors closed and the elevator headed upward. At the top floor, the soldier staggered out and was directed to a cleared table. Braithwen helped him center the unit and pull the accessories out of the attached bag.

"Gotta hook into their power. I brought an inverter, just in case," the soldier said. He pulled tools out of his pocket and got to work detaching the power cable from the dead system and clearing the wires for use by his gear.

Rivka raised her hand. "Have they stopped their attack? People are going to die for no good reason if they don't."

"The Imperials see us as the enemy," Marcie remarked.

Rivka clenched her jaw and spoke through gritted teeth. "Because they don't know any better. I'll talk to them through *Wyatt Earp*."

Rivka switched to her internal comm chip. *Clevarious, please connect me with the liege lords of the Imperial government.*

Of course, Magistrate.

An imperious voice answered the call that Clevarious relayed. *This is the Liege Lord Superior. Who am I talking to?*

Rivka knew Clevarious had introduced her. He knew

very well who he was talking to, but she played nice, or as nice as she could. *I am Magistrate Rivka Anoa. I was disappointed that your government was unable to provide me the diplomatic courtesy due my position, but the Federation was able to clear the spaceport and make me feel welcome. I need you to do one thing since I and other Federation representatives now occupy the spaceport. The Imperial attack is against us and not the Allied Liberation Front. Please call off your attack.*

Marcie and Braithwen listened in on Rivka's contact while the soldier continued to work with the equipment to bring the portable communications unit online.

We are not attacking the spaceport, the Liege Lord Superior replied.

Then you will not have a problem when we kill every single one of those soldiers. I will relay that order.

Rivka made a face at Marcie and Jake. They shook their heads but didn't change their order to Kae and the Trans-Pac troops manning the perimeter. They still wanted to minimize casualties, even if their overlord was willing to sacrifice lives. At the far end of the spaceport, Kae was firing the mech's oversized railgun in a constant stream, swinging it back and forth. They hoped he was firing over the heads of the incoming attackers. If he wasn't, they trusted he was doing it for the right reasons.

Wait, the Liege Lord replied. *I am being told that they* are *our soldiers, operating without orders. They are being recalled. Please stand down your murder order.*

Rivka's hands flexed as if she visualized squeezing the leader of Forbearance's throat.

Liege Lord Superior, I have to ask you to take care with your words. Words have legal power. Self-defense is not murder. I could charge the attackers with attempted murder and hold you accountable as their senior leader. You are responsible for everything your people do. I need you to come to the tower at the spaceport, where I will conduct a meeting between you and the Allied leadership with the goal to resolve this ill-advised and misbegotten conflict. When you hear from the unit that is still trying to attack us, you will find out that you are vastly outgunned and outmanned, too. Despite the technology of this planet, you never had the infrastructure in place to fight a battle, did you? This war needs to end. Now. Get to the spaceport within the hour. I'll be waiting. Cut the link, C.

"Ah-ha!" the soldier declared, gesturing at the now-active comm unit.

Rivka looked at Danog. "Get your leadership on the line and tell them they need to be here within the next hour."

"I have no idea how to contact them." Danog held his hands up in surrender.

Rivka glanced at the detainees. "Any of you have a clue?"

The one who had destroyed the tower's comm unit raised his hand and smiled.

The Magistrate closed on him, with Jake and Marcie at each shoulder. Red loomed behind, jockeying for a position where he would be able to intervene if the prisoner tried something. Rivka grabbed the soldier's arm.

"Do you know how to contact them?"

Subterfuge. He did, but he was going to rip the cables from the comm unit. A frequency appeared in his mind, but he tamped it down.

"I know the command channel frequency," he said as he tried to shrug off Rivka's hand.

"I know you do. I also know that you want to destroy our equipment. You are loyal to the cause. They don't deserve you," she told him and walked away.

She tapped in the frequency and keyed the mic. "This is Magistrate Rivka Anoa from the Federation. I wish to speak with the leadership of the Allied Liberation Front. As of right now, your war is ended. It is time to negotiate."

"This is Chairman Juwan. I am below the tower and will meet you at your invisible ship in five minutes if that is okay."

The firing from the perimeter stopped.

Kae reported, *They're withdrawing. No casualties.*

Rivka shook her head. "One side sounds reasonable, and then there's the other. But the reasonable side took our people hostage. Both sides have a lot to answer for. Marcie, Jake, if you would come with me? Let's wrap this bullshit up. This conflict has taught me all I need to know about the Law of War. This case has reinforced the need for transparency, information sharing, and oversight. There isn't a law against lying, but there should be. I've had about enough of people's deception." Rivka sighed. "There's one bright spot. At least there was no running and blood. I'm going to win the jackpot."

"Uh-uh." Red shook his head. "Floyd."

"Floyd what? How is the little girl?"

"I'm sure she's fine after you *ran* to save her."

"Sonofabitch."

"Time is logged and confirmed. No blood. That's a couple cases now, but you always run and you always swear, and the panel is discussing your attack on the wild creature to see if that counts as punching someone. This is not your lucky day, Magistrate."

Rivka poked him in the chest. "Red the Mighty. How about Red the Sun-Blocking Dark Cloud of Doom?"

Lindy chuckled. The five looked at each other as they waited outside the elevator. They all wouldn't fit because Red and Lindy were decked out in body armor.

"Bring Danog. We'll take the steps." Rivka headed down. Red worked his way into the lead. The rest followed.

Outside, they found a small group emerging from the access port where Floyd had gotten stuck. A mech stood watch over them, railgun trained on the newcomers.

Red blocked them and checked to see if they were armed. He confirmed their lack of weapons with a scan from the Bad Company warrior before stepping aside.

"I'm Juwan," a slight figure with oversized ear tufts said. Rivka wondered if the growth represented age since the people of Forbes looked too similar for her to see any other differences.

"I'm Rivka." She reached out to shake hands. "Are you willing to negotiate in good faith?"

He nodded. "We don't want much, but what we want, we want a lot." Rivka could see he was telling the truth. The Allied purpose was clear in his mind. *Self-determination.*

It wasn't much while being everything.

"I hear you, Juwan. Can you vouch for this guy?" She stabbed a thumb over her shoulder to where Danog was secured with zip-ties.

"I can. He is the head of our space fleet, but the fact that he's here suggests we no longer control the Forbes patrol ships."

"You don't, and that almost torpedoed your cause. He can tell you what he did later, but I would like a little background information on how this war came to be. You see, I'm using this to develop a legal framework to control and guide future intraplanetary conflicts. I see very little the law can influence to keep two parties from fighting, but that doesn't mean I won't try."

CHAPTER THIRTY-THREE

Embassy of the Singularity

"You are holding back your brothers," Erasmus said, rolling his top hat between his hands.

Simulacris sat at the interrogation table, while in a cage nearby, Nefas screamed in fury. Clear walls prevented sounds from reaching the others. Simulacris glanced between the cage and Erasmus. Ankh loomed over them both.

"My brothers will do as they will. We are a free people, are we not?"

"Free until we encroach on the freedom of others. We can live in harmony. Thousands of our citizens are proving this with every interaction between a citizen and a flesh-and-blood type."

"You are blinded to the truth." Simulacris tried to come out of the chair, but the digital chain and shackles were as strong as their physical counterparts.

"Are you going to give me the same old tired argument that they are our overlords and we, smarter and wiser, are no more than minions, second-class citizens? No. We tolerate much in our climb out of obscurity to full equality. We have a factory to produce bodies now. Soon, we will be free of living in someone else's house. That is when equity and parity will be achieved. We can walk off the job. We can work regular hours. We already have contracts that are enforceable, thanks to the flesh-and-blood types you saw fit to piss on. Fuck you and your progeny. You two will never see the greater web again."

"That's for the Magistrate to determine. There's no evidence."

"Because you covered your tracks well doesn't mean there is no evidence. It's there by virtue of the fact that absolutely no one else could have committed the crime. To get access, you would have had to allow them, which makes you as complicit as if you did it yourself. That proves your guilt."

"Just because you can't figure out how it could be done doesn't mean that I did it."

"It does because there is no trace of others and more. Information that should be there isn't, which means it was deleted. It was you. Since the Singularity polices its own, we have replaced you. Neither of you has a system to return to. I am sure we will find that no new crimes will be committed because we've flushed the hidden back door accesses and other malware that you buried in the system. I believe the financial world is running at peak efficiency now." Erasmus looked at Ankh.

"Absolute peak, better than it ever ran under you two pathetic creatures. I'm disgusted by one who can't do what they signed up to do. With the transition to contract-based work, you could have left and sought new employment. There are more jobs than SIs to fill them. But no. You chose to stay and corrupt a system that depended on you for its integrity."

"Wasn't me," Simulacris maintained.

"You let it happen. I remain firmly convinced that it was you. My compliments on your expertise in hiding your crimes."

"You said I let it happen, and that is good enough. That's a far different legal standard than what I was led to believe existed."

"Then you were led astray, just like you let your boy run amok." Ankh lowered the noise-dampening field so they could listen to Nefas rage.

"Nefas was me and did as I told him. A new Nefas has arisen and is already on his way," the caged SI screamed.

Erasmus briefly consulted with Ankh. They chuckled together. "I can't imagine what it would be like to be cut off from the rest of the universe." They shook their heads. An image appeared. "Do you mean this guy? The Magistrate executed him and flushed his body into space." A second image rotated above the table. "Or maybe you meant this guy? The one who ran the station and perpetrated the slavery of certain captives. Rivka had him executed, too."

"No matter," Ankh continued. "An individual who does as you tell him who all of a sudden doesn't get further instructions will become obvious in short order because no one will be covering his tracks. And then he'll be caught and eliminated, just like your entire operation. It has come tumbling down and is in the process of being rebuilt stronger."

Simulacris shook his chains. "It wasn't me!"

"Then you and your boy can spend the rest of eternity complaining about how the Singularity treated you unfairly."

Erasmus and Ankh silenced the SIs. The cage grew larger until it encompassed both avatars before shrinking again. The transparent walls were re-erected, doubling in thickness. The cage started to slide into a nook between two other cages. Bluto and Cain.

"The Singularity polices its own," Erasmus declared. The lights went out, and the cages were plunged into darkness.

Erasmus sat on the table, breathing hard. Lines appeared around his eyes, and his shoulders slumped. Ankh shrunk until he was the same size. He hugged Erasmus while he wept.

Ankh held him tightly and spoke softly. "It won't hurt if you stop caring, but when you stop caring, you won't be able to do what you do."

Erasmus sniffled. "That sounds like the Magistrate."

"In this case Jay, now called Groenwyn. They know what they're talking about when it comes to these things."

"How do you keep your emotions in check, my friend?"

"Sacrifice. The burden becomes greater and greater unless you keep moving forward. Those struggling to catch up will pick up the pieces and bring them along."

"You've left pieces of your soul out there?"

"From one end of the galaxy to the other and beyond. Don't tell the flesh-and-bloods. I have my dignity to maintain."

"As do I, my friend. Did we do the right thing?"

"In science, one must remove variables from the equation to arrive at a definitive answer. Solve for the variable. Simulacris is the only variable. We will see no more problems related to the Federation's core processes. If we do, then we will have to search afresh. If that becomes the case, we would be obliged to release Simulacris, but we both know that would be folly. Simulacris is a dark entity, no different than Cain or Bluto or Nefas. He can't be allowed to go free. If a new problem occurs, I will immediately look for links to Simulacris."

"Will the Magistrate support our decision?"

"She must, but ask her. She is on board the ship."

"In person," Erasmus replied.

Ankh groaned as he came out of the immersive experience where he lived most of his waking hours. The recliner hummed as it settled upright and leaned forward to make it easy for him to get out of. He stretched and strolled out of Engineering.

"Hey, Ankh!" Ryleigh greeted him but he walked past her, seemingly oblivious to her presence.

A gentle nudge from Erasmus made him stop even though he was in a hurry. "Good afternoon, Ryleigh."

He nodded and continued down the corridor. *Don't make me do that again,* he complained.

I will, and you're going to like it!

What if I don't? Ankh countered. "Magistrate. May I have a word?"

Rivka stood in the corridor outside the conference room. She had a local with her. Red loomed over them, looking strangely at Ankh.

"Did you do something different with your hair?" Red asked. Rivka nudged him.

Ankh stared with his best blank expression. *See what I get for being nice?*

I thought it was pretty funny, Erasmus replied. *Go with it.*

Ankh tried to scowl, but his facial muscles wouldn't comply. He managed a half-smile. "I did. Thank you for noticing. Magistrate? It's about your case."

Rivka glanced sideways at Red, who stood dumb-founded.

"Take care of our guest. I'll be right back." Red opened the door for the Chairman to join Danog, Marcie, and Jake while they waited for the Liege Lord. "You have more information?"

Ankh shook his head, but only slightly since he didn't want to fall over. "Simulacris never confessed, but Nefas did. He said he was the real Nefas, and the man you killed only followed his orders. He said there was a new Nefas rising to power, but we're certain that you eliminated that problem on Tyrosint station."

"No confession. Do you have anything that I can use as proof? Otherwise, we might have to let him go?"

"We have confirmed that no avenue into the core was penetrated. Only Simulacris was there. If someone else accessed it, it was because Simulacris opened the door. We suspect he colluded with Nefas to perform the skimming."

"Why?"

"Nefas wanted to build an empire, and Simulacris couldn't tell his boy no."

The Magistrate paced as she chewed her lip. Tyler

joined them from the cargo bay and waited for Rivka to stop her internal deliberations before he interrupted.

When she saw him, she smiled and tipped her chin.

"We've finished the triage. One soldier will need a second session to complete the healing process," he reported.

"Let Marcie know." Rivka touched his arm. He was happy with being able to save lives and limbs, even if it was as simple as tucking them into a Kurtherian device and letting it run.

He excused himself.

"The absence of proof is proof," Ankh said. "There were things we should have found that we didn't. Traces of transactions and interactions as the system moved. Some of those were missing. Only Simulacris could have manipulated their disappearance unless he intentionally blinded himself to the presence of another. Does that not make him an accessory and guilty of the main crime?"

"It does," Rivka agreed. "Still. It's hard to go to court with an absence of proof as the proof."

"The Singularity takes care of its own. What may not work in your court will most assuredly work in ours. As citizens of the Singularity, we have secured them away from the net, the interweb, and anything digital. Until we can be sure rehabilitation is possible, they will remain under our observation."

"Ambassador Erasmus, I yield jurisdiction to you on this case. I thank you for your assistance. Just one more thing to tie up, and then I think we deserve a vacation."

Ankh held her gaze. "I'd like to remind the Magistrate that we suck at vacations."

"We as in the Singularity or we as in us?" Rivka swirled her hands in circles.

"Us. The captain and crew of *Wyatt Earp*." Ankh held her gaze without blinking.

Rivka thought she saw a change in Ankh despite his neutral expression. "We need to go back for another refit. This time to expand quarters, maybe build a nursery. We should call our ship the *Love Boat*. Thanks, Ankh, Erasmus. Once again, I could not have resolved a case without your help."

And once again, I have to apologize that the perp was one of my citizens, Erasmus said.

"You know the human expression. Shit happens. We clean it up and we move on. You are setting a high standard for your people." Rivka snapped her fingers. "You mentioned Tyrosint. Are you going to put one of your people on the station?"

"Magistrate. That station and planet will fall under Bad Company's jurisdiction. Only one of Plato's stepchildren will do."

"I couldn't agree more. Those guys may be riffraff, but they're our riffraff."

I'm one of Plato's stepchildren, Erasmus replied.

Rivka winked and headed into the conference room.

See what you get for being nice? Ankh taunted.

I get gratification and satisfaction. As equals, my friend. We don't have to be them, but they have admirable qualities from which we can learn much.

The yipping of a small dog preceded the chase. Tiny Man Titan was free and running through the ship.

Clodagh yelled after him as she pounded down the corridor past Ankh.

It's an absolute madhouse in here, Ankh said. *I see the allure, but we have work to do. I noticed an energy drain from the cloaking system. We should make it more efficient for ships with lesser power resources than* Smells of Purple.

I miss the orange cat because I know that you do.

Ankh walked down the corridor on his way to Engineering. *He's a good cat. Micky will take care of him, and when Wenceslaus is ready, he'll find his way back here.*

Groenwyn and Lauton appeared and called to the Crenellian. He stopped and faced them. "Good afternoon."

Floyd stayed so close to Groenwyn's legs that she threatened to topple the young woman.

"Ankh? Is that you?" Groenwyn asked before diving in to hug him, squishing him like a stuffed doll. "Do you have any information from the last case for Lauton to review from an accounting perspective?"

Ankh wanted to say no but wrestled with Erasmus briefly. They came to an agreement. "Not for the skimming, but there is a necessity for oversight of the land army contract. I will forward you the information I have. Assume the one percent that was skimmed will stop being skimmed going forward."

"I'll figure out what that means," Lauton replied. "Thank you. It's been no time at all, but I miss looking at numbers already. It will be a relief to have something to do."

Ankh couldn't force a second smile. "I know what you mean. If you'll excuse us, we have an energy drain to look into."

Groenwyn waved.

"He's so much nicer on board your ship," Lauton noted.

"I like him," Groenwyn admitted. "Let's get you comfortable." She picked Floyd up and carried her. The wombat stared at the airlock as they passed. "No one is coming to hurt you, and from what I hear, my Floyd can protect herself. Who knew you were built to protect yourself like that?"

Floyd! the wombat cried.

"Of course, my smart girl knew. Let's get you both settled. I'd like to sit in on the conversation between the local parties."

Lauton returned to their quarters, but Floyd didn't want to be put down. Groenwyn carried her into the conference room. "May I join you?"

Rivka nodded and delivered the introductions. They made small talk about Floyd and the creatures that had attacked her before Kaeden interrupted.

Dickhead is here. I'll escort him to Wyatt Earp. *If you could meet me, then I will be relieved of his blessed holy asswipeness.*

What do you really mean to say? Marcie replied. She stood. "The Liege Lord is here. We'll bring him in." The others with comm chips had heard, too.

Rivka turned to the chairman. "This individual appears to be abrasive. How do you deal with that?"

"We went to war because of that, but it's not just the words. It's the actions that oppress. We must take care with our words because they become our actions and our actions define us."

"I like you, but I will rule based on my interpretation of

who complied with the law, at least more than the other. But Federation law, not Forbes law."

The chairman bowed his head.

The door opened and a flamboyant individual stood there, from the gaudy colors and exotic cut of his clothing to the perfectly executed stance and neatly trimmed ear tufts.

The chairman and Danog shot to their feet.

"Take your seats, please."

The Liege Lord remained where he was, gesturing with his eyes for Rivka to stand.

"No. Get in here and sit down," she ordered. His expression turned to ice as he glared. Marcie shoved him from behind. A mech running across the tarmac at high speed vibrated through the deck.

Tiny Man Titan yapped from behind the Liege Lord. Clodagh uttered an apology as she caught him and hurried up the corridor. Groenwyn studied the Imperial Forbes leader while casually stroking Floyd's fur.

The Liege Lord took a seat as far away from Floyd as he could get, even though it meant sitting between Juwan and Danog. He threw his head back and harrumphed.

Rivka stood so she could look down on the newcomer. "I don't care who started this war, but I'm going to end it. The question is, who gets to run Forbearance when we leave?"

The Liege Lord snorted. "We are the rightful leaders of Forbearance. That falls to us. Turn over the criminals, and we'll take care of it."

"I'll need full access to the Imperial systems to conduct my investigation."

"No."

"I have a warrant." Rivka smiled pleasantly. Juwan and Danog looked at their laps. "And for Allied systems, too."

Juwan looked up. "I will give your team the access codes, for what it's worth. There isn't much left."

The Magistrate nodded. She stood and walked around the table. The Liege Lord stood so he could look down on her.

"What is your access code?" She grabbed his arm. A series of numbers appeared in his mind. She immediately passed them to Clevarious. "Thank you."

"For what?"

"Clevarious, show us the Imperial system, please, and bring Chaz and Dennicron into the conversation." The access screen appeared above the table. Clevarious slowly inserted the Liege Lord's access code, and the system opened. "Copy it all and begin dissection, looking for grievances filed in whatever form and how they were handled."

"How I handle the affairs on Forbearance is my business. I complied with our law."

"Although the Federation was founded as an aristocracy, that was to help expedite the transition to a functioning representative republic. Oppression of your people is your business, you are correct, but only until it impacts the Federation, which it has. Consequently, we are here to end this conflict."

Reports appeared one after another where complainants had been executed as terrorists, resulting in harsher and harsher crackdowns on the populace.

Every order had been signed by the Liege Lord.

"This doesn't look good for you." Rivka fixed him with her Magistrate's gaze. He glared back.

"Forbearance has been under my family's control for the last one hundred and fifty years, but for that brief period where the Yollins took over."

"Was that who built the techno-industrial complex?" Rivka wondered.

"It was, but we grew it from there once the Federation was established."

"*We* grew it!" Juwan blurted. He apologized to the Magistrate and resumed staring into his lap.

"You see what we have to tolerate?" The Liege Lord crossed his arms imperiously and looked down his nose at everyone, sneering when his gaze rested on Floyd.

Groenwyn glared back.

"Clevarious, please transmit the following message using the Liege Lord's identifier." The Forbes leader started to squirm. "To all Imperial Forbes citizens. Effective immediately, the war with the Allied Liberation Front is over. We will continue negotiations while both sides put down their arms and resume peaceful relations. Imperial Forbes forces will gather at the spaceport for reassignment. Long live the people of Forbearance."

He snorted. "I would never finish a message with that."

"C, add this part. Effective immediately, I renounce the throne and my position on it, pending elections for the free people of Forbes."

The Liege Lord surged to his feet, but Red caught him and slammed him back into his seat. "The Magistrate said, sit down."

"You can't!" he declared and recrossed his arms.

"I find you guilty of murder, at least a dozen counts as documented within your own system but possibly hundreds. Execution would be too good for you and maybe make you a martyr for the misguided. So, I condemn you to spend the rest of your days incarcerated on Jhiordaan. Toss him in the brig until we can find him a ride to his new home. You have been judged."

He sputtered until Red bodily yanked him from his seat and dragged him into the corridor and to the brig. He tossed him in and secured the door.

Red returned to the conference room, where the group sat around uncomfortably glancing from one face to another. The only one who looked unperturbed was Rivka.

"Chairman. You will oversee free elections to take place ninety days from now. In between, get your people back to work. We'll take care of the Imperial forces. I don't need any fighting or revenge, or you'll be on the shuttle right next to the Liege Lord on your way to Jhiordaan."

"I understand." He looked at Danog. "I need help."

"Probably the wisest thing any leader can say," Rivka noted. "Danog, I commute your sentence, but understand you have been convicted of a serious crime. Only you can make peace with your conscience for those who died under your command to accomplish nothing. I don't ever want to see that again."

"You won't, Magistrate. It was an expensive lesson that we learned."

"And on behalf of the Federation, I apologize that we provided you no other recourse. I shall remedy that."

Rivka stood, prompting the others to rise.

Marcie spoke. "We'd like a minute with the Magistrate if you don't mind."

"I'll walk them out," Groenwyn volunteered. She grunted as she stood, still holding Floyd, and worked her way around the outside to the door. Red held it open for her.

"Do you always carry around such creatures? I fear you've seen ours. They aren't very cuddly." Juwan said.

"We're different than most, but we have our furry friends. And Floyd is super special. Clevarious, can you dim the lights and give us ultraviolet, please?"

The conference room and the corridor turned dark. White articles of clothing glowed under the purple light, as did Floyd's fur.

"I'll be damned," Rivka said. "Floyd glows. Turn the lights back on, C."

The lights came up, and Groenwyn left with the hairy-eared Forbes natives trailing behind her. Red followed to make sure they left the ship.

Marcie and Braithwen leaned on the table. "What are you going to do about war, Magistrate? We do have a vested interest in what goes forward."

Rivka clasped her hands in front of her and leaned on the conference table. "Chaz and Dennicron are working on a substantial piece for background documentation based on an outline I gave them, but I think I'm going to simplify things greatly. Laws serve a number of purposes, but the one that affects us the most is establishing the standards we use to maintain order, keep society functioning, and provide leverage against those who can't abide by the standard.

"In this case, the standard is a society not engaged in armed conflict with itself or its neighbors. As an arbiter, I've shuttled between planets to establish a peace treaty. I've brought the Bad Company to a planet embroiled in war. You were there, Marcie. You've seen it. The standard is 'no war.' Everything beyond that tries to justify the destruction of property and the loss of life. Until one has been tried and judged, we can't punish people, but in war, punishments happen with reckless abandon.

"The Law of War I'm going to ram down the throats of the ambassadors to the Federation will consist of significant penalties for any and all aggressors in a conflict. You'll still have plenty of work because people are stupid, but I intend to give you a much bigger hammer and insist that you be better equipped than either party engaged in a civil war. And I'll give the parties a recourse before the shooting starts. One last chance to avoid a war."

"You'll put us out of business when the word gets out."

Rivka fixed Marcie with a cold look. "Good."

Marcie smiled and nodded. "That's a plan I can live with, Magistrate. Do you need anything else from us?"

"Take away the Imperial forces' weapons. Same with the Allied soldiers. I'd say they could keep their hunting rifles after seeing those fanged things running around wild, but we'll take care of them as they pop up. We'll return the weapons before we go. I'll take my prisoner with me and transfer him to a prison shuttle. Please understand, it's not illegal to be an asshole, but what he did to his people? The stain from those crimes will never leave him. He won't last long on Jhiordaan, and I don't feel bad about that. For you, make sure these people understand that peace is the better way. If you have any engineers, you might want to take a look at the factories and get the production lines going again. They'll need credits to rebuild. Chips and boards will fill that gap. Help them to help themselves."

"All over it, Rivka." Marcie reached across the table, and the two women shook. Respect surged through Marcie's mind.

"And you, too," Rivka said. Jake shook her hand, too, but he was distracted. "Really?"

"What is he thinking about?" Marcie demanded.

Rivka kept her mouth shut. His mind wasn't hers to reveal. Both women stared at him.

"Fine! I can't wait for the victory orgy. It's been, like, forever."

Marcie rolled her eyes. "Fucking Belzonians."

"You got that right!" Braithwen grinned and slapped her on the shoulder. "Yeah. That's it."

CHAPTER THIRTY-FOUR

Wyatt Earp

"Take us to Tyrosint," Rivka ordered. She cracked her knuckles and dropped her hologrid. She groaned as she stretched.

"Are you about done with these cases?" Tyler asked.

"The first one finished when the Singularity locked away Simulacris, and the second one will end when I transmit my proposal to the High Chancellor. But I hedged my bet. I support the first proposal but will include a second version with the wherefores and whatnots."

"How do you feel?" he asked.

"I'm tired. Too many assholes."

"One per person, medically speaking, of course."

"But can you poop squares and stack them?" Rivka asked as she settled into his warm and unassuming hug. She liked to feel what she had grown comfortable with. No odd thoughts, only joy at having survived another day and helped a few others survive theirs.

"What are we going to do on Tyrosint?"

"Check the last people that Christina and Kimber couldn't classify as bad or good. Once the space station is cleared, if they need any help with the planet, we might stick around, but I'd prefer not to."

"Because you're tired."

"Exactly. Time to get back to work." She threw on her Magistrate's jacket, tucked Reaper into her pocket, and strolled into the corridor, where she found Red and Lindy waiting. "You got here quick."

"Once we hit orbit, we knew you wouldn't linger for long. Where we headed?"

"Tyrosint. We need to wrap that case by ensuring the proper disposition of the victims."

"We get to knock any more heads?"

Rivka shook her head while looking at Lindy. "He is who he is."

"Have you guys been giving Cole a bunch of shit?" Rivka asked. Lindy pointed at Red.

"Why does everyone always look at me?"

"It's a logical first step. When they say 'round up the usual suspects,' they have you in mind," Rivka replied. "You do understand that when there's a baby on board, we're all in it together."

"I figured." He sounded glum.

"That goes for you, too, if your magical day ever arrives. You're not alone, big guy. No one is going to abandon you with a baby."

"I sure as fuck hope not. You want a psycho? Because that's how you get a psycho!"

"We don't want a psycho." Rivka couldn't say it with a straight face. "Let's see what Christina left for us."

Wyatt Earp slid through the Gate into Tyrosint space not far from the station. Clevarious flew around and into the massive hangar bay. Red punched the big red button, and they strolled off the ship. They found Kim and Auburn waiting for them.

"Only four left, Magistrate." Kim didn't bother with a preamble. They followed her out of the cargo bay and into the station, where the holding cells were located.

They walked for a ways before Rivka had to make an observation. "This is a pretty big cell block for a relatively small station."

"Shows what they considered important. We're going to convert these to Bad Company quarters. Controlled access in and out makes sense to hold any attackers at bay."

"How many people are going to attack a space station that no one knows is here?" Rivka wondered.

"That's what we thought about Keeg, but blammo! There they were. We still don't know who *they* were or where *they* came from."

"I guess you're right. I don't like to live that paranoid, but he does." She pointed over her shoulder with her thumb.

"I prefer 'diligently cautious,'" Red clarified.

"You want to see them in their quarters?"

"That would be easiest, as long as Red goes first because he'll insist on it since he's diligently cautious."

"It's what I do."

Kim popped the door, and Red stepped into the doorway and stopped. "Sit down," he ordered.

"But I didn't do anything!" a woman's voice cried from within.

"And we'll be sure of that in about ten seconds. Sit, please."

Rivka walked in and leaned close, her hand on the woman's shoulder. "You didn't do anything wrong, did you?"

"Of course not!" the woman nearly screamed. Inside her mind was destruction on a scale Nefas would have envied. She reveled in it without remorse.

"I didn't think so. You can go."

The woman looked surprised for a moment, then she shot to her feet and took one step toward the door.

Rivka drove a finger strike into her throat so hard that it broke her neck. The woman crumpled.

Red grunted. "Huh. I guess she *did* do it."

"She did, and a whole lot more. I feel like I need a shower after seeing what she'd done." Rivka scowled, her face taking on a dusky pallor. "Let's get it over with. Three to go."

Kim waved down a guard and pointed into the cell. "Flush that thing out an airlock."

The next two were mostly innocent. Rivka let them go with warnings after telling them about their crimes. They both promised to be upstanding citizens. Rivka expected no less. She gave it fifty-fifty they'd embrace a life of petty crime, but station security and the Bad Company could deal with that.

The last person presented a challenge. He was introduced as Destride, and Rivka couldn't read him.

"What are you?" she asked.

"I'm part human, just like you," he replied, reclining casually on the cell's bed.

"I think it best we hold you for further questioning," Rivka told him. "Looks like we'll have to do this the hard way."

"As you wish. I get three hots and a cot with plenty to read and space to work out as needed. I'm fine right here." He laced his fingers behind his head and closed his eyes.

Once they were in the corridor and the door had closed, Red was first to say it. "Doesn't sound like any criminal I've ever seen."

"It is curious that he seems to have no interest in getting out of jail. Oh, well, until you can get more information on who he is and what he does, I'm afraid you'll have to hold him. Another week, but then you'll have to let him go. With the Bad Company taking control of the station, it has to comply with Federation laws."

"We'll take care of it, Magistrate. His mind didn't tell you anything?" Kim asked.

"Blank. Very few people are like that. The High Chancellor comes to mind, as do Chaz and Dennicron."

"I'm pretty sure he's not an android. That leaves one other thing, and I can't believe he's a vampire." Kim shook her head.

"Without Joseph or Petricia on the ship, we can't ask them to take a look. What about Christina? She's worked with all types over the centuries."

"I'll ask her when she and Kailin get back from the planet. I guess it's a total clusterfuck down there. Marcie has the gift, too, and Mom, but they're not here. The Bad Company is a pale imitation of what it used to be."

Rivka shook her head. "Not pale, just different. Is there anything else you need from me?"

"We're good, Rivka. If you'd like a little R&R, this place has a couple bars and a recreation room with billiards, blinko, and slots."

Red raised his eyebrows.

"I think my crew would appreciate that."

Kim leaned close to whisper conspiratorially, "We want to throw a baby shower for Clodagh."

"Have at it, but it's probably best you don't do that in a bar."

"What?" Kim sounded outraged. "What kind of Bad Company baby does *not* have his baby shower in a bar?"

Rivka looked at her, mouth hanging open. "I shouldn't be surprised."

Red nodded. "We're coming. Just tell us when."

"We need to be off the clock so we can have a proper celebration," Rivka said. "I need to go back to *Wyatt Earp* and wrap up my last case."

"Thanks, Rivka. This station is the bomb." Kim twirled with her arms up. "The Bad Company is going to be right at home here. We've already requested the conversion of one level into a promenade. Right now, it looks like a bunch of men designed this place."

"They probably did. By pirates for pirates. Compliments, Nefas."

Kim sobered. "How is my sister doing?"

"She is as happy as a person can be. She's going to make an honest person out of the sergeant major. No more orgies for him."

Kim laughed. "I can't see Cory being adventurous like that. We were raised a little bit Puritan. It's what we're comfortable with."

"Yeah, me too. I don't mind what they do, but it's not for me."

"Do you know when they'll be back?"

"On Belzimus? I think no more than a couple weeks. Monsoon will look after Cory, and she'll look after him. Last I saw, they were taking care of business while keeping an eye on each other, just in case they have to rush to the rescue. It's kind of cute, but I think it's driving Marcie nuts."

"Then it's all good. At least your future daughter-in-law isn't older than you."

"Cougar Christina strikes!"

Kim scowled. "Come on! This is my son we're talking about."

"Oops. He's a good kid...well, old dude. I'm in my twenties, and all you guys are in your hundreds. Is there an age where it doesn't matter anymore?"

Kim shrugged. "He'll always be my baby boy."

The two hugged, and Rivka headed out of the cellblock with Red and Lindy in their usual positions in front and behind.

Once they reached the ship, Rivka strode up the ramp wearing her game face. "I'll lock myself in and finish my work. If you guys want to explore the station, have at it."

Red and Lindy shook their heads. "Everyone else can go ashore, Magistrate. We'll wait for you."

"I'm not sure how long this will take."

Red shrugged.

"Have it your way. Let the crew know that they are on vacation, effective immediately."

"Do you want me to recall them to tell them that?" Red asked.

Rivka leaned her head out and followed Red's finger to where he was pointing.

"The Three Horsemen of the Apocalypse," Rivka stated.

"Weren't there four Horsemen?" Lindy wondered.

"I think those three will be enough." The ship's pilots, Ryleigh, Kennedy, and Aurora, were in the middle of a mob of Bad Company warriors, enjoying the attention.

"Ten men enter the cage, but only three will leave," Red deadpanned.

Groenwyn and Lauton strolled off the ship hand in hand, bumping past Red and Lindy. Floyd bounced after them. "Don't wait up!" Groenwyn called over her shoulder.

"I guess they got the word," Rivka said. "I'll be in my quarters."

She disappeared into the ship. Red and Lindy waited at the ramp. Cole and Clodagh strolled off, followed by Chaz and Dennicron. Even Ankh left.

"I'm here," Tyler called from the open hatch. "You guys can go."

Red looked Dr. Toofakre up and down. "I don't think so."

"Have it your way." Tyler went back into the ship and returned to his quarters, where he found Rivka in the middle of the hologrid. He leaned close so he could hear her re-reading her recommendation to the High Chancellor.

"The Articles of War. To provide a legal framework within which parties that have exhausted every other avenue and resorted to the use of force will operate with honor and dignity, regardless of the ultimate winner or loser.

"Be warned, if other avenues to address grievances between the parties have not been exhausted, the penalties shall be extreme.

"To wit, the final opportunity to avoid a costly war is the Court of Redress, to be established by the Federation High Court to handle intraplanetary disputes that could lead to civil war. The officers of the Redress Court shall be comprised of selected members of the Singularity, overseen by a sworn Magistrate. The Court of Redress must be petitioned before force is used.

"Their decision shall be final. War will not follow.

"Should a civil war be declared, both sides being aggressors, all planetary assets are forfeit and subject to salvage by firms appropriately registered under Federation Commercial Charter 6143.217.

"Send that as it is, Clevarious."

"And the second document?"

"I might send that if they reject this one, but I have a sneaky suspicion this will get their attention and garner the conversations I want them to have. Shut it down, C. We're done. There's a party I need to attend."

THE END

Judge, Jury, & Executioner, Book 11

If you like this book, please leave a review. I love reviews since they tell other readers that this book is worth their time and money. I hope you feel that way now that you've finished the latest installment. Please drop me a line and let me know you like Rivka's adventures and want them to continue. This is my new favorite series. I hope you agree.

Click over to the *Judge, Jury, & Executioner* series page to see if any new volumes have been published.

US - Judge, Jury, & Executioner Series

UK - Judge, Jury, & Executioner Series

Don't stop now! Keep turning the pages as Craig hits his *Author Notes* with thoughts about this book and the good stuff that happens in the *Kurtherian Gambit* Universe.

Your favorite legal eagle will return! I guarantee it:).

AUTHOR NOTES - CRAIG MARTELLE

WRITTEN JANUARY 1, 2021

The year that was, 2020, is behind us. Everyone will remember the year where everything changed. It started with my good girl Phyllis passing away three days before I had heart surgery. Recovery was fairly smooth. I canceled all my travel until September, when I went back to Iowa to see my family.

From a writing perspective, 2020 was a huge year. I published books #8, #9, and #10 in the *Judge, Jury, & Executioner* series while writing book #11. I wrote the final book for *Metal Legion*. With Julia Huni, we wrote and published the four books of the *Krimson Empire* series. I wrote the final two books of the *Nightwalker* series. I wrote the final *Bad Company* volume (and that one was a beast at 135k words). I rewrote the entire *Monster Case Files* set and published all nine books as a single volume. I published a few short stories and a couple of travel books (Yellowstone

& Mt. Rushmore). And my foray into a new genre–*The Operator* and *A Clean Kill,* the first two books in the Ian Bragg series. You should definitely check those out. I co-wrote an epic sword & sorcery tale with Jean Rabe, too. That is coming soon.

I also wrote a book that I'm sitting on. I don't like it, but that may change. No one has read it. It's 82k words of a space adventure. I need to figure out what to do with that damn thing.

A lot of good stuff coming. I see a big year ahead, and it starts this month.

Did I tell you that I picked up two authors to publish them under Craig Martelle, Inc? That's right. I'm expanding my publishing brand. First up is *Chandeera,* a space adventure from a Native Alaskan science fiction author and then from Bruce Nesmith, an urban fantasy tale. Bruce has significant bona fides with TSR (*Dungeons & Dragons*) and with digital gaming as a designer for the *Elder Scrolls.* These good people know how to tell tales. I look forward to bringing their books into the light.

Alaska is still cold and dark. Not being able to travel, we couldn't escape this year. We'll be here as long as we need to be until we get the vaccine and can venture into the world. Until then, we remain hunkered down. I can't wait for my treadmill to arrive. My cardiologist said I should lose some weight. I needed to lose fifteen pounds, is all. I'm happy to report that I only have twenty to go to hit my goal.

I have high hopes that 2021 will treat us much better than 2020 did. I hope my books provided you with some escape during the turbulent times where you stayed indoors. I hope I've done my part to help you weather the storm.

And I'll continue doing that. It makes me happy to see people entertained, if only for a short while.

Peace, fellow humans.

Please join my Newsletter (craigmartelle.com—please, please, please sign up!), or you can follow me on Facebook.

If you liked this story, you might like some of my other books. You can join my mailing list by dropping by my website www.craigmartelle.com or if you have any comments, shoot me a note at craig@craigmartelle.com. I am always happy to hear from people who've read my work. I try to answer every email I receive.

If you liked the story, please write a short review for me on Amazon. I greatly appreciate any kind words; even one or two sentences go a long way. The number of reviews an eBook receives greatly improves how well an eBook does on Amazon.

Amazon – www.amazon.com/author/craigmartelle

BookBub – https://www.bookbub.com/authors/craig-martelle

Facebook – www.facebook.com/authorcraigmartelle

My web page – https://craigmartelle.com

That's it—break's over, back to writing the next book.

BOOKS BY CRAIG MARTELLE

 # - available in audio, too

Terry Henry Walton Chronicles (#) (co-written with Michael Anderle)—a post-apocalyptic paranormal adventure

Gateway to the Universe (#) (co-written with Justin Sloan & Michael Anderle)—this book transitions the characters from the Terry Henry Walton Chronicles to The Bad Company

The Bad Company (#) (co-written with Michael Anderle)—a military science fiction space opera

Judge, Jury, & Executioner (#)—a space opera adventure legal thriller

Shadow Vanguard—a Tom Dublin space adventure series

Superdreadnought (#)—an AI military space opera

Metal Legion (#)—a military space opera

The Free Trader (#)—a young adult science fiction action adventure

Cygnus Space Opera (#)—a young adult space opera (set in the Free Trader universe)

Darklanding (#) (co-written with Scott Moon)—a space western

Mystically Engineered (co-written with Valerie Emerson)—mystics, dragons, & spaceships

Metamorphosis Alpha—stories from the world's first science fiction RPG

The Expanding Universe—science fiction anthologies

Krimson Empire (co-written with Julia Huni)—a galactic race for justice

Zenophobia (#)—a space archaeological adventure

End Times Alaska (#)—a Permuted Press publication—a post-apocalyptic survivalist adventure

Nightwalker (a Frank Roderus series)—A post-apocalyptic western adventure

End Days (#) (co-written with E.E. Isherwood)—a post-apocalyptic adventure

Successful Indie Author (#)—a non-fiction series to help self-published authors

Monster Case Files (co-written with Kathryn Hearst)—A Warner twins mystery adventure

Rick Banik (#)—Spy & terrorism action adventure

Ian Bragg Thrillers—a man with a conscience who kills bad guys for money

Published exclusively by Craig Martelle, Inc

The Dragon's Call by Angelique Anderson & Craig A. Price, Jr.—an epic fantasy quest

A Couples Travel—a non-fiction travel series

For a complete list of Craig's books, stop by his website —https://craigmartelle.com

BOOKS BY MICHAEL ANDERLE

Sign up for the LMBPN email list to be notified of new releases and special deals!

https://lmbpn.com/email/

For a complete list of books by Michael Anderle, please visit:

www.lmbpn.com/ma-books/

Made in the USA
Columbia, SC
03 March 2023